PRAISE FOR ANDREWS & WILSON

"Fans of Frank Peretti will enjoy this action-packed inspirational."

PUBLISHERS WEEKLY on *Dark Intercept*

"*Dark Intercept* is a fantastic blend of supernatural thrills, crisis of faith, and military thriller all rolled into one. . . . A unique crisis of faith novel that is sure to be a hit!"

MYSTERY AND SUSPENSE MAGAZINE

"*Dark Intercept* is a masterpiece of a military thriller with remarkable heart and depth. No one in the genre writes grittier and more authentic action than these two authors, and yet *Dark Intercept* also deals with the intriguing questions of spirituality and the human condition, making it a spellbinding page-turner that will leave you both thrilled and enriched by the experience."

MARK GREANEY, #1 *New York Times* bestselling author of *Relentless* and the Gray Man novels

"A blistering page-turner of a thriller . . . that effortlessly transports the reader from the adrenaline-filled highs of the battlefield to the soul-searching lows that follow."

JOSHUA HOOD, author of Robert Ludlum's Treadstone series

"The characters are unforgettable and unique, promising a blockbuster Shepherds series. Andrews & Wilson write with the authenticity that can only be achieved through boots-on-the-ground downrange experience. Whether you're military connected or not, reading this novel will make you want to enlist with these spiritual warriors. Un-put-downable."

K.J. HOWE, internationally bestselling author of *Skyjack*

"In *Dark Intercept*, Andrews & Wilson flawlessly weave a tale of spiritual and natural warfare as riveting as it is inventive. By combining the grittiness and veracity of their bestselling military thriller series with an unabashed focus on the eternal struggle between light and darkness, Andrews & Wilson inject a shot of adrenaline into faith-based fiction. Frank Peretti has company!"

DON BENTLEY, author of the Matt Drake thriller series

"A thrilling and gripping ride through the eyes of those who strap on the uniform and serve, [this book] helps us see what true leadership looks like. . . . You'll enjoy this crackling adventure and learn some valuable things along the way."

DANIEL DARLING, bestselling author of *The Characters of Christmas* and *A Way with Words*

"Andrews & Wilson strategically position the physical realm with the spiritual in this edge-of-your-seat thriller. . . . This novel captures perfectly the spiritual warfare raging around us, in a way that is both entertaining and chilling. Expertly woven and crafted, *Dark Intercept* is sure to have you view the world around you with a different set of eyes. A must-read!"

EDWIN E., military ministry leader and former Green Beret

"From the jaw-dropping opening chapter to the pulse-pounding climax, *Dark Intercept* is an emotional thrill ride of cinematic proportions. Expect to be blown away and entertained but also left thinking and talking about this book for weeks after you turn the last page. With *Dark Intercept*, Andrews & Wilson usher in a new era of Christian thriller fiction!"

CRAIG ALTMAN, lead pastor, Grace Family Church

"Shifting constantly between the fast-paced thriller and thought-provoking moments of personal challenge, *Dark Intercept* will take you to a new dimension of fiction that changes your reality. Take the journey!"

CHRIS BONHAM, senior executive pastor, Grace Family Church

THE SHEPHERDS SERIES

DARK ANGEL

ANDREWS & WILSON

Tyndale House Publishers
Carol Stream, Illinois

Visit Tyndale online at tyndale.com.

Visit Andrews & Wilson online at andrews-wilson.com.

Tyndale and Tyndale's quill logo are registered trademarks of Tyndale House Ministries.

Dark Angel

The Shepherds series logo designed by Andrews & Wilson and used with permission.

Authors' photograph taken by Wendy Wilson, copyright © 2019. All rights reserved.

Cover designed by Faceout Studio, Jeff Miller

Interior designed by Dean H. Renninger

Edited by Sarah Mason Rische

Published in association with the literary agency of Talcott Notch Literary, LLC, 276 Forest Road, Milford, CT 06461.

Dark Angel is a work of fiction. Where real people, events, establishments, organizations, or locales appear, they are used fictitiously. All other elements of the novel are drawn from the authors' imaginations.

For information about special discounts for bulk purchases, please contact Tyndale House Publishers at csresponse@tyndale.com, or call 1-855-277-9400.

Library of Congress Cataloging-in-Publication Data

A catalog record for this book is available from the Library of Congress.

ISBN 978-1-4964-5139-2 (HC)
ISBN 978-1-4964-5140-8 (SC)

Printed in the United States of America

28 27 26 25 24 23 22
7   6   5   4   3   2   1

For Emma and Larkin

NOTE TO READERS

We've provided a glossary in the back of this book to define the acronyms, military lingo, and abbreviations used in this series.

★

PART I

For we do not wrestle against flesh and blood, but
against the rulers, against the authorities, against the
cosmic powers over this present darkness, against
the spiritual forces of evil in the heavenly places.

EPHESIANS 6:12, ESV

CHAPTER ONE

LA SANTÉ PRISON

42 RUE DE LA SANTÉ

MONTPARNASSE, 14TH ARRONDISSEMENT

PARIS, FRANCE

1158 HOURS LOCAL

Nicholas Woland, known simply as "l'américain" to prisoners and guards alike, sat on the edge of his hard, narrow cot, hands resting idly on his knees. With eyes closed, he began four-count tactical breathing to ready himself—a practice he'd acquired in the Army, during his ten years of service as a Green Beret. Most of the things he'd learned in his former life he'd jettisoned, the way a space capsule rids itself of a booster rocket once attaining orbit. But *some* things he'd kept.

The tactically useful bits . . .

After two rounds, his pulse slowed and the knots of tension he stored in his neck and heavily muscled shoulders began to relax. Today was the day, and he needed to be both physiologically and mentally prepared to do his part for the plan to succeed. There would be no second chances, of this much he was certain.

His cell, located on the third floor of D-block, was spacious compared to most—a luxury he'd *earned* after his third cell-mate had been found dead on the floor at reveille. Directeur de Prison August Chauvin had ordered Woland placed in solitary confinement as punishment. But after forty-five days, he'd been relocated to D-block while retaining his *sans roommate* status. A simple white placard that read *Puni* was affixed to the outside of his cell door, a visible signal to all that he was being punished in perpetuity. It was nothing more than an administrative exercise, however, so Directeur Chauvin could satisfy the lawyers and the army of French human rights activists to whom he was obligated to bend the knee. Chauvin was a politician, not a true prison warden, and aptly named—his head as bald as an egg. That his infamous American charge had killed three inmates under his care was a potentially career-ending black mark for Chauvin. Woland knew the feckless director would do whatever it took to salvage his career, even if that meant leaving one rack permanently empty in Woland's two-man cell.

Before the renovations, living conditions had been far more bar-baric at France's most storied prison. But calls for reform had put an end to the inhumane living conditions and brutal treatment of inmates at La Santé. Parisian sensibility, it seemed, was as tena-cious as it was naive and had proven so by performing an HGTV "home makeover" on the prison that housed France's most dangerous criminals. Yet despite the reforms, he'd had enough of this place.

Nicholas Woland was no man's caged beast.

And he would gnaw off his proverbial paw if that's what it took to be free.

Footsteps echoed in the corridor, getting louder and closer until finally stopping just outside his door. A Klaxon sounded, loud and jarring, announcing that Woland's cell door would be opening momentarily. He continued his four-count breathing, anticipating what was about to happen next.

André was about to happen next.

André was a holdover from pre-2015, a veteran prison guard who had somehow managed to survive the purge and La Santé's reorganization into a kinder, gentler corrections facility. In the new system, Woland suspected that André's chances to exorcise his demon came fewer and farther between, which meant he never wasted an opportunity to punish l'américain. Woland fantasized regularly about killing the man and had come close to doing so on more than one occasion. But self-discipline had stayed his fists every time, preventing him from crossing the one line—murdering a corrections officer—that would permanently seal his fate. And so he would respond as he always did, with silence and passivity, until André had had his fun and left Woland bruised and bloodied on the floor of his cell. Whatever punishment André meted today, Woland would absorb it with stoic indifference, because today was the last day the sadist would ever touch him.

The Klaxon blared a second time, followed by a magnetic snap signaling his cell lock releasing. Only then did Woland open his eyes and turn to see André smiling at him from the open cell door.

"On your feet, American," André barked in French, smacking the baton in his right hand into the palm of his left. Woland stood, but André glanced back toward the entry at the end of the hall and shouted again, "I said on your feet!"

Then it began.

André whipped the baton around in an arc. It whistled through the air before careening toward him. Woland could have easily blocked the blow—could have taken the club and beaten the man to death in seconds, long before his fellow guards could reach them—but instead he tightened his core. The rubber baton slammed into his left buttocks, sending an explosion of pain into his lower back and down his leg. He resisted the urge to turn and glare at the guard—that would guarantee a second blow—and instead bowed his head in deference.

"That's better," André said for whoever he thought might be listening to their exchange, seemingly rewarding Woland's compliance.

André was unpredictable, and Woland put coin-flip's odds on whether the guard would beat him into the ground. When a second blow did not come, he slowly turned and held out his wrists for André to cuff. Cowed and shackled, he shuffled out of his cell, with André repeatedly prodding him in the lower back with the baton. They continued down the hall to a large gate that clicked open and slid into the wall. A second guard waited for them, his own baton out of its loop by protocol but hanging nonthreateningly by the man's leg.

"It is your day for some sunshine, yes?" the guard said, smiling at Woland and seemingly happy to practice his English.

Woland forced a smile. "This is the one and only thing I've been looking forward to."

Given his conviction as a terrorist, Woland's meals were served in his cell, he bathed alone, and his outdoor exercise periods were limited to the company of only five other prisoners. He rarely saw the same prisoners more than once, and usually those he did encounter were the ones in solitary near the end of their stretch. Apparently if you were convicted of a terror attack resulting in the deaths of thirty-seven French citizens and you killed three inmates, you lost more privileges than ordinary murderers.

C'est la guerre.

The second guard, known as Pet—the origin of the nickname unknown to Woland—fell into step on his left. Behind him, André loomed, ready and willing to deliver a blow with the baton to Woland's kidneys at the slightest provocation.

"I hoping you are enjoying your outdoors time, Nicholas Woland," Pet said, recycling their only conversational option.

"*C'est magnifique.* It's going to be a soiree," he replied with a wry grin.

Pet laughed.

Poor fool . . .

They passed through another magnetically locked gate, then walked down two flights of stairs, emerging into a final, gently downward-sloping corridor. At the end of the hall, beyond a final gate, sunlight streamed through double glass doors—no doubt ballistic glass, based on the thickness. Woland squinted against the glare with his poorly light-accommodated eyes. Before the renovations, the prison had been even more dimly lit, but on D block lighting was still an issue. He blinked several times while the gate swung open and Pet removed his restraints.

"You are having one half hours of the outdoors exercising," Pet said, still smiling at Woland's soiree "joke."

The man didn't seem the prison guard type, Woland thought as a third guard issued firearms to Pet and André for the upcoming courtyard patrol. Perhaps Pet was better suited to running a florist shop or bookstore. Unlike André, who would not hesitate to gun down any inmate he perceived as a threat, Woland found it hard to imagine Pet pulling the trigger . . . even if his own life depended on it.

Well, we're about to put that to the test, aren't we?

André shoved Woland in the back to get going, and he marched out the double ballistic glass doors into the courtyard. The cool midday air contrasted sharply with the warm sun on his face and made him tilt his head back and smile at the sky like a kid. After briefly savoring the moment and reclaiming a modicum of his humanity, he drifted right along the exterior wall of the D-block building, one of four buildings sticking out from the center of the courtyard like the spokes of a wheel. During the renovations, the last of the guillotines—the most infamous and iconic feature the courtyard was known for—had been removed. The last execution by guillotine at La Santé was more recent than he would have imagined—November of 1972—after Roger Bontems and Claude Buffet had been sentenced to death for their escape attempt during which a number of hostages had been killed. For these men, being the last to have their heads separated from their bodies at the prison was their only real claim to fame. They had been mundane criminals, unlike so many other prisoners incarcerated here. Including the infamous terrorist assassin Ilich Ramírez Sánchez—Carlos the Jackal—who'd called La Santé home until 2006.

Before my time . . .

Woland stopped and stretched his back, noting the position of the third guard who'd issued rifles to Pet and André. Instead of lingering at the door, he walked into the crux formed by the intersection of two buildings. André stood directly beside the south wall, which ran along Rue Jean Dolent and separated the prison from the row of apartment buildings towering across the street. Woland was no expert on the matter, but he knew of no other maximum-security prison located in the heart of a city the likes of Paris. The security constraints imposed by La Santé's urban location—such as line of sight into the courtyard from elevated positions nearby—were about to be exploited.

Woland paced back toward the double doors, smiling and nodding at Pet as the third guard walked across the yard, heading for a cluster of three prisoners talking together. Per the rules, all prisoners were to be isolated from one another, and guard number three was on his way to break things up.

But he didn't make it.

The first explosion hit hard. The shock wave funneled through the courtyard, blowing out windows in a cascade of raining glass. The pain in his ears was so acute, Woland thought he might have burst his eardrums, but there'd be time for worrying about that later. He glanced left to see a gaping maw in the stone wall on the street side of the courtyard. The blast had also collapsed and mangled a ten-foot swathe of heavy steel fence that served as the inner barrier.

The operator in Woland took over, and he scanned the courtyard for threats. Instead of running for freedom and risking being shot by the riflemen still manning the two corner towers, he double-timed it to where Pet lay motionless on the ground, covered head to toe in blood. Woland suspected that most of the blood was not Pet's and instead had come from the trio of prisoners and guard number three who'd been standing in the blast zone and whose body parts were now scattered about the courtyard.

"*Qui est là?*" Pet said, staring up with unfocused eyes.

"It's me, Nicholas," he said, taking a knee beside the man.

A heartbeat later, both guard towers exploded in beautiful, simultaneous precision—struck by RPGs from the apartment buildings across the street.

"Are we under attack, Nicholas Woland? I cannot see anything," Pet said, a tear spilling onto his cheek.

Gunfire erupted in the courtyard as two other prisoners, sprinting toward the hole in the fence, were gunned down from behind. Woland glanced over his left shoulder and ID'd the shooter. André stood ten yards away, rifle up and a mirthless grin on his face as he unloaded his magazine.

Woland picked up Pet's rifle and, with practiced fluidity and precision, put three rounds in André's torso. Then he stood and looked down at Pet.

"It's okay, my friend," Woland said, smiling pitifully. "Help is coming."

"*Dieu te bénisse,*" Pet said and squeezed his eyes shut. "God bless you, Nicholas."

Woland leveled the muzzle at Pet's forehead, squeezed the trigger twice, and watched the man's skull deflate like a torn basketball on the ground.

"I rather doubt that," he said with a chuckle, turned, and sprinted toward freedom.

He passed through the inner and outer barriers easily, ditching his rifle on the sidewalk after clearing for police threats. Just as he'd been told, a utility van was parked a half block away, its passenger-side panel door hanging wide-open. He ran to it, jumped in, and slammed the slider shut. Inside the cargo compartment, he stripped off his La Santé uniform and changed into jeans, a sweatshirt, and leather jacket. He stuffed his uniform inside a large toolbox and then crawled through the gap into the driver's seat. He turned off the van's hazard lights, opened the driver's door, and exited onto Rue Jean Dolent.

Across the street, as promised, an idling ambulance waited. Woland walked around to the back, climbed inside, and shut the door behind him. A middle-aged man wearing paramedic attire sat beside the treatment cot, waiting for him.

Woland greeted the man in French.

"Take off your jacket and lie down," the man replied in German-accented English as the ambulance swerved from the curb, sirens blaring. "I'm not French, in case you were wondering. You prefer English, *ja?*"

"Yes," Woland said, shrugging off his jacket and then stretching out on the cot. "But I also speak French, Pashto, Arabic—even your native German."

Unimpressed, the man simply grunted and taped an IV catheter to Woland's arm, though he did not actually break the skin nor insert it into a vein. Next, he tore open Woland's shirt—buttons popping and clattering to the floor—and taped a bulky, blood-soaked dressing to his chest. Lastly, he sprayed Woland's face with water, mussed his hair, and had him don an oxygen mask.

"When we arrive at hospital, I want you awake, but do not

speak. You should appear confused and in pain. The pulse oximeter will display very low oxygen, so they will roll you into the trauma bay. But don't worry; we have someone waiting to take you where you need to go."

The German placed a large pistol, equipped with a suppressor, into Woland's hand, then covered him with a thick green blanket. "Just in case things don't go according to plan."

"And what is the plan?" Woland asked.

"The attendant will wheel you past the doctors' locker room. You roll off the gurney and go inside. Locker number four has everything you need, including new clothes, keys to a car in the pant pocket, and a wallet with new identification. Go to Hotel Henri IV, Rive Gauche. I have programmed the location into the car's GPS to make it easy for you, but it is located on Rue Saint-Jacques, north of Boulevard Saint-Germain and across from the Église Saint-Séverin cathedral. Park the car on the street. You have a key card in the wallet for room 415."

"Got it," Woland said over the wailing siren. "Then what? Where do I meet Victor?"

The German laughed, his expression softening for the first time.

"What's so funny?" Woland said, irritated.

"You must be important, *ja*? This is above my level. Check into your room, order room service, have a drink. Someone will come and tell you what to do next."

As the ambulance swayed into a right-hand turn, the German looked up and glanced out the small, square windows in the back doors.

"We are arriving," he said and, with an evil, twisted smile, slipped an additional magazine under the blanket and into Woland's right pant pocket. "If you are detected, kill everyone who sees you at the hospital."

"My pleasure," Woland said, then let out a theatrical groan, changing personas into the role of a confused, injured patient.

As the ambulance braked to a stop, he adjusted his grip on the weapon under the blanket and, for the first time in his life, actually hoped that this time, he wouldn't have to shoot anybody.

CHAPTER
TWO

TRINITY LOOP TRAINING COMPLEX

15 MILES WEST OF NASHVILLE

SOUTH OF ASHLAND CITY, TENNESSEE

0714 HOURS LOCAL

A new hope swelled in Jedidiah Johnson as he turned south onto Cross Hill Road. The last time he'd felt this excited and nervous was . . . well, *never.* Okay, maybe his first day of BUD/S when he started his journey to become a Navy SEAL. Of course, the indoctrination program he was about to enter was nothing like the meat grinder the SEAL instructors had put him through in Coronado. He imagined today would be mostly a paperwork drill, along with several hours of safety and indoc videos and time on the range to document his firearms proficiency. The days of being subjected to grueling physical training, sleep deprivation, mind games, emotional abuse, and swimming until he got hypothermia or hypoxia were long past.

At least they better be, he thought with a chuckle as he navigated his brand-new pickup truck through the serpentine switchback that led to the security checkpoint at the main gate. A quick scan of the guardhouse and surroundings validated that the Shepherds organization took security seriously. To the untrained eye, the hidden countermeasures probably wouldn't be obvious, but thanks to his operator pedigree, Jed knew what to look for: the tortuous path through the concrete security balusters that prevented an approaching vehicle from entering the complex at high speed like a missile; the hydraulically operated, retractable steel crash plate the guards could raise instantly to block the road; the hidden shooter's nest disguised as second-story office space over the guard shack, and so on. Nobody was getting into Trinity Loop without an invitation, that was for sure.

He eased his black-on-black Silverado High Country to a stop at the gate and put the transmission in park as a uniformed security guard stepped out of the building to greet him. The guard nodded as Jed rolled down the driver's window. Unlike some of the less-than-intimidating physical specimens Jed had encountered over the years at security checkpoints, this dude had a lean V-shaped torso, heavily muscled forearms, and an operator's bearing.

"Howdy," Jed said, looking at his own reflection in the crimson mirror finish of the guard's Wiley X sunglasses. He handed his ID to the guard while he glanced at the embroidered name patch on the man's right chest, which read *Sanderson.*

Instead of taking Jed's driver's license, Sanderson lifted a tablet computer in his left hand and aimed the camera at Jed's face. After a beat, he said, "Welcome, Senior Chief, to Trinity Loop. They're expecting you."

"I guess that means you don't need my ID?"

"From now on, your face is your ID," Sanderson said. "Do you know where you're going?"

Jed shook his head. "Nope, first time here."

Sanderson tapped on the tablet a couple times before turning the screen to face Jed. "You're here at the main gate on Cross Hill Road. Continue straight. The first stop sign you'll hit is where Cross Hill intersects Trinity Loop Road. At that stop, hang a right. Trinity Loop Road is, in fact, an actual loop that runs through the entire complex. So even if you get lost, all you ever need to do is find your way back to Trinity Loop and you'll eventually get where you're trying to go."

Jed nodded, committing the displayed map of the complex to memory. "Roger that."

"Your destination is the training barracks, which are located here," Sanderson said, pointing to a cluster of buildings shaded in green on the map in the southwest quadrant of what Jed could see was a sprawling campus—one that appeared to rival Constellis Group's thirty-six-hundred-acre flagship training facility and proving grounds in Moyock, North Carolina. "Check-in for basic is at 0730, so I suggest you hurry. You're the last new recruit to arrive."

"Basic? New recruit?" Jed said with a chuckle. "I think you might have me confused with someone else."

"You're Jedidiah Johnson, are you not?"

"That's correct."

"Then the system identified you correctly." Sanderson glanced at his watch. "You really should get a move on. You're definitely gonna wanna change into your PT gear before they get started."

"Hold on. I work for Ben Morvant. I'm just here to complete the indoc paperwork this morning."

Sanderson's lips twitched into a wry, crooked grin—like somebody had just tugged up on an invisible thread connected to the left corner of his mouth. "Huh . . . is that what they told you?"

"Well, not verbatim. I mean, it was implied," Jed said as a heaviness settled into his gut.

"You've got eight minutes, Senior Chief. I wouldn't waste any more of it jawboning with me." Sanderson took a step back and pointed down the road toward buildings in the near distance. "First right at Trinity Loop Road. Circle around until you see the sign that says Jericho Training Facility. That's you."

"Thanks," Jed said and, suddenly feeling very grumpy, put the transmission in drive and piloted his truck onto the complex. He left the window down, propping his left elbow on the sill as he drove toward whatever amateur-hour boot-camp baloney they apparently had planned for him today.

If Ben thinks I signed on to get screamed at by some retired drill sergeant reliving the glory days, he's got another think coming, he thought with an irritated exhale. *I'm already an operator. I've got nothing to prove to these people.*

He hit the Trinity Loop Road intersection a few moments later and turned right as Sanderson had instructed. As Jed looped around the heart of the complex, he scanned the buildings and decided it looked like a mash-up of Camp Peary in Virginia and Vanderbilt's main campus, if such a thing was possible. A brick clock tower with a white cupola and spire—reminiscent of the one atop Independence Hall in Philadelphia—dominated the central quad. His seat vibrated as the Silverado's lane departure system warned him and automatically course-corrected, preventing him from drifting off the road.

Crashing my truck and showing up late . . . definitely not the first impression I want to make, he thought, grateful he'd let the salesman talk him into splurging for the safety and technology package.

After looping a quarter of the way around, the training complex that Sanderson had shown him on the map came into view. A long, low, flat building emerged over the rise, set back from the perimeter loop twenty yards or so. This building was flanked by three smaller buildings, which he guessed to be a canteen, a gym, and classroom space. Beyond, he spied a hard-core–looking obstacle course, a cross-country track that looped around a man-made lake, a firing range with both indoor and outdoor facilities, and finally a massive, warehouse-style building that he'd bet money was a kill house. Confirmation that he was in the right place came an instant later in the form of a green sign embossed with the words *Jericho Training Facility*.

Jed braked and turned in to the complex, scanning for signs of life and a place to park. Just then, his mobile phone vibrated inside the armrest cup holder. He glanced at the caller ID and it read Unknown.

"This is Jed," he said, taking the call.

"Park in the lot behind the barracks, then double-time it to the west side for check-in," a gruff male voice said. "You're late, Johnson."

The caller hung up before he could answer.

Jed swallowed down his irritation at being henpecked and did as instructed. After parking, he shoved his phone into his pocket, shrugged his go bag onto his right shoulder, and jogged around the north side of the barracks building and into the heart of the horseshoe-shaped training complex.

These guys don't mess around, he thought, surveying the multimillion-dollar setup.

"Johnson," barked the same gruff male voice who'd called him on the phone. "Quit gawking and get over here."

Gritting his teeth, Jed turned and walked over to meet his antagonizer—a fit, silver-haired dude with a high-and-tight haircut and a face that was a dead ringer for Stephen Lang's villainous character in the movie *Avatar.* Jed had four inches and thirty pounds on the guy, but something told him the old-timer could go toe-to-toe with him either in the ring or on the impressive obstacle course across the way.

"I'm looking for Ben Morvant," Jed said, forcing a smile onto his face. "I was supposed to meet him here this morning to go over some paperwork."

The man was decked out in a navy-blue T-shirt with *Instructor* printed in bright-yellow letters across the chest, a pair of khaki UDT-style shorts, and Nike trainers. He fixed Jed with a steely-eyed glare and said, "I work for Ben. Don't worry; we'll get to that paperwork when we get to it. In the meantime, looks like you've got three minutes to find your rack, get changed into PT gear, and fall in with the rest of your team out there on the plot. See those seven bodies over there? They're waitin' on you."

Jed followed the instructor's outstretched finger to where a cluster of folks—five men and two women—all dressed in PT gear were warming up. "You're serious?" he said, turning back to the instructor. "We're really going to do this?"

A self-important grin—the likes of which Jed hadn't seen since BUD/S—spread across the other man's face.

"Evil never rests, young man, and neither do we. Hallelujah and hooyah, frogman. Welcome to Jericho Basic."

CHAPTER THREE

Jed resisted the urge to pick a fight with his new instructor and decided to play along . . .

For now.

He quickly found his assigned rack in the barracks, changed into his PT gear, and jogged back out to join the cluster of others waiting for him on the lawn. As he got closer, he was surprised to see a few familiar faces in the group. He recognized four Shepherd operators but only knew two of them by name. Strange that over half of the supposed "new recruits" in this class were the same men he'd fought shoulder to shoulder with only a few weeks ago when they'd foiled a terror attack at the Cathedral of the Incarnation and then a second at Cross Landing Church in the Nashville suburbs.

"Eli . . . Grayson . . . what are you guys doing here?" he said with a grin as he joined the group.

"Hey, Jed," the easygoing operator named Eli said and stuck out his hand. "Long time, no see."

Jed clasped the man's bear paw of a palm, then did the same with Grayson's outstretched hand.

"Dude, are you sure you're ready for this? As I recall, you took quite a beating at the Yarnells' house that night," Grayson said with legitimate concern on his face.

"Yeah, man, I'm all good," Jed said while he scanned the other faces looking at him. "I'm a quick healer—it's a SEAL thing."

Grayson and Eli, who Jed knew were both former Army Special Forces, looked at each other and shook their heads.

Two more operators walked up to say hello, men he recognized but didn't know by name. "I'm Carl," one of them said, a power-fully built Black man who had a large, ornate cross tattooed on his left forearm and a Marine Corps eagle, globe, and anchor inked on his right. "I was on the Smoky Mountain rescue team, but we never got a chance to talk."

"I remember," Jed said, shaking hands. "Nice to officially meet you."

"And I'm Johnny," the other familiar face said. "I was on your stick when we stopped the hit at the church."

"Good to see you again," Jed said, shaking Johnny's hand as well.

"Let me introduce you to the other nuggets." Johnny turned to the three strangers dressed out in PT gear. "This fella is Hyeon," he said, pronouncing the name *yun* like *fun*. "He's Korean."

"Actually, my parents are Korean. I'm from Montana," the man said in perfectly unaccented English and turned to Jed. "Hey, Jed, good to meet a fellow frogman."

"Back at you," Jed said with a nod, noting the bottom half of a bonefrog tattoo on Hyeon's left deltoid just visible beneath his shirtsleeve.

"I'm Bex," a very blonde and very buff woman said, stepping in front of Johnny to shake Jed's hand. "Heard you were with SEAL Team Ten?"

"Yeah, that's right," Jed said.

"I was an IDC with an FRSS team in Iraq and then a few years at Four, before getting recruited to the JSOC element," she said, revealing her pedigree as a combat medic with tactical chops who'd worked with the Tier One SEALs in a single, elegant sentence. "Just retired from SA-2 at Group Ten. They wanted to take me out of NSW and assign me to Portsmouth Naval hospital, but I said no thank you, ma'am."

"I hear you."

"Probably know some of the same people," she said with an insider's smile.

"Probably do," Jed said, returning a grin of his own.

"And I'm Nisha," the last member of the group said, a strikingly attractive woman with skin the color of caramel and hair as black as night. Instead of stepping up to shake hands, she simply waved at him from where she was standing. She had the leanest build of the lot, but like everyone in the group, she stood with square-shouldered posture and exuded a been-there-done-that aura. But unlike the others, she didn't share any of her background or have visible tats that hinted at her pedigree.

"Hi, Nisha," he said, wondering if perhaps he'd seen her face somewhere downrange.

"All right, this ain't the first day of youth group summer camp," their instructor said with practiced indignation. "Time to knock off the chitchat and get to work. Johnson!"

"Sir?" he said, turning to the salty instructor. "Unless there's something else you'd like me to call you."

The silver-haired man grinned. "Oh, that's right. You were late, so you missed my introduction."

"Everybody just calls him the Colonel," Carl whispered. "I've been here six years and he's never told me his first name."

"I heard that, Carl," the Colonel said and then dragged his laser beam gaze across the group. "That's the difference between you and me. I'm not here to make friends. I don't care if you like me. I'm here to stress-test each and every one of you to failure and then watch and see if you can knit yourselves back together."

Jed suppressed a grin. *Man, he's really getting into character. I wonder how long they're going to keep this cosplay boot camp act up.*

"Johnson, take us out on a five-mile run to get everyone's muscles loosened up before we start the day's PT," the Colonel said and chopped a hand in the direction of Trinity Loop Road.

"Roger that, Colonel," he said. "Does this unit have a name?"

"Jericho Basic, Alpha platoon."

"All right, Alpha. Buddy up and let's get sweaty," Jed said and took off at a jog toward the parking lot access road leading to Trinity Loop.

Grayson fell in beside him at the front of the column and the rest of the platoon formed up in pairs behind them. "Trinity Loop has a two-and-a-half-mile circumference," Grayson said. "I know math is difficult for you SEALs, so a five-mile run is two laps."

Jed chuckled, happy to see that interservice rivalry and ribbing was alive and well even here in the Shepherds. "Thanks for that pro tip."

"Anytime. Army has your back, frogman," Grayson said with a grin.

Jed glanced over his shoulder, unable to resist verifying that everyone in the platoon was where they were supposed to be and pounding the pavement on pace. Their spacing was perfect, of course, and no surprise the Colonel was keeping stride in trail.

"Can I ask you something?" he said to Grayson as he brought his eyes back front.

"Fire away."

"What gives? I came here today expecting indoc, not boot camp. I'm a blooded, fifteen-year special operations veteran. You guys have seen me operate. Ben knows what I'm capable of. Seriously, dude, what is this?"

Grayson glanced sideways at him, with a wry expression on his face. "I'm going to be really annoying and answer your question with a question: What was the best thing about being a SEAL?"

The answer came to Jed like reflex. "The brotherhood."

"Why?"

"C'mon, man, you were a Green Beret. You know why."

"Uh-uh, no shortcuts. Say the words. Tell me why," Grayson said.

"Because we fought together, we bled together, we laughed together, we cried together . . . whatever challenge the command or the bad guys or life threw at us, we overcame *together*."

"Exactly, which is why every new hire is run through basic. Logistically, it's a lot of work and a huge time suck, but it's necessary. Only through shared adversity in training can we forge the kind of bonds required to face the adversity waiting for us outside the wire."

"Are you saying that you and Eli and the other veterans are going through the program again, alongside me and the other newbies?" Jed asked, legitimately surprised.

"Yep. Our recruitment classes are small. How else would we become a team if we didn't? You more than most should be able to appreciate the rationale. There are no shortcuts, Jed."

He glanced at Grayson and saw that the operator was smiling—a real, genuine, no BS smile.

He considers this a badge of honor . . . like a renewal of vows.

"How many times have you done it?" Jed asked.

"Jericho Basic?"

"Yeah."

"This will be my sixth."

"Whoa . . . were they all under Colonel Avatar back there?" Jed said with a grin.

Grayson laughed and looked over his shoulder at Eli, who was running in the pair behind them with Hyeon. "Bro, Jed just called out the Colonel for looking like the dude from *Avatar*."

"See, I'm not the only one," Eli said.

"It's an inside joke we have," Grayson said, turning back to Jed. "But to answer your question, yes. The Colonel's been here since the beginning . . . not the *beginning* beginning, like in the Middle Ages—the dude's old but not *that* old—but since before the beginning of Trinity Loop."

"Interesting."

"Yeah, in fact, building this complex was his idea. He donated family land for it."

"Ah, so he's Jericho," Jed said, connecting the dots. "The training center and the program are named after him?"

"Bingo," Grayson said. "You'd be surprised how long it takes most people to figure it out. Heck, Johnny still hasn't made the connection. But Johnny was Navy, so there's that . . ."

A powerful new respect took root in Jed's mind for the man he'd written off as a drill sergeant wannabe reliving the glory days.

"I didn't realize Navy SEALs ran so slow," a gruff voice hollered from the back of the column. "My mother is eighty-two years old and she runs faster than this, Johnson."

"Hooyah, Colonel," Jed hollered back as he lengthened his stride and picked up the pace. Everybody in this group clearly had a superior level of fitness, but he had a feeling none of them had any idea what Jed was physically capable of.

I'm going to make Colonel Jericho think twice about doing that again, he thought as a devious grin spread across his face. *Maybe this is going to be fun after all.*

CHAPTER FOUR

Maria Perez resisted the urge to run her fingers over the incision sites on her abdomen and focused on looking natural in the small but posh lobby of the boutique Parisian hotel. The stitches in her belly button were driving her crazy. So very, very itchy. She'd taken a bullet while managing an operation at the Yarnell home in Nashville—not in an official capacity as a metro police detective, but in service of her *other* job. The trick, however, was making sure everyone believed otherwise. Yes, she'd been on duty that night. Of course she'd arrived just in the nick of time to save the girl. She'd become quite the actress over the years, and it appeared she had everyone fooled, including the Yarnells.

This trip to Paris, which she'd played off as necessary for psychological reasons, was also in service of her *other* job. The order had been given and she was in no position to decline. Once you were in, refusing was no longer an option. *There's no reason to be paranoid,* she told herself. *I'm not the target of the manhunt . . . at least not yet.* If Interpol and French police thought that Nicholas Woland was hiding out in this hotel, it would have been obvious by now. If she knew anything, it was how to recognize a sting operation in progress.

She crossed the lobby, her low heels clicking on the tile floor, and smiled at the stern-looking woman behind the reception desk. The woman, whose hair was pulled back in an impossibly tight bun, gave a half smile and held up a finger as she finished on the phone. After ending her call, the receptionist rested her hands on the ridiculously Parisian, faux-gold inlaid desk, which was positioned in front of a wall covered with a matching gold foil.

"*Oui, madame. Comment puis-je vous aider aujourd'hui?*" the woman asked, tilting her head in a way that reminded Maria of a Labrador retriever.

"English?" Maria asked hopefully. She was bilingual and fluent in Spanish, but her French was only middling. This was Paris, after all, where the privilege of speaking French was reserved for Parisians.

"Of course, madam," the woman said, her lips smiling but her eyes suggesting this to be the dumbest question of the day. "How may I help you?"

"I'm Anna Mayberry in room 413. Have any messages arrived for me while I was out?"

At this the woman's face showed genuine surprise. Perhaps in the age of cell phones and tablets, no one left messages with hotel desks anymore. Nonetheless, the woman dutifully scrolled through a box with dividers labeled with room numbers, then looked up and smiled her saccharine-sweet smile again.

"No, madam. No messages."

"Thank you," Maria said. "Have a nice day."

The receptionist gave a curt nod but didn't answer, and Maria headed for the elevator, where she was met with more obnoxious gold leaf. Once inside, she pressed the number four and the doors slid shut. Had the surveillance team detected anything of concern, she would have been aborted with a message at the desk. Moments later the bell chimed and the doors pulled open on the fourth floor. She would be glad to be back on task in Nashville, hunting the Shepherds and prosecuting the latest threat—the Navy SEAL who from all evidence had not, as promised, returned to Virginia Beach after helping rescue the Yarnell girl. Multiple attempts to find him the usually useful, much more supernatural way had failed. Even Victor himself was having difficulty finding his way into the man's mind.

Until the Nashville Metro Police cleared her to return to duty—at least another few weeks from the looks of it—she had the flexibility to serve her master however he saw fit. It was flattering to be tasked to a high-profile operation like this one. Victor had taken a tremendous risk breaking this man out of La Santé. Whatever he was planning for Nicholas Woland must be big, and she wondered what skills the man possessed that other Dark Ones did not.

Maybe one day the answers to such questions would no longer be above her pay grade.

She swiped her key card, heard the click, and let herself into room 413.

The room was small, comfortable, and annoyingly Parisian in that it had the same pretentious style as the lobby. As she walked to open the curtains, she paused at the door connecting to the adjoining room 415. She felt a flutter in her chest, which was out of place given her years of service. She'd been in many more dangerous situations than this. Her task was simple—escort Woland across the border into Switzerland while posing as his wife. If they were stopped, her presence would help bolster the validity of Woland's new identity. On paper it made sense, but she also suspected Victor had a secondary motive. He wanted someone he trusted to keep an eye on the freshly liberated Dark One—an asset Victor had left to rot in jail for far more years than anyone, probably including Woland himself, had anticipated.

As she tried to convince herself she had nothing to worry about, anxiety clawed at her. The assignment felt bigger than it should. Darker, riskier . . .

Staring at the connecting door, Maria felt a visceral unpleasantness—as if malice was seeping in from the room next door and somehow tainting the very air she breathed. She quick-stepped to the window and flung open the curtains to let in the light. Shadows fled and the room instantly felt cleaner.

Sanitized.

It's not the mission . . . it's the man, a second voice seemed to say, not hers, and she shivered.

Then she made an annoyed *tsk* sound and shook her head. She was acting like a schoolgirl new recruit. She'd been with *Victor* of all people—or whatever he really was—and there was no one more malignant and powerful. Nicholas Woland was but a man. She took a long, deep breath and then let it out through pursed lips. Even after centering herself, the compulsion to retrieve the pistol from her luggage was overpowering.

It's okay, she told herself. *We're on the same side.*

With a resigned exhale, she walked to the connecting door and unlocked the dead bolt. After opening her slab, she rapped twice with her knuckles on its twin.

"It's open" came a relaxed and refreshingly American voice from the other side.

Maria pushed and sure enough, the door swung easily into the adjoining room that was the mirror image of her own.

Woland sat at the small table, legs crossed at the knee and a stub of a cigarette between the first and second fingers of his right hand, a thin tendril of blue smoke rising beside his chiseled jawline. Both forearms were wrapped in sleeves of tattoos. The left, an image of Lucifer, wrapped around the thick, sinewy forearm. The image was gorgeous: gray skin, glowing eyes above a gleaming smile on the thin face, gold scars covering the lean, muscular body, which was also studded with horns on the shoulders and arms.

"You like the art, I see," Woland's deep voice boomed, just a hint of east Texas accent around the edges.

"It's magnificent," she said, then tore her eyes from the mesmerizing tattoo, immediately regretting how her voice sounded like a fangirl meeting her favorite musician.

"It cost a fortune," Woland said, uncrossing his legs and stubbing out the remains of his cig. "It covers an old tattoo that no longer suited my life choices. A perfect recasting, I thought, considering my pedigree."

"I'm sorry, but I don't know what you mean," she said, her voice now back to normal.

He smiled, and it occurred to her how similar the smile was to the image inked on the man's arm, an image of Lucifer straight out of her mind when she'd read Dante's *Inferno*.

"Lucifer was the ultimate fallen angel, don't you think? God's right-hand man. There's a saying—the bigger they are, the harder they fall. Well, that's a far fall and one that led to his incredible power. Kinda like me, right?"

He rose and she noted how his broad chest and shoulders tugged at the seams of his dress shirt, which he wore untucked over black jeans, the denim also stressed to contain the muscles beneath.

She forced herself to hold his penetrating gaze.

"I'm afraid I'm not fully read in," she said, searching for control over this conversation. *She* was the handler here, not the other way around. "I don't know your pedigree, nor do I care. My job is to get you safely to Bern. We're to pose as a married couple for the trip, a half day's drive on the A6. I'm just filler for your NOC. Six hours—that's all we are to each other."

"Mmm-hmm," he said, stepping toward her. She felt her pulse quicken with both fear and desire as he did. "This is not my first rodeo. I know you work with Victor, and if he sent you, then you must be good."

He took another step, closing the interpersonal gap, and his scent flooded her nostrils. An unsettling and almost-uncontrollable lust flooded over her as she held her ground.

"After the Paris attacks when you were arrested, we were all shocked," she said, forcing herself to breathe through her mouth. "I'd never seen Victor so angry . . . I have to confess I was surprised he orchestrated your escape. So much rests on the success of your next mission."

She hoped the comment knocked Woland down a peg. At the same time, she also wanted to suggest she had knowledge of the upcoming operation for which this man had been freed from La Santé, but in reality she had no idea what Victor was planning.

The imposing operator took another step closer.

This time, Maria had no choice but to take a step back, but her heel hit the wall, leaving her nowhere to go.

"I never doubted Victor would come for me," he said, placing a hand on the wall behind her, leaning in as he did. She closed her left hand into a tight fist to stop the trembling. "You see, like Lucifer, I am a fallen angel, sweetheart," he said and used his free right hand to sweep a wisp of hair that had fallen onto her face and tuck it behind her ear. "That's why Victor needs me."

She placed both hands on his chest and shoved him hard enough to make him stumble. He caught himself, then looked her up and down, surveying her like one might a new car on a lot while deciding whether to take it for a test drive.

She crossed her arms. "We're all fallen angels of one sort or another. I can promise you that whatever you imagine your value to Victor is, you have miscalculated. If you die here, he has plenty of other fallen angels ready and willing to serve the cause. And I also promise you this . . ." She leaned in toward him. "If you touch me again, I will kill you."

He surprised her by laughing—a deep, genuine laugh—before

returning to the table to take a sip of whatever cocktail he'd been drinking.

"I apologize," he said, eyes suggesting he regretted nothing. "Incarceration takes a toll on a man."

She gave a curt nod. "We leave in two hours. Have another drink if you like; I'll be doing all of the driving, so no issues there."

"Two hours." He raised his glass in toast to her and then drained the remainder of his cocktail.

She'd turned to head back to her room—where she fully intended to lock the connecting door, though she doubted that would prevent anything with this man—when he called after her.

"Young lady," he said, the honorific both demeaning and inscrutable as he looked no older than she was.

"Yes?" she said, turning to find him tugging his left sleeve up over a bulging bicep to reveal yet another tattoo.

"Victor doesn't have another fallen angel like me."

Her mouth dropped open and her eyes went wide at the iconic inked symbol—a Christian cross, with a sword and a shepherd's crook behind, surrounded by laurel. Speechless, she forced her mouth closed and met his lascivious gaze.

"That's right, sweetheart," he said, eyes glowing like the image of Lucifer on his forearm. "I was a Shepherd."

CHAPTER FIVE

As usual, Jed was wrong.

Jericho Basic was not fun . . . not fun at all. The Colonel ran the program with the inhuman cadence of a metronome and was tougher and more physically fit than Jed's most generous initial prediction. Six days into the program, Jed's muscles were trashed. He hadn't been this sore since BUD/S. The Colonel was relentless, and Jed couldn't help but wonder if the man was a cyborg.

He was not alone in this assessment.

"I'm telling you guys: the Colonel is not human," Hyeon said, walking out of the men's bathroom toward his rack, talking with a toothbrush still in his mouth. "Fifty bucks says if we could see under that tan, leathery skin of his, we'd find a Terminator endoskeleton."

"Totally," Bex chimed in. "Remember that scene in *T2* when Arnold uses a pocketknife to carve around his forearm and then rips off the flesh to show everybody his robot hand? My nightmare is that at the end of basic, the Colonel is going to call us all together and do that."

"That scene was so nasty," Carl chimed in from his rack, already horizontal with the Bible he'd been reading lying open and facedown atop his expansive chest. "It's one of those things you can never unsee."

"I've been here four years," Johnny said as he slid his trainers under the foot of his rack. "And I've never seen the dude doze off or get tired or nothing. I'm pretty sure while we sleep, he plugs himself into a charging station."

Jed chuckled at the comment as he pulled down the top sheet and blanket on his rack in preparation for getting some desperately needed shut-eye. He looked up just in time to see Nisha, who was sitting on the mattress on the rack to his right, lift the T-shirt she was wearing up and over her head. Beneath she was wearing a black athletic bra, which she slept in along with a pair of hip-hugging, fitted workout shorts. Despite himself, he let his gaze pass slowly over her, finally locking onto her rich, espresso-colored eyes. The corners of her lips curled ever so slightly while her eyes narrowed just a twinge to send him a definitive message—one part chastisement, one part satisfaction.

Busted.

The sleeping quarters were coed, but the barracks had separate men's and ladies' toilet and shower facilities at the opposite ends of the rectangular hall. In the Teams, he'd served with plenty of women in support billets, but there had been no female SEALs. His BUD/S class had been exclusively male as had been every bunk room he'd slept in during his time in the Navy. He wasn't sure how the Army and Marines managed the nitty-gritty of gender integration, but this was his first coed berthing experience. Obviously the decision had been made here at Trinity Loop to integrate the classes to the maximum extent possible using a gender agnostic model. Over the last several days, he'd often reflected on his conversation with Grayson during the first run about shared adversity, bonding, and brotherhood. To have a separate women's program with a dedicated female instructor and separate barracks would— even if born from the best intentions—foster an us-versus-them mentality.

This way was better.

And it was working. They were bonding, and the interpersonal banter was way up over the past week.

The Colonel had made Jed platoon leader on the first day, and he'd decided that so long as nobody felt uncomfortable, or the behavior didn't cross the line into sexual intimidation, harassment, or fraternization, he would let it ride. They were all adults here . . . so long as everyone's behavior stayed professional, well-mannered, and good-intentioned, the system worked. They needed to be comfortable with each other, and they needed to be able to trust one another. That trust and comfort level came only by becoming intimately familiar with each team member's personality, habits, and most importantly, their physical, emotional, and spiritual strengths and weaknesses.

The family that plays together stays together.

Besides, it wasn't like he was trying to manage a bunch of hot-tempered, overconfident, and inexperienced E-1s and E-2s. Half the class were veteran Shepherds and the other half were highly vetted and decorated frontline operators.

It's all good, he thought and glanced at his watch.

"Lights out in three mikes," he announced, but a quick look around the bunk room revealed that he was the last man standing. The rest of the team was either already in their racks or kneeling at their bedsides in prayer. Jed, it seemed, was the only one who didn't pray every night before chasing sleep. It wasn't that he didn't *want* to pray—he'd felt the power of prayer during the operation to find Sarah Beth Yarnell. He felt the familiar but still-distant faith growing inside him. He guessed, more than anything, he just wasn't sure what, exactly, to say to the God he'd walked away from back in Tennessee so long ago.

Jed sighed and remembered that guilt was a tool used not by God but by . . . *others.*

He closed his eyes, let out a long breath, and tried to think of what to say. After a moment, when nothing profound came to him, he thought simply, *Thanks, God.*

Despite not meaning to, he looked back at Nisha, catching her as she swung her legs up onto the mattress and disappeared them under the top sheet.

"Good night," Nisha said in something that was becoming a ritual between them.

"You too," he said. "0600 is going to come quick."

"It always does," she said, her slight accent more noticeable to him when she was tired at the end of a hard day than in the morning.

Based on her accent and physical appearance, he pegged Nisha as Punjabi, but which side of the Indo-Pakistani border she hailed from was a mystery. She'd still not shared anything about herself with him—neither professional nor personal. This trait, however, was a clue in and of itself and lent strong credence to his growing belief that she had come to the program from the "spooky" side of the counterterror community. She projected a spy's discerning manner—always collecting and assessing information without leaking any clues about her own history or intentions. She ran like a triathlete, handled firearms like a pro, and never drew attention to herself. Only on the obstacle course did she consistently falter, where her ratio of upper body strength to weight lagged the others, including Bex. This was a normal and, unfortunately, disqualifying criterion for most women wishing to enter the special operations community. Gender dimorphism was a reality of the human condition and the primary reason why there were no female SEALs—at least not yet.

In combat, especially in spec ops, raw physical power mattered.

The lights in the bunk room automatically turned off at 2200 hours, plunging the room into momentary darkness until individual reading lights flicked on, first in Carl's rack, then in Bex's. They both liked to read the Bible before turning in, and this little rule bend was another example of something Jed would tolerate and only curb if it became a problem. Eyes open, Jed stared at the ceiling. He listened to the crickets and tree frogs singing outside. He listened to the breathing sounds of his Jericho Basic family. He could tell that Nisha and Eli—his right and left side bunkmates—were already asleep. They were both usually out cold within sixty seconds of lights out. Jed took longer to decompress and quiet his internal monologue before he could fall asleep.

Probably because sleep, most nights, was not his friend . . .

Carl's light clicked off first.

Bex's light followed five minutes later.

Jed rolled over and stared at Nisha, her features barely discernible in the heavy dark of the bunk room. She was exquisite to look at, and it bothered him terribly that he found himself wanting to.

Eventually sleep did find him . . . and so did his demons.

He awoke, but inside a nightmare, to the sound of his first love and high school girlfriend screaming.

"Rachel!"

Her cries were coming from the basement. He turned to David, his best friend, standing at his side. Instead of finding courage, David's eyes were filled with fear . . . because there were other sounds coming from the basement.

Inhuman sounds—primal and wicked.

Jed charged down the wooden staircase to find Rachel on her back, legs forced apart and torso pinned beneath a broad-shouldered thing in a varsity letter jacket that was attempting to savage her.

"Get off of her!" he screamed and grabbed Rachel's attacker by the hair and pulled.

Kenny Bailey turned to look at him, but the boy's face was consumed by another—a grotesque, demonic visage superimposed atop his classmate's real face. The demon face snarled at Jed, eyes glowing the color of flame.

Then it spoke.

"You can't hide from me. I'm coming for you, Jedidiah . . . coming for you and everyone you love."

Jed sat bolt upright in his rack, chest heaving and his entire body covered in gooseflesh.

"Jed, are you okay?" an unfamiliar woman's voice asked nearby.

"Where am I?" he said, scanning the room.

"You're in the bunk room," the woman said and slipped toward him like a night shadow.

He drew his fist back to strike, but as he did, his wits returned to him. "Nisha?" he whispered, straining to make out her features in the dark.

"Yes, it's me," she said, taking a seat on the edge of his mattress. "You were having a nightmare. A pretty terrible one from the sound of it."

A reading light clicked on in Carl's rack. "Everything okay?" the Marine asked, sitting up.

"Yeah, I'm sorry, guys," Jed said, addressing everyone who was now awake, which was pretty much the entire platoon. "Didn't mean to wake everyone. Y'all can go back to sleep."

Carl clicked off his reading light and Jed heard the rustling of sheets and creaking of cot springs as his drowsy teammates repositioned and went back to sleep.

Nisha lingered. "Do you want to talk about it?" she whispered.

He shook his head. "Not really."

"I can relate. The Dark Ones invade my dreams as well."

"They do?" he said, turning to look at her.

"Oh yes," she said with a pitying little laugh. "Maybe tomorrow it will be your turn to comfort me."

He smiled at her.

She smiled back, then wordlessly returned to her rack, where she rolled onto her side, facing away from him. He exhaled through pursed lips, reclined, and knit his fingers together beneath his head under his pillow. The last time he'd had that dream had been while sleeping in a hollow in the woods during the infil to rescue David and Rachel's kidnapped daughter, Sarah Beth. A shiver chased down his spine.

Why am I having it now? he wondered.

He'd been doing so well lately, keeping his thoughts off Rachel. Since he'd started basic, he'd not thought of the Yarnells once. But it wasn't just reliving the basement incident that bothered him . . . Something had changed in the dream. Tonight, the demon had spoken to him directly: *You can't hide from me. I'm coming for you, Jedidiah . . . coming for you and everyone you love.*

That was new.

New and disturbing . . . because he recognized the voice. It was the same voice that had invaded his mind at the compound in the woods during Sarah Beth's rescue. The same voice that had talked him into putting his pistol muzzle underneath his chin and almost convinced him to pull the trigger.

Victor, it would appear, has found me.

CHAPTER SIX

Woland savored the comforting, familiar burn in his back, shoulders, and forearms as he alternated curls, upright row, Arnold press, and lunges with the heavy dumbbells. His warm-up had been a hundred push-ups and a hundred sit-ups, something his muscles barely registered these days. Having no access to a gym in La Santé, his daily routine had consisted of dozens of supersets of push-ups, handstand presses, crunches, and isometric exercises. He could manipulate his body weight with the ease of an acrobat, but it wasn't enough.

There was simply no substitute for weight training.

He placed the dumbbells back on the rack with a satisfying clunk and rolled his head to stretch out his tight neck as he glanced at the clock on the wall. He needed to get back to his hotel room so he didn't miss the call. He felt eyes on him and turned, the young woman on the treadmill flushing red at being caught ogling him before turning away. Then she glanced over again and smiled.

If only I had more time . . .

Perhaps they'd cross paths again in the hotel bar later this evening. If not, there were so many other women he could target. This was Rome, after all.

Woland wiped the sweat from his face, sucked down two cups of cold water from the cooler by the towel dispenser, tossed his cup, and then, with a final smile to the girl on the treadmill, he walked out of the hotel gym.

Back in his room, he tossed the towel and his key onto the black sofa with its pretentious salmon-colored piping and glanced at his watch. He still had five minutes before the scheduled call, but he retrieved the satellite phone from the room's lockbox to be certain. Seeing no missed calls, he walked to the balcony and opened the glass slider. A blast of air rushed through the gap—real, outdoor air—and he inhaled. Though tainted by the obnoxious odors that came with big-city living, the experience felt decadent after so long breathing the stale, institutional air at La Santé. Even better was having a balcony at all, with its view of the small courtyard below. At check-in, he'd almost demanded a room with a view of the Tiber River across the Lungotevere dei Mellini, but a courtyard view was safer and tactically prudent.

Woland laughed. Even La Santé had not been able to strip his love of luxury and decadence. What was the point of living if one abstained from sating the carnal pleasures? *Ironic,* he thought. *I used to be perfectly content to sleep in the mountains of the Hindu Kush with a rock as my pillow.* Content . . . so long as he was on the hunt. Perhaps that was where the lust for killing had taken root. He'd fought it—that craving to take another man's life—long and hard. Then he'd convinced himself that the killing was just a tool—a means to an end—and that his real love was duty, honor, and country. Eventually he'd been forced to admit that while those things had mattered to him early in his military career, it was the rush and joy from killing that drove him.

As a man raised in the Methodist church, he'd hoped, and at times even prayed, that working with Ben Morvant and the Shepherds would shake loose something spiritual inside him and help him combat feelings and fantasies born of murder. But that hadn't happened. It had been a hard transition to free himself from the shackles his Christian upbringing had placed on him. Truth be told, he didn't believe any less in God now than he had as a young Green Beret or even as a Shepherd. He'd just picked another side—the winning side. Because if God loved His children as much as His Book claimed, why didn't He rescue them from the horrors Woland had witnessed in war? Why did Victor exist at all? Only under Victor's tutelage had Woland completed his evolution.

Only Victor accepted him for what he was.

A grin spread across his face and he took another long breath of Rome's city air. He had learned to embrace his identity as a killer, and any lingering doubts fostered by his time locked away in the Parisian prison had dissipated as he'd killed the five people—three men and two women—in the trauma bay at Hôpital Cochin in

Paris. For the sake of anonymity, he'd wanted and even intended to avoid further bloodshed, but he hadn't been able to help himself. As the blood had sprayed onto the wall of the doctors' lounge from his sixth victim—a cleaning woman who'd picked the wrong time to empty the bin of soiled scrubs—all he'd managed to think had been *She shouldn't have looked at me that way.*

That was who he was—a man willing to murder for a look.

The satellite phone chirped, breaking his rumination. He picked it up, punched in his encryption code, and pressed the green button to connect.

"Yes," he said.

A pause stretched out; then a familiar, oily voice said, "Nicholas . . . so nice to hear your voice."

"And yours," he replied, trying to hide his surprise.

As if anything could be hidden from Victor . . .

When Victor didn't answer, he continued, "Though I was surprised to not hear from you sooner. Two years is a very long time."

He immediately regretted the misstep. And as the silence stretched out, he worried he'd offended the man. A chill ran down his spine at the notion.

"Surprised? You shouldn't have been. I didn't need you until now," Victor said finally. "You exist to serve me, not the other way around."

It suddenly struck Woland that if a serpent could speak, this was exactly what it might sound like.

"Of course," he said, forcing humility into his voice as best he could and tamping down a rage he felt flicker inside him. "I only meant that I might have imagined your needing my unique skill set sooner than this. I exist to serve."

"Yes," Victor said and then sighed. "We both know that isn't entirely true . . . but I do need you now. Have you deduced the target?"

"Yes," he replied with certitude. "The Vatican. It's why you sent me to Rome."

"Indeed," Victor replied. "This is a mission for which you are uniquely qualified. Your familiarity with and connections inside mercenary networks in the Middle East and Africa will need to be exploited for this operation. Equally important, your intimate knowledge of the Shepherds tactics, communication protocols, hierarchy, and personnel will be critical for the plan to succeed. Are you ready to prove your worth?"

"Yes," Woland replied, knowing that Victor's appraisal of his knowledge and contacts were a stretch of the truth. The Shepherds' security protocols would have changed immediately after his defection. Still, he knew how Ben Morvant thought, didn't he? He could guess easily what he would have done and what changes he would have made. Morvant was predictable. Empathy and compassion were his biggest weaknesses—weaknesses Woland knew how to exploit and, hopefully, could ultimately use to destroy the man.

"Excellent," Victor said, his voice a hiss. "Because this operation must penetrate every layer of Vatican security—both tactical and spiritual. Holy blood must be spilled."

Woland drew in a breath as Victor explained his malign vision for the operation. What the dark angel was describing sounded like a suicide mission, but a mission that excited Woland nonetheless. With the proper team and sufficient planning, he certainly would not need to sacrifice his *own* life. Still, to be part of such an audacious plot, one whose cries would echo around the globe, would be so . . .

Satisfying.

And he knew Victor well enough to know that an initial operation would precede the one at the Vatican.

". . . but another element is necessary," Victor continued. "Before spilling holy blood, we must first set the stage. Two operations will work in tandem to foment hate, manifest division, and turn brother against brother on a global scale. This is the ultimate goal. Do you understand?"

"Yes," Woland said, his mind already working the tactical aspects of the operation.

"Prove to me you understand by explaining how."

Woland laughed. "By making the Vatican operation look like retribution—a jihad perpetuated by radical Islamists," he said softly, his lips turning up in a smile. "We need an attack on a Muslim target first. A mosque in the Middle East—Syria perhaps, or in Iraq—using only western fighters, American or British ideally. And it must have heavy civilian casualties. Women and children especially. Blame and outrage are the goal."

"Precisely. The groundwork is already being laid," Victor said with both satisfaction and irritation that Woland had passed his test.

"Of course it is," Woland said and snorted a short laugh.

"It will happen in Iraq, very soon. Your operation will take place shortly after. But you have much work to do. Your job is to find a weakness to exploit within the Holy See. You need to focus."

The jab irritated him. He was focused.

"I need intelligence on Vatican City," he said, his mind racing and his heart following suit. "And the details of the other operation. It is imperative we make the two attacks appear directly linked. The Vatican attack must be perceived as retribution for the other."

"Very good, Nicholas. You have come a long way, my son. A courier will deliver a memory stick with a full brief on the mosque attacks and our entire dossier on Vatican security in the coming twenty-four hours."

"Thank you," he said. "That will be very helpful."

"Yes," Victor replied. "The Shepherds aren't the only ones with assets inside the Vatican."

The line went dead. Woland placed the phone back in the drawer, an enormous smile on his face. Then, charged with a new sense of purpose, he changed to go for a run.

CHAPTER
SEVEN

"At least the food is good here," Hyeon said from the chair next to Jed as Alpha platoon ate lunch together. "Otherwise, I'd be as grumpy as the Colonel."

Jed, who was in the middle of chewing a mouthful of sub sandwich, nodded with enthusiastic agreement. So far, all of their meals had been prepared at the central campus cafeteria and delivered to the chow hall on the training annex, but they were fan-friggin'-tastic regardless. The sandwich in his hand had triple the cold cuts and veggies one would expect from a catered lunch. For big boys like Jed, both quality *and* quantity were important. Putting away two Subway footlongs for lunch was his SOP, but this monster sub the Trinity cafeteria had prepared would do the trick.

"Does anybody want to trade an apple for my potato chips?" Nisha asked, scanning the table for takers.

"Are those cheddar and sour cream Ruffles?" Eli said, squinting at the bag.

"They are indeed," she said, holding up the bag like a spokesmodel presenting the latest and greatest thing on QVC.

"I definitely want in on that action," Eli said and tossed her his apple.

Nisha caught the flying Granny Smith with her left hand and slid the bag of potato chips down the table to him.

Despite a mouth full of food, Jed chuckled at the horse-trading banter. It reminded him of the good old days in middle school when he and David and Rachel—the three musketeers back in that simple time—swapped snacks from their lunch boxes. Whether it was four Oreos in exchange for a Little Debbie Swiss roll or a half PB and J for a whole banana, important culinary calculus went into such things. Not to mention a good deal of poker-faced gamesmanship. A warm nostalgic feeling buoyed his spirits momentarily, before the memory turned on him and soured his mood, as thoughts of losing Rachel to David always did. But he'd lost more than Rachel, hadn't he? He'd lost the life he'd planned—a marriage and a ministry that David had stepped in to usurp. He now understood and accepted that it was the Dark Ones who'd driven him from his friends and his God, but thoughts of David living the life meant for him still brought feelings of bitterness and envy.

"What's that look for, Jed?" Bex asked from where she sat directly across the table from him. "You look like you just bit into a lemon."

"Pickle," he lied and forced a smile back onto his face. "Too many in that bite for my taste."

"Here's what I want to know," Grayson chimed in. "Why did people start putting pickles on sandwiches in the first place? I mean think about it: you've got this perfectly delicious sandwich with fresh-baked bread, salty ham, spicy salami, and rich, creamy slices of cheese and then some clown says to himself, 'You know what would make this better? A slimy, ugly slice of green that tastes like rotten vinegar.'"

Eli shrugged. "I don't know. I think they taste pretty good, especially on burgers."

"You *would* think that, 'cause you're like a human garbage disposal," Grayson said, tossing Eli a bag of potato chips from his own tray. "Dude, if you didn't work out every day, you'd weigh three hundred pounds."

"You're just jealous of my sexy bod." Eli stood up and started rubbing his stomach, which he puffed out like a potbelly for effect.

Jed and everyone else at the table laughed at the show. The dude was strong as a bull, but like so many senior operators, Eli was now making the lifestyle decision to trade in his six-pack for a pony keg if he kept eating like he did. Jed got it. He wrestled with his own life-is-too-short gremlins too. On that cue, he glanced down at the slab of frosted chocolate brownie on his plate, which he had every intention of devouring.

Someday my metabolism will hit a wall and when that day comes, I'm gonna have a pony keg of my own.

"Freidus, sit down before you give everyone indigestion," the Colonel piped up from the far end of the table, where he was sitting off by himself. Most of the time he ate alone, preferring to take his meals in his office, but not this lunch.

"Aw, Colonel, I was just getting warmed up," Eli said with his trademark lazy grin as he settled back into his chair.

"Y'all got ten more minutes; then I want everyone in the classroom for indoc," the silver-haired instructor said, pushing his chair back from the table and rising with his tray.

"Indoc?" Bex said, screwing up her face. "I thought we were already—"

"You thought wrong," the Colonel said, cutting her off. "There's a mandatory video you need to watch and someone who'd like to say a few words to you."

"Roger that, Colonel," Jed said. "Ten minutes in the classroom."

The Colonel checked his watch. "Nine minutes, Johnson. Keep up," he barked and walked out of the chow hall.

Jed turned to Hyeon. "I knew there was a video. There's always a video."

"Did they make you watch that one at Little Creek with the narrator who talks like James Earl Jones?" the former SEAL said, grinning from ear to ear.

"Yeah, that one's a classic," Jed said and then, doing his best James Earl Jones impersonation, said: "'In 1962, the US Navy formed the first SEAL Teams—sea, air, and land—to meet President John F. Kennedy's mandate to develop unconventional warfare capabilities. The mission: to conduct clandestine operations and counterguerilla warfare insurgencies in maritime environments and denied areas around the globe.'"

"Dude, that was spot-on," Hyeon said through a laugh. "When you retire from this place, you definitely have a future in voice-overs."

"When I retire from this place, I'm gonna be drinking beer on the beach in the Virgin Islands every day, and the only impersonations I'll be doing are of the world's most interesting man as I order another Dos Equis."

The comment earned him a fist bump and an *amen* from Hyeon, and then the banter ended because Jed still had an apple and that brownie to wolf down.

After everyone's places were cleared and trash put away, they walked as a group to the classroom building on the training annex. Eli held the door for everyone as they entered. Off to the side of the building's spartan lobby, the Colonel was talking with a man whose back was to the door. Despite not being able to see the man's face, Jed immediately recognized the visitor. With a smile, he vectored to join the twosome and say hello. He'd not seen Ben Morvant since the attack at the Yarnells' a month ago. A part of him thought it odd that he'd had zero interaction with the man who'd recruited him to the Shepherds since his arrival, but he'd chalked it up to this whole boot camp, basic training model they were using. Seeing Ben now, however, he couldn't pass on the opportunity to say hello.

". . . Interpol issued a red notice on him, but so far Woland's managed to slip through the net," Ben was saying in a low voice as Jed approached. Then the former SEAL and Shepherd leader stopped talking abruptly and turned to greet Jed with the smile of a parent who'd just been interrupted at the grown-ups table by one of his kids. "Hey, Jed."

"Heck of a facility you've got here," Jed said, trying to ignore the awkwardness. "To be honest, this training complex rivals what we had at Little Creek. I haven't toured the main campus yet, but it's a lot bigger than I expected. How many folks work at Trinity Loop?"

Ben smiled patiently while Jed rambled and then said, "I'm glad to hear you're settling in, Jed. There'll be time to catch up later. See you in the classroom."

The Colonel, for his part, fixed Jed with his default drill instructor's glare but added nothing.

Jed hesitated a beat at the not-so-subtle brush-off and said the only thing he could say. "Sure, I'll see you inside."

Red-faced, he turned and walked into the classroom, where the rest of the team was getting settled. The room was windowless, with a speaker's podium at the front, a massive whiteboard on the wall behind it, and a ceiling-mounted projector. The rest of the space was occupied by a half-dozen three-person tables in lieu of individual desks. Jed followed the pattern established by his teammates, who were sitting in pairs, and took the right-hand spot at a table with Hyeon, leaving the middle seat empty.

"Something's definitely up, dude. I can feel it," Johnny was saying to Carl behind him as Jed settled into his chair. "Have you heard anything?"

"Yeah, I heard a rumor," Carl whispered back. "But this ain't the time or place to get into it."

Jed was about to turn in his seat to engage the veterans and ask them about the red notice and the name he'd heard, *Woland*, but the Colonel and Morvant walked into the classroom.

"I know everybody just ate lunch," the Colonel began, "and that means when I turn off the lights and start this mandatory indoctrination video, some of you yahoos are going to be tempted to fall asleep. Yes, Johnny Rawlings, I'm looking at you. But I strongly advise you resist doing so because all that will do is force me to start the video over. Every single one of you will watch this video—from beginning to end—even if I have to restart it a hundred times. Is that understood?"

"Hooyah, Colonel," Johnny barked, beating Jed to the punch for once.

"Good, but before I start it, this distinguished gentleman standing up here with me has a few words he'd like to say to you. Ladies and gentlemen, say hello to Ben Morvant—commander, Shepherds North America."

The four veterans in the room banged their fists on the tabletop in three quick, synchronized beats and popped to their feet. The four nuggets, Jed included, missed the table pound but followed their brothers' lead and snapped to their feet as well.

Ben shook his head and waved a dismissive hand at them as he stepped behind the podium. "Sit down, you jokers." He swept his gaze sequentially across all the faces before continuing. "Most of you know me, but I see a couple of new faces—Bex and Hyeon . . . did I get the pronunciation right, son?"

"*Yun* like *fun*—you nailed it, sir," Hyeon said.

"Nisha, Jed, and my fellow veterans—it's good to see all of you. The Colonel tells me this class is already starting to gel, which is good news. But you've got a long road ahead and plenty of PT and training yet to do, so don't lose focus."

The veterans banged their fists on the table three more times, obviously some inside joke or tradition they had with the Shepherd commander, earning another smile from Ben, this one a little less bright.

"Now I imagine some of you new people might be wondering what the heck you've gotten yourselves into. That's both natural and sensible at this stage of your recruitment because at Jericho Basic we hit the ground running—literally—and the Colonel refuses to take his foot off the gas long enough for you to ask questions and get your bearings. Well, that's why we have this session. For the next hour, I'm making the Colonel pump the brakes. The video will answer most of the questions you might have, but I want to make myself available for a few minutes so you can ask your more burning questions of me personally and get those much-needed answers. So fire away."

For an awkward moment, nobody said anything or raised a hand.

"This is your one and only chance, people," the Colonel said, his voice ripe with irritation. "If you don't ask the man questions, then he says goodbye and I turn on the video."

Bex raised her hand.

"Yeah," the Shepherd commander said, nodding at her.

"Before I got recruited, I didn't even know the Shepherds existed, and I consider myself someone who has her finger on the pulse of the clandestine world. I knew about Trinity—just like everybody in the biz knows about Triple Canopy and Academi—but I'd never heard of the Shepherds. So I guess I have two questions. First, this is not a small operation—how have you managed to keep the secret? And second, nobody has succinctly explained to me what our charter is. Do we have, like, a mission statement or something?"

Morvant smiled. "Those are keen observations and great questions and I'll do my best to address all of it. As you deduced, Trinity—or Trinity Global, as far as the lawyers are concerned—is the official cover for the Shepherds organization. Governments and companies around the world contract with us for legitimate training, security, and risk mitigation services, and that allows us to move our people around easily and travel with authentic paperwork. This facility, Trinity Loop, is the training nexus and headquarters for that operation, while simultaneously supporting the North American Shepherds organization."

"Isn't that risky? I mean, how do you keep the two separated?" she asked.

Ben chuckled. "We don't. Everyone who works on this campus is read in on the mission. We're all on the same team."

"Global is where real Shepherds like us get put out to pasture," Johnny piped in.

Ben shot him a look. "I'm going to pretend I didn't hear that."

"But there must be more to the story," Bex said. "I mean, when did this all start?"

"Ours is an ancient and storied organization with roots dating back to the Middle Ages, which you'll see in detail in the video. The very first Shepherds were German monks who filled their ranks with young men who demonstrated the gift of second sight—specifically the ability to see into the evil hearts and minds of men, giving them the ability to predict evil deeds before they happened."

"Interesting," Jed said. "So the first Shepherds were actually Watchers."

Ben nodded. "And they quickly ran into a problem I imagine all of you can guess."

"That bad guys aren't afraid to fight back," Hyeon said.

"That's right. They were men of God, but they lacked the physical armor and skills to defend themselves and stop the criminals, rapists, and murderers they were trying to prosecute preemptively.

So the head of the order made a difficult decision—one that would change the fate of the organization and mankind forever. He engaged knights to train his monks in the art of combat. It didn't take long, however, before the monks and the knights realized this arrangement was suboptimal for both parties—with neither the monks nor the knights putting their best skills to use. And so a partnership was forged in faith between warriors and holy men to work together to find and stop evil as a team. This early charter is the same one that guides us today."

"Whoa, that's pretty friggin' cool," Hyeon said.

"I know," Ben replied. "For centuries, this is how it was, an alliance between men of God and warriors of faith, working together in secret, their partnership a promise, their mission a holy vow to stave off the efforts of the Dark Ones who are trying to keep mankind from God. As times changed, so did the Shepherds—branching out, putting down roots outside of Europe, while constantly evolving to maintain their anonymity and effectiveness. Funding, recruitment, and secrecy were and still are the three greatest logistical challenges we face. With the rise of information technology, we are more at risk of discovery now than ever before. It's one of the reasons our vetting process takes so long and why we compartmentalize the way that we do. Before we invite a new member into our world, we must be absolutely certain we've made a sound decision."

"Quite a tall order considering the size of the operation. How many Shepherds are there?" Hyeon asked.

"Globally there are five hundred Shepherds supported by another five thousand leadership and support staff, Watchers, Keepers, and men and women of God."

Hyeon whistled.

"Five thousand, wow," Jed said. "How many are Watchers?"

"Watchers cycle through based on the emergence and loss of their abilities. Most are recruited at eleven or twelve and then age out by twenty at the top end," Ben said, but he looked at Jed with a strange smile. "So the number varies, depending on where they are in their training cycle and when the degradation process begins. On average, though, about 5 to 10 percent of the support staff are active Watchers, with another 5 to 10 percent in various support roles."

"And the leadership?"

Ben smiled mysteriously this time. "The numbers and roles of the leadership staff worldwide are available only on a need-to-know basis. Suffice it to say that we have leadership personnel on campus for training and operational control, but a significant number embedded in governments, industry, and faith venues across the globe. Our funding comes from private donations, faith-based organizations, industry, and even federal sources—all of it procured by leadership read in to our operations. I know that's vague, and the topic is glossed over in the video for obvious security reasons, but that's the best we can do today."

"How long has this unit here been in existence?" Nisha asked.

"The North American unit has existed since the earliest days of the American Republic, but we've been operating from this campus for eleven years. The current war on terror across the globe afforded us the opportunity to bring everyone under one roof, so to speak, as the world is now a place where a task force–style DoD contractor raises little or no eyebrows. We needed to centralize for training as well as to grow our operational footprint, and with rising activity by the Dark Ones, it was becoming too difficult to protect everyone, everywhere, all the time. The OC, or official cover, for this facility is exactly what you see online. To the world, Trinity Loop is a private defense contractor specializing in the training and professional development of law enforcement and paramilitary civilian contractors. Whether you're looking at us from outer space or from outside the front gate, we look and behave just like Academi's Moyock facility in North Carolina. Inside the wire, as you all have come to learn, we are something else entirely."

Morvant fielded a few more questions from the group, artfully navigating some of the stickier topics he didn't want to get into and outright dodging a question from Carl about a rumored jailbreak in France.

Need to know and all that jazz, Jed thought. *Been there, done that.*

"All right, folks, I'm going to step out now and leave you to watch your indoctrination video in peace," the Shepherd commander said, gave a little nod to Jed, and walked out.

While everyone fidgeted in their seats—their overly taxed and sore muscles making it difficult to sit still—the Colonel dimmed the lights and turned on the projector. The Trinity Loop indoctrination and safety video began with music and a sweeping aerial view of the campus that zoomed in on a platoon of fit men and women working their way as a team across the Jericho Training Facility obstacle course. Then the epic voice-over began.

"Trinity Loop, the nation's premier training facility for civilian and contract security personnel, offers new recruits state-of-the-art . . ."

With a grin on his face, Hyeon leaned over to Jed and whispered, "Morgan Freeman?"

Jed chuckled, not surprised. "Oh yeah, no mistaking that voice . . . you totally called it."

CHAPTER EIGHT

Jed jerked awake in his rack, woken by a deafening, repetitive, metallic banging.

"Out of your racks, boys and girls," the Colonel shouted as he walked down the center aisle between the parallel rows of bunks, banging a metal trash can lid with a hammer. "Fall in on the kill house armory for your zero-dark-thirty live-fire evaluation. You have five minutes."

Adrenaline burned away the fog of sleep within a microsecond, and Jed was on his feet conducting a head count to make sure he wasn't missing anybody. He'd participated in plenty of devious scenario-based training drills over the years and wouldn't have been at all surprised to find one or more of his teammates "missing" at kickoff.

One, two, three, four, five, six, seven . . . all accounted for.

"All right, Alpha," Jed said the instant the Colonel stopped beating the trash can lid. "You heard the Colonel. Kit up, buddy up, and move out."

"Oh, man, are you nuggets in for a ride," Johnny said, running in place with high knees beside his rack. "Better get your muscles warm and blood flowing 'cause this ain't your granddaddy's kill house."

Jed turned to Eli. "What's Johnny talking about?"

Eli, who was taking his sweet time getting dressed, flashed Jed his trademark easygoing smile. "You'll see."

"Thanks, Eli. As always, you're very helpful," Jed grumbled and slipped his kit over his head.

Four minutes and forty-five seconds later, an adrenaline-charged Alpha platoon was formed up outside the locked door to the kill house armory. The energy was positively palpable as Jed scanned his teammates—most of whom were smiling and chatting excitedly with their neighbor. This evolution was Alpha's first trip to the kill house, a warehouse-size facility that dominated the southwestern quadrant of the training complex. Jed had asked a half-dozen questions about the building since the first day of Jericho Basic, but all he'd managed to get was confirmation that it was, indeed, a kill house. The lack of details, coupled with the cryptic smiles and knowing glances shared between the veterans, was revealing in its own right. Jed suspected this facility was something special, maybe even the crown jewel of the Trinity Loop complex itself.

A magnetic lock clicked and the armory door opened from the inside.

"Well, don't just stand there, Johnson—get your people inside," the Colonel said, standing in the doorway. "The bad guys aren't going to shoot themselves."

Jed, whose teammates had taken the initiative and were already heading inside, resisted the urge to roll his eyes at the unwarranted dig. This was how the game was played; the Colonel was just trying to get under his skin and fluster him prior to commencing what would undoubtedly be a graded evolution. Every interaction with his instructor—and the veterans, too, for that matter—was a leadership trial. Jericho Basic was designed to stress-test his mental toughness and emotional stability, not only as a Shepherd candidate but also as platoon leader. During SEAL training, he'd learned to manage such things, and most of the time the insults and potshots rolled off him like water off a duck's back.

Most of the time . . .

He stepped last into the armory and checked that the door shut and locked behind him before joining the rest of his teammates in a semicircle around the Colonel, who was standing in front of a wall of equipment and weapons. Long guns, pistols, helmets, chest plates, magazines, and night-vision goggles were all displayed in cradles across neatly arranged rows.

"This is a Sig Sauer MCX Virtus SBR," the Colonel said, pulling a slick-looking assault rifle from the rack. "But it's no ordinary Virtus . . ." He turned the weapon to show what appeared to be an aftermarket kit integrated into the upper receiver. "It's been modified with a precision, safe-targeting computer that uses a built-in gyroscope, the weapon's optics, and proximity sensors to prevent trigger pulls during live-fire exercises when the muzzle is aimed at a friendly or tracking toward a conflicted line of fire."

"Does it rely on body sensors or is it entirely AI driven?" Hyeon asked.

"Good question," the Colonel said, returning the Sig to its rack and pulling a nylon harness with flattened, hexagon-shaped devices the size of saucers on the front and back. "The answer is both. Every one of you will be wearing these sensor vests when you step foot into the kill house. The vest pings your location to the control room computer, which manages the scenario, but these hexagon sensors automatically signal an opposing operator's targeting computer when painted by that operator's laser sight."

"Double redundancy," Grayson said, nodding at Hyeon.

"Very cool," Hyeon said.

"Now I know that this is not your first rodeo. Each and every one of you has spent time in a kill house before. Some of you, undoubtedly a lot of time," the Colonel said, his gaze settling on Jed. "But no matter how many targets you've plinked, or how many kill houses you've cleared, I guarantee you've never seen anything like what you're about to experience."

"Rumor is they spent twenty-five million on it," Jed heard Johnny whisper to Bex, who was standing beside him.

The Colonel picked up one of the helmets with earphones, a boom mic, and a funky-looking goggle rig where NVGs would normally be on a tilt bracket. "This helmet is equipped with everything you need. The radio is built-in, with rotary dial controls on the outside behind the right ear: volume, channel, and mode selector switch."

"Are those NVGs or something else up top?" Bex asked.

"Something else," the Colonel said with a grin and flipped the goggles down. "Say hello to the world's first battle-zone augmented-reality goggles. Some of the imagery you see is real; some is computer generated. It is very difficult to tell the difference with your eyes alone."

"Whoa," Bex said, turning to Johnny.

"Told ya," Johnny said with a grin. "It's like the freaking *Matrix* in there."

"And all the gear is pretty much knuckle dragger–proof," the Colonel said, his gaze again going to Jed. "But the veterans can help get you sorted out before going in. Any questions?"

"Yeah, what's the OPORD for this evolution? First, are you just running us through sequentially as singles or in teams? And second, is there a mission objective we need to brief or is this just us plinking targets?" Jed asked.

"About time you asked that," the Colonel said, ever intent on busting Jed's chops. "This first time through will be as singles plinking targets so everybody can get familiar with the setup and equipment. Next time through we'll mix it up and make things a little more interesting."

"Roger that, Colonel," Jed said. "All right, everybody, let's get fully kitted up and ready to rock and roll."

The veterans paired up with the rookies and helped everyone get their gear sorted out while the Colonel disappeared to the control room to ready the course. As platoon leader, Jed volunteered to go last. He watched and waited with growing and eager anticipation over the next hour as his teammates cycled through the kill house. One by one, they returned to the staging room—exhausted but wearing Cheshire cat grins on their faces.

"Dude, Jedidiah," a sweaty-faced Hyeon said, clapping Jed on the shoulder after returning from his run, "get ready to have your mind blown."

"He's right—it's incredible," Bex said. "I can't wait to go again."

"You're up, Johnson," the Colonel's gravelly voice said in Jed's earphones.

"Check," Jed said into his boom mic. He gave his kit a final once-over, checked his weapon, and headed into the blacked-out tunnel leading from the staging room to the kill house.

Halfway through the tunnel, he flipped the AR goggles down from his helmet and into place in front of his eyes. In addition to turning night into day with instant full-color illumination, he noticed a heads-up informational overlay—like something a fighter pilot might see—as part of his field of view. At the top of the display was a compass heading that scrolled seamlessly as he swiveled his head right and left. The comms channel his radio was tuned to was indicated in the upper-right quadrant, along with his call sign for the run, which was Eight.

"I'm going to give you a five-second look at the route you need to take," the Colonel said in Jed's ear. A new visual indicator appeared in the upper-left side of his field of view identifying the incoming caller as *Papa*. The indicator disappeared when the Colonel's transmission ended and a three-dimensional overlay appeared in the center of Jed's visual field. The map overlay depicted a relatively complex serpentine path through the kill house that included staircases with up-and-down arrows. He quickly swallowed down his awe and studied the route, which snaked this way and that, as well as up and down stairs. At each major decision point, he assigned a simple action: *Right, straight, right, left—up, left, straight, left—down, left, right, left.* Then he created a chunky mnemonic—a memory tool that he'd learned in the Teams and honed during his career: *RiSR Left—ULoSe Left—DeaLeR Left.*

The map disappeared just as he repeated the impromptu mnemonic for the second time. It wasn't perfect, but it was what his brain generated organically in the moment and his best chance to remember the complex course.

A digital stopwatch appeared in the upper-right corner of his vision field: 00:00.

"Your run kicks off on my mark," the Colonel said, prompting Jed to step up to the glowing horizontal line on the floor at the end of the tunnel.

As he did, he clicked on his optical target designator and a green laser line appeared, streaming from the end of his rifle, which he could see in nonaugmented reality through his goggles.

"In three . . . two . . . one . . . go!"

Jed's rifle came up and he smoothly advanced in a combat crouch. The instant he stepped across the starting line, the world around him transformed into an urban setting with him standing in a deserted alleyway. He scanned left and right, looking for threats in what he presumed was a simulation of a generic third-world city. With only one way out of the alley, he quick-stepped toward the cross-street exit, drifting right to hug the side of a shanty building. Before he reached the street, a pair of armed insurgents swept around the corner directly in front of him. He engaged them, immediately dropping each with a single head shot. The imagery was so photo-realistic that after firing the shots, he hesitated, concerned he might have just killed two red-team actors.

But the fighters dematerialized before his eyes, decomposing into piles of ash on the dusty street.

Movement at ten o'clock in his peripheral vision caught his attention. He sidestepped right while rotating left and swept his targeting laser to bear on a shooter on the roof of a two-story building. Tracers zipped past Jed's left temple as he squeezed the trigger and dropped the target. The body tumbled off the roof and landed in the street, where a man in a black tunic picked up the shooter's AK-47 and turned it on Jed.

Trigger squeeze. Trigger squeeze.

Jed dropped the opportunistic jihadist with a double tap to the chest.

Light and shadow moved in his right peripheral vision. Jed whirled to see a white panel van tearing around the corner. It screeched to a halt in the middle of the street while the side slider door drifted open. Jed tagged the driver just above the left ear with a shot through the driver's window. The man slumped forward, his head hitting the steering wheel and sounding the horn in a loud, continuous bleat. Inside the cargo compartment, a black-clad insurgent appeared behind a deck-mounted .50-cal. Jed cursed and hit the deck as the shooter wildly strafed the street. Tracers flew over his head as Jed brought his muzzle up and fired a three-round burst into the van from a prone position. The gunner jerked and collapsed behind the .50. Jed hesitated a beat, but he kept aiming into the cargo compartment of the van, expecting another fighter to take his brother's place behind the mounted heavy gun.

He was not disappointed.

A second fighter stepped out of the shadow to man the .50, but Jed dropped him with a head shot before he could get set.

Movement to Jed's right drew his eye and he shifted his aim that direction. Years of trigger discipline stayed his index finger as a woman and a small child crossed the street in a huddled run. She glanced at him as she crossed the beam of his targeting laser and he saw terror in her eyes.

Real terror.

How is that even possible? he thought as he popped to his feet.

He shook off the distracting thought and scanned for emergent threats. An explosion thirty yards ahead washed out his vision, thundered in his headset, and shook the ground. Jed took a knee, sighting over his rifle and waiting for his goggles to refresh. Two assaulters clad in body armor and fatigues emerged from the smoky haze, bearing down on him with long guns.

Instead of reflexively firing, Jed queried the Colonel. "Papa, I've got two possible tangos heading my direction. Look like friendlies, but please advise."

"Shooters are blue," the Colonel came back, confirming Jed's instincts.

Jed swept his scan past the simulated operators who streamed by, engaging targets behind him. In the upper-right corner of the visual field, he saw the exercise timer scrolling away. He'd barely made it past the first turn, already fired ten rounds, and was burning time like mad.

Man, this is nuts, he thought and recalled his mnemonic. *RiSR Left—ULoSe Left—DeaLeR Left.*

He'd executed the first right and advanced straight, which meant he needed to be looking for the next right turn. He scanned ahead and spied another alley that intersected this main street he was on.

That has to be it, he thought and sprinted to the corner, where he paused, pressing his shoulder against the side of a stucco wall. Crouching low, he quickly sighted around the blind corner and pulled his head back.

No visible threats.

He exhaled hard and took the corner, leading with his rifle and fully expecting bad guys to swarm out of the woodwork any second. As usual, the bad guys did not disappoint. A metal door swung open on his left with a shooter inside. He capped the dude and swiveled back to center just in time to drop an insurgent running toward him with a knife.

Next turn is left, the SEAL inside reminded him as he advanced down the alley, which appeared to be a dead end. *And don't forget to check your six.*

Jed glanced over his left shoulder in time to see a jihadist with an AK-47 charging around the corner at the alley entrance behind him. He brought his rifle around but not before the fighter squeezed off a burst that sent rounds and tracers screaming inches from his helmet. Despite shooting second, Jed's three-round burst made contact first, crumpling the shooter in his tracks.

Half a mag burned.

Seeing no other threats, he swiveled to front and charged toward the end of the alley, praying he'd made the correct decision turning down this street in the first place. When he reached the dead end, he spied a wooden door on his left. He assumed it was the back entrance to the two-story stucco building he was now standing outside. Jed fell in beside the door, his back against the wall in the breacher-ready position. Heart pounding and lungs heaving, he pulled a flash-bang from his kit and counted himself down: *Three . . . two . . . one . . .*

On *go* he kicked the door open, tossed the flash-bang inside, and juked back clear of the doorway. Automatic-weapon fire erupted and tracers screamed out the open door into the alley for a full second before the flash-bang went off, silencing the onslaught. In the lull, Jed slipped through the opening and into the room, scanning for targets.

He found three.

Trigger squeeze. Trigger squeeze . . . trigger squeeze.

A baby wailed nearby—the child's cry so real that gooseflesh stood up on his forearms. Dread instantly blossomed in his stomach, as this training scenario was suddenly hitting a little too close to home. A flashback of a mother and child being held hostage by her armed and angry Taliban father in the Hindu Kush popped into his mind. With gritted teeth, he boxed the gruesome memory and purged his mind.

Keep your head in the game, Jed . . .

He advanced into the next room, where he encountered a staircase leading up to the second story. He registered that with this staircase he was transitioning to the second chunk of his mnemonic, with *U* for *up*. His heart rate picked up and he ascended the staircase quickly and quietly, controlling his footfalls to minimize noise. As the upper level came into view, he came face-to-face with a woman, cradling a child in her arms, and a bearded man standing behind her. He had one arm wrapped around her neck and held the point of a gleaming six-inch-long blade beneath the child's chin.

"Don't let him hurt my baby," she begged, tears streaming down her cheeks in twin rivulets.

The baby let out a second, gut-wrenching cry just as Jed locked eyes with the knife-wielding hostage taker.

"Go back or I kill them both," the man growled in broken English.

"Let them go or you die here," Jed said, positioning his green targeting dot in the middle of the man's forehead.

"If I let them go, you will shoot me," the man said, fiery hate burning in his eyes. "You leave; then I let them go."

Jed put tension on the trigger. The last time he'd been in this situation, he'd tried to talk the angry father down and the man had prematurely cut the mother's throat when he tripped while dragging her backward. Jed refused to make that mistake again.

The hostage taker took a step back . . .

Jed squeezed the trigger.

The round flew true and hit the knife-wielding maniac between the eyes. The woman screamed as he released his grip and crumpled into a heap behind her. "Thank you," she said and then she and her baby dematerialized right before his eyes.

"Eight, this is Papa. Exfil in five mikes at the LZ," the Colonel said. "Better get moving."

Apparently this is a timed evolution . . . Thanks for telling me now!

"Check," Jed said, keeping his voice neutral. He glanced at the timer in the upper-right corner of his visual field: 05:12. He'd burned over half his time and he wasn't even halfway through the course yet. If things kept up like this, there was no way he'd complete it under the ten-minute limit. He scanned the hallway and saw two doors, one on the left, one on the right.

ULoSe Left, he reminded himself. *I already went up . . . left next, then straight, then left again.*

Sighting over his rifle, he quick-stepped to the door on the left side, which was shut—because of course it was—thereby requiring another time-consuming breach. The compulsion to hose down the room through the door from the outside was overpowering, but he knew better. If he did that, he'd undoubtedly find a room full of shot-up kids when he went in.

No shortcuts, he reminded himself and pulled a flash-bang from his kit.

Wishing he had a buddy for this evolution, Jed repeated the standard entry protocol all by himself—kicking the door in, tossing the flash-bang, and breaching the room. Two men dressed in tunics were bent at the waist, clutching their ears and disoriented from the flash-bang. Each man had an AK-47 hanging from a sling around the neck. Jed popped them with head shots before they had time to recover their wits from the blast and engage.

The rectangular room he was standing inside had no other doors, just a lone window on the far wall. *Now straight,* the SEAL inside reminded him. But he couldn't go straight . . . at least not very far. Jed exhaled and turned in a circle, scanning for something he might have missed while replaying the sequence of turns and moves he'd made.

I went up the stairs and took the first left to enter this room. . . . Next I'm supposed to go straight. After that it's left, then down to start the next chunk. But this doesn't match up.

He charged across the long rectangular room, wondering if he got his mnemonic wrong, and arrived at the lone window on the opposite wall. He looked outside, through the dirty panes, and to his surprise saw a metal balcony extending off to the left with a fire escape ladder at the far end.

Okay, maybe across the room was the straight leg; the balcony is left; then down is the fire escape ladder.

Decision made, he reached to lift the windowpane, but before he could, the glass exploded with incoming gunfire. Jed dropped low and crabbed out of the line of fire, pressing his back to the wall beside the now-blown-out window. He held, weighing his options, as alternating volleys of gunfire continued to stream through the gap.

Sounds like two shooters. Probably on the rooftop across the street.

He blew air through pursed lips and weighed his miserable options. With two shooters sighting on the window, exiting to the balcony was a death wish. He didn't know where they were positioned, which meant he'd have to scan to find them *while* they were shooting at him. And even if he was lucky enough to get one of them, he wouldn't get both before getting sniped himself. Then an intriguing idea occurred to him. The simulation had tested him once already, tempting him to err with friendly fire on simulated operators. Maybe now he could summon those same friendlies to his aid.

"Papa, this is Eight," he said into his boom mic. "I'm pinned down by two enemy shooters and unable to advance to exfil. Are blue forces still in situ? Need covering fire."

"Copy, Eight. Let me make a call . . . ," the Colonel said and Jed could practically hear the smile in his voice. "Standby, Eight, blue shooters en route to your pos. Get ready to move on my mark."

"Roj, standing by."

A few seconds later, fresh gunfire erupted outside in a heated back-and-forth exchange that lasted twenty seconds.

"Eight, this is Papa," the Colonel said. "The snow has been plowed. Exit now."

Grinning large, Jed popped to his feet and climbed out the window onto a rickety metal balcony. He did a quick scan of the rooftops and then the street below, where he saw a lone friendly operator kneeling behind a dumpster scanning for targets. Knowing his good fortune would not last long, Jed ran across the balcony that stretched to the far corner of the building. As soon as he got to the ladder, he quickly slung his rifle, took a knee, and tried to compress his massive frame through the circular hole cut in the metal grate. Gunfire erupted all around him, just as he'd squeezed his shoulder through. Bullets pinged and sparked off the metal balcony overhead and the ladder rungs. With gritted teeth, he shifted his feet from the rung he was standing on to grip the outside of the rails with the arches of his boots. Then, fast-rope style, he executed a rapid descent—sliding down the ladder rails to the ground below using friction to control his speed.

He landed with a thud, his legs taking the impact like shock absorbers, and settled into a deep squat. Palms burning from the slide down, he brought his rifle up and scanned for threats and the source of the incoming fire. During his scan, he saw that both his blue team companions had been shot and were lying, unmoving, in pools of blood, which meant he was on his own for the rest of the scenario. He found the enemy shooter a heartbeat later, a teenager firing at him from behind a pockmarked car parked twenty meters away. Jed fired a three-round burst at the car, driving the shooter into cover and giving Jed time to find cover of his own.

DeaLR Left, he reminded himself. *Six rounds left in this magazine.*

He'd just descended, which meant it was time to go left. After that right, then left to exfil. He glanced at the counter in the upper right of his visual field: 08:23.

Almost out of time.

He sprinted left in a tactical crouch, making for a metal dumpster. He dove behind it just as AK-47 fire strafed the ground behind him and ricocheted off the side of the dumpster. In the distance, he could hear the thrum of helicopter rotors pounding the air and he knew it was his ride out of here. He didn't have time to play Whac-A-Mole with this kid taking potshots at him from behind. He scanned down the street for the next possible right turn. He spied an intersecting street a half block away, but to reach it he'd have to cross to the other side of the street he was on, opening himself up to being shot in the back. Once again, if only he had a buddy, they could provide covering fire for each other and take turns making the cross. Situations like these were the reason SEALs never operated alone. Maybe that was the point of the Colonel sending each member of Alpha platoon through this ballbuster of a course alone—to remind each of the rookies of the power of being a team.

A fresh salvo pinged off the side of the dumpster.

He glanced at the counter: 09:02.

Less than a minute remaining.

Screw it. It's now or never.

Jed popped out and fired a three-round burst at the parked car and took off in a sprint at an angle toward the corner. He'd only made it halfway across the street when the kid behind him opened fire. Tracers zipped past as he took aim behind him, holding his rifle out with one arm. He squeezed off another burst of fire, emptying his magazine. Call it God or good fortune or almost two decades of training, but his salvo connected, hitting the shooter center mass and dropping him. Maybe he imagined it, or maybe not, but for a split second Jed could have sworn he heard the Colonel laugh on the comms circuit.

Lungs heaving and quads on fire, Jed ejected his spent magazine and reached for a spare on his kit as he rounded the corner. He slammed it home and indexed the charging handle as he sprinted onto a new street where four new insurgents were waiting for him. With no time for finesse or caution, Jed flicked the fire-selector switch to auto and strafed the group from left to right, dropping all of them without breaking stride. He sprinted through the carnage, his thumb switching the rifle back to single shot.

One more left turn . . .

He glanced at the counter: 09:35—only twenty-five seconds remaining.

At his ten o'clock, he saw a Black Hawk flaring in for a landing just beyond a row of low buildings. He dug deep and found that extra gear to sprint toward the final turn. He rounded the bend, sighting over his rifle, and found himself staring into a central city square with a paved courtyard and fountain in the middle, ringed by shops and cafés on three sides. The helo had landed in the commons. The rotor wash was kicking up dust in bilateral swirling arcs, knocking over bistro tables and chairs and scattering civilian bystanders who were running in all directions. Jed marveled at the realism, feeling the vibration from the rotors in his chest and wind in his face.

How is this even possible? he thought as he ran toward the helo's wide-open cargo door.

Inside the Black Hawk, an operator dressed in fatigues was

waving Jed to hurry. The pilot turned to look at Jed through the side cockpit window and Jed saw that the man's face was Colonel Jericho's smiling at him.

"On your right," the Colonel said.

He whirled right and saw a black-robed jihadist step out of the darkened doorway in a building across the courtyard holding an RPG on his shoulder. Jed stopped, took a knee, and sighted in for the long shot. As the terrorist took aim at the helo, Jed took aim at the man's chest.

Trigger squeeze.

The black-robed fighter fell backward into the doorway, firing the rocket-propelled grenade as he did. The ordnance slammed into the adjacent building and exploded in a fireball, sending debris and dust flying. With a victorious grin, Jed popped up to his feet and turned back to the helo and the familiar-faced smiling pilot.

The counter in his goggles reached 10:00 and the world around him dematerialized—the Black Hawk, the courtyard, and all the people blinking out of existence. Heart pounding, Jed let his rifle hang by the sling around his neck and put his hands on his hips to catch his breath. The inside of the massive kill house was dark, but not too dark to make out the actual structures he'd navigated and climbed over. The metal balcony and ladder had been real, attached to a real two-story building. Other structures and buildings were present as well, making the inside of the cavernous space look like an indoor Hollywood movie set.

"The simulation is over, Jed," the Colonel's voice said in his ear. "Exit straight ahead."

Having no idea where the control and observation room was located, Jed simply gave a two-finger salute to the ether and jogged into the tunnel with the glowing red sign that said Exfil instead of Exit over the doorway. Grinning like a kid on Christmas morning, he pushed through the door and stepped into the staging room to rejoin the rest of Alpha platoon.

"So what did you think?" Grayson asked, speaking for the others, who were all staring at him with anticipation.

"That was friggin' unbelievable," Jed said, shaking his head. "I've never seen anything like it."

"So cool, right?" Eli said, giving Jed a slap on the back.

"So cool," Jed echoed.

"Well, you ain't seen nothing yet," Johnny said and let out a whistle. "That was just level one. The Colonel has a whole bag of kickass he's going to unleash on you nuggets in the next round. So get ready."

As if on that cue, the Colonel emerged wearing his typical judgment-from-on-high expression. "Well, congratulations," he said, walking over to a TV monitor on the wall and turning it on. "You all passed your indoctrination run—some better than others."

The TV screen displayed a list of everyone in the platoon, their names organized in a vertical column. Instead of being listed in alphabetical order, they were ranked based on something called an APS score. Jed's name was listed first with an APS score of 302. Eli was second at 289, followed by Grayson at 267, Carl at 259, Johnny at 241, Nisha at 238, Hyeon at 227, and Bex last with a score of 212.

While Johnny cursed both his displeasure and disbelief at the leaderboard results, the others stared at Jed with wide-eyed disbelief.

"Congratulations, Jed," the Colonel said. "You just set a new, all-time aggregate performance score record for the indoc run."

Not sure what to say, Jed simply nodded and humbly took in the moment as everyone congratulated him and gave him fist bumps and backslaps.

"That's it for tonight," the Colonel said. "Stow your gear and get some sleep. Sunup comes early."

"You heard the Colonel," Jed said as he safed his weapon for storage. "Lights-out in fifteen mikes."

Everybody got busy stripping off and stowing their gear except for the veterans, who had walked to the far end of the staging room to caucus in private. Jed glanced that direction, catching the evil eye from Johnny as the four blooded Shepherds talked in heated whispers.

"What do you think that's all about?" Jed said, turning to Nisha, who was taking off her sensor vest.

She glanced at him for a second, then shrugged. "Bruised egos maybe . . . but don't worry. I'm sure it won't be long before we find out."

Jed nodded and told himself she was right. He'd done well tonight, surprising both himself and everyone else with his performance. This was a good thing and proved to the Colonel that someone had made the right choice picking Jed as platoon leader. Clearly Johnny wasn't pleased with his own performance, and he was projecting his anger onto Jed. This was a competitive crew, operators accustomed to being the best of the best and performing at the highest level. Individual excellence was nothing to feel guilty or ashamed of. Jealousy and jockeying for position was normal.

It would all sort itself out in time.

Take the win, dude, the SEAL inside said. *You earned it.*

CHAPTER
NINE

The Colonel, Jed decided, might just have an empathetic bone in his body yet. He'd not let the team sleep any later, nor had they been exempted from a grueling PT after their late-night training op in the high-tech kill house, but now he'd been told to assemble his team for a didactic session—though the topic for the class instruction was left a mystery. Jed funneled in behind his team to room 101 in the square building labeled "Classroom Block" in simple font burned into a wood plaque above the door, though the more formal sign on the corner of the brick building called it BLDG 1223.

"I think you'll like this," Eli said, clapping him on the back.

Jed was drawn to the easygoing former Green Beret, and he now found himself depending heavily on their growing friendship as he got his bearings in this new life. He'd not yet asked Eli why the seasoned Shepherd operator wasn't heading up the team instead of himself, fearful there might be some reason Eli would be uncomfortable sharing—some failure or weakness in his past. But whatever it was that kept him from leading, it sure didn't stop the man from operating. Eli proved on every evolution that he was the gold standard of special operators—whether in terms of fitness, tactical prowess, or his never-in-doubt attitude.

"What is this that I'm going to like so much?" Jed asked as he slid into a seat beside the Shepherd—one of the four seats in the front of six rows of long, desk-like tables. He looked down to find a pad of paper, a pen, an electronic tablet, and a leather-bound Bible at his and each of the stations.

"What?" Eli said, tugging at his beard with one hand and pulling his long hair behind an ear with the other. "And ruin the surprise?"

Behind the podium at the front of the room was a split whiteboard on either side of a monitor used to show pictures and videos, he imagined. The door to his right of the boards opened, and he felt a smile broaden as Ben Morvant walked in. The smile turned to confusion and then irritation when two other men followed him in and took seats in two of the three folding chairs along the wall behind the podium. Jed felt his pulse quicken and his chest tighten at the sight of David Yarnell.

Man, I don't need this today.

"Welcome, Jericho Basic twenty-two zero one, Alpha platoon," Ben said, his tone formal and all business, using the numerical designation for their training class Jed had heard only once before. "I was happy to hear everyone performed well on the first kill house evolution last night." He looked up and gave a subtle nod to Jed, which Jed returned with a smile. "This morning we are shifting gears. Please log in to your tablets and set your biometric log-in and password."

Jed watched Ben step over to David and the man seated beside him who, like David, looked completely out of place in a room full of blooded warriors. The man was small in stature and slender in build, though his rugged face suggested he was no stranger to the outdoors. Ben spoke to them in hushed whispers, but Jed's eyes stayed on David, who, suddenly noticing him, lifted a hand in a subtle wave. Jed gritted his teeth and gave David a curt nod, then looked down at his tablet, forbidding himself from taking another unproductive stroll down memory lane.

When he tapped the screen, a dialog box opened, prompting him to enter his full name and ID number, the latter of which he had to find on the CAC card hanging from the lanyard around his neck. The screen then took him to a window to set in his finger-print access and backup password and reminders. He pressed his left thumb and then right forefinger on the reader, and the tablet told him his fingerprints had both been accepted and prompted him to enter a secure password. He tapped characters into the dialog box with two fingers:

8r0keFr0gR828

Broke Frog, Romans 8:28.
He wasn't sure what random part of his brain had produced

the Scripture—once his favorite, but now, so many years later, uncomfortable for some reason. But he knew it felt right.

Had his life truly been one of good, letting all things in his path be used by God for His purpose? If so, it had been all God and not him these last seventeen years.

"All set, team?" Ben asked, bringing him back.

His gaze once again drifted to David. A sudden flash of irritation welled up inside him.

Why did David sitting in the front of the room bring him so much doubt? The bitterness and regret, those feelings he understood—but why the doubt? God had made it abundantly clear that David had a role to play in his life, and yet Jed felt like this new journey as a Shepherd should be his and his alone to take.

"Please open the icon labeled TSL and then open block one lesson. For those of you new to the term TSL, these are the tactical spiritual leaders, whom we partner with our combat team leaders—David and Jedidiah respectively for this platoon. We believe that pairing spiritual guidance and tactical expertise is the ideal combination to fulfill our charter."

Jed couldn't resist the urge to lean over and whisper to Eli, "Because what spec ops team *doesn't* have two commanding officers?"

Eli shook his head but grinned.

"A fair point, Senior Chief Johnson," Ben said, somehow having heard Jed's snide comment. "Jed brings an important leadership question to the table. Everyone here has considerable tactical experience, along with a variety of traditional combat and counterintelligence skills. In a conventional conflict, all of us recognize the vital importance of having one clear, unified chain of command.

So why did we choose to muddy the waters with this leadership pair concept?"

No one answered, and Jed leaned back, folding his arms on his chest.

Finally Eli raised his hand. "Because there are often two distinct faces to our enemy."

"Correct," Ben said. "As a veteran, Eli has obviously heard this before, but it's the truth. Jed, you recently augmented a Shepherd team in the field on two real-world operations; you must certainly agree that there were physical as well as spiritual elements which needed to be considered, quickly and effectively, to make the right tactical decisions when facing off against the Dark Ones."

Jed felt eyes on him, as the rest of the nuggets on the team were no doubt learning for the first time that he had previous combat experience with the Shepherds. He ignored the stares and focused on the matter at hand. Whatever doubts Jed still harbored about faith and his relationship with God, he could not deny that spiritual warfare played a critical role in every engagement with their enemy. Still, he didn't remember Ben receiving counsel from anyone—much less some "tactical spiritual leader." Certainly not in real time, anyway. His mind suddenly went to the terrifying and overpowering urges used by the Dark Ones at the target compound in the mountains, when he'd rescued Sarah Beth. He remembered placing the gun under his chin, the voice in his head at once his own and also not, urging him to pull the trigger.

"There are definitely spiritual influences at work for which I'm not well prepared. I can see how those pressures . . . ," he said, shaking away the nauseating memory, "could affect my ability to make a tactical decision."

The admission was difficult but true, and he let his eyes flick over to where David was leaning in, the man beside him whispering something in his ear and his former friend nodding.

"I, too, require counsel from my own TSL, Jed. And while you may not have seen or heard Pastor Mike during those operations you augmented, he was present and in lockstep with me. The strength of the relationship between the combat team leader and his TSL can determine whether an operation is a win or a massacre."

"Just like we could easily be killed in an ambush without the eyes of our Watchers," Jed said.

"That's the second time you've mentioned the Watchers," Nisha said, turning to Jed. "During the indoc session, you brought them up and there was some discussion about them aging out as adolescents. I'm not familiar with this role or program. Care to elaborate?"

Jed looked to Ben, who nodded for him to field the question.

"The Watchers are incredibly talented and very brave young people who are our eyes and ears on the enemy," Jed said, thinking back to Corbin, the teen girl who had guided not only Sarah Beth as they'd hunted Victor in some other, spiritual plane he didn't understand, but also provided real-time spiritual ISR for the Shepherd team. He still didn't understand how it all worked, but he certainly knew that, without them, they would have been blind.

"Indeed," Ben said, "but that's a discussion for a later class. Phase two of your training will include Watcher integration . . ."

Jed wondered suddenly how many phases Jericho Basic entailed, and how long phase one would last.

"We will also, in phase two, get deeper into how the TSL pairing works functionally with respect to the chain of command. Today, however, we want to focus on the spiritual warfare component of being Shepherds and why it's so critically important. To that end, let me introduce you to someone far more qualified to speak on the matter, Pastor Mike Moore."

The man seated beside David rose now, and Jed immediately noticed two things. The first was that the man, while small compared to the burly operators in the room, moved with the catlike grace of an ultra-athlete—or perhaps a warrior? And the second he noticed was a tattoo on the man's right forearm identical in design to the logo he had seen on the wall of the admin building on arrival. A block-style cross sat in the middle of a crest of laurel leaves. Behind the cross, a sword and a shepherd's crook crossed one another to form an X. The logo, for some reason, made him think of his own Navy SEAL Trident tattoo.

The man took off his eyeglasses as he approached Ben at the podium. Jed noticed that his face was chiseled like a warrior's, but his brown eyes were soft and compassionate like those of a pastor. The two men hugged in the brief, backslapping embrace common to military men before Ben took a seat and Mike took his place at the podium.

"Welcome, everyone. I'm Mike Moore, head of the tactical spiritual leader program and Ben's TSL," Pastor Mike began. "You are men and women of service, each with an exemplary record of putting God and country before self in either the Armed Forces or intelligence community, but your presence here means you've been called to a higher purpose. Before we get into that, let me tell you a little bit about myself. Before I was Pastor Mike, I was Major Moore, Army Ranger in the Seventy-Fifth Ranger

Regiment. Like you guys, I saw things in my decade in the regiment that at times shook my faith and at other times strengthened it. I had doubts—not about the existence of God, but the nature of God. I asked the 'why' questions that people like us—people at the tip of the spear who have encountered Satan's evil firsthand—inevitably ask. Often, the unanswerable questions get folks like us in trouble spiritually. After running from those questions for a long time, I finally summoned the courage to ask them out loud. I skipped the preacher middleman and shouted them directly at God . . ."

Pastor Mike looked over at Ben and smiled.

"But that's a story for another time. Soon after, a man came to me and told me that God had answers for me if I would be willing to serve Him by putting my Ranger skills to work for a higher purpose," Mike said, and Jed watched the man's eyes drift to the memory. "I joined the Shepherds and became a combat team leader like Jed. After a couple of years serving at the tip of the spear, God called me to shift roles once again. I took a break in service for seminary and became a pastor. Then I rejoined the unit to work closely with Ben in a leadership capacity. I guess you could say I was the first TSL, but we didn't officially coin that term until later—after an event occurred in our ranks that showed we needed a program to provide both spiritual guidance and oversight to our tactical teams."

Jed raised his eyebrows in surprise at the cryptic reference, glancing over at Eli, who nodded and mouthed, *"Later."*

"As a Ranger and an officer, I know that the idea of a team concept for leadership seems foreign. But trust me when I tell you, having been on both sides of leadership here for a long time and having survived a failure of spiritual leadership a few years ago, that this concept is absolutely mission critical . . ."

Jed wondered again what had happened. He watched Ben look at his feet and shake his head, saw Pastor Mike's finger unconsciously drag across his shirt, tracing some injury to his abdomen, Jed thought. Beside him, Eli sighed.

"If you came here looking to be a contract operator, to be a physical warrior like you were before but without the burden of government oversight, then you've come to the wrong place. Tell me now and we'll release you with a simple NDA and a good-luck pat on the back. If you are unwilling or incapable of embracing the concept of spiritual guidance, if you don't heed the lessons we're teaching, then you will fail your mission and most likely not survive here. So . . . are you all in on continuing or does anyone wish to be excused?"

He crossed his arms as if daring someone to volunteer to be excused. Jed, for one, had come too far to ring this bell, despite any doubts or uncertainties he still harbored. Pastor Mike waited for the murmurs of Jed's teammates to subside and then continued.

"Very well, then, let's move on." Pastor Mike put his glasses on, looked down at his tablet computer, and read aloud the verse beneath the header B1L1: "'For though we walk in the flesh, we are not waging war according to the flesh. For the weapons of our warfare are not of the flesh but have divine power to destroy strongholds.' That's from 2 Corinthians 10—it's the divine truth of what we do here. Paul is telling us something vitally important about the nature of our battle and the powers we have in this realm. He's warning us that if we try to wage war against the enemy using only the weapons we perfected in our Ranger regiment, our Marine unit, or our SEAL Team, then we will fail. If you try to fight the Dark Ones like a conventional soldier, evil will prevail nine times out of ten."

The pastor stepped away from the podium, his eyes passing over the room and letting the weight of his words sink in.

"Does everyone here believe that?" he asked.

Do I? Jed asked himself. He took a deep breath and then a big leap of faith and closed his eyes. *I do, God. I don't understand half of this, but I believe.*

"Hooah," one of the Army dudes said from behind him.

"Yes, sir," Jed chimed in and felt without seeing Eli's smile beside him as a warm sense of peace seemed to settle over him like a comfortable sweatshirt. "Hooyah."

"Good," Pastor Mike said, returning to the podium and putting his glasses back on yet again and reading the next line as Jed followed along. "'Put on the whole armor of God, that you may be able to stand against the schemes of the devil. For we do not wrestle against flesh and blood, but against the rulers, against the authorities, against the cosmic powers over this present darkness, against the spiritual forces of evil in the heavenly places.' That's from Ephesians and it's important too. For those of you whose faith background forgot to teach you about Satan, here it is: He . . . is . . . real." Pastor Mike tapped the podium loudly with his left index finger, punctuating each word. "The devil is real and is here on earth. He is crafty enough to seduce people to him by appearing to be the light, just as it says in 2 Corinthians. And just as real are the angels cast out with him, the dark angels who serve him still, as described in Matthew 25 and Revelation 12. . . . Your team leader, Senior Chief Johnson, can vouch for that, having had his own close encounter with one of Satan's dark angels."

The former Ranger looked up over his glasses and held Jed's eyes.

Jaw tight, Jed gave a curt nod.

Pastor Mike went on. "As Shepherds, we are the guardians of the gates holding chaos at bay. Everywhere you see corruption and cruelty, massacre and mayhem, Satan is present. Through his instruments—the dark angels and their followers—he sows seeds of uncertainty, fear, and suffering. These are not vapors about which I speak, but people who have surrendered their will and their body to Satan and his evil. If you have not encountered one of these dark servants in the field, then prepare yourself, because you will, and you must be ready when you do."

A chill chased down Jed's spine. He'd already faced off against the Dark Ones, on several occasions now, and Pastor Mike's words resonated with him. They were human but at the same time vessels for something inhuman—a ravenous power barely contained and burning inside. In each encounter, Jed had barely escaped with his life, and he couldn't help but wonder how many of his other teammates had had similar experiences and lived with the secret inside.

"Now, I want to introduce you to David Yarnell," Pastor Mike said and gestured to David, who stood and walked over to stand beside him at the podium. "David is going through his own version of Jericho Basic and will serve beside Jedidiah as the team's TSL. He's going to walk you through a number of Scriptures that you have on your tablets. Afterward, you'll break into groups of two and work together to come up with a plan on how you will, as a team, apply these Scriptures to real-life combat and your every-day life. Questions?"

Behind him someone whispered softly, "Yeah, why do we have a combat team with a nugget team leader *and* a rookie TSL?"

"Shut up, Johnny," someone else whispered.

"All right, then. David, take it from here."

Jed watched as David took the podium, his face uncomfortable but not lacking in confidence.

"All right," David said, a fire in his eyes that Jed hadn't seen since their youth. "I'm David Yarnell and God called me to be here. Let's get into this."

Jed did his best to put aside the bitterness. David was working on his master's in divinity, had been recruited by Ben Morvant, and was now being mentored by Pastor Mike. As a SEAL, Jed had served with plenty of guys who weren't his friends in the "real world" but were his brothers on the battlefield. It would have to be that way with David, he supposed. Because Pastor Mike had reminded him why he was here and why he would stay.

If leadership had faith in David, then Jed should trust that David had knowledge to share that he needed to embrace.

No matter how upside down that made the world feel.

CHAPTER TEN

Maria Perez kicked off her comfortable flats as she pushed through the door to her apartment, tossing them with a flip of her toes against the door to the hall closet. She dropped her keys on the pass-through bar and her leather bag onto the corner barstool and then made the very conscious decision to leave her roller bag where it was. She would unpack tomorrow. Tonight, after twenty grueling hours of traveling, she would drink a nice bottle of red wine, watch some mindless TV, and try not to pick at the laparoscopic incision in her navel. She grabbed a bottle of Justin Isosceles from the rack, a wine goblet, and a corkscrew, then padded across the hardwood floors to the sofa. After untucking her shirt from her designer jeans, she all but collapsed onto her sofa, aware of the grunt she made as she did. She kicked her feet onto the coffee table, used the electric corkscrew to uncork the bottle, and gave a generous pour into the widemouthed crystal wineglass.

With the TV remote in her lap, she took a long pull on the dry wine and stared out the angled, oversize windows to the east. For a moment she contemplated a quick shower and then a walk to "The District," the twenty-square-block epicenter of Nashville's downtown nightlife, where music was always playing and drink was always flowing. Hunger gnawed at her. She'd not eaten since her flight across the Atlantic, but her spartan fridge and pantry had little to offer. The Ainsworth around the corner had a killer chopped salad, and she could order a stiff cocktail, which strangely seemed more palatable in her fatigued state than red wine. Male companionship would find her, without any effort on her part, and that would certainly help distract her mind from where it kept sneaking away to.

Melded into the sofa as she was, however, mobilizing to go out felt like a Sisyphean effort.

She sighed, took another sip of wine, and leaned her head back into the cushion, suddenly feeling the ache of the bruises on her shoulders and back—souvenirs from the night spent in bed with her dark companion in Paris.

And the demon or demons that now called the man home.

Her hand went to the bite mark that still burned on her left shoulder and she smiled, a crooked and lustful smile.

Nick Woland.

Then the sudden and unwelcome face of her grandmother snuck into her head.

No tiene por qué ser así, pequeña. Nunca es tarde para Dios . . .

Maria laughed out loud at this, and the image of her dead grandmother's kind face evaporated.

"I'm afraid it does have to be like this, and it's much too late for your God, *abuela*," she shouted at the memory, trying and failing to muster a sardonic laugh.

She liked to imagine her life a black comedy, but there was no satire in her past.

Her mood souring, she gulped down her wine while wishing desperately that she had hard liquor in the apartment.

Had her *abuela* not died, would it have been different? She would not have been abused while in the keeping of two different foster families. She might not have been raped when she started hanging out with other teens as tragic as she had become. But wouldn't she have ended up here anyway? Wasn't this her fate? The world was dark and hope was pointless.

You have to embrace the dark to survive.

And she had.

The phone rang.

Not the phone in her pocket or even the one in her bag.

The other phone. The one in the small office she had beside the spare bedroom, which she'd converted into an exercise studio. She worked out hard and regularly, trying to fight off time after recently passing the big 4-0 landmark. It was also imperative she maintain a combat-ready level of fitness because she was playing in Victor's world now.

She set her glass on the coffee table and rose, feeling the need to move quickly. Not because there was any chance of missing the call—he would let it ring until she picked up—but because she was terrified to make Victor wait.

"Hello?" she said, panting into the phone.

"How was your trip, my dear?" Victor's oily voice asked.

"Everything went well and as expected," she reported, aware that he knew this already. Still, hating silence for even seconds when on the phone with him, she continued her data dump. "As you directed, I stayed with the target in Bern long enough to confirm the pickup and then followed him south as far as Spiez, as backup against unforeseen interventions." She squeezed her eyes shut tightly at the poor choice of words. Victor hated the implication that there were things he could not foresee. But there must be, or why have her escort Woland at all?

And why the failure with the Yarnell girl?

Her eyes flashed open wide at the unwanted thought, and she gasped at her mistake.

But Victor said nothing, and after a few seconds, she slowly let her breath out.

"You did well, Maria," he said, his voice low and even and impossible to read, "as I knew you would. Did you enjoy Nicholas?"

Not *Did you enjoy meeting him?* . . . but *Did you enjoy him?* His meaning was clear, but she refused to play that game.

"He seemed healthy and motivated for whatever task you have for him."

"Of course he is," Victor said, but she could hear the taunting smile in his voice. "And now it is time for me to put you to better use than babysitting. How long until you are returned to active duty?"

"I'm not sure," she answered honestly. "It's up to the medical board. I'm ready to go back now, but they could decide to follow the surgeon's guidance and keep me sidelined another two weeks."

"Very well," Victor said. "The task I have for you is better performed while you are on your convalescent leave, in any case. I assume you have contact information for Jedidiah Johnson?"

"Yes," she said, intrigued, "but I'm having trouble locating him. He doesn't seem to be in Virginia Beach as we were led to believe."

"It is *my* understanding that he has returned to Tennessee, Maria. We knew they would try to recruit him, and I believe they have succeeded."

"I'm sorry," she said and meant it, though for what reason she felt unsure.

"I'm not," he all but hissed. "This will work into our plans perfectly. All our efforts to infiltrate Trinity Loop have failed. Until Paris, I had no idea you were such the seductress."

She closed her eyes and flushed with something—fear, maybe—at the remark. Not about her sleeping with Woland—had she really lured him, or had it been the other way around?—but at the insinuation. If she'd not misheard, he wanted her to infiltrate the Shepherds operation in Nashville and use Jedidiah Johnson to do it.

"You need not be afraid, Maria. You are a loyal soldier. Your sacrifices are not unnoticed, and your commitment is clear," he said, and she could picture him staring with those black eyes at the long nails on one of his thin, bony hands. "Never forget we're playing the long game, my dear. This battle began thousands of years ago and we are in the fight until the bitter and glorious end. But we have an opportunity here to disrupt the biggest impediment in our path at the moment. Obviously that is the Shepherds. And I believe you are the best soldier I have to capitalize on this opportunity."

"What do you want me to do?" she asked, but her mind was already developing a game plan as Victor described what he wanted.

Jedidiah Johnson's empathy and compassion were his weakness. And his loneliness and regret.

She smiled. *This might even be fun . . .*

"I won't disappoint you," she said.

"You never do," Victor said, and the line went dead.

Maria sat a moment, her mind running through the conversation she would have, her eyes closed and her smiling lips parted slightly. Then she snapped the encrypted phone into its cradle and headed back into the living room. She sat on the sofa, legs folded beneath her, and unbuttoned two buttons on her expensive blouse, setting a mood for herself. Then she took a slow sip of her wine, pictured Jed in her mind, and felt a stirring that she liked.

She pressed the number she had saved on her cell phone under Jed Johnson.

It went to voice mail without a single ring.

"Hey, it's Jed. I'm not available but leave a message and I'll call you back."

Maria pouted her lips and thought a moment, then spoke softly into the phone, making sure to sound both excited and nervous.

"Hi, Jed. It's me . . . I mean it's Maria . . . Perez. It's Maria Perez. Detective Perez from Nashville Metro PD." She let a pause stretch out. "This is not a business call or anything. I just . . . Okay, the truth is I was thinking about you and wondered how you were doing. I know you're back in Virginia but thought maybe if you might be coming back to Tennessee soon, we could get together and catch up?"

She smiled, rising from the couch and pacing, the nervous energy no longer an act.

"Ooookay. So that's like the most embarrassing voice mail I've ever left. So . . . all right, give me a call when you get this . . . if you want to. Bye."

She disconnected the call and grinned.

Not bad. Even if he's not interested, he'll call back. He's too much the knight in shining armor not to.

She paced to the window, looking out at the city lights. Empathy and compassion were Johnson's weaknesses, but she knew of another . . . the girl.

She scrolled through her contacts until she found Rachel Yarnell's name.

It would take a little time, but it would be time well spent. She would call the woman in the morning and ask about Sarah Beth. She'd build a rapport with the traumatized mother and learn what had become of the gifted young Watcher. The bond between the Yarnell child and Johnson was strong, so strong that instinctively Maria knew she needed to exploit it.

It was a good plan.

One way or another, she would worm her way into Jedidiah Johnson's heart, and once she was in, she would turn it as black and calloused as her own.

CHAPTER ELEVEN

Jed felt . . .

Off.

Something he couldn't articulate. A phantom itch he couldn't scratch. On top of that, his body seemed out of sync. During their morning PT he'd felt sluggish and had gotten winded during the five-mile run. He'd even felt a burn in his hip for several strides, which worried him. But that wasn't possible because his hip was healed.

Unless . . . it wasn't.

What if Ben's "healing" it all those weeks ago had been nothing more than placebo effect? What if this whole time he'd simply been imagining it?

No, that's impossible, he thought, shaking off the idea. *The arthritis was so bad I could barely walk when I got out of bed in the morning. I wouldn't be able to do any of these things if it wasn't healed. Ben is the real deal. Period. End of story.*

"Hey, Jed, everything all right?" Nisha asked, stepping up beside him as they walked from the barracks to the kill house.

"Yeah, everything's fine. Why do you ask?"

"I don't know—you just seem quiet today."

He shot her a sideways glance. "Quiet? Is that spook code for dragging tail?"

"No," she said with a polite chuckle, "but now that you mention it, I did notice you clocked us in at our slowest morning run since day two."

"Yeah, well, the Colonel has really put us through the grinder these last couple days. I figured I'd dial it back a little today—you know, for you guys."

"How benevolent of you."

"If I didn't know better, I might think you're making fun of me, Nisha."

"Me, make fun of you?" she said. "I would never dream of teasing a big, volatile former frogman such as yourself."

"Wow, I didn't realize spooks had a sense of humor," he said, tossing it back at her.

"They don't," Bex said over her shoulder from a few strides ahead. "It's surgically removed at the Farm as part of their indoc."

"It's true. They do it laparoscopically," Nisha said, theatrically pulling her onyx ponytail aside and showing him her neck. "If you look closely, you can see a tiny incision at the base of my skull."

This comment got a real laugh from everyone and he suddenly felt better.

When they reached the entry door to the kill house, Eli punched in the access code. The veteran held the door open while everyone in Alpha platoon stepped inside. The Colonel was waiting for them in the staging room, but today he was not alone. A young woman with a backpack, whom Jed instantly recognized, was standing beside the silver-haired instructor. She locked eyes with Jed, smiled, and gave him a self-conscious little wave. Jed smiled back at her while the Colonel made introductions.

"For today's exercise, we have a very special guest. Everyone say hello to Corbin Worth, one of our most talented young Watchers over at St. George's. She's going to be providing tactical coordination for blue team today. With her is her Keeper—her mentor and handler for activities with our unit—Pastor Margaret Murphy, a legendary Watcher in her time."

The woman beside the teenager gave a tight smile and curt nod to the team. The message was clear, at least to Jed. Pastor Margaret was no doubt all the things the Colonel said, but she was more than that. In the gritty world of special operations, even in the Shepherds, this woman was as much chaperone as she was mentor. And who could expect less? Who would allow their child to work and travel with the operational teams without such checks in place? Jed wondered if most of the Watchers had other family members working in the community in various capacities. Was Pastor Margaret a mother to a Watcher of her own? Did the gift of second sight run in families? His mind turned to Sarah Beth . . .

"Hi, guys," Corbin said, blushing and looking down at the floor as soon as all eyes fixed on her.

"Hi, Corbin. It's awesome to have you here," Jed said, addressing her for the group. "We're so glad you're going to be a part of the exercise today."

She nodded. "Yeah, it's going to be fun."

"I don't know if *fun* is the right word for what y'all are about to experience," Johnny said under his breath.

The Colonel shot Johnny a *You and I are gonna have words later* look before continuing, "For today's exercise, we're stepping things up to the next level. This is a red-on-blue event, with four veterans on the red team and the four nuggets on blue. Red squad are assaulters and blue squad are defenders. Corbin will be the Watcher for blue squad, providing real-time ISR and tactical guidance. Red squad will be working for me and embedded as part of the scenario with other virtual shooters. Veterans, kit up and join me inside. Blue squad, you guys stage here. Once you're kitted up, your Watcher will brief you on your mission objective. As far as rules of engagement, for today's exercise you'll be using Simunition 9mm FX cartridges. For those of you who are unfamiliar with this product, it is a nonlethal marking munition specially designed for close-quarter man-on-man training exercises like the one we're conducting today."

"In other words, paint rounds that hurt like the real thing," Eli chimed in.

"Thank you, Mr. Freidus, for that profound insight," the Colonel said. "The marking munitions are nonlethal, but like your mama used to say, 'If you're not careful, you'll shoot your eye out.' So keep your visors down at all times. Anybody who doesn't will be escorted off the property by yours truly. Is that clear?"

"Hooyah, Colonel," Jed said with an exaggerated bark, unable to resist.

The Colonel pursed his lips at Jed and turned to leave. "Red team, meet me outside the control room in five."

The veterans quickly kitted up and left for their red team brief with the Colonel. On his way to the door, Eli clapped Jed on the shoulder and wished him good luck. The sentiment was sincere but the concerned look in the man's eyes set Jed's nerves on edge. Clearly they were in for a real ballbuster of an exercise.

Splitting the platoon, marker munitions, a Watcher serving as coordinator . . . I wonder what else the Colonel has up his sleeve, Jed thought.

He scanned the staging room, checking on his squad. Everybody was kitted up and ready except, of course, Corbin, who stood back from the group beside Pastor Margaret, both with arms crossed over their chests. The fifteen-year-old Watcher looked smaller and younger than he remembered. Her nerves of steel and David-versus-Goliath performance the last time he'd seen her in action against the Dark Ones had obviously colored his memory of her. He shook her hand with a nod to Pastor Margaret, who gave a genuine smile for the first time, and then he turned to face the others, standing tall at her side.

"Corbin, let me introduce you to the rest of the team," he said and gestured as he spoke their names. "Say hello to Nisha, Bex, and Hyeon."

Nisha spoke first. "Hi, Corbin. It's nice to meet you. I've never worked with a Watcher before, so I'm very excited for this opportunity."

"Nice to meet you too, Nisha," Corbin said. "That's a pretty name. It means *night* . . . doesn't it?"

"That's right. You speak Hindi?"

"No . . . that would be cool, but I'm really bad with languages. *Muy bueno* and *hasta la vista* are pretty much all I've got."

Nisha chuckled. "Then how did you translate the meaning of my name?"

"I sensed it," Corbin said, tucking an errant strand of hair behind her ear. "It's kind of what I do."

"Whoa, that's crazy," Bex said, stepping up to shake the young Watcher's hand. "Can you do that trick with my name?"

Corbin held Bex's hand and cocked her head just so while staring at the former combat medic. "Bex is your nickname. Your real name is Becky, but the captain of the track team started calling you Bex and it stuck."

"That's amazing," Bex said, shaking her head in disbelief.

"Wanna try for the hat trick?" Hyeon said, stepping up to greet Corbin.

Corbin took his proffered hand and closed her eyes. After a second, she smiled. "You're trying to lock me out . . ."

"I know. Is it working?" Hyeon said, chuckling despite his knit eyebrows and the strained expression on his face.

"Not really, O *virtuous* one," she said, her smile victorious.

"Wow, that's impressive," Hyeon said, shaking his head with wonderment. "She got it. Hyeon means *virtuous* in Korean."

Jed glanced at the digital clock over the tunnel door that led into the kill house arena. "All right, folks, as fun as 'try to stump the Watcher' is, the Colonel has us on the clock. We've got less than ten minutes to brief this before the exercise starts. Corbin, the Colonel mentioned that you would be briefing our mission objective; is that true?"

The young Watcher looked at her Keeper, who nodded.

"Yes," Corbin said, turning back to Jed.

"Good, because the Colonel didn't tell us jack," Bex said.

Corbin looked around the staging area and then nodded at one of the two round tables at the far end of the room, where the water cooler and snack bar were located. "Let's go sit at that table and talk."

Jed and his three fellow rookies settled into the molded plastic chairs bunched on one hemisphere of the table while Corbin shrugged off her backpack and took a seat opposite them, Pastor Margaret beside her still standing. From her backpack, Corbin retrieved a sketch pad, set it on the table, and began flipping pages. This was not the first time Jed had seen the girl's sketch pad and her preternatural artistry. He'd first met Corbin after Sarah Beth's rescue, at the safe house east of Pigeon Forge, where she'd carried this same notebook full of pencil-and-ink sketches. The detail and accuracy of the figures she drew reminded Jed of Leonardo da Vinci's famous anatomical drawings. But unlike Da Vinci, Corbin's skill with the pen was intertwined with her divine gift of second sight.

As a Watcher, her mind's eye was not constrained to the confines of her own imagination. Corbin, and the others like her, could look outside herself into the beyond . . . into the minds and thoughts of others and, Jed suspected, into futures and pasts not her own. She was a modern-day prophet in some ways, sharing images given to her from God or taken from others with a gift from the Holy Spirit. As she flipped through the pages, she gave them a peek into her Watcher's world—a headspace filled with competing imagery, intimate beauty interwoven with demonic horror. Finally finding the drawing she wanted, she flipped the sketchbook around to face them, showing off a magnificent landscape drawn in detailed perspective over a two-page spread.

"Hold on—did you draw that?" Bex asked, her mouth agape. "Because if you did, that's beyond incredible."

Corbin's cheeks went rosy. "Yeah, and, um, thanks."

"That's St. Peter's Square," Hyeon said, leaning in to study the page. "See here—these are the statues of the saints looking down from atop the Doric colonnades. At the center of the *ovato tondo*, we have the obelisk, and in the background, that's St. Peter's Basilica."

"That's right," Corbin said.

"And that's us," Nisha said, pointing to four tiny figures drawn running in a diamond formation across the world's most famous cobblestone courtyard.

"Very good."

"So wait a minute," Nisha said, looking from the sketch pad to Jed and then to Corbin. "What is this sketch? Do you already know what's going to happen? I mean, is this like a scene from the simulation . . . a simulation we haven't run yet?"

"The answer is complicated. I saw this happen, but I don't know what future it belongs to. It came to me like a snapshot, without context or explanation. The Colonel briefed me on the exercise, and I know the mission objective, but I don't know all the details. And like the rest of you, I have no idea what's going to happen once you actually get in there. As your Watcher, I'll share everything I see and feel, but I'm not even close to omniscient. Does any of that make sense?"

Jed nodded and so did the others.

"Okay, good. Here's what little I know. Vatican City has been breached by terrorists. Our mission objective is to enter the Vatican, eliminate the enemy infiltrators, and rescue any civilian hostages," Corbin explained.

"Oh, is that all," Bex said, her voice oozing with fatalistic sarcasm. "I was worried the mission was going to be difficult."

"I guess that's why Johnny was laughing at us when he and the other veterans were walking out with the Colonel," Hyeon said. "He's probably been through this scenario a bunch of times and knows how impossible it is."

"Corbin, do you know what size force we're facing?" Nisha asked, skipping the banter. "In other words, besides the four veterans in red team roles, how many simulated tangos are we up against?"

"The Colonel told me if you asked that question, to tell you a dozen, but my experience with these exercises is that we should consider that a very soft number. The simulations are fluid and the Colonel likes to change the rules as he goes along, just like the Dark Ones tend to do in real life."

"That's a great observation, Corbin, and sound advice to keep in mind, people," Jed said, shifting his gaze from her eyes to the sketch pad. "Do you have any other ISR you can provide us before things kick off, like the best infil route, locations of the bad guy shooters, where civilians might be clustered, that sort of thing?"

Corbin nodded and shared everything she knew. After she'd fielded all their questions, Jed glanced at the countdown clock over the tunnel door. Seeing it had only fifty-seven seconds remaining, he scooted his chair back from the table and said, "All right, Alpha, let's grab our helmets and rifles and go save the Vatican."

The other three rookies loudly expressed their mutual enthusiasm for the challenge ahead and followed Jed to the equipment rack. Corbin and Margaret stayed behind.

"Aren't you coming with us?" Bex asked, looking back at them as the four operators clustered by the tunnel door.

Corbin shook her head. "Nope. My post is here."

"But how are you going to—?" Bex stopped midsentence. Her mouth gaped open as she stared at the high schooler. "Shut the front door . . . are you kidding me?"

"What's happening?" Hyeon asked, looking from Bex to Jed.

"Corbin just talked inside my head," Bex said.

"Have you never worked with a Watcher before?" Jed said, looking from Bex to Hyeon.

"No," Hyeon said.

"Yeah, about that . . . Corbin doesn't need a radio," Jed said with an insider's grin.

"Try it with me," Hyeon said and then his mouth dropped open. "Whoa, I can hear you, but your lips aren't moving."

Corbin smiled. "First time is always weird, for both of us actually, but you'll get used to it."

"Last time we worked together, you did your thing, but you also wore a headset. Are you going full mind talker for this op or will you have a radio too?" Jed asked.

Corbin pulled a radio and headset from her backpack. "No, don't worry. I'll be looped in on conventional comms the entire time."

"Good. I'd prefer redundancy just in case things go south," he said.

"Which they always do," Nisha added.

Hyeon pressed the silver cross he wore on a chain around his neck to his lips and said the operator's prayer. "Dear Lord, please watch my six."

Bex stuck out her fist to Hyeon for a bump. "Amen to that."

"It's time," Corbin said, donning her headset with boom mic. "Good luck."

Jed nodded at her and, still feeling *off*, led his team into the tunnel.

CHAPTER
TWELVE

Jed stopped at the white line on the floor at the end of the tunnel and stared into the darkness beyond. A shiver snaked down his back as a familiar yet foreboding presence danced just outside his consciousness.

His hip twinged, and he reflexively adjusted his stance to shift the weight to his other leg.

Next, his operator's swagger seemed to leave him—leaking away like water slipping through cupped fingers. He tried to shake it off, but self-doubt bored into his brain the likes of which he'd not felt since his very first op as a SEAL.

You don't know what you're doing, said a voice in his head. *Your uncertainty is going to get your teammates killed. Your lack of faith is your weakness—*

He cut the voice off, checking in with Corbin on the radio. "Watcher, this is Alpha One," Jed said. "Radio check."

"I read you Lima Charlie, One," Corbin came back. "Alpha sound off."

Nisha, Bex, and Hyeon chimed in as Alpha Two, Three, and Four.

"Check," Corbin came back. "Good comms."

At the same time Jed heard her in his earphones, Corbin said something entirely different in his mind: *One, are you okay?*

He answered her with a thought: *I'm fine.*

You sure? I'm feeling something different from you, she said.

No, really, I'm good . . .

She didn't answer right away, and he thought for an instant he'd lost her connection. He was about to reach out when she said, *I've got your back, One. You can count on me.*

Roger, Watcher. Thanks.

A timer with all zeroes appeared in the upper-right corner of Jed's augmented visual field, indicating the exercise was about to begin.

"No matter how many times I do this, this part still freaks me out," Bex said as their helmets synced to the control room network and their augmented-reality visors came to life.

"I know—this part is crazy," Hyeon chimed in.

Inside Jed's helmet, the blackness of the kill house started being painted over, replaced with a bright, sunny day as he and his three teammates were magically transported to Vatican City in the heart of Rome. Instead of landing on Via della Conciliazione—the famous promenade leading into St. Peter's Square, where Jed had expected to begin the op—he found himself standing on an asphalt path in the middle of a green enclave. Trees dotted the landscape, providing a patchy shade canopy, while expertly manicured shrubs and neatly mowed lawn stretched off in all directions. In the background, multiple buildings with Italian Renaissance architecture dotted the landscape.

"Watcher, One—where are we?" Jed said into his helmet mic as he brought his rifle up and began a scan for threats.

"You guys are in the Vatican Gardens, which cover fifty-seven acres inside Vatican City. Hang tight. I'm pulling up a map to determine your exact location," Corbin said.

"We're sitting ducks here, boss," Hyeon said behind Jed. "We should relocate to a covered position."

"Agreed," Jed said. "But we need to get oriented first."

"I've got you," Corbin came back. "You're halfway between the Tomb of St. Peter, to your northeast, and the Governor's Palace, which is west-southwest of your position."

Jed scanned, his head on a swivel as she spoke, identifying both of the landmarks while locking in his cardinal directions.

"I've got new intel coming in," she continued. "Shots fired inside the Governor's Palace. Enemy shooters have breached the building."

"Copy," Jed said and chopped a hand toward the back side of the sprawling building. "Alpha will breach the Governor's Palace building from the rear and prosecute the threat. Make sure you notify the Swiss Guard and Gendarmerie GIR of our presence," he added, remembering the names of the Vatican security forces from the cursory brief they'd received. "GIR may have snipers on rooftops and I don't want us getting plinked."

"Roger, One, deconfliction in progress," she said.

Jed led Alpha squad off the asphalt path and onto a stretch of lawn.

You're going the wrong way, a voice said in Jed's mind.

Say again, Watcher?

I didn't say anything, One, Corbin answered in his mind, the ethereal quality of her disembodied voice feeling very different from the one he'd just heard.

Rifle fire suddenly erupted on both sides of them.

"Somebody sees us, but I don't see them," Bex said, scanning for the source of the incoming fire.

"Get low and head for that grove of trees over there," Jed said, chopping a hand and vectoring for cover in a low combat crouch. Tracers screamed overhead in all directions as he led his team toward a thick cluster of evergreens behind a four-story building.

"We're in a cross fire," Hyeon shouted.

"I know," Jed hollered back as they wove their way into the cover behind tree trunks and a dense spread of low branches.

"I'm hit," Nisha cried and collapsed on the bed of pine needles and mulch.

"I got this," Bex said as they clustered around Nisha.

In Jed's visor, a medical alert flashed: *Nonlethal injury to team member. Mobility impacted. Blood loss will become critical without intervention.*

"Talk to me, Bex," he said, taking a knee and scanning through the gaps in the foliage for converging threats.

"She took a round to the left thigh," Bex said, pulling an actual blow-out kit from a cargo pocket. "Looks like it punched straight through. Applying a tourniquet to stanch the blood flow."

The alert in Jed's visor updated a moment later. *Team member blood loss stopped. Medevac required in thirty minutes or less.*

"I'm in the fight," Nisha said, and Jed wondered what her visor status was telling her. He'd been in countless training simulations over the years, and he knew the round Nisha had taken in the leg was Simunition, not an actual slug. She was not *really* injured, but when he glanced at her leg, the wound and blood looked as real as any he'd seen in combat.

"Can you move?" he asked as fresh gunfire tore through the branches all around them.

"Yes, but with a 50 percent reduction in mobility," she said.

"Watcher, Alpha—we're in a real jam here. We've got one wounded and shooters converging on our position," Jed said, breathing heavy. "Talk to me."

"You've got two pairs of shooters coming at you—one pair from the east and another from the west. Plus, I hold a sniper on the roof of the Ethiopian College, which is the building right next to you guys. I'm trying to read him to find out if he's a friendly or not."

"Understood, but we can't stay here. We need options."

"I think your best option is to try to make it inside the Ethiopian College. You'll have better cover and can regroup inside. But before you can move, you've got to deal with the converging shooter pairs moving in on your position."

"Check."

He made eye contact with Hyeon and gestured for the former SEAL to cover the east approach while he covered west. Hyeon nodded and they both crabbed through the foliage until they found prone shooting lanes to defend their hide. As Jed scanned over his rifle for the incoming assaulters, more unsolicited negative thoughts began to barrage him.

You're a terrible leader. You're going to get your entire team killed.

He blinked and shook his head, trying to regain his focus.

You're weak. You don't have what it takes to be a Shepherd, the voice taunted.

With gritted teeth, he reached out to his Watcher: *Corbin, can you hear that?*

Hear what? she answered.

There's somebody else here with us, somebody inside my head. A Dark One, maybe. Can you help me?

The taunting voice returned. *Now I know your Watcher's name. Now I can hunt her too. You're a fool, Jedidiah. . . . You're weak and stupid.*

Corbin screamed—loud and long and terrible—but Jed couldn't tell if the scream was in his head or being broadcast on the radio.

"Four, did you hear that scream?" Jed said.

"Negative," Hyeon replied.

Jed, help me! Corbin cried, and this time Jed could almost feel her pain.

Hot rage erupted in his chest.

Don't you touch her! he screamed in his mind.

Operating on pure reflex, he closed his eyes and followed an invisible thread tugging inside his head. As he did, he soon realized the thread wasn't tied to Corbin, but rather to the source of his torment. At the end, he found a figure made of light but ringed in shadow. It had no features to speak of—just blinding light where a body was supposed to be.

Show yourself, you coward! he shouted at it.

You shouldn't have come for me, the voice said. *You left your team vulnerable and unprotected.*

Instead of feeling malice or hate from the figure, Jed felt a different emotion, one he did not expect . . . disappointment.

A bullet whistled past Jed's left ear, snapping his consciousness back into himself and what he was supposed to be doing, defending their western flank. He saw two operators converging in low tactical crouches, sighting over compact machine guns. At this close range, he could see they were dressed in tactical gear and had GIR patches in bold white letters emblazoned across their otherwise-black antiballistic vests.

"One, Four—I've got incoming Gendarmerie," Hyeon called. "Are these guys legit or bad guy impostors?"

"I don't know," Jed yelled back. "But I've got a pair incoming on my side."

"What's our ROE, bro? We've got like fifteen seconds and we're dead."

Jed centered his targeting laser on the forehead of the lead incoming shooter and put tension on the trigger. Only Corbin could answer that urgent question. He queried her one last time, praying she was back engaged. "Watcher, Alpha One—we've got incoming GIR. They're targeting us and we need to know if we can shoot back. Need you to deconflict. Watcher, do you copy?"

Corbin didn't answer.

The incoming GIR shooters opened fire on their position, splintering wood and sending pine needles and bark raining down on Jed's head.

Corbin won't be helping you anymore, Jed, the voice said with final judgment. *She's mine, and now you and your team are dead.*

He decided to engage the GIR shooters, but four rifle cracks in rapid succession behind him and a punch to the back of his helmet killed the command before he could make it. A giant red warning flashed in the middle of his visor: *FATAL GUNSHOT WOUND TO THE HEAD. ALPHA ONE KIA.* With a defeated, angry groan, Jed rolled onto his back and looked up to see Eli, Grayson, Johnny, and Carl standing over them with rifles pointed at Jed's team.

"Poor, clueless little nuggets," Johnny said with a Cheshire cat grin. "Y'all're dead."

"Where the heck did you guys come from?" Hyeon said, getting up to his feet.

"From the Collegio Etiopico building. Flanked you from behind while the converging avatars kept you distracted on the wings," Eli said.

Jed sat up and laid his rifle across his lap. Unable to meet the veterans' gaze, he said, "Yeah, looks like I dropped the ball pretty bad on this one."

"Yes, you did," a baritone voice answered, but it wasn't Eli.

The simulation melted away and the shadowy, elaborate innards of the airplane hangar–size kill house came into view. Jed lifted his head to look in the direction of approaching footsteps to find the Colonel marching toward them with a drill instructor's glower on his face.

"And the other three of you didn't impress me either," the Colonel added as he stopped in front of the group and crossed his arms over his hard, muscular chest. "I want you all to stow your gear and meet me in the training classroom in fifteen minutes for a debrief. And after that, I think we're all going for a little run."

Without waiting for Jed's reply, the Colonel stormed off.

"Well, I, for one, think that went really well," Hyeon said, doing a solid Ryan Reynolds impression. "Got our butts kicked in record time."

"Yeah, maybe there's a ribbon for that?" Bex added as she safed her weapon.

Eli extended a hand and helped pull Jed to his feet.

"Thanks, bro," Jed said, still unable to meet the veteran's eyes.

"Let's go for a little walk," Eli said, clamping his arm around Jed's shoulder and leading him away from the group and toward the middle of the expansive kill house.

Jed glanced over his shoulder as he turned and caught Nisha's eye. She gave him a tight-lipped smile and mouthed, *"Next time."*

Next time, he thought. *Two simple words with so much implied meaning. Next time we'll know what to expect. . . . Next time we'll do better. . . . Next time we'll win.*

Eli marched him out of earshot and then took a seat on a rock the size of a lounge chair—one of several scattered about in this section of the course. Jed found his own rock and sat, discovering as he did that what he'd judged to be a rock was actually a carved piece of hard foam painted to look like a rock.

"What's on your mind?" Eli said without a hint of judgment in his voice.

"Is Corbin okay?" Jed asked, his mind going to the one teammate he'd not been able to put eyes on.

"She's fine."

"Are you sure? She screamed in my mind and it felt real."

Eli nodded. "I promise she's fine. In fact, one might say that she was wearing two hats for this exercise—a blue hat *and* a red hat."

"I'm not sure how to take that, but okay."

"C'mon, Jed. Talk to me. Give me your unfiltered opinion on what just happened."

Jed blew air through pursed lips. "What's there to say? I screwed up, and I've gotta own that."

Eli chuckled. "Dude, I'm not looking for the party line. I said unfiltered. I wanna know what's really on your mind. Be honest."

"Fine, you want me to be honest? It was a bogus exercise. We had basically zero advance ISR and the tasking was vague to the point of negligence. On top of that, my team was essentially teleported into the middle of an engagement already underway, in the open, with a Watcher who had no access to traditional TOC resources. In other words, the Colonel knowingly sent us into an unfair fight with one hand tied behind our backs. How's that for honesty?"

Eli chuckled.

"What's so funny?" Jed snapped, looking at his teammate for the first time.

"You're right. It was unfair and that, my friend, was the point," Eli said. "You were *supposed* to fail this exercise."

Jed shook his head as if to clear his ears. "Huh?"

"Yeah, the Colonel and Ben designed it that way on purpose. All the things you said were true. The odds of you snatching victory from the jaws of defeat on this op were less than 5 percent."

"Hold on. The Colonel *and Ben* designed it that way on purpose? Was Ben here for this exercise?"

Eli answered the question with a smile.

"So that's who was in my head," Jed murmured, the final puzzle piece clicking into place. Conflicting emotions washed over him at this realization. On the one hand, he felt immense relief. During the exercise, he'd been convinced that a Dark One, possibly Victor, had found him and was probing his mind. Thank God that was not the case. But on the other hand, learning that Ben was the one harassing him was kind of disturbing. He knew the man had gifts, but this had felt . . . *dark*.

"It's not so easy to concentrate when you've got Ben Morvant mucking around in your headspace, is it?"

"Then you know what it's like? You know how it feels?" Jed asked, surprised by Eli's comment.

"Of course I do. Every Shepherd needs to know what it's like to have their thoughts hijacked—especially team leaders. And every Shepherd needs to learn how to rebuff psychic attacks. Remember Pastor Mike's talk? If we don't train and learn how to resist the weapons and tactics used by the enemy, we'll fail in real-world combat. So yes, Jed—I know exactly what you were up against. Does that make you feel any better?"

"Actually, it does," Jed said, finding a smile for the first time since he'd stepped out of the tunnel.

"Good," Eli said, getting to his feet. "And on that note, we should probably get going. We don't want everybody waiting on us."

"Roger that," Jed said, rising from his "rock" and heading for the tunnel. "And, Eli . . ."

"Yeah?"

"Thanks for reading me in."

"Easy day," the Shepherd said, pulling a bag of sunflower seeds from a cargo pocket. "That's what I'm here for."

CHAPTER THIRTEEN

Imam Sayed Hassan al-Hajjaj couldn't help but smile as he looked around the *muṣallā,* or prayer hall, at the large crowd filing in for the Fajr salat. This, the official third of the five daily prayers, had always been his favorite—even more so lately because worshipers had come to the mosque at the sound of the call to the third salat, full of hope after so many years of hopelessness and fear. With the defeat of ISIL had come destruction and, in the aftermath, anxiety over what new opportunistic brutality would emerge to fill the power vacuum.

ISIL had razed the countryside as they forfeited control to Iraqi and coalition forces, leaving misery and mistrust in their wake. This mosque had been damaged but thankfully spared total destruction like so many that ISIL had blown up or burned to the ground—houses of worship the brutal extremists had deemed apostate to their radical views. The peace-loving Muslims that had been trapped under ISIL extremist rule in Tal Afar had cheered their liberators: coalition soldiers and the bearded warriors of America's special forces. The imam's congregation was grateful to the soldiers who had rid them of the terrorist menace and now were ready to get on with their lives.

Slowly they had rebuilt, but more slowly was the return to emotional and psychological security he sought for his congregation. The smiles as men filled the *muṣallā* and women passed through to take the stairs up to the *makhphil*, from which they would offer their prayers to Allah, told al-Hajjaj they were making great strides. They were seekers of peace, families who wanted what all humans want—safety and security for their loved ones, the freedom to make a living without risk of violence and death, and the ability to worship in peace. And now, it seemed, they were finding their way back to this and the happiness that came with it.

"As-salamu alaikum, Imam," a familiar voice said. *"Allah maak."*

He turned to see the smiling face of the young man whom he had been mentoring this past year. Only thirteen years old, this son of a cobbler running a shop in Tal Afar had spent hours studying the Quran with him and then cleaning the *muṣallā* between prayers. This, in and of itself, seemed a great measure of the improving spiritual health of his flock.

"They seem happy, Tariq," he said in his native Arabic to the boy he'd come to love. "I thank you that your service to Allah makes this a place that is so welcoming for them."

"I am honored to serve Allah and you, Imam," Tariq said, his right hand over his heart.

"I wish for you to take your place here, up front," al-Hajjaj said and gestured from the minbar—the raised dais where he delivered his sermons.

The boy's eyes widened and his mouth turned up with delight. "I am honored, Imam," Tariq said, his voice quivering with excitement. He nearly skipped to the front row, where al-Hajjaj's assistant winked at him, then called out to Tariq.

"Pray beside me, Tariq," he said.

In a few days, on Friday, he would deliver the khutbah message at the Zuhr salat and had plans already to speak about love and service, using young Tariq as an example. He could imagine the boy's father beaming with pride. He had turned ahead of his congregation, ready to roll out his prayer rug to face the mihrab, the nook that faced Mecca, when he heard shouting outside. He spun around to face the entrance and saw a half-dozen soldiers forming at the rear of the prayer hall, spreading out beneath the three open arches leading outside, rifles up and at the ready. He sprinted toward the man who appeared to be in charge, left hand out and visible and his right on his heart.

"Please, please," he said, finding a softness in his voice somehow as anger rose inside him. "It is our time of prayer. We welcome you, of course, and thank you for your protection, but ask that you please let us perform the Fajr salat before we offer you our assistance. Then we will serve you however we can."

"We ain't here for your help, bro, and sure as hell not for your

protection." The soldier wore a tan vest packed with extra magazines, as well as a brick-like radio with a wire to the headset he
wore. On the center of the vest was an American flag, just visible
above the assault rifle he was clutching in his hands. "And we don't
have time for your devil prayers. We're here for Imam al-Hajjaj."

"I am Imam Sayed Hassan al-Hajjaj," he said, hand still on his
heart and his nod nearly a bow. "I am happy to help you but again
ask I first be allowed to deliver the prayer for my congregation."

The blow came out of nowhere, a sharp crack to his left knee,
presumably from the special forces soldier beside the leader. Pain
consumed him and he collapsed to the ground, belatedly aware of
the howl of agony that escaped his lips. He raised both hands in
the air immediately.

"There has been a mistake," he cried.

The next blow was from the leader, and he felt his collarbone
shatter under the butt of the man's short rifle but this time managed not to scream at the pain streaking through his chest and
shoulder.

"The only mistake here is you deciding to help ISIS bomb
maker Muhammad al-Madir, you dirty liar," the man said.

Another soldier tore open al-Hajjaj's robe and began to frisk
him. He found his phone, pulling it roughly from his pocket and
then handing it to the leader, who opened it, apparently delighted
that it required no security code. Then he passed it to another
soldier, who raised it as if about to take a picture.

"Don't hurt our teacher!" said a voice al-Hajjaj recognized—
a young but strong voice speaking in English.

Al-Hajjaj was about to turn to warn his young pupil back, but
the lead soldier's face caused the words to catch in his throat. The

operator flashed the boy a delighted, malevolent smile while his eyes flared with an orange-red glow. In his peripheral vision, the imam saw the other soldiers were fanning out and moving into the prayer hall crowded with kneeling men and their prayer rugs.

Dread consuming him, al-Hajjaj forced his gaze from those glowing eyes to Tariq, who was striding boldly toward them.

"Tariq, no!" he shouted, but it was too late.

The crack of gunfire from behind him made him jerk as the American's bullet tore through Tariq's chest. The boy fell backward, landing on the ground beside an old man who had his hands up in surrender. Screams and chaos followed, from the women on the *makhphil* above and the men in the *muṣallā* who moved to huddle together instead of running toward the only exit. He turned back to see the lead operator gesture with his left hand and raise his rifle. Pressing his cheek into the stock and sighting in on the crowd with his now bright-red, glowing eyes, the American soldier let out an evil, maniacal laugh.

These men cannot be the Americans. They would never do this.

Gunfire erupted all around the imam as he screamed in horror, turning to watch as the worshipers, trapped between the shooters and the minbar and mihrab, were cut down. Blood spattered the floor and walls all around the ornamental niche that pointed toward Mecca. Unable to stomach the horror, he pulled his eyes away and covered his head with his arms, his collarbone screaming in pain as he waited for a bullet to mercifully end his life.

The gunfire persisted for what felt like an eternity before finally going silent. When no bullet ended his misery, al-Hajjaj raised his head and saw two soldiers moving through the crowd of corpses. With the men slaughtered, they turned their weapons up into the *makhphil*, where the screaming women were still trapped. He watched as the soldiers fired burst after burst up into the women's prayer room, laughing as they did, their glowing eyes wide in bloodlust. Then one of them pulled out a can of spray paint and headed toward the mihrab at the far end of the *muṣallā*. Al-Hajjaj watched from the ground as the man painted large Christian crosses on the decorated walls.

With great agony, al-Hajjaj pulled himself to one knee and turned to face the leader of this band of killers. Beside the leader, the soldier with the imam's mobile phone panned in a circle, recording the massacre—for what purpose, al-Hajjaj couldn't possibly fathom.

"Why?" he gasped, tears streaming down his cheeks and into his beard. "I would have done whatever you asked of me. We have no weapons. We are on the same side as you. There was no reason for this—none."

The leader fired his rifle in the air as if signaling to his troops that their work here was done. The soldier who had been recording dropped the imam's phone and crushed it underfoot.

"Oops, looks like you just died, Imam," the leader said with a mirthless chuckle.

"I don't understand," he sobbed. "I don't understand any of this."

The leader raised his rifle, and al-Hajjaj stared into the black eye of the barrel.

"You don't need to," the American devil said. "But know you served a higher purpose today, Imam."

There was a flash of light . . . immense pain . . .

Then darkness.

CHAPTER FOURTEEN

Sheets balled up in his fists, Jed stared out through panicked eyes he knew were not his. This was a nightmare but not the kind he was used to. Instead of reliving the night of the senior bonfire and the incident in Kenny Bailey's basement, tonight he was not himself. These eyes belonged to someone younger, an adolescent boy in a mosque where soldiers were weaving their way through a sea of kneeling worshipers with arms raised above their heads in terror.

Jed could feel their panic and the terror inside the boy.

Watch. Learn. Remember, because this is important.

The voice was his, but he knew it wasn't really. It was that *other* voice that came to him sometimes—the voice he'd denied for years as a warrior's intuition. Almost every operator developed a "sixth sense" and they sometimes talked about it, without ever wading too deep into the muddy waters where spirituality and combat intersected.

His heart was pounding in tempo with the boy's, driven to an uncomfortable and unnaturally high cadence by fear. Jed tried to bring his pulse rate down, but his operator training seemed to have no effect, for the body having this experience was not his own. He watched the congregation's imam approach the lead soldier, and he felt anxiety and love for the man.

"I am Imam Sayed Hassan al-Hajjaj. I am happy to help you but again ask I first be allowed to deliver the prayer for my congregation."

The man spoke in heavily accented English, and the soldier in front of him, kitted up like an American special forces operator, just laughed as the operator beside delivered a crippling blow to the imam's left knee, dropping him to the ground.

Is this the past? Is this happening right now?

Jed felt his fear—the boy's fear—give way to rage, rising from a dark, carnal place. He glimpsed a flash of a memory of a bearded man in a black tunic beating a woman with a stick—his mother perhaps—and this time he would not stand by and do nothing. His feet were moving . . .

A second blow was dealt to his mentor, a rifle butt breaking the imam's collarbone with a sickening crack.

"The only mistake here is you deciding to help ISIS bomb maker Muhammad al-Madir, you dirty liar," the American said.

But that was wrong—he and the boy both knew it. Imam al-Hajjaj despised the jihadists. This wasn't about a bomb maker—

so why were the Americans doing this? The next thought wasn't a shared thought, but Jed's and Jed's alone.

They're wearing American flags, but these guys aren't American special operators. These guys are something else . . .

As if to confirm his suspicion, the man looked up and laughed again, and Jed saw the orange glow in his eyes. A soldier tore open the imam's robe and pulled out his mobile phone, using it to film the massacre that followed.

"Don't hurt our teacher!" he screamed at the lead soldier, fists balled with defiance as he moved to challenge the leader.

"Tariq, no!" the imam cried.

Jed watched, impotent, as the operator brought his rifle up and the muzzle flashed blinding-white light. He didn't feel the bullet impact, but he felt himself falling backward. Then he was staring up at the arched ceiling of the mosque, full of terror and rage as innocents screamed and rifle fire echoed around him . . .

Jed sat bolt upright, his hands burning with the pain from his own fingernails tearing into his palms. Mouth agape, he panted, trying to get his breathing under control before he woke the others. He'd done that enough already.

The vision was over, but like the wind whispering in the eaves on a stormy night, an oily voice taunted him.

I'm coming for you . . . and you're too weak to stop me.

Fiendish laughter followed, then faded into the sounds of actual wind blowing through the trees outside the barracks.

Jed reclined back onto his pillow, closed his eyes, and practiced several rounds of four-count breathing to slow his pounding heart. Once he was calm, he looked at his watch—2332.

Remember . . .

Remember what?

The mosque could be anywhere, though he knew instinctively it had to be located in the Middle East—Iraq or Syria.

The faces of the fallen . . .

He had not seen the boy's reflection and only glimpsed the imam for an instant. The face of the Dark One pretending to be an American special operator—now that was a face he could remember. That and the feel of the place. Its spiritual signature . . . if there was such a thing.

Exhaustion settled over Jed like a weighted blanket, and despite the emotional turmoil he'd just suffered, he drifted slowly back to sleep . . .

"Everybody up!" a baritone male voice called.

Jed's eyes popped open to the blinding light in the room.

"Everyone up—let's go," the voice commanded, and Jed registered it wasn't the Colonel bullying them out of their racks but the Shepherd commander himself. "Eli, head over to the theater and tell IT that I need a secure link to the main side TOC. I'm going to be briefing the entire command."

"Roger that," Eli said and disappeared.

Jed glanced down at the Suunto watch on his wrist: 0445.

He'd somehow managed to log five hours of sleep since his nightmare. Swinging his legs off the side of the bed, he looked over at Nisha as she arched her back to work out the kinks from sleep.

This is exactly what I need, more sleep deprivation and another stress test exercise.

He heard her voice clear as day, but her lips weren't moving.

"It's not a stress test," he said before he could catch himself.

She scrunched up her face, confused. "I didn't . . . ," she started to say but didn't finish the thought.

His cheeks flushed as he looked away, pretending like it never happened.

Minutes later, he and his team were hustling across the courtyard between the barracks and the chow hall toward the admin building. Grayson and Johnny were keeping pace beside Jed.

"This isn't part of the training, right?" he asked, suddenly doubting everything he'd just experienced.

"Nah, we've not done anything like this before," Grayson said, running a hand through his short hair and readjusting his ball cap to keep it in place.

"Something real is going down," Johnny said.

Moments later, they streamed into an indoor amphitheater with tiered seating. The performing arts–size auditorium was already packed with several hundred people, and Jed shook his head in surprise.

"Who are all these people?" he asked Grayson, whom he followed down the central stairs until an open row presented itself.

"What do you mean?" Grayson asked, surprised. "These are the tactical teams. These are the Shepherds."

Jed suddenly remembered the Q and A session with Ben the other day when he described the size of the global operation that rivaled all of Naval Special Warfare Group 2, including boat teams and support and logistics.

"What did you think? We fight all of the devil's bad guys with just a handful of dudes out of Ben's house?" Grayson whispered and then laughed.

The Shepherd commander walked up to the podium as

commotion to Jed's right made him look that way. David Yarnell was squeezing past his teammates in the row as they pulled their legs tight against their seats to let him by. Grayson got up and shifted one seat left, and Jed did the same, reluctantly freeing up the seat beside him for his TSL and team colead.

David flopped down into the seat and leaned toward him. "Sorry I'm late. They told me to join my team but didn't say why."

"You're all good, bro," Jed whispered back, struggling to tamp down his knee-jerk negativity at David's presence.

"What's going on?"

"No idea. We just got here."

Ben tapped the podium microphone, an electronic-style plunk filling the auditorium, and the room hushed.

"Thank you, ladies and gents, for getting here so quickly," Ben began. "I know some of you are on leave and others are in training block, so I appreciate your getting here on little notice. I felt it best to get everyone up to speed at once, no matter who responds to the current situation."

Ben craned his neck as the movie theater–size screen behind him filled with a gruesome image that made Jed's chest tighten— bodies stacked on top of each other inside a very familiar mosque. The walls were riddled with bullet holes and spattered with blood. In the background, a man in white robes was lashed to a pillar, his arms pulled behind him, his head lolled to one side, and a bullet hole in the center of his forehead.

Imam al-Hajjaj . . .

The image switched to another view, this one of the far end of the worship room—the *muṣallā*, a memory reminded him— where the walls had been spray-painted with bright-red crosses.

Jed strained his eyes, looking for the foot of the boy who had fallen somewhere in this frame.

"This is the Farouq Mosque in Tal Afar, Iraq," Ben said, raw emotion in his strained voice. "The site of a horrible massacre early this morning local time, where the attack was recorded in real time."

The picture now shifted to an erratic video, bouncing wildly, as if a victim were filming while trying to escape. Bodies were falling all around whoever held what Jed assumed to be a phone camera, crossing rapidly across the image of what appeared to be two soldiers firing into the crowd. The recording lacked audio, but Jed knew all too well what the screams sounded like.

"This video was posted several hours ago by a human rights organization—or at least that is the claim. It reportedly shows coalition forces firing into a crowd of worshipers at morning prayer. The phone purportedly belonged to the local imam who filmed the attack before being gunned down."

No, Jed thought. *That's wrong. I saw a soldier—a Dark One posing as a soldier—take the phone and begin to film.*

"Survivors claim that the attackers were American military and from the description, they appear to be American special operations forces. However . . ." Ben paced away from the podium, hands behind his back as the screen went dark and then was replaced by the Shepherds logo. "We have reason to believe that this was a staged attack, meant to indict the coalition forces and foment anger and hatred. Obviously spray-painting crosses on the mihrab would succeed wildly in that regard."

"Were there any SOF units operating in the area?" someone asked from the front row.

"No. I've been in conference with both the task unit commanders and the JSOC unit commander, and there were no operations in Tal Afar at the time. Obviously that can—and will—all be spun up as a cover-up. In addition, we have chatter picked up by our Watchers suggesting there was an important operation going on in Tal Afar last night."

Jed wondered suddenly what that meant. In his old life, spooks talking about "chatter" meant signals intelligence—bits and pieces of communications, emails, and social media posts suggesting activity of concern. What constituted Watcher chatter, he still did not fully understand.

"The evidence is thin, but we have been in prayer and believe strongly this was a false flag operation conducted by the Dark Ones designed to fan the flames of hatred and anger in the Middle East as the tensions have been waning since of the defeat of ISIL in the region. An op like this is right out of the Dark Ones' playbook. The crosses are meant to imply Christian liability for this attack, obviously, thereby provoking retaliation in kind. They want holy wars; they want jihad." He walked back to the podium, grasping it with both hands, his jaw twitching in anger. "If we're right, this is likely only the first in a series of coordinated operations. We expect additional attacks—both retaliatory strikes against coalition forces and de novo attacks on Christian minorities and additional Muslim targets. Expect Christian or Jewish calling cards to be left. Do not be surprised if Western and Israeli forces are jointly implicated, reviving the whole 'two devils' theme that's been successful in sowing hatred and violence the last decades in the region."

Jed watched Ben sigh heavily. The man seemed tired, a side Jed had not yet seen from the Shepherd commander.

"We will be spinning up Gideon Bravo Team in the coming hours for deployment to Iraq and specifically the Tal Afar region. The NOC," he said, referring to the acronym for "nonofficial cover" or a cover that would not be known or avowed outside of the origin unit, "will be a joint counterterrorism task force, investigating an ISIL or al Qaeda link to the attack. This will get a lot of cooperation from the JSOTF in the region, who undoubtedly feel they're in the hot seat here, having been accused of this atrocity and already convicted in the court of public opinion. Our job is to confirm the Dark Ones are responsible and how they successfully carried out this attack."

Jed suddenly realized how vital it was that he share his nightmare with Ben. The thought of sharing his vision—which meant accepting that it had really happened at all—was overwhelming but necessary.

He leaned over to Grayson. "I need to speak with Morvant."

Grayson raised his eyebrows in surprise. "What? Why?"

Right—I get it. What could a nugget still in Jericho Basic have to say at a time like this?

"It's important, bro," he said. "It's related to what he's briefing us about."

"I want everyone to head to their team rooms, where you will review the details of the attack and other intelligence we have from the Watchers Middle East as well as our own program. Find what we're missing. Involve your TSLs, please. Their spiritual guidance is crucial on this. I expect another briefing in just a few hours, back here, and will assemble you through your team leaders. Gideon

Bravo, be ready to roll out in the coming hours; assemble gear and stage it in your team room. I know you have questions, but we don't have the answers yet. But if we don't figure this out and get ahead of what's coming next, there will be an explosion of religious violence in the Middle East that will make 2004 to 2007 look like child's play."

And then he strode off the podium, the wiry Pastor Mike falling in step as he left through a side door at the front.

"I'll take you," Grayson said.

"I need Eli there, I think," Jed added as they rose.

"Okay," Grayson said. "I'll grab him and meet you outside the main doors."

The operator shuffled off to the left, exiting the far end of the row and heading quickly toward the exit. Jed looked over at David, who eyed him with something—not suspicion, maybe, but a high level of curiosity and something else.

Despite all his bitterness, which he knew could easily be a tool of the dark forces, Jed met David's gaze. "I need you to come with me."

"What?"

"I have to talk to Commander Morvant about something— something important. And I need you there."

"Really?" David said, surprised but apparently also pleased. "Why me?"

Jed forced a grin onto his face. "You're my TSL, right?" he asked. "We're supposed to do all of this together."

David nodded. "Okay, let's go."

As they shuffled out behind the rest of the team, David grinned at Jed over his shoulder. "Kinda like old times, only this time you can't blame the mess on me?"

It was David who'd gotten Jed into the vast majority of troubles he'd experienced as a kid. He'd always been the wild and crazy one to Jed's calm walk of faith—the yin to his yang.

But this was beyond anything either of them could even have imagined.

Jed nodded but couldn't keep a nostalgic smile from creeping onto his face as he followed David and the rest of his team toward the exit.

CHAPTER FIFTEEN

Ben settled into the chair at the conference table beside his desk with a heavy sigh. He leaned back and scrubbed his face with his hands as a weary groan escaped his lips.

He was tired—so very, very tired—a feeling he neither liked nor was accustomed to.

His years deploying as a Navy SEAL, with all their intensity, violence of action, and emotional and physical sacrifice, had been nothing compared to the last decade with the Shepherds. And the last almost five years now as the leader of nearly a thousand combat, spiritual leader, and support personnel for the North American command had been the most draining of all. He was at the pointy tip of the spear in a war that had raged on for thousands of years and would rage on until Christ returned. Whether the Second Coming would happen in his lifetime or not was up to God.

My contribution is both small and finite.

Conversely the Shepherds' contribution was vital and evergreen. Their impact, by disrupting the operations of the Dark Ones, provided the hope and stability that brought millions to God. In the end, that was their real charter—to provide safety from the evil of Satan and his dark angels so as many people as possible could come to know God before the final tribulation. Wasn't that what he'd learned from his study of the most important book in the world? Eternity . . . that was what they were fighting for. The mission was too important for him to be tired.

But he was tired nonetheless.

A long sigh slipped from him as his mind went, unbidden, to a place nothing good could come from—to Nicholas Woland and the greatest failure of his life. His thumb and forefinger found the skin between his eyes at the bridge of his nose and squeezed while he wondered, for the millionth time, what he could have done differently. But as always, the answer was the same.

At first, Woland had been exactly what he seemed to be: a very talented operator from the uber-elite First Special Forces Operational Detachment-Delta—aka Delta Force, the Unit, and CAG. The best of the best. He had excelled throughout training, saying and demonstrating all the right things. And yet it had all been a deception. Woland had joined in service of his own agenda, not God's. Despite their safeguards, a faithless man had snuck into their ranks, and Ben had missed it.

Oh, the irony—the head Shepherd unable to spot a wolf in sheep's clothing.

Anger swelled inside him as regret and self-blame were replaced by something darker. It wasn't just his personal failure that ate at Ben; Woland's betrayal of faith, of God, and of the brotherhood upset him as well. Woland's jailbreak preceding the massacre at the mosque was no coincidence. The innocent lives snuffed out today were only a prologue for something much bigger and more diabolical. Woland's defection to the ranks of Victor's army was a clear and present danger to the Shepherds organization. Yes, protocols had been changed and security measures taken, but the wolf had spent much time with the flock.

Right or wrong, he closed his eyes and said a short prayer that he would find the former Shepherd, confront him, and defeat him before it was too late. He knew it was a selfish prayer—Christ never demanded retribution for Pontius Pilate—but this was different. Wasn't it? God had him on a path of service fraught with violence of action in a hot war between good and evil, so wasn't his reaction expected? Acceptable? Perhaps he should be praying for Woland's soul. But he wasn't. Instead of asking for the man's salvation, he prayed for divine justice—for Nicholas Woland to be delivered to the company of his dark fellows in the fires of hell as swiftly and expeditiously as possible.

The thought caused a flutter in his stomach, as he couldn't help but wonder if the man was truly beyond saving.

Maybe there's still time to turn him back to the light.

No . . . don't go there.

One last sigh and he opened his eyes.

Reflexively he grabbed his favorite picture from the corner of the large desk where he almost never sat, preferring the conference table instead. The picture was ancient. His son, Jason, was barely a year old in the picture, sitting in Christy's lap, grinning a big-cheeked baby grin and staring at the camera with those blue-gray eyes. Christy called them his storm eyes, or sometimes his Ben eyes, and he guessed that was right. Jason was starting middle school soon and now had a baby sister—jeez, little Elizabeth was almost six—to take care of. And take care of her Jason did, with the passion and commitment of a Navy SEAL.

He remembered the day the picture was taken—just a few weeks into his recovery from injuries he'd sustained in a raid against the Dark Ones in Africa. He'd had no idea what that even meant at the time but knew he'd defeated a great evil that day, healed his teammates Reed and Chris, and then nearly died from his own wounds. But God had had other plans for him. Like a paraphrase from the great Mark Twain, he chuckled as he thought, *The rumors of my crippling demise are greatly exaggerated.* He'd medically retired from the Teams, but instead of the life in a wheelchair he'd been promised by VA doctors, he'd rehabilitated himself and completed Jericho Basic. Six months later, he'd deployed for his first time as a Shepherd under the leadership of Mike Moore.

He'd confronted his fears and nightmares and defeated the Dark Ones on that op.

And again, on the next op.

And the one after that.

And the one after that . . .

The memory of Christy's question asked from the pillow next

to him when he'd climbed out of bed in the middle of the night still tugged at his heartstrings.

"Do you think you'll be gone long?" she'd asked, her eyes saying, *Please don't go.*

"That's God's call," he'd replied, using their family catchphrase . . . a catchphrase that he knew was beginning to wear thin with her.

A knock on the door straightened him up in his chair, and he placed the picture back on the desk and wiped an unexpected tear from his cheek.

"Come," he commanded.

The door opened and Pastor Mike walked in, gave a nod, and then dropped into the seat across the conference table from him. "You okay?" his TSL asked, his voice more Ranger than pastor.

"Five by," Ben replied, forcing the fatigue from his mind—and his soul. "Just need a power nap and maybe a PowerBar."

"I hear ya," Mike laughed. "I'm getting closer to sixty than fifty and I'm starting to feel it." Then he rolled his head, enjoying a satisfying crack Ben could hear. "But I can still whup your sorry, crippled butt, so don't get any ideas."

"Right," Ben said, not up for their usual Army-Navy banter just now.

And besides, it might just be true.

"So you're sending Gideon Bravo to Iraq?" Mike said, leaning on his elbows.

"Yeah, they're on the short fuse, 0300 rotation beside Raphael Alpha."

"But you've got Michael Alpha and Charlie nearby in theater already," Mike pointed out.

Ben smiled at him and raised his eyebrows. "You're the spiritual leader here, right?"

"Right," Mike said, then laughed out loud. "Hard to stop being a Ranger, you know."

"I can't even imagine," Ben said. "And believe me, I value your advice as my former commander as much as I do as my spiritual mentor." He sighed. "And friend, of course."

"Of course," Mike said, eyeing him uncomfortably with those brown eyes he often felt bored right through to his very soul. "Do you want to talk about—?"

A sharp knock on the door stopped Mike midsentence.

"Come," Ben barked. The door opened, and to his surprise, one of his best operators, currently doing a run through Jericho Basic, stuck his head in. "Eli? What's up, brother?"

"Sorry to interrupt, boss," the Shepherd said. "But I've got Jed Johnson here with me, and he needs to talk to you. It's urgent."

"Related to . . . ?"

"The developing crisis and operation in Tal Afar."

Ben exchanged looks with Mike, who pursed his lips as he often did when he found something particularly interesting.

"Send him in," Ben said, feeling a renewed energy for some reason. "And you come on in too."

Eli nodded and Ben watched the six-foot-four former Navy SEAL step through the door behind him, all but coming to attention at the doorway. Ben had been distant and all business with Johnson since he'd arrived—as was the protocol with new recruits—and it showed, but something told him he needed to drop the wall. The key was to know when to be leader and when to be brother—both tactically and spiritually. He relied more heavily on the Holy Spirit for this part of his job than any other. Being gifted with the ability to hear people's thoughts and feel their emotions didn't hurt either.

"Relax, Jed," he said. "Come on in and take a seat, brother."

Jed took a seat, with Eli sliding into the chair beside him, and everything about his new Shepherd screamed fear and confusion. Behind him, David Yarnell stood, hands clasped in front of him, and rocked back and forth on the balls of his feet.

"What's up, Jed? Is everything going okay in Jericho phase one? You're not having second thoughts, are you, bro?" Ben asked with a good-natured smile.

Jed looked tentatively between Mike and Eli and then said, "I had a nightmare, or I thought it was a nightmare until your presentation in the auditorium . . ."

Ben felt his weariness disappear in a flash. Once again, Jedidiah Johnson surprised him.

"Jed, just tell us what you saw—unfiltered. It could be terribly important."

Ben listened as Jed described in great detail how he had watched through the eyes of a boy inside the mosque during the massacre. His heart skipped a beat as the former frogman described intimate details of the attack he'd learned but not shared during his briefing. Jed ended by claiming he had seen at least one of the attackers—well enough to recognize the man.

"Hold on," Pastor Mike said. "What time did you wake up from this nightmare?"

"Around 2330, sir," Jed said with an uneasy exhale.

Jed, it seemed, was not enjoying his new gift.

I remember that feeling, Ben thought, remembering how viscerally such visions had affected him in the early days.

"That means you were—"

"Yeah," Ben said, cutting Mike off. Better to lead Jed to his new reality slowly. He'd witnessed the attack through the eyes of the boy who'd been killed in real time, just like a Watcher. This was a seeing, not a memory or a prophecy.

"Jed, this has been hugely helpful, my friend." Ben rose and paced a moment, saying a silent prayer in his head.

"There's one thing more," Jed said. The SEAL shot an uncomfortable look back at David, but his TSL was lost in thought and didn't notice. "I think that Victor has been inside my head."

"What do you mean?"

"Well, at the end of the nightmare, after the boy was shot, I think he spoke to me."

"What did he say?" Mike said, concern and fire in his voice.

"He taunted me," Jed said.

"Tell me *exactly* what he said," Ben pressed.

"He said, 'I'm coming for you . . . and you're too weak to stop me,' and then he laughed."

Ben resumed his pacing, debating. *Holy Spirit, guide me here. I have so many emotions clouding my judgment—fear, relief, a longing for my family. Please let me know this is the right call . . .*

And He did. An almost-euphoric sense of peace swept over Ben as he prayed. He opened his eyes and smiled.

Thank You, Father.

"Jed, I need you to get your team together and let them know you're heading out. I'm sending you downrange to Tal Afar. You're going to help us sort this whole mess out."

"What?" Jed's voice rose higher than he probably meant it to. "You're sending us? We still haven't completed basic."

Jed's follow-up thought came to Ben like a loudspeaker: *I'm not ready. I completely failed the last kill house evolution.*

"That's true," Ben said, addressing both Jed's spoken and unspoken thoughts. "You still have more work to do and additional skills to learn, but God has His own timing and sometimes His own training program. He doesn't gift us without purpose, Jed, and your vision and connection to the mosque attack are more valuable to the mission than squeezing in another evolution at the kill house."

Jed nodded.

Ben leaned over, palms on the cool surface, and looked into the gifted SEAL's eyes. "Jed, the second kill house evolution is designed for failure. We throw that curveball to open your heart and your mind to the types of stressors and tactics you will face confronting the Dark Ones that are beyond the reach of your combat skills. I failed it too—everyone does. But you learned a valuable lesson. The Dark Ones don't play fair. They don't care about SOPs, rules of engagement, or the Helsinki Accords. Being a Shepherd is not about being a perfect operator. No matter how tough you are, no matter how physically fit you are, no matter how tactically proficient you are, you are never going to be enough to defeat the enemy we face. Not alone. Not even with your team."

"I thought God never gave us more than we could handle," Jed grumbled, stroking his chin, brow furrowed in thought.

"That's a lie," Ben said, standing up straight. "God allows us to carry more than we can handle, alone, all the time. But there is no such thing as more than *He* can handle. That's the lesson of the kill house exercise. Without God, you'll lose, every time."

The SEAL looked up and nodded, apparently satisfied with that answer.

"Enough with the preaching," Ben said, ending the discussion for now. "Get your team kitted up and ready to roll out. As of this moment, you are no longer Jericho Alpha. You guys are now Joshua Bravo, and you are officially operational."

"You got it, boss," Eli said and rose.

"David," Ben said.

The pastor started as if shaken from sleep. "Yeah?"

"Go with the team and get kitted up. Then come back here to spend some time with Pastor Mike and me. We've got some things to brief you on as well."

"Yes, sir."

Jed rose to his feet, but the uncertainty on his face was undeniable. "Ben, I'm going to be honest. I'm not sure I'm ready yet. And after the kill house . . ."

"Let go of the kill house, Jed," Ben said, making another decision and already dreading telling Christy. "You're ready when I say you're ready. Nevertheless, I'll be deploying with Joshua Bravo on this op—as a mentor and consultant—but the team is yours to lead. And Mike will be coming along as well, to work with David."

He saw David's shoulders drop with visible relief.

"Roger that," Jed said, his eyes more confident and having regained some of their fire.

Marching orders received, Jed, Eli, and David departed, leaving the two old friends alone once more.

"Jed *is* ready, and I know you'll get Yarnell up to speed in short order. They're both exceptional," Ben said.

"Don't do that," Mike said, a grumpy edge creeping into his voice.

"Do what?" Ben said, all innocence.

"Read my thoughts. You know I hate it when you do that. And if you think he's ready, then *hooah*, but the nightmare has me concerned. It sounds to me like Jed experienced second sight through the eyes of a boy at the mosque."

"I know. That's why Jed and his platoon are going on the trip."

"At his age? Besides, he's not a Watcher, and no Shepherds have the gift of second sight. I mean other than you, obviously."

"With God, nothing is impossible." Ben smiled. "Aren't you the one who told me that's the difference between a gift and a skill? Gifts are given to us. We can't control who gets what gifts and how long they are available to us. Young people are most receptive to second sight and the gift fades with time, but not always. Tobias, for example, has never lost the power to see. And in my case, the gifts manifested later—they were given to me when I needed them. I don't know God's plan for Jed, but my heart tells me his path might be similar to my own. With respect to second sight, this could be a one-off or an awaking; only time will tell. The thing is, Mike, we don't know what else he's capable of. During the kill house evolution, he found my thread and confronted me. No other Shepherd has done that before. Ever."

"You didn't share that little detail with me before," Mike said, and Ben could see the gears turning in his head.

"I meant to; we've just both been busy. We need to make more time to talk."

"I'd like that."

"You know, Jed collected a ton of intelligence during that vision, and it's all crammed into that anxious headspace of his. It's up to us to help him figure out how to get it out. I'm hoping David might be of some assistance to that end."

"Agreed. I'll talk with David about it." Then, tugging at his chin, Mike said, "Victor's visit at the end of Jed's vision was certainly no coincidence."

Ben nodded. "This isn't the first time Jed has tangled with Victor, but I think you're onto something. He sensed Jed's presence and went after him. If he's monitoring the scene, I think it's safe to conclude he was the architect behind the attack."

"The dark angel sure loves his false flag operations."

Ben nodded and locked eyes with his counselor, mentor, and friend. "You okay heading to the sandbox with me for this one?"

But he didn't need to read Mike's thoughts to know the answer. There was still a larger-than-life warrior inside this man.

"Are you kidding? I wouldn't miss it," Mike said with the wave of a hand and smile on his face. "Besides, Beth will be happy to have me out of the house for a while. She's always saying how I try to take over all her projects."

Ben nodded as he picked up his keys from the desk and grabbed his ball cap.

"Going to go tell Christy in person, huh?" Mike asked.

"Now you're reading my thoughts, is that it?"

"*Pffftttt*, I wish. The only gifts God saw fit to give me were this chiseled face and anatomical perfection."

Ben laughed out loud at this. "Amen, brother."

Mike had confided in him, on more than one occasion, his

frustration at not being on the receiving end of supernatural gifts. And compared to Ben's bounty, for Mike it certainly had to feel like a feast-or-famine dichotomy. Yet Ben was well aware of the amazing gifts God *had* given Mike—analytical foresight, the ability to inspire, and aptitude for recognizing and developing the gifts in others. Without Mike, Ben would not have found his true calling. Without Mike, he would have never risen to lead the Shepherds.

He headed out the door and down the hall where his Jeep waited just outside the main door, a lead weight in his stomach. He dreaded telling Christy the news. But when he explained why, she would understand, and she would support him.

She always did.

It was why God had put them together.

PART II

There are different kinds of gifts, but the same Spirit distributes them. There are different kinds of service, but the same Lord. There are different kinds of working, but in all of them and in everyone it is the same God at work.

1 CORINTHIANS 12:4-6, NIV

CHAPTER SIXTEEN

Woland was a contemplative sadist.

The most gifted sadists usually are.

For a man to effectively damage another, he must first study the inner clockworks of a human being until he intimately learns all the vulnerabilities of the mind, body, and soul. Only through this process of diligent probing and experimentation can a sadist know how to optimize the psychological, emotional, and physical damage he can inflict. Prison had been his doctoral program, La Santé his laboratory. He entered as a special forces operator, reformed Shepherd, and gifted servant of the Dark One.

He exited as something much more.

Only then did Victor break him out.

During his years in prison, he'd learned that the best time to challenge authority and stress-test security protocols was at the end of the workday—when the staff was tired, hungry, and done caring until tomorrow. Willpower is not an infinite resource. Nor is it a muscle that can be made harder and stronger through training as some people liked to believe. No, all the popular metaphors for willpower were self-deception. Willpower is a child on a journey . . . enthusiastic and energetic at the onset but quick to tire and lose interest.

As a Shepherd, he'd wrestled with his willpower—or maybe the converse was true—every day. He'd discovered a lot about himself through those trials and learned many of the exploits he now used against others. He'd also learned that the rudimentary demands of the flesh were enough to erode most people's willpower. Hunger, thirst, the need to satisfy a caffeine or nicotine habit, the need to sleep, the need to relieve oneself . . . all enemies of willpower. Simply interfering with one or more of these basic biological evolutions started the erosion process. Depravity alone was enough to undo those with the weakest spirits. For stronger, disciplined men, more extreme and calculated measures were required . . .

His target for this engagement, Rector Feiven Senai, was an Ethiopian scholar in residence and the head of the Pontifical Ethiopian College. Since his call to Rome two years ago, it was rumored that Senai had become both a friend and frequent counselor to the pope. The sitting pope was known for his sense of humor, collegial nature, and open mind. He made friendships easily and was trusting by nature—a pair of weaknesses that Victor felt made him more vulnerable. This made Rector Senai a logical target for exploitation. The fact that Senai had a twin brother who lived back in Ethiopia with a wife and three children, whom the rector adored, made him the perfect candidate.

Woland, dressed as a priest in a black suit, clerical vest, and Roman collar, walked casually down Borgo Pio toward the Porta Sant'Anna entrance to Vatican City. Located north of the crowded St. Peter's Square on Via di Porta Angelica, the tall, elaborate wrought iron gate—flanked by a pair of double stone columns topped with eagle statues—functioned as the secure entry point for vendors and guests with appointments. Policed and administered by the Swiss Guard, tourist access to Vatican City via St. Anne's Gate was strictly prohibited. Humming "Für Elise," Woland strolled across the threshold as if without a care in the world. Within three strides, he was hailed by a pair of Swiss Guards. As they moved to intercept him, he had to force himself not to smirk at the flamboyant tricolor uniforms and black berets worn by the famed pontifical protection force. These two young men looked like brightly colored clowns, not elite soldiers.

"This is the business entrance for Vatican City. Entry is permitted by appointment only," the taller of the two guards said in accented English.

"Yes, I'm aware. My name is Father McTierney and I have an appointment with Rector Senai at the Ethiopian College," Woland said, voice neutral but tinged with an Irish accent.

"Do you see that small building twenty meters up the street on the right?" the guard asked.

He clasped his hands together behind his back. "Yes, I do."

"That is the security checkpoint. Provide them with your

identification, and if your name appears on the approved visitors' list, you will be permitted entry."

Woland nodded, thanked them, and walked toward the little security building, not much bigger than a kiosk. Humming, he casually scanned for cameras, sniper hides, and spiritual threats. As a Shepherd, his quest to develop spiritual gifts had been frustratingly slow and unrewarding. But after offering his body as a vessel to a fallen angel, everything changed. As a Dark One, the power and the rage were instantly accessible. The beast inside him was always gnawing and clawing just beneath the surface, and its predatory gifts were offered freely. In fact, it was not tapping the power that was the problem, but rather the opposite . . . restraining himself was the challenge. Since his emancipation from prison, it had been increasingly difficult to keep the beast at bay.

It wanted out.

It wanted to do very bad things.

With great effort, he forced himself back into the calm and pious state of mind that his NOC, Father McTierney, exemplified. The odds were high that he would cross paths with a Shepherd in a NOC similar to his own. Like a cancer, the Shepherds had infiltrated the ranks of the most powerful institutions around the globe. The Vatican was no exception. He knew there would be Shepherds serving covertly inside the pontifical guard as well as in the Gendarmerie Corps, but this information had been wisely compartmentalized, so he didn't know names or numbers. During his tenure at Trinity Loop, he'd not been read in to all of the organization's secrets. This lack of trust—lack of faith in him—had been one of the reasons he'd abandoned them. Yet, having served and lived with them, he knew their means and methods. He knew how they thought and reacted. He recognized their movements, the way they carried themselves, their arrogance. They reeked of piety and their stink was forever imprinted on him. He could pick Shepherds out from a crowd with a high degree of accuracy now.

Hopefully, the converse was not true.

Today's mission was a critical test. The next phase of the operation hinged entirely on his ability to penetrate Vatican City security, deliver the ultimatum to Rector Senai, and not get caught. If detected and detained, that was the end of the road for him. Even without saying the words, Victor had made the stakes perfectly clear. Satan himself had no tolerance for incompetence, and no quarter was granted in defeat.

He reached the tiny shack and stepped inside. Unlike the gate, this checkpoint was manned by the Vatican police dressed in the standard gendarme uniform of a white short-sleeved shirt, navy-blue trousers, and Italian-style police hat. He presented his forged credentials and introduced himself to the guard responsible for in-processing. The guard glanced at his Irish passport and then handed the forged document to another officer, who left with it and went into the building next door . . . not a good sign.

While he waited, Woland chatted politely with the guard seated at the reception counter. The man asked him where he grew up in Ireland, and memories came to him of a small town populated by people he'd never met. He was seeing through the eyes of someone else. A pub, a fight, a mutilated body behind a dumpster . . . he conveyed none of this. Instead, he harvested the useful details about the place with theatrical nostalgia. Eventually the guard with his passport returned.

Woland sniffed.

Something about the scent of this man was off . . .

"Is there a problem?" the reception guard asked the returning guard.

The second guard glanced at Woland, then handed his passport back to the other seated behind the counter. "Everything checks out. Is he on the list?"

"Yeah, I was just about to clear him."

"Did you call Rector Senai to confirm the appointment?"

"I did not. Would you like me to?"

The standing guard shifted his gaze to Woland. "Yes."

"Okay," the seated guard replied and then, turning to Woland, said, "It will just be a moment, Father."

"Take your time. One can't be too careful these days. 'Keep your heart with all vigilance, for from it flow the springs of life,'" he said with a smile, surprised how readily the Word of God came to him.

"Proverbs," the guard said.

"Indeed."

The seated guard rotated in his chair and used a desk phone to call Rector Senai. As Woland listened to the one-sided conversation, a bead of sweat ran from his armpit down his left side, taking him by surprise. He relaxed his brow and the muscles around his eyes and jaw. He centered himself and waited patiently, all the while trying to ignore the sweet, sickly stench of the suspicious guard.

He's a Shepherd, he decided, and the beast inside fantasized about ripping the man's throat out with his teeth.

"Rector Senai is expecting you, Father," the seated guard said, hanging up the receiver and handing Woland back his passport.

"He will meet you at St. Joseph's fountain. Do you need me to show you on a map where it is?"

"That would be kind of you," he said, curious as to the route they would send him on.

The guard drew a red line with a pen up Via Sant'Anna, across the parking area inside Belvedere Courtyard, and drew an X on the opposite side. He then drew a circle around overlapping blue dots in the garden labeled St. Joseph's fountain.

"An escort will meet you here, inside Belvedere Courtyard, and lead you under the museum and out into the garden. This works for you?" the guard said, handing him the paper map.

Woland nodded. "It does. Thank you and may the Lord's peace be with you."

The guard nodded back and gestured to the exit door. Woland did not trade glances with the standing guard as he left, but he felt the man's eyes on his back. With a victorious grin, he stepped outside and into the pleasant late-afternoon air. He walked up Via Sant'Anna onto Via Belvedere and passed three patrolling Vatican police officers—each of whom eyed him coldly. Upon reaching the complex of buildings that made up the Apostolic Palace, library, and famed Vatican museums, he walked through an arched passage which was paved and just wide enough for automobile passage. Belvedere Courtyard, it turned out, was used as a parking lot.

He walked across the lot and was soon met by a uniformed officer with a radio clipped to his belt and a microphone handset clipped to his left shoulder lapel. The guard asked for his name, and when he introduced himself as Father McTierney, the man led him through a locked door, down a hallway, across a small courtyard, and through yet another arched passage that put him on the garden side of Borgia Tower in the Square of the Furnace.

"Follow this road, Via del Governatorato, toward the Palace of the Governatorate. The fountain is on the right in front of the building," his escort said. "Do you need me to take you the rest of the way?"

"No, that won't be necessary," Woland said. "Go with God, my son."

The young man nodded, turned, and walked back in the direction they'd come from, while Woland strolled along the paved road into the Vatican Gardens. He ignored the chirping birds and paid no mind to the manicured lawns and shrubbery. He found the whole "beauty in nature" mentality pointless and absurd. Nature was a war zone, every single creature engaged in a daily battle for survival. Darwin had had it right when he'd coined the term *survival of the fittest*. Only the strong and clever and adaptable survived. This was an eat-or-be-eaten world, and to say otherwise was disingenuous. The Dark Ones understood this.

The Dark Ones weren't afraid of the truth.

He reached St. Joseph's fountain a few minutes later. Made of marble and granite, the fountain featured a two-tiered elliptical pool fed by a small rock waterfall built into the hill behind it. Six bronze sculpted frieze panels were displayed on an arcing back wall celebrating the life and work of Jesus's human father, Joseph the Nazarene. Woland scowled at the image depicting the angel visiting Joseph to explain his wife's miraculous conception.

"What a fool. Cuckolded and proud of it," Woland murmured as he turned his attention to his target, an Ethiopian man dressed in a long black robe and wearing a flat-topped, brimless hat.

"Rector Senai," he said, addressing the man of God with a vulpine smile. "I'm Father McTierney."

"I know what you are, and I know what you are not," Senai said in accented English. "Let us not waste time with pretenses. I could have you arrested right here and right now."

Woland shook his head. "We both know that is a hollow threat . . . otherwise we wouldn't be having this discussion *right here and right now.*"

The rector scowled at him. "Make your demands."

Woland retrieved the mobile phone from his pocket and opened the photo library. He indexed through the photographs to the one he knew would have the biggest impact—an image of Rector Senai's eight-year-old niece with tears streaming down her face and a bloody lip, sitting at the feet of a burly man pointing the muzzle of an AK-47 at the back of her head.

"Take a look at these," he said, passing the phone to Senai.

The rector's eyes went wide and a look of horror spread across his face as his sheltered mind registered the reality of what he was seeing. Using his thumb, he swiped through the photographs depicting all five members of his brother's family in captivity, all after being physically abused to different degrees. Senai's twin brother was barely recognizable, his face badly swollen and bloodied from the beating prior to the photography session. This was a one-shot opportunity with Rector Senai, so Woland had advised his colleague in Ethiopia that they needed to put on a good show.

"Monsters . . . monsters . . . you're all monsters," Senai mumbled as tears began to stream from his eyes. "What do you want? I have no money, no influence, no power in Ethiopia . . ."

Woland had to resist rolling his eyes. "Don't be ridiculous. You and the pope are friends, are you not?"

Senai looked up from the phone for the first time and met Woland's gaze. "No. The answer is no."

"Very well," Woland said and extended his hand to take the phone back. "I will inform them to tell your brother of your choice before he is executed. They will all be made to suffer before they are permitted to die, even the children."

"They are innocents—children who have never done anything to you," Senai growled, clutching the phone in his hand.

"Did it matter when your precious church burned heretics alive in town squares across Europe? Did it matter when young women were accused of witchcraft and hung on Christian gallows? In this war we're waging, innocence has never mattered. Now give me the phone back. You've made your choice."

Senai shook his head. "You can't do this."

"Stop telling me what I can and cannot do. This is *your* doing. This is *your* choice."

Woland yearned for what was coming next . . . Senai's grand betrayal. He wanted it. Needed it. Like a junkie needing a fix, this was what he lived for now. The desecration of principle. The sullying of the soul. The moment when another human being turns away from the light and betrays himself, his creed, and his God. It was so thrilling to watch them fall and so fulfilling to see them loathe themselves in the aftermath of their choice.

It was in the choosing that the corruption took place.

Free will was the key.

Free will was the turnstile between heaven and hell.

The rector glanced around—whether seeking help or checking

to see if they were being watched, Woland couldn't tell. The man's whisper settled the matter an instant later.

"What specifically must I do?"

A surge of pleasure flowed through Woland at the words. "Invite the pope to lunch at the college."

Senai hesitated a beat, and Woland saw the gears of self-deception begin to turn in the man's head. "That's all I must do to save my brother's family . . . invite the pope to lunch?"

"No, the pope must *attend* the lunch, or a breakfast or a tea service—I don't care what it is—so long as he leaves the papal residence and sits down with you at the college to break bread."

"That's all that is required and your people will let my brother and his family go without further harm?"

Woland nodded. "That's all."

"How do I know I can trust you?"

Woland considered the question for a moment, and instead of his reflexive laconic response of "You don't," he gave a different response, one his instincts told him was required to win this man's lasting commitment and prevent a reversal after his departure. "As a show of good faith, I will order your two nephews and your sister-in-law released after you invite His Holiness. Your brother and niece will remain hostage until after the meeting."

"How about the reverse: my brother and my niece are released first?" Senai said, still clutching the phone.

Woland chuckled. "Even the pious value human life subjectively. . . . The answer is no. You're lucky I'm even giving you this."

Senai nodded.

"The phone, Rector," Woland said, his voice going hard.

The rector handed him the mobile phone, which Woland powered off and shoved into his pocket.

"How do I contact you?" Senai asked.

"You don't. Post the event on the college's online calendar and say nothing of this to anyone. Do not mention the pope in the post, simply call it lunch or tea with Rector Senai. It must happen no sooner than five days from now and no more than eight. I will know if you betray me, and the result will be a horror you can't imagine—nor will you have to, as I will provide you more than ample videos of the result. We have eyes and ears inside these forty-foot walls. Don't test me, or instead of getting proof of life in your in-box, you'll get the opposite," Woland said as he turned to leave.

Senai said nothing else, but Woland could feel the man's angry eyes on his back, making him smile. As he strolled down the tree-lined path, birds singing overhead, he began to hum—"Ave Maria"—as loudly and as badly as his baritone vocal cords would permit.

CHAPTER SEVENTEEN

Jed arched his back as he moved forward in the cargo hold of the enormous Air Force plane—the same model he'd logged hundreds of hours in traveling to the world's hot spots during his time in the Teams. Despite the wide, large cabin, traveling in cargo planes of any size was not well suited for the big boys of the special operations community. But at least he could stand up straight. He maneuvered around the up-armored Humvees chained to the metal floor, rolling his neck and stretching his back. As he rounded the last truck and headed toward the lavatory, he gave a nod to Ben, who sat on an orange canvas bench seat, his forearms on his thighs, talking in hushed tones with Pastor Moore.

"You five by, frogman?" Moore asked as he passed by.

"Hooyah," Jed replied.

The pastor gave him a curt nod, then leaned back, adjusted his glasses, and crossed his wiry arms across his chest. "And your team?"

"Excited and nervous to be downrange together, I think. Everyone has a decade or more of experience, but the first time together is always an unknown. Glad I have Eli with me."

"And David Yarnell?" Moore asked, his voice not unmasking anything behind the question.

"He's good, sir," Jed said, casting a glance back to where David sat alone, reading beneath a light. "I'll help get him bonded into the team," he added before either of his bosses came up with that jewel on their own.

He continued forward to the head, thinking about David. Honestly, while he had opened his mind to having a TSL on the team, he still didn't really see what purpose they served downrange. In the modern era, they could provide spiritual insight from back in Tennessee, using the vast technology to stay connected.

But not as well as if they're tightly integrated into the team. They have to be part of the brotherhood.

He shrugged at the voice, maybe his own, and grudgingly admitted it was true. And, he supposed, he should admit to himself that his own bias about working beside David, and the constant reminder of the love and life lost, made Jed the last person to see the matter clearly.

The vacuum system flushed the toilet with a loud rush of air that popped Jed's ears, and then he washed his hands and headed back aft, intent on making himself sit with his childhood friend and check in on him. On his way, he passed Ben and Mike Moore again and eavesdropped just long enough to catch them talking about Woland—the same name he'd caught Ben talking with the Colonel about. They fell silent when they noticed him loitering. Red-faced, he nodded an apology to Ben and went to find David.

"You good?" he asked, settling down on the deck beside David.

David made a show of scanning the belly of the C-17, which was crammed with trucks and Pelican cases full of equipment and weapons, and said, "I definitely feel like a fish out of water."

In that moment, Jed saw David like he remembered him—his skinny best friend with whom he'd spent countless hours making forts in the woods and playing ghost in the graveyard after sundown with Rachel.

We were the three musketeers . . .

"It's a good metaphor," he said at last. "I feel the same way."

David shook his head. "How can you say that? You spent seventeen years doing this. Me . . . I never left Nashville. This is your world—a warrior's world—not mine."

"That's partly true. But the Shepherds are not the same as the SEALs. This is *our* world, bro," Jed said, forcing a smile on his face and trying to see the frightened teammate beside him instead of the childhood friend who was living the dreams he'd once had for himself. "The enemy we're facing is nothing like insurgents with IEDs and AK-47s. The malice we're battling is the same dark force that I—"

Ran away from all those years ago, he thought, finishing the hard part of the sentence in his mind.

David nodded, and Jed wondered if he'd somehow heard the unspoken confession.

"The Dark Ones are terrifying," David said. "But you don't need me telling you that. I know what evil you faced when you saved Sarah Beth . . . both times."

Jed swallowed and changed the subject back to David. "Back at Trinity Loop, are you getting any weapons training at all?"

"They qualified me on a pistol—a Sig Sauer P320—and also on a Virtus. I can handle both safely and put rounds into static targets."

"You always were a deadeye shot with a BB gun," Jed said with a chuckle. "Same principle, different caliber ordnance."

"Do you remember that day we were plinking cans and I shot you when it was your turn to run out and set them back up?" David said with a wry grin.

The long-lost memory suddenly came to Jed and he could practically feel the sting in his butt cheek. "You were such a little punk back then."

They both chuckled at that and spent a moment feeling their way out of the comfortable shared nostalgia back to the awkward present.

"We'll be staging at special forces FOB and you and Mike will be inside the wire the entire time. You'll be completely safe. But if you're interested, when we get back, after I'm done with basic, I can run you through some drills . . . maybe even talk the Colonel into letting me take you through the kill house."

"I've heard rumors about that kill house. Is it really as cool as people say?"

"Badassery of the eleventh order," Jed said, shaking his head. "It's insane."

"Cool," David said, but Jed could tell the man's mind was still on the mission and anxiety about the possibility of facing combat.

If David were any other teammate, Jed would next ask him about family. But he just couldn't do it. He couldn't bring himself to ask about Rachel. Walking away from her after "the event" at the senior bonfire so many years ago was the one regret he refused to let go.

The truth was, he still loved her.

Or loved the person she'd been, anyway. He supposed he didn't really know her now, right?

He started to get up, then decided there was one thing he *could* ask—wanted to ask, in fact. "How is Sarah Beth doing?"

A smile spread across David's face. "She's doing great. She loves St. George's, but it's so hard for Rachel and me having her away. We're allowed to visit whenever we want—after school hours, that is—and that first week, we were there every night." He chuckled. "Finally she told us she wanted us to just come on the weekends and one evening during the week, because she was falling behind on homework."

"I'm glad she likes it, David," he said and meant it. He missed Sarah Beth. The bond they'd formed during her rescue had been understandably powerful—magnified, he supposed, by the trauma and horror they'd survived together—but he'd not seen her since he returned to Nashville after his move from Virginia Beach.

"It's easier for Rachel," David said, glancing away, perhaps sensing that talking about his wife would be uncomfortable. "They have that thing where they can share thoughts. Me, I feel more disconnected from her than ever . . ." He sighed and looked like he might tear up, and Jed fidgeted in his seat. He'd done more than enough here, perhaps. "She asks about you, Jed. All the time. She said she's glad we're working together because she thinks God wants us to be a team."

Jed chuckled. "She's probably right about that one," he said, rising from the canvas bench. "Because here we are, against all conceivable odds. Please tell her I asked how she was doing when you talk to her next." He turned to head aft, then paused. "And tell her I'll visit her at St. George's when we get back, okay? I mean, if it's okay with you, of course."

"Okay, sure."

The strange look on David's face wasn't enthusiasm. Jed definitely picked up something from the man . . .

Jealousy?

Sarah Beth might think she'd rather have a Navy SEAL for a dad, but unlike Jed, I've always been there for her. I'll never run away and leave her.

And there it was.

Jed felt a flash of empathy for the man, but it was quickly eclipsed by irritation bordering on anger. Jed hadn't forced his way into their lives. Quite the opposite, David had begged him to come. Begged him to save Sarah Beth. With Rachel's blessing. They'd come to him, not the other way around.

Instead of reaching down and squeezing the man's shoulder or saying something like "You're a great dad, David," as a voice inside was urging him to do, Jed simply walked away and headed to where his team was camped out by the ramp. He was doing the best he could, and not picking a fight was going to have to be enough.

Eli lay stretched out on a sleeping bag and a poncho liner, Carl on one side of him on his own camp-style setup, and Bex and Hyeon on the other. Behind him, halfway up the ramp, Grayson lay with his legs crossed at the ankles, a beanie cap over his face, his snoring suggesting he found their mode of transportation quite comfortable.

"Where's Johnny?" Jed asked, and Eli jerked a thumb to the starboard side of the aircraft where several hammocks had been strung. Jed guessed that the large lump in the farthest one must be the former SEAL operator, and beyond the hammocks Nisha sat on the canvas bench seats, either watching or reading something on an iPad.

Jed dropped to the ground, sitting cross-legged on his own rolled-out sleeping bag—something he'd not been able to do for years, until Ben had healed the pain and scar tissue where the Taliban 7.26mm round had torn through his hip—and leaned back on his arms, palms behind him on the cool metal floor.

"Can I ask you guys something?" Jed said, looking back and forth between Eli and Carl, the former MARSOC Marine.

"Anything," Eli said with a shrug.

"Who is Nicholas Woland?"

Both operators froze, then exchanged surprised glances.

"He's a Dark One, right?" Jed asked.

"Oh, he's a Dark One all right," Carl said, a troubled look on his face. "And a very dangerous man."

"Nick Woland is a terrorist who just escaped from La Santé Prison in Paris," Eli continued. "We snagged him during a counter-terror operation in France a little over two years ago. He's killed a lot of people. I don't have any idea how he escaped, but there's no doubt he had a lot of help, which means . . ."

"Which means that something really big and horrible is coming our way," Carl said, finishing the thought. "Tell him the rest."

Eli shot Carl a look but then turned back to Jed. "Before working for Victor, Nick Woland was a very talented operator. He was Army SF and I knew him briefly when I was at CAG."

With that comment, Jed learned something new about Eli. That he'd been an operator with the Army's elite JSOC Tier One unit, a sister unit to the Navy's Special Warfare Development Group, said everything about the guy. But the revelation only added to Jed's confusion about why he was leading Joshua Bravo and not Eli.

"Hold on—Woland was a former Delta?" he asked.

"Yep," Eli confirmed. "I didn't really know him very well then. I was going through selection and training and he was deployed. He came back as I joined the Unit, but he separated from the Army shortly after."

"How does a guy like that end up working with the Dark Ones?"

"Look, Jed, there are all kinds of guys in special operations. There are guys there for God and country, guys who fight for the safety and security of their families, and guys just there for the action and adrenaline rush. Now and again, someone makes it into the program who just craves the violence. We screen the bad apples out at each level, but they happen. Y'all have had a handful of guys in Naval Special Warfare who've strayed from the path if I'm not mistaken."

Jed nodded. He'd even fought beside guys that were there for the wrong reasons, guys he considered brothers on the battlefield but wouldn't hang out with back home. And he knew of a few very rare cases of bad actors who made it all the way to Tier One.

"But I'm afraid it's worse than that," Eli said.

Bex and Hyeon leaned in now, fascinated, arms wrapped around their knees as they listened.

Eli combed his fingers through his long hair. "Nick Woland was also a Shepherd."

"What?" Jed said, shocked at the revelation. "How is that even possible?"

Eli let out a heavy exhale. "In Matthew 13, Jesus tells the parable of the sower . . ."

"I remember that one very well," Hyeon chimed in. "Many seeds are scattered, but not all thrive. The seed on the path gets eaten by birds. The seed in the thornbush gets strangled by the worries of the world. And the seed on the rocky ground sprouts quickly but doesn't survive because it is unable to put down deep roots."

"That's right," Eli said, smiling. "People come to and leave God for all kinds of reasons. Some folks are raised in the church but never make the commitment of their own accord. Others start with God but are seduced by the devil's lies and lured away. Some come to God in times of tragedy or weakness, but when the crisis is over, they forget about Him. Others come because they fear death, and the promise of eternal salvation is comforting, and still others come because the message appeals intellectually."

"And for Woland?" Jed asked.

"Power," Eli said with a forlorn look. "This isn't the official word from the Shepherds head shed, ain't something I ever talked with Ben or anyone else about. It's just something I believe, after struggling to understand the betrayal myself. In Delta, Woland had a reputation as a fearless, high-speed operator. But he was arrogant and that hurt him with leadership, which was why he left instead of serving out a twenty-year career. He simply wasn't going to advance, and for him, that was unacceptable. When I got to the Shepherds, Woland was already here. He talked the talk of his faith, but I believe that what he found attractive was the power. He used to quote Luke 10 all the time. I think he had it tattooed on his arm. Luke 10:19, it was. That's where Jesus gives authority to the disciples, where He tells them they will have power over the enemy. I think that's what Woland really wanted. And Ben seemed to be grooming him into leadership. He was already the XO of Gideon when I arrived, but he made no bones about telling anyone who'd listen that he wanted to be in charge of one of the entire teams. Morvant had some big talk with him—none of us ever heard the details—and man, was Woland pissed. Just a couple of months later, he disappeared and shortly after showed up on the battlefield—fighting for the other team."

"He advertised himself as a mercenary for hire, but there was never any doubt he worked for Victor," Carl said, anger and bitterness obvious in the former Marine's voice. "It's the very charter of the Dark Ones—spreading hatred and fear through violence and division. Making people doubt God. Turns out, Woland is a master at it."

"No doubt," Eli said, his gaze far away.

"I just don't see how that's possible," Jed said, shaking his head. "We have Watchers, and Ben reads people so well he can practically see through us. How does a black heart like Woland's go undetected?"

"He didn't exactly go undetected," Eli corrected. "He wasn't a mole. He was a true Shepherd, all in and on the team. But then he defected . . ."

Jed looked up to see David had joined them at some point, his face in awe of the conversation.

"More like Judas," David said.

"A fallen Shepherd," Jed mumbled, still unable to wrap his head around it.

"You mean a dark angel," Carl snorted.

"A dark angel?"

"Sure." Eli changed position, sitting cross-legged, the sense of being at summer camp now complete. "It's like in Revelation 12, right? There was this war in heaven and the archangel Michael is fighting against Satan. And when Satan loses, there's no place for him in heaven anymore and he's cast out and sent down onto the earth. But not by himself—God tells us through John in Revelation that Satan's angels were cast out with him."

Jed looked up at David, who nodded.

"Anyway," Eli sighed. "That's when things changed for all of us in the Shepherds."

Jed nodded as the pieces fell into place. Something had happened that made them develop the accountability system he now knew as the TSLs—the spiritual leaders coming up beside the combat team leaders in a command role. This was it—the defection of Nick Woland.

"Pastor Mike had become the spiritual leader for Shepherds North America already," Eli continued. "So he and Morvant decided to replicate his role at the team level, assigning spiritual leaders to each combat element."

"To monitor the Shepherds for evil in their midst," Jed muttered.

"Not at all," David said, speaking quickly. "That's not what I'm trained to do, Jed. I'm not here to spy on anyone or keep tabs on people's faith. My job is to provide spiritual and biblical insight during the planning and operational phases of every mission and to help the team be a tightly knit group of believers when we're not operating. A wolf in sheep's clothing might be able to fool us individually, but not collectively if we're attuned together."

"Exactly right," a new, familiar voice said, and Jed turned to see Ben Morvant walk up and then stop at the fringe of the group, crossing his powerful arms on his chest. "The Holy Spirit illuminates the path, but God gives us free will to decide. It's up to us to listen and choose whether or not to accept counsel. The TSL is the glue that cements the group together spiritually so you and your team can hear the calling of the Spirit in moments of chaos."

There was a simplicity and a purity to the concept. By not having combat responsibilities, the TSL was unburdened to keep the focus on God in the heat of the moment when the operators would be the most distracted and overwhelmed. And during downtimes, the TSL provided a different set of eyes to look at the spiritual health of the team without the bias of being an operator.

"Speak with you privately for a moment, Jed?" Ben asked. His eyes and his voice were soft, so Jed didn't think he'd done anything wrong.

Not yet, at least.

He scrambled to his feet. "Yeah, of course, boss," he said, then followed the legendary SEAL back toward the front of the aircraft, where they both took seats on a bench.

"Pastor Mike going to join us?" Jed asked, looking around.

"He's checking in on Corbin and her Keeper," Ben said, gesturing with his head to the camper-size truck across from them, which looked like a command and control vehicle a suburban SWAT team might use. "We keep the Watcher team separate from the operational team as much as possible, for a variety of reasons, but not the least of which is the young age of the Watchers. In this case, as Corbin's a teenage girl, it's particularly important. The families of these kids sacrifice a lot and no doubt live with legitimate fear for their children. We owe it to them to do everything in our power to protect them."

Jed nodded understanding. He was glad the Watcher was Corbin, but obviously having a fifteen-year-old girl side by side with a blooded combat team could be complicated for both sides of the equation.

"What's up, boss?" he asked, leaning forward, forearms on his thighs.

"Well, I have something important to talk to you about, Jed. I'm sure you feel strange being at the head of Joshua Bravo, especially with seasoned veterans like Eli, Carl, and Grayson on board, and I wanted to talk to you about that decision."

"Okay," Jed said slowly, not sure where this might be going.

After an awkward pause, Ben leaned back on the bench, folded his arms, and crossed his legs at the knees. "Are you familiar with Romans 12?"

Jed shifted uncomfortably. He really was trying, but he was in constant catch-up mode when it came to Scripture.

Ben held up a hand. "It's okay. It's not a test. In Romans 12, the apostle Paul discusses the various spiritual gifts we, as Christians, receive. The context of the passage, however, is that a community of believers needs diversity, with different people and different gifts to make the community—or the church—a whole and able to do many different things."

"Is this the passage where he compares people with different gifts to different parts of a body?" Jed asked, Ben's description sparking a memory from long ago.

"Yeah, that's the one exactly," Ben said. "The point he's making is that every part of the body is important for the whole body to work properly. Another analogy might be that while it would be cool to be a neurosurgeon, if you have a community with only neurosurgeons, then good luck getting your car fixed or running your grocery store or having a fire department come in an emergency. Paul wanted believers to know how important embracing individual gifts was—not just their own but those of others. It came at a time when there was lots of jealousy in the early church, and he wanted everyone to understand that diversity of gifting is not God having favorites but needing all the jobs to be done—each important to the whole community."

"Okay," Jed said. "So as a leader, I think I hear you telling me you want me to flesh out the gifts and talents of my teammates so that we, as a team, can work most effectively."

Ben smiled a big, genuine smile and then patted Jed on the shoulder. "That's a lesson I'm sure you learned long ago. No, I'm talking about you here—and specifically, the spiritual gifts you seem to have."

Jed raised his eyebrows, even more uncomfortable now. He hated how it made him feel different—like a freak, he might have said in high school.

"Jed, do you ever feel like you know what people are thinking?"

Jed let out a long, sighing breath. "Sometimes. I've always sort of been able to tell what people are feeling, like an empathic kind of thing, and at times felt like I knew what they thought. But lately . . . well, lately I seem to actually hear the thoughts—in my head, sort of, but like it's out loud."

"Do you do that when you want to?"

"Not really. It just sort of happens, you know?"

"Oh, I do indeed." Ben chuckled. "What else?"

"What do you mean?"

"What other things—supernatural things—are you experiencing?"

Jed clenched his jaw. He supposed if there was anyone he could share this with, it would be Ben. "Sometimes, I just . . . I don't know, sort of just know things."

"Can you give me an example?"

"At Team Ten, I was known as the ambush detector. I would get these feelings, or sometimes I would even . . ."

He hesitated but held Ben's eyes.

"Hear a voice?" Ben asked.

"Yeah, sort of. I always assumed it was my own inner voice. I chalked it up to warrior intuition. But when the voice said *move*, I learned to move or people were going to get hurt."

Jed shared a story about his first deployment to Iraq. On one of their early missions, they were hitting a target where a notorious bomb maker was supposed to be. The team was split into two, and on the approach, Jed just *knew* that the building was rigged to explode.

A new thought occurred to him.

"You know, later, on that same op, we had the bomb maker in the back room and were doing an intelligence collection sweep before pulling him off the X. And he spoke to me—in my mind. I always thought I imagined it, but I remember thinking that his eyes were glowing. Just like the Dark Ones we fought in Nashville. I never saw that again until I got tangled up with all of this stuff with Sarah Beth and you guys."

Ben seemed more than intrigued; he seemed delighted. "I want to talk a moment about the nightmare you had—the vision from the attack in Tal Afar."

"Okay," Jed said but felt himself start to relax a little.

"From what you described, it seemed like you were seeing the events through the eyes of someone present at the attack."

"A young boy," Jed said, his voice tight. "I believe he was killed."

"Okay," Ben said softly. "The timing of your nightmare suggests that you were seeing this in real time—occurring pretty much exactly when the attack occurred."

"So what does that mean?"

"It means that you were having a seer vision, Jed. Not a prophecy of something that would happen or images from something in the past, but seeing it, in real time, through someone else's eyes. This is one of the most important gifts that our Watchers use to provide ISR for us."

"But you guys said this gift occurs in adolescence and always disappears by late teens or early twenties, right? So why would I have it now?"

"Did you ever have it when you were a kid?"

"I don't think so," Jed said finally. "I had a traumatic experience in high school, but that was different."

"Okay," Ben said, shooting him a comforting smile. "So to answer your question, yes, the seer gift generally comes in adolescence and almost always fades by age twenty. But there are exceptions."

"Are there other operators in the unit with this . . . gift?" Jed asked quietly, looking to the rear of the plane.

"Only one that I know of."

Jed looked up from where he leaned over now, rubbing his hands together, forearms on his thighs. He raised his eyebrows expectantly.

"It's me, Jed," Ben said. "I have that gift as well. Like you, I still have it, and like you, it came to me later in life—on that mission in Africa for which I became tragically infamous in the SEAL Teams."

Jed felt pieces slip into place. "Can I ask you something?"

"Anything."

"In the kill house—those feelings and thoughts. The dysthymia and the sense of being taunted. That was you, right? Because it felt so much like Victor, I . . . I just need to know if it was you."

"Yes, that was me," Ben said. "It's part of our training to expose every Shepherd to the psychic forces you may encounter in combat. The Dark Ones, the powerful ones like Victor, especially, will try and use these tricks against you in the heat of battle."

"It's not the only time," Jed said, memories flooding over him of the night in the Tennessee mountains, his own gun under his chin and a voice wooing him to pull the trigger.

"That was Victor," Ben said. "The night at the compound in the mountains—Victor was in your head."

"How did you know about . . . ?" Jed clenched his jaw and

shook his head. "Never mind." He folded his arms now, defensively, across his chest.

"Jed," Ben said softly, "I went through all the things you've described and more. But unlike you, I didn't have anyone to guide me through it and it took me forever to figure out the faith element. My grandmother had tried, when I was younger, to explain it to me, but I didn't get it, and by the time it mattered, she had passed away." Jed watched the Shepherds leader as his mind seemed to travel to some faraway past. Then he shook his head gently and continued, "Anyway, the gifts you're describing—and perhaps others you haven't mentioned or experienced yet—these are gifts of the Spirit."

"How many people have more than one gift like this?" Jed asked.

"We are the only ones I know of in the North American Shepherds organization," Ben said. "And also unique to us, as far as I know anyway, is the gift of reading minds and projecting thoughts at such an older age. Additionally, I have some other gifts . . ."

"Like healing," Jed said, rubbing the hip Ben had laid his hands on.

"Yes," Ben said. "I also have the ability to penetrate the minds of the Dark Ones. That made me pretty unique here at the Shepherds until you showed up."

Jed sat up now, leaned back, and let out a long whistling breath.

"I'm telling you this, Jed, for a few reasons. First of all, if your journey is like mine, you may have other nascent abilities that have yet to present themselves. Knowing that may make you better prepared both to handle the emergence of a new skill and exploit it tactically. Second, it might help you accept and understand why you are leading Joshua Bravo. You are a skilled operator, but so are the veterans on your team. The difference is you have gifts they don't, and when it comes to facing Dark Ones like Victor, that is both an advantage and a burden that only the team leader should have to bear."

"Sure," Jed said, unconvinced. "But I don't have any control over my abilities. The vision came while I was asleep. Hearing people's thoughts seems to happen mostly at inopportune times. It's annoying and awkward and embarrassing. And as far as penetrating Victor's mind, no way I could win that mental dogfight. Last time I barely escaped with my head intact . . . literally."

"Which brings me to my third point." Ben placed a hand on Jed's shoulder. "I'm here for you, bro, as a mentor but also as your friend. I went through this alone, but you don't have to. You will, in time, gain control. I promise. Pray about it. Study the Word. But you also gotta let me know what's going on, okay? I can't help you unless you confide in me, and that includes letting me know if you're struggling. God called us to this community for a reason. We need each other for counsel and accountability, but also for fellowship and support."

"Okay," Jed said and then met Ben's eyes. "But I don't have to share any of this with the team right now, do I?"

"Not until you're ready. But embrace your gifts, Jed. Don't fight them. It's why you're here. It's why David reached out to you that fateful day when Sarah Beth was taken. I firmly believe that," Ben said and stood to leave.

The Shepherd commander's closing comment hit Jed like a bucket of water to the face. He'd not considered that possibility. And now David was his TSL. How had he not seen it?"

"That's right," Ben said, reading his thoughts. "Chew on that for a while and then try to get some shut-eye. We're landing in a couple hours, and we'll be busy as soon as we're on the ground."

"Roger that," Jed said, feeling more like someone who'd just been told he had cancer than someone given amazing spiritual gifts. "I'll try."

Ben gave him a parting nod.

Jed exhaled and slow-walked back to his sleeping bag, feeling more unsure than ever about the burden he was being asked to carry.

CHAPTER EIGHTEEN

Jed felt a powerful wave of nostalgia as he watched the ten CAG operators dismount from three Toyota Hilux pickups, one with a 50mm technical mounted in the rear bed. The bearded men were clad in slicks—unmarked cammies, free even of the identifying camouflage patterns—but their beards, kits, and helmets gave them away. They were American operators from the Army's elite Delta Force, Tier One warriors who were the very best of the best. The SEAL in Jed knew instinctively that these were *not* the men from his vision, but he scanned their faces anyway. Finding none that matched the murdering masqueraders at the mosque, he relaxed.

The tallest man of the group stepped to the front and extended his gloved hand. "Denny," the operator said, smiling broadly. "I'm point man for this band of merry men."

"Jed," he replied, releasing the man's powerful grip. "Did you guys have a successful night?"

"Yeah, well, you know," Denny said with a chuckle, turning toward a tan building similar to a double-wide trailer. "The definition of success is dynamic in this theater, bro."

"Amen to that," Jed said, waving his Shepherds to follow. His tours in Iraq had never taken him this far north, but he'd heard of the intense action faced by troops at the FOB formed at the southern edge of a former Iraqi air base, surrounded by some of the most inhospitable terrain in Iraq. Miles of flat open desert in one direction, rising hills in another, and to the north the densely populated city of Tal Afar made the base both strategically important and dangerously vulnerable to attack. The base had at one time been a hub of CIA and special operations activity at the height of Operation Iraqi Freedom, then had been abandoned to become a center of operations for ISIS, before being routed by coalition and Iraqi forces and taken over again. Now it was an Iraqi training base and, more secretly, a staging area for Tier One special operations in the region.

"Y'all hungry?" Denny asked, clipping his helmet to a carabiner on the left side of his kit and then tearing away the Velcro cummerbund as he kicked through the wooden door into what Jed had correctly assumed to be a team room for the unit. The

Green Beret set his rifle and kit inside an oversize cubby along the wall, his men following suit, and then the man grabbed a bottled water from a brick inside a lift-top refrigerator, holding it out to Jed with his eyebrows raised. Jed nodded and the man tossed the bottle to him, and then the rest of both teams, before cracking the top of his own.

"We could eat," Jed said with a smile, though he didn't feel particularly hungry. Sharing a meal was a great way for teams to bond, he knew.

"They love us here these days," another operator said, clapping Jed on the back as he passed before running a hand through the thick hair plastered to his head from hours inside a tactical helmet.

"Yeah, they used to," said another grimly.

Jed felt Denny's eyes on him.

"I'm assuming that's why y'all are here, right?" the operator said pointedly. "Because we were in theater operating when the mosque massacre happened? Here's the deal—we were with our Iraqi partners hitting a little compound thirty-five miles northwest of here. But we can't say that, because we were operating across the border in Syria without permission."

I'm not letting you guys hang my men out to dry. Not a chance.

The Green Beret's inner monologue echoed in Jed's head, and he had to refrain from responding to the man's thoughts directly. Then, without warning, more voices—full of anger and fear— filled his head from the other SF operators. He winced, not sure how to turn it off.

"You all right, bro?" Denny asked.

Jed nodded, trying to shut the voices out like squeezing his eyelids tight against a bright light. "Fine, just have a headache coming on. . . . Anyway, we're not investigators looking for somebody to hang. We're operators just like you. This is not about optics; it's about truth. Our task force is here to identify and prosecute the people responsible for the attack." He glanced over at Ben, who'd been letting Jed take the lead until now and whose expression suggested Jed was doing fine. "We're assuming, based on the very limited intelligence we have, that this was a false flag operation designed to stir up both religious and sectarian violence."

"Yeah," Denny said, his voice sounding relieved but still a bit unsure, "that's what we thought, too." He took a long pull on his water bottle as his men spread out behind him, kits now secure and arms on their chests. "But this wasn't a bunch of hajis—I mean, locals," he corrected, with a self-conscious glance at Nisha. "I'm sure you saw the video. Those boys looked like American operators."

"Agreed," Jed said, the voices suddenly going quiet in his head. He was unsure whether it was because of something he did or because the Green Berets' anxiety was dialing down. "Which makes it all the more important that we find and prosecute them quickly and effectively. If they're trying to stir things up, we need to end them before they strike again. The appearance of coalition involvement puts your mission here at risk and makes your work far more dangerous."

If my team finds these murdering posers, they're going to regret the day they were born.

"If we work together, we can make that happen," Jed said.

"Can make what happen?" Denny asked, his eyes narrowing.

Ben gave Jed's arm a squeeze. Jed turned and met his mentor's disapproving gaze.

"Sorry," Jed said and faked a cough. "If we work together, we can clear up this mess and you guys can get back to doing the work you were sent here to do."

"I like how that sounds," said an operator standing just behind Denny. "Fortunately, our partners here don't think we had anything to do with it. I'm Edwin, by the way."

"Good to meet you, bro," Jed said, shaking the man's hand. "I'm Jed." He then gave a round of first-name introductions to the rest of Joshua Bravo.

"Eddy here is our weapons sergeant," Denny said.

"Great to meet you guys," Eddy said, "and if you can help us find and end whoever did this, then you're more than welcome. But the thing is, what we do better than anyone in the world is engage and partner with locals," the man continued. "It's what sets us apart from SEALs like you," he said, guessing correctly and grinning. "We have a very robust OGA contingent working with us here, and they have no intel on this hit. And those boys have a deep and dark network of local assets they manage who kind of love us now that we helped boot ISIS out of town. We eat like kings whenever we meet with locals, and the kids flock around us like they used to back in the day. We just haven't found much in the way of non-friendlies in Tal Afar. Most of the terrorists left with ISIS, because the locals rose up, partnered with us, and fingered the bad guys."

"That's why we're making hits to the west," another Green Beret chimed in.

"And the east," added another operator, a younger guy with a thin, patchy beard. "And why we were far from here when the massacre happened. Fortunately, we had a bunch of Iraqi SF with us who did a great job of letting the locals know it wasn't us."

"But there is still a ton of fear and suspicion . . ."

"And anger," a Green Beret near the couch added, spitter in hand.

"Patches is right," Denny said, nodding to his young soldier. "Mosul is still another whole thing. We're guessing that a false flag like you suggest could have originated in Mosul, but again, that video is pretty damning."

"Those guys looked and talked like Americans," Patches said, shaking his head. "I don't get it."

"And that's not even the most confusing element of the footage," Nisha said.

"Let's sit for a minute, since we're laying it all out," Denny suggested.

They moved en masse over to a long wooden conference table covered with maps and used water bottles half-filled with tobacco juice. A nearby living area off to the side reminded Jed of every FOB he'd deployed to, replete with beat-up couches, a pristine big-screen TV, multiple gaming systems, and a watercooler. The plywood walls were emblazoned with a mix of posters, graffiti, and captured enemy memorabilia tacked up like trophies, including two different black, shot-up ISIS flags.

"Sorry to cut you off there, ma'am," Denny said, looking expectantly at Nisha. "I didn't catch your name."

"I'm Nisha," she said as they all took seats, some of Denny's operators remaining standing to make room for Jed's team at the table. "And you can think of me as the N2 for my team," she said, identifying herself as the intelligence officer.

That seemed about right to Jed.

"Pleasure to meet you, Nisha," Denny said. "What were you getting at a minute ago?"

"Well," she said, appearing to choose her words carefully, "there are a lot of competing interests in this part of Iraq these days. Not many of them seem interested in allowing the rampant, third-world terrorism that ISIS brought to continue, but who leads Iraq and eastern Syria out of that climate matters both politically and financially."

"Are you suggesting that Russia might be involved?" Denny said, fascinated.

"Not specifically, but they would certainly be on the list. There are other players, including factions within Turkey as an example, with significant interest in this dusty little corner of Iraq. The point I'm making is that finding Western-looking mercenaries to play the part of American operators just isn't that hard any-more. Whether the strings in the puppet play are pulled by ISIS, al Qaeda, Russia, a radical Turkish faction, or someone else, the first step is to find the men who executed the operation. If we do that, then we can follow the strings to their puppet master."

Jed was impressed and gave Ben a subtle nod. Nisha had just done something Jed had failed to consider—she'd provided Denny and his crew with a plausible counternarrative to explain the mas-sacre without having to read them into Shepherds territory. They would need that, because in their world, an explanation that Dark Ones with glowing eyes were behind the attack simply wasn't going to cut it. Jed understood this better than anyone.

"It's a good plan, but a tough place to start," Denny said, exchanging glances with the operator called Eddy, who seemed like his number two. "'Cause we got nothing on the shooters."

"That's right," Eddy said. "Our spooky friends used image cap-ture from that video and ran multiple images through the DoD facial recognition database. They got zilch. No matches, which in my mind supports Nisha's theory."

"Interesting," Nisha said, glancing at Jed with an inscrutable look in her eyes.

"That's right—no matches to active duty or former military operators in theater, including contractors," Denny said. "The contractor bit surprised me. I thought for sure them boys were hired guns."

That actually *did* surprise Jed. Like Denny, he'd assumed that the killers from the massacre really were American, but just guys who'd landed in the camp of the Dark Ones. A collection of those bad apples Eli had talked about. But if they'd run the images through the DoD database, then his assumption that the killers were former American military seemed less likely now.

"I'd love to meet with the OGA shop and exchange information," Nisha said. "We also have our own—" she paused and looked at Jed, who nodded—"team, back at the jet, who can help us vet data."

"Why is it that you spooky task force dudes—and ladies," Eddy corrected quickly with a nod to Nisha and Bex, "always have supersecret squirrel stuff back on the jet?"

This comment garnered a laugh from everyone, including Nisha, and it did the much-needed job of breaking the tension. Moreover, the well-timed smack talk did wonders breaking through the us-versus-them mentality. He liked Eddy, he decided.

"Truth is, we're all on the same team," Denny said, taking the reins. "And we can use all the help we can get. We need to wrap this up so we can get back to work. Local engagement is impossible with this dark cloud hanging over our heads."

"I can imagine," Eli said sympathetically.

"You look familiar," Denny said, cocking his head and looking carefully at the former Green Beret. "You were at the Unit for a time, right?"

The corner of Eli's mouth ticked up. "Yeah, I spent a few years at CAG. Got scooped up by this task force a few years ago, but you look familiar as well."

"I think I was in selection when you were still operating. Five or six years ago or so?"

"Closer to seven, maybe?"

"Yeah, that's about right. Good to see you. How's the other side?"

Eli laughed. "Same as CAG mostly. A few more resources, a little spookier . . ."

"Maybe we could have a sidebar sometime," Eddy said. "I'm coming up on twenty and thinking about the next chapter."

"Sure," Eli said.

"I'm starving," Denny said, getting to his feet and ending the conversation. "Let's head to the main side chow hall and introduce Nisha to our OGA partners, either before or after, whatever she wants."

"Before is fine," Nisha said. "I'm not hungry and I'm ready to get to work on this."

"Roger that," Denny said.

The Green Berets grabbed their pistols and rifles as they headed out the door.

Jed was glad they'd been permitted to carry their own weapons on the compound as well. Green-on-blue attacks happened in Iraq, no matter how much the locals claimed to love you. And now that he'd seen a whole different side of the good-versus-evil battle raging just beneath the surface, anything was possible.

CHAPTER NINETEEN

TWENTY & GRAND APARTMENTS

2000 GRAND AVENUE, WEST END

NASHVILLE, TENNESSEE

1635 HOURS LOCAL

Maria's medical board was scheduled in two days and the waiting was driving her crazy. She was eager to get back to police work.

Lately, she'd had difficulty deciding which job was her real job—which life her real life. Was she Detective Perez who moonlighted on the side for the Dark Ones, or was it the other way around? Police detective was her official cover, but she'd earned the title on her own. Yes, she exploited her position in her quest to do Victor's bidding, but the truth was, she loved being a detective. Solving puzzles, of one sort or another, was an escape for her and had been since before her grandmother passed.

Her mobile phone rang and she glanced at the screen, hoping to see Jedidiah Johnson's number. The incoming call wasn't Johnson, but it was a call she'd been waiting for.

She tapped the green button on the screen, then put the phone to her ear. "Hello?"

"Hello . . . Is this Detective Perez?" a woman's voice said.

"Yes, it is. How can I help you?" she asked, feigning that she didn't recognize who was calling.

"Hi, Detective. It's Rachel. Rachel Yarnell."

"Omigosh, Rachel!" she exclaimed, using the more intimate first-name approach on purpose. "Rachel, it's so nice to hear your voice. And please call me Maria."

"Okay, Maria," Rachel said, and Maria could practically hear the woman smiling.

This is going to be easier than I thought.

"So how are you? How is everyone doing?"

"Well, we're good," Rachel replied, but her tone said otherwise. Something with her husband, David, maybe? Maria would love to have had gifts like Victor's—the ability to reach into people's minds. Nonetheless, her detective's intuition was generally more than enough. "I got your message calling to check on Sarah Beth."

"Yes," she said, "I haven't been able to stop thinking about that night. I've been worried about her and really wanted to know how she's doing. I hope I didn't overstep by calling you."

"Not at all. I was flattered that you even thought to check on her. We owe you so much."

Maria rolled her neck, then carefully put just the right mixture of guilt and remorse into her voice. "You're too kind. I just wish that were true. I can't help but think that if I'd been better at my job . . ." She let the words drift off and counted slowly to three—the perfect amount of time for an awkward pause, but not enough for Rachel to think of something to fill it. "Anyway, I feel just awful for everything you've been through. How is Sarah Beth coping?"

"Very well. We've enrolled her in St. George's Academy, and I think boarding school is the best thing that ever could have happened to her. She's never alone. She's around kids her own age 24-7, with structured activities and, you know, campus security," Rachel said, her voice bright now. "We miss her terribly, but those are things she simply wouldn't have had otherwise. I think it's important that she's not alone . . . you know, after what she's been through."

"Yes, yes, definitely," Maria said, narrowing her eyes at the thought of the girl surrounded by so many Watchers.

"And we see her every weekend and drop by occasionally during the week. This is a tough week, because David is—" Rachel stopped midsentence.

"David is what?" Maria asked, curiosity piqued. "Please tell me he's okay?"

"Oh yes, David's fine. . . . He's just out of town this week for work."

"Well, that's a relief," Maria said, wondering where Rachel's divinity student husband could have possibly gone for *work*. She forced herself to hold her tongue, as pressing for details would be a mistake.

"It just makes it even harder to have Sarah Beth gone when I'm all alone."

"I hear you. I'm on convalescent leave and the boredom—and

loneliness—is killing me. I'm not married and not seeing anyone. At the rate I'm going, I'm not sure if I'll ever get to be a mom," she said and put as much regret into her voice as she could possibly fake. She waited a beat, until the thought might have occurred to Rachel as well, and said, "Hey, I have a great idea! Would you like to get together and have coffee or something? I mean, I certainly don't want to intrude or anything. I just thought . . ."

"I would love to grab a coffee," Rachel said. "How about tomorrow? Ten or maybe eleven o'clock?"

"Perfect, Rachel. Thank you so much."

"Not at all," Rachel said, her voice warm and excited. "You saved my family—and almost died doing it. I would love to get to know you better."

"If you'd like, I can just swing by your house and pick you up," Maria offered, smiling at how easy it all was. "I live in the West End just minutes away from you, and don't worry—I won't show up in a squad car."

"Well," Rachel said, and Maria sensed something awkward and uncomfortable in her voice. "To be honest, we moved recently. With everything that happened in that house . . . I'm sure you get it."

"Oh, for sure," Maria said but bit the inside of her cheek. *How did we not know that?*

"We're a bit out of the way now. It would be better for me to meet in town. I have to be over that way anyway. You pick the place, and I'll meet you there."

A malign grin spread over Maria's face.

"We could meet at the Vandy bookstore right down the street. Obviously you know how to get there." She pictured Rachel's eyes closing at the emotional images that would have brought to her—images of her little girl snatched from her outside the bookstore—then added quickly, "Omigosh, that was terribly insensitive of me. I wasn't thinking, Rachel . . ."

Rachel laughed good-naturedly. "It's okay, really," she said. "And to be honest, given everything that happened *after* the bookstore, I don't really even have a negative association. Let's meet there, in fact. It'll be cathartic."

"You sure?"

"Yeah."

"Well, great," Maria said, her smile broadening.

Victor will be pleased with my progress after all. Not only will I have a backdoor connection to Jed, but I will have an avenue by which to keep tabs on Sarah Beth—for both intel and opportunity.

"So I guess I'll see you tomorrow. I can catch you up more on Sarah Beth then," Rachel was saying, proving her instincts correct.

"Great," Maria said and meant it more than Rachel could possibly know. "See you then."

"I really look forward to getting to know you better, Maria."

"Me, too," she replied, then disconnected the call and smiled. *You have no idea how much.*

CHAPTER TWENTY

"I'm just trying to understand," Denny said, his frustration bleeding through. "We really appreciate everything you've done so far. And I get that y'all have your own, super spooky secret squirrel stuff going on. But trying to run a joint op with dual comms, while keeping your intel eyes separated from my command element here in the TOC, makes no sense. Just bring your people in here, everyone can work together, and we can go kill us some bad guys."

Jed nodded and sighed. He got it. As a SEAL, he'd spent

countless hours of frustration dealing with "task force" guys—
teams of operators from some spooky, unnamed organization with
operational control over a mission that his team would have to
risk everything for. Nothing pissed off an operator more than not
being fully read into an action they might well die for. But Jed
also now saw the other side of that coin. There were secrets that
needed to be kept for a variety of reasons. And the secrets of the
Shepherds "task force" were beyond the norm.

"Denny, brother, I completely understand. I do. This time last
year, I was a white-side SEAL downrange and dealing with the
same kind of 'other government agency' BS as this. But listen—
brother to brother—I need you to trust me on this, man. There is
a legitimate reason why it needs to be this way, I promise."

Jed could only imagine the reaction in the JSOC TOC if they
marched in fifteen-year-old Corbin and her Keeper, the latter of
whom looked far more like a schoolteacher than a counterterrorism
analyst. And that was before trying to explain how Corbin was
passing on intelligence she was collecting in real time with her
mind, not available to satellites or drones overhead. And to top it
all off, there was no way that a teenage girl should be exposed to
the JSOC TOC environment. That Corbin was a field asset at all
still blew his mind. To whatever extent possible, she needed to be
shielded from personal risk and all unnecessary interactions.

"This is pretty irregular protocol, even for a bunch of spooks,
Jed—or whatever your real name is," Denny said.

The comment made Jed grin inside.

"For what it's worth, my name really is Jed, and I really was
a SEAL at Team Ten. And I really do know how much you hate
the position we're putting you in. But I promise you it's necessary.

The technology—" he grimaced slightly at the word, as Corbin was not a piece of tech—"that we have access to in this task force is highly classified. If this camp is not the right target, then we'll *know* it with a certainty like . . ."

". . . the Word of God," Eli said with a smile.

Jed smiled back.

"Exactly. The Word of God." He turned to Denny. "And to be honest, don't most of the spooky guys coming through make these silly changes to your protocol and then sit here and sip coffee while you guys are out in the suck?"

"Yeah," the operator said and seemed to relax a touch. "You got that right."

"Well, we're going to be out in the suck with you, brother. We're doing it the way we have to, but we're side by side." He studied the man's face. "Hooyah?"

Denny smiled now and reached out for the hand Jed extended.

"Hooah, bro," he said, mirroring back the Army version of the SEAL exclamation, just as the door hissed open and Ben and Nisha came in, followed by a dour-looking man dressed in khaki cargo pants, a 5.11 Tactical fast-drying shirt, and hiking boots—clearly a representative from the CIA unit supporting the JSOC team. The newcomer was clenching his jaw and didn't look happy.

"We've got an update," Ben said with a knowing glance at Jed as he waved everyone over to the conference table. Nisha took a seat at the head of the table, where she plugged a laptop into a port coming up from a rough-cut hole in the table. She tapped on her computer and a monitor on the far wall mirrored the image on her screen for all to see.

"This is the target site, occupied by—" Nisha said but was interrupted before she could even get started.

"Hold on. I thought this group was ruled out by OGA and our intel shop. Wanna tell me what changed?" Denny said, crossing his arms over his expansive chest, covering up the Redneck Riviera whiskey logo on the T-shirt he was wearing. Behind Nisha, the team's affiliated CIA case officer just shook his head and looked at his feet.

"As Jed alluded to before, we possess some very advanced SIGINT capabilities," Nisha said, which was technically not a lie. Of course, she couldn't dare explain that the "signals" they were intercepting were conversations from inside the heads of the bad guys.

Jed watched Eddy and Patches exchange skeptical looks while Denny came back at her.

"So do we. We've got a direct line to real-time feeds from NSA. We have guys who place listening devices disguised as rocks in the backs of pickup trucks. We have laser mics that can pick up vibrations off a glass of water on a table to listen in on conversations. But you're saying you have something more advanced than that?"

"Yes," Nisha said simply and confidently. "We're using tech not yet available to NSA."

"And you won't tell us how, show us the tech, or give us access to the raw data. Is that correct?"

"That's correct," Ben said, asserting himself for the first time. "This is a hard line, gentlemen. End of discussion."

On that cue, Jed said, "Remember we're gonna be out there on the tip of this spear with you—risking our necks on our intel."

Denny pursed his lips and let out a long sigh before saying,

"That's not lost on me, my friend, but I'm still responsible for my men and their safety, and you're asking a lot."

Jed felt the room changing, and then he heard another voice—Eddy, he was pretty sure—inside his head.

And when it all goes bad, you guys will disappear and leave us holding the bag. No way I'm shooting potentially innocent American contractors on your muddy authority.

"Gentlemen, we take this operation, your safety, and the integrity of this mission more seriously than you can imagine. None of us wants to be wrong, especially when it could involve shooting what might be innocent American contractors," Jed said, switching to his business voice as he held Eddy's eyes. The operator's eyebrows arched in surprise, and Eddy shifted uncomfortably in his chair. "The group who did this tried very hard to make it appear that your unit was responsible. It was calculated, intentional, and by design. Their goal is to escalate regional tensions and animosity and draw our forces deeper into a hopeless conflict. We can stop it by not just finding and ending these guys, but by revealing to the world that it was *not* American special forces behind the attack."

"Then tell us who it is," Denny said.

Jed leaned over the table, staring deep into Denny's eyes. "If you feel the stakes are too high for your team to participate, then no hard feelings. We'll conduct this operation on our own and provide cover for you. As far as our command authority is concerned, we'll say we made the unilateral decision to cut you out of the operation."

Denny shot Jed an *oh, please* look and said, "On your own with, what, like six of you?"

"Eight," Nisha corrected and crossed her arms.

"Eight," Denny said, nodding and then looking over at Eddy, who nodded back at him. "Okay, well, that ain't enough. No way we're letting you guys go in there without backup . . . especially handicapped as you are with a couple of Navy SEALs on your stick."

Eli laughed and gave Denny a fist bump. "Took ya long enough."

These guys are in, Jed decided as soon as he saw the crooked grin on the Green Beret's face.

"We're briefing this a little backward, I guess, but let me share with you what new signals intelligence we have, and then I'll turn it over to Bill here," Nisha said and nodded at the unit's CIA intelligence partner.

Bill waved a hand for her to continue.

"Over the last several hours, we were able to intercept several communications between a team of contractors working in Tal Afar and a non-state actor. The contractors work for Dark Horizon—a security company working under a State Department contract, which Bill will give you more details on later. The order to attack the mosque was given from a command authority we have determined is *not* inside or in any way related to State."

That part's not entirely true. I need to get with Jed about that later, Nisha thought.

Jed put a finger to his temple and massaged. He was beginning to hate the unwanted and sometimes-unwelcome intrusion of other people's thoughts into his head, even when it was useful.

"Hold on," Denny said, stopping her. "What are you saying? That these dudes are, like, double agents? On Monday they work for State as legit contractors, and on Tuesday they put on their mercenary hats and turn into a murder squad for hire? I've never heard of anything like this before."

Ben answered for her. "We have strong evidence that the non-state actor pulling the strings is one we've been tracking and targeting for a very, very long time . . ."

Like hundreds and hundreds of years . . .

Jed blinked away Eli's thought.

"We can't, unfortunately, disclose more to you about this group at the present time, but disrupting their activities is the primary charter of our task force," Ben continued. "What I can say is that they are very skilled at covering their tracks, pay very well, and also use extortion and blackmail to motivate their *hires.*"

Denny scowled at the horribly vague explanation, and behind Nisha, the OGA man named Bill rolled his eyes.

"Continue, Nisha," Ben said.

"Unfortunately, there's more. Time-sensitive intelligence indicates that this merc team has been tasked with a second attack."

"What?" Eddy said, sitting up in his chair. "Where and when? We gotta hit 'em before they do something else that looks like Americans are murdering innocent people over here."

"We agree, which is why we need to put something together immediately," Ben said.

"We believe, with a high degree of certainty, that there will be an attack on a second mosque during morning prayers tomorrow," Nisha said.

Denny looked at his watch. "That's in less than seven hours."

"Correct," Nisha confirmed. "The attack is scheduled for just ahead of the salat al Fajr at the al-Imam Khayat Mosque to the east of town. We have every reason to believe it will go down just like the first one."

"Blame American SF and paint crosses on the walls," Eddy said.

"Precisely," Nisha agreed. "This is designed to stoke fear, mistrust, and then violence against both coalition troops and Christians."

"To what end?" Denny asked.

"Simple," Ben said, interrupting whatever Nisha was about to say. "To destabilize the region."

"Which is why you think it could be the Russians?" Denny asked, his voice one part awe and two parts disbelief.

"I didn't say this was the Russians," Nisha said quickly. "I said there were a variety of state and non-state actors with a vested interest in who controls Iraq and Syria. But stopping this attack and taking some of the compromised shooters off the X could help answer that question."

Jed hated the tightrope they were forced to walk here, but Nisha was doing about as well as anyone could.

"Translation—don't hose everyone down," Eddy said with a nod. "Gotta have a few live ones to disappear down some dark hole to squeeze intel out of."

"Something like that," Jed said.

"We should hit them at their compound right now. I think that's obvious. It will be easier and safer, especially for the surrounding communities," Denny said, a new urgency in his voice.

"I wish it was that simple," Nisha said. "Unfortunately, we have reason to believe that two advance teams are already in place, staged for the hit near the mosque. If we hit the compound now, those teams will be in the wind."

"Then we split up and hit the compound and the advance teams simultaneously," Denny said.

"That's one option for sure," Nisha agreed. "But let me turn it over to Bill to brief you on the most up-to-date satellite imagery and head counts in the compound and around the mosque. Then we'll brainstorm the best way to make the hit. Agreed?"

"Cool," Denny said, and Jed watched as all of the operators—both the Green Berets and his Shepherds—leaned in attentively.

He winked at Nisha as she turned over the laptop to Bill, and she smiled back.

Then he leaned in with his Army brothers as the battle plan began to take shape.

CHAPTER
TWENTY-ONE

Jed stopped at the corner and held up a closed fist, *feeling* the operators spreading out behind him and scanning their individual sectors. His joint five-person squad—call sign Sword—included Grayson and Bex, along with Eddy and Patches from Delta. Eli led the other stick—call sign Spear—with Johnny, Hyeon, and two Green Berets. Together, they were assigned to intercept the disguised Dark Horizon assaulters before they could attack a second local mosque.

The remainder of the blended team, call sign Shield, had Denny at the helm with three Delta shooters and Carl and Nisha representing the Shepherds. The plan was for Shield to hit the Dark Horizon compound to the north, kicking off the op, while operating on a separate channel to deconflict comms during simultaneous engagements. Further complicating matters was the need for the Shepherds to manage comms from their own TOC—aka the Watcher trailer inside the Air Force C-17 parked at the Tal Afar air base. Ben and Corbin would be providing "gifted guidance" that was certain to raise some eyebrows by the end of this thing.

It is what it is, Jed thought. *Completing the mission and keeping my team alive is the priority. I'll deal with how to spin it later.*

"Variable, this is One—Sword is Studebaker," Jed whispered into the boom mic beside the corner of his mouth, reporting they'd made the first checkpoint. Johnny had floated the idea of using Old Testament battle sites for checkpoints, but Jed decided it was too overt of a hint to use with their Green Beret partners. So vintage autos it was.

"Copy, Sword is Studebaker," Ben came back.

"One, Two—Spear is Hudson," Eli reported a minute later from his own checkpoint, six blocks to the east, where he was approaching at an opposing forty-five-degree offset from Jed's team.

"Variable, One—sitrep," Jed whispered, asking for an update on the enemy assaulter positions.

"We hold two six-man teams mustering east and west of you. We'll call their movement, but you've infilled inside their perimeter without detection as we hoped. You should intercept them outside of Cadillac," Ben said, Cadillac referring to the mosque.

"Roger," Jed said. He was glad Ben was keeping Corbin off the radio. Her young voice would surely bring unwanted questions.

A distracting thought from Eddy popped into Jed's head unbidden.

How do they know we're undetected?

He glanced back at Eddy, who was scanning their six, not looking at Jed.

It's already starting, Jed thought to himself. *We're going to have to be more careful.*

On that cue, Corbin piped up in his head for the first time.

One, I'm reading four different Dark Ones on the assault team. I have good eyes and ears. They have no idea you're there. Promise.

He smiled. Now that was intel definitely not fit for the open comms channel with the Green Berets.

Thanks, Watcher One.

My pleasure.

And now came the waiting. Before they could engage, Denny and his stick needed to hit the compound, removing the bad guys' command and control. Then, in the ensuing confusion, Sword and Spear would ambush the assaulters moving on the mosque. This was an authorized capture/kill mission. The goal was to take captives, but if there was any perceived risk to the local worshipers or to the team, orders were to neutralize that threat.

Why do we come up with lines like "neutralize the threat"? Jed thought. *We're going to kill them.*

His thoughts went to Nisha, the only one who hadn't deployed with a special operations direct-action team. He was glad she was with Carl, an experienced operator and Shepherd, but truth be told, she'd proved she could handle herself by outscoring half her male counterparts in multiple evolutions during Jericho Basic. On top of that, he knew she'd been in more than a few intense firefights in her day, something he felt guilty for knowing, since it had come to him unsolicited from her mind.

She'll be fine, Jed, Corbin said in his head.

Stop that, he replied with a tight grin.

"Dark Horizon just got the green light and are moving. Hold until I have Shield breaching," Ben reported.

Jed's heart rate ticked up and tension spread through his muscles as his body readied itself for action. He raised and circled his hand and felt the other four operators press in on him in preparation for the go, which came seconds later.

"Shield is inside the compound. One, green light," Ben said, communicating volumes with an economy of words.

"Go, Two," Jed said and chopped a hand forward.

Rising to a combat crouch, he led his squad around the corner of the two-story brown stucco building. Grayson drifted to the south side of the dark, narrow street, leading Bex and Patches while pressing against the wall. The trio matched Jed and Eddy step for step; they shuffled quickly along the north side. Scanning through their NVGs, the five operators moved through the shadows as one, their IR target designators crisscrossing the night like laser beams as they searched for targets.

Fifty yards to the intersection where the bad guys were converging.

"We have good eyes, One," Ben reported. "Both types," he added cryptically. "Thermals confirm six tangos spread out but moving down the center of the street."

That made sense. The enemy had no reason to think they would meet any opposition on their approach to slaughter innocents at the mosque. The worshipers would already be crowding into the worship hall at the mosque, oblivious to the evil descending upon them.

"Two, hold. You have six tangos in your cross fire in five seconds," Ben reported.

"Check," Eli said, his voice tight.

Jed signaled his team to pick up the pace. The gunfire about to erupt to the east would alert his target that something was wrong and spoil the engagement.

"One, your tangos are repositioning south into cover along the building wall. Shield has the command compound secure, but they may have—"

Gunfire behind Jed shredded the early morning stillness and cut off the message from Ben, but Jed connected the dots and accelerated his team to the intersection. Leaning in on his Sig Sauer M400, he sighted around the corner of the stucco building, dragging his green beam IR laser to where Ben had reported the enemy assaulters. But before he could engage, a white flash from incoming fire in his NVGs made him get small and low. When his NVGs refreshed, he found the target—a figure on a knee beside the building. With practiced efficiency, he placed his targeting laser center mass and pulled the trigger. Then he watched, suddenly unsettled, as the kitted-up operator pitched backward against the wall.

Father God, please don't let us be wrong.

We're not wrong, Jed, Ben's voice said in his head.

The gun battle quickly escalated as the enemy returned fire. This adversary was far more capable than local insurgents, and they were equipped with the same high-tech weaponry as Jed's team. IR designators crisscrossed the street, like a lightsaber battle, as both groups of operators shot and scrambled for their lives. Seeking cover, the five remaining tangos retreated through a gate and behind a low wall surrounding the courtyard in front of the building.

"We need to split," Grayson barked. "Pincer assault in case they try to squirt out the back of that building."

"Agreed," Jed said. "Give us covering fire to reposition."

Grayson led Bex and Patches to the corner and unleashed heavy fire, driving the enemy down.

"With me," Jed called to Eddy, and he sprinted across the street, eyes on the gate and the stucco wall behind which the enemy was holed up. As long as they could keep the bad guys pinned down in a cross fire, they might be able to force a surrender without killing everyone. Seconds later, they'd crossed the intersection and were crouched behind a low covering wall. Jed watched Bex take her turn at the corner, firing two three-round bursts at the Dark Ones posing as American fighters.

Eddy popped up, fired, then dropped and shifted left to a new spot.

Fire and move. Combat 101.

Jed popped up next and fired, aware of the green beam flashing in his vision and jerking left as gunfire chewed up the wall where his head had been, spraying concrete fragments against his cheek. It was a different proposition fighting an enemy with parity. He wiped a hand across his face where chunks of cement had sprayed his cheek but found no blood.

He heard two more bursts of fire from across the street where Grayson, Bex, and Patches were still dug in.

Grayson just dropped a second shooter, Corbin said.

Check.

"One, Two—Spear is secure," Eli announced from the site of the other gun battle east of them. "No crows. Moving to your pos."

"Roger, Two."

No crows meant Eli had taken no captives. The Dark Ones fought to the death, it would appear.

"One, we can't reposition," Grayson reported. "Too much fire."

"Check," Jed said. "Hold for Spear."

"One, you have a tango entering the building. Looks like he's trying to squirt out the back," Ben reported.

"We're on it," Jed said and instantly Eddy was up beside him. They sprinted low, hugging the perimeter wall to loop around to the back of the building, hoping to cut off the bad guy's escape.

Finding no gate on the back side, Jed vaulted the wall while Eddie provided cover. He landed with a thud, but his once-ruined hip had answered the call without a whimper. He immediately took a knee, scanning the back of the building while Eddy repositioned to join him. Half a block away on the other side of the street, the gun battle with the dug-in Dark Horizon shooters raged on.

"What do you think?" Jed said to Eddy, not taking his eyes off his scan. "Breach and go get him, or hold here and plink him when he squirts?"

"Your call," Eddy said.

"Spear is in position. Ready when you are, Three," Eli reported, informing Grayson they had additional firepower to engage.

"Check, ready for covering fire," Grayson said.

Controlled gunfire erupted on the other side of the building.

"Three, hold!" Corbin suddenly said on the radio, the fear in her voice making her sound like a child. "You've got a bomber!"

A wave of vertigo washed over Jed, and for an instant he saw the scene from Grayson's eyes—a dark figure catapulting over the wall and sprinting toward Grayson, Bex, and Patches, who were just beginning to cross the street.

"Get down!" Bex screamed, backpedaling beside Grayson to the Green Beret, who was still advancing. Then, the puzzle pieces clicking into place, Patches dropped prone as the explosion rocked the street.

The powerful blast from the suicide bomber traveled like a rolling shock wave, the energy deflected by the ground and kicking up dust to cloud his vision. Jed snapped back into his own head—his last borrowed visual that of Bex, his team's combat medic, surging forward to take a knee beside Patches.

Whoa . . . what just happened?

"Patches is five by," Bex announced as Jed got his bearings.

"How did your people know about the bomber?" Eddy demanded. "And who was that girl on comms?"

"One, your tango is on the move," Ben announced, saving Jed from Eddy's question. "He's jumped to the next building."

Jed chopped a hand forward and sprinted for the corner, where he took a knee and held up a closed fist. Eddy stopped behind him, scanning their six as Jed peered around the back corner of the neighboring building.

"Variable, One—sitrep," he whispered into his boom mic.

"One thermal a meter on the other side of the wall," Ben said. "You're practically on top of each other."

Jed was swiveling, looking for a window or a door the shooter might use, when Corbin came on the line again.

"He's coming down on you!" she yelled.

Jed saw a shadow in his peripheral vision, dropping from the sky.

He shifted his aim up but too late to fire. The falling figure landed on top of Eddy, both men tumbling to the ground as a feral scream ripped through the night air. Jed sidestepped left, trying to open a lane of fire as the two operators rolled and fought on the ground. Unable to shoot without risking hitting the Green Beret, Jed slung his rifle and pulled the bowie knife from the scabbard on the side of his kit. Blade glinting in the moonlight, he advanced on the thrashing tangle of arms and legs.

Eddy grunted as he grappled on his back with the fighter on top of him, his rifle pinned between and useless. As the blows flew with savage velocity, Jed prepared to leap onto the attacker's back only to freeze when Eddy howled in pain. Jed watched, stupefied, as the fighter bit into the cord of muscle between Eddy's neck and shoulder.

"You're too late, Shepherd," a deep and otherworldly voice growled, turning to look at Jed, eyes glowing like red-hot coals in a winter fire, blood dribbling over the chin.

Then the Dark One leapt off Eddy, rising an impossible six feet into the air before kicking off from the wall to redirect his vector toward Jed. Arms outstretched like a pouncing jungle cat, the dark soldier came straight at him. Jed dropped his left shoulder and slashed in an arc, connecting as he spun. He felt a rush of hot wetness on his hand as he tucked his shoulder and somersaulted clear. The Dark One landed with a thud but sprang to his feet with inhuman reflex. Chin up, he lifted his head and let out a wet, raspy laugh despite the arterial blood spraying from where Jed's blade had opened his throat.

Then the twisted thing charged, coming at Jed again with impossible speed.

In his peripheral vision, Jed saw Eddy roll into a kneeling firing stance and take aim. The muzzle flashed and the dark fighter's torso jerked as the bullet tore through him. But despite the damage, the possessed man stayed on his feet, blood soaking his entire front. Jed's mind flashed back to the Dark One he'd fought in the Yarnells' driveway, a demon soldier with the same glowing eyes who'd fought with superhuman strength, attacking mercilessly even after Jed had broken its arm.

Face contorted with rage, the shadow soldier rushed Jed.

Jed shifted his stance in preparation to deliver yet another kill strike, but Eddy fired again. This time, the Dark One fell—hitting the ground face-first with a wet splat like two hundred pounds of wet cement. It lay still for a moment, but then like a scene from a horror movie, it began to move. Eddy startled backward as the dark warrior tried to rise, before falling and rolling onto its back.

Jed and Eddy moved in together, both with rifles raised, two green dots of IR light beside each other on what was left of the man's face. The one remaining eye still glowed red, but as Jed watched, the light faded. Then it happened—a demonic double visage appeared over the fighter's wrecked face, as if a snarling and ghoul-like hologram was being projected onto the dead man. It flashed orange and the glowing demon face disappeared, leaving a horrible stench in its wake.

"What the hell just happened?" Eddy said, punctuating each word as he stared transfixed at the corpse.

"What do you mean?" Jed asked, buying himself a second or two as he decided what to say to the terrified Green Beret.

"What do I mean?" Eddy said, gesturing wildly with his left hand. "Are you telling me you didn't see that? You didn't see the . . . the . . . thing on his face? You didn't see the glowing eyes?"

"I'm not sure what I saw," Jed said.

"That dude dropped on me from the sky and transformed into a monster. . . . That was some Stephen King–level terror, bro."

"He jumped on you from an open window," Jed said, seeing his fellow Shepherds coming around the corner toward their position.

"Whatever, dude," Eddy said, exasperated. "His eyes were glowing and he jumped like ten feet vertically and then flew through the air like a friggin' supervillain. He kept fighting after you opened his throat and I shot him in the head. How is that possible?"

"Two, One—I could use a hand," Jed said, prompting Eli to hurry up, as he had no idea what he was supposed to do here. "The dude was obviously on drugs," he said, turning back to Eddy, trying to put the same awe and fear in his own voice. "PCP or something."

"Yeah, maybe," Eddy said, shaking his head, wanting to believe the lie. "But what about . . . ?" He lowered his voice to a conspiratorial whisper and tipped his boom mic up and away from his mouth. "What about the *face*?"

"What face?" Jed asked, all innocence, just as Eli stepped up.

"That dude had two faces and one was . . . not human."

Jed was about to feign ignorance again when Eli slapped Eddy on the shoulder.

"You good, bro?"

Eddy shot Jed a look that said *Please don't say anything to the command or they'll think I'm crazy.*

"We're good, bro," Jed answered for them both. "One is Packard," he said into his mic, giving their TOC the jackpot call sign. "But no crows, I'm afraid."

"Roger, One, understand Packard," Ben said. "We need to bring the bodies back to the compound. Vehicles moving toward you for both sticks at Hudson. Collect everything you can and exfil in five mikes."

"Copy all."

Jed watched Eddy, his rifle dangling from his right hand instead of in a combat carry, set off in a daze up the road toward where Patches was standing with Bex. He couldn't leave Eddy like that. After Jed's first encounter with a Dark One in Kenny Bailey's basement, he'd had no one to talk to, and it had sent his life into a tailspin. He refused to let the same thing happen to Eddy.

But he needed counsel from Ben first.

He glanced at Eli, who tipped his mic up.

"Everything okay?" the veteran Shepherd asked.

Jed nodded. "Yeah, I think so. Eddy is just freaked out. Unfortunately, he saw the eyes and the face."

"What do you mean *the face*?" Eli asked, and at first Jed thought he was screwing around, but his teammate's expression showed real confusion.

He leaned in closer. "You know, the double face—that thing that happens just before the demon leaves the body."

Eli shook his head. "I've seen the glowing eyes, but I've never seen the demon face you're talking about. Maybe that's a gifted skill? I don't know. You'll have to talk to Ben about that one." He reached down and grabbed the corpse by the kit. "Help me with this piece of garbage, won't you."

"Yeah," Jed said and helped his brother haul the body of the dead shooter down the road to where the rest of the team was pulling the other corpses into neat rows.

We need to talk, Jed, Ben's voice said in his head. *I didn't know dark angels were revealing themselves to you.*

Yeah, Jed answered back, *we definitely need to talk.*

As the adrenaline from the battle ebbed, a feeling of relief washed over him. There would be no massacre of innocent civilians today. They'd stopped this attack and whatever else Victor had hoped to accomplish with it. Jed's first mission leading Joshua Bravo team was a success.

Take the win, bro, he thought to himself and let a victorious grin spread over his face.

CHAPTER TWENTY-TWO

JOINT TRAINING TASK FORCE ACTIVITY TAL AFAR

FOB SYKES

TAL AFAR, IRAQ

0552 HOURS LOCAL

Jed watched Eddy carefully as they rode in the back of a pickup truck back to base. The Delta operator sat on the bed floor, hands folded on top of the rifle in his lap, staring out at nothing for the entire ride. Jed knew that look. Eddy wasn't going to be able to let it go . . .

Grayson, who sat beside Jed on the rail, gave him an elbow and leaned in. "Awesome work, bro. I wasn't sure about putting a nugget in charge, but you did good."

Jed smiled and gave his teammate a nod, wanting to relish the moment, but he couldn't. He shifted his gaze to Patches, who was seated beside Eddy and babbling on and on about the op, apparently oblivious to the fact that Eddy wasn't hearing a word. The younger Green Beret's face was riddled with tiny cuts from the explosion, but miraculously he was otherwise unscathed.

The truck rolled through the retractable gate, drove onto the compound, and jerked to a stop beside the low building that served as the TOC for the Green Berets. Jed spun around and dropped off the side rail, his boots hitting the dusty, hard-packed ground with a double thud. The front passenger door opened and Bex slipped out of the cab, an Army SF driver hopping out on the other side.

The door to the TOC swung open, and Ben made a beeline for Jed, with Mike Moore and David Yarnell quick-stepping in his trail.

"Quick word, Jed?" Ben said, pulling him aside and around the corner of the building.

"Sure," Jed said as if he had a choice.

"First of all, great work," Ben said as they moved out of earshot of the others. The Shepherd commander's face was practically beaming like a proud daddy after watching his kid hit his first baseball, so Jed knew the words were genuine.

"Thanks," he said.

"What happened there at the end?" Pastor Mike jumped in, getting straight to business like the Seventy-Fifth Ranger commander he once was. "Tell us exactly what happened. Don't leave anything out."

A lump formed in Jed's throat. "I'm sorry if I screwed up how I handled it with Eddy, but what am I supposed to say? We got up close and personal with a Dark One. I mean, you guys know how hard it is to kill the possessed. It's like fighting the undead."

"It's a nightmare, I know, but that's not what I'm talking about," Moore said, exasperation creeping into his voice. "On comms we heard you guys talking about a demon double visage. Did the demon show itself to you, Jed?"

Jed folded his arms across his chest. "Um . . . yeah."

"Was this the first time that happened?"

He shook his head. "Every time I've gone toe-to-toe with one of those bastards, I've seen the demon face."

Pastor Mike swallowed hard and looked at Ben, and unless Jed's eyes were playing tricks on him, the wiry pastor looked a couple shades paler.

"Guys, you're making me uncomfortable," Jed said. "Can somebody please tell me what's going on?"

"Jed, is that what you saw in the basement on the night Kenny Bailey tried to rape Rachel?" David asked, his expression oddly dispassionate and self-assured given the subject matter. "Did you see a demon in Kenny?"

"Yes, of course," Jed said, a chill chasing down his spine. "Didn't you?"

"No, Jed, I did not," David said and then he did something Jed did not expect. He reached up, clasped a hand on Jed's shoulder, and looked him in the eyes. "That explains a lot, my friend . . . a lot."

Jed felt his eyes rim with unexpected tears. He blew out a sharp exhale. "So all this time, you thought I beat Kenny to near death just because . . ."

David shook his head. "I knew something wasn't right with

Kenny that night, but if I had seen what you did, I wouldn't have been able to self-deceive the way I did. I told myself what I saw was my brain playing tricks on me. The glowing eyes . . . that was just light from the stairwell reflecting off his eyes in the dark. The inhuman noises were just Kenny grunting in the throes of carnal aggression. But if I had seen what you saw, if I had seen a demon, it would have messed me up real good. I probably would have done what you did . . . I probably would have run away."

Jed nodded, but inside, he was experiencing an emotional earthquake. The foundation upon which he'd built his temple of guilt and regret was the belief—no, not the belief, the *assumption* that David and Rachel had witnessed the same unnatural phenomenon, the same bone-chilling evil that night. But they hadn't.

They didn't see the beast . . .

David let go of Jed's shoulders and flashed him a tight-lipped smile.

"Jed, look at me," Ben said, his confident voice pulling Jed out of his headspace and to the present. "The Dark Ones show their true face to very few people. As far as Pastor Mike and I are concerned, what you experienced is strategically important."

"I still don't understand," he said.

Ben exhaled. "Now I've never had a sit-down with Satan, the CSO of their head shed, but I like to think of him as the ultimate playground bully. Every bully is insecure, afraid, and deep down hates himself. So what does a bully do to make himself feel better? He torments other kids, tries to tear them down so they feel like he does, miserable and afraid. Most of the time bullies go after the easy targets—the loners, the shy, the weak. Kids that won't fight back. But eventually that low-hanging fruit loses its flavor, forcing the bully to go after a worthy adversary—someone who, if he succeeds in breaking, is a real win for his malignant ego. Which is why most bullies develop a fixation on a happy kid with friends and self-confidence. To torment and break a kid like that is truly satisfying. Is any of this resonating with you?"

Jed nodded.

"Strategically, Jed, we think the Dark Ones work the same way," Pastor Mike said. "They target the spiritually weak and emotionally vulnerable, but they fixate on the strong and the powerful. You'd never open yourself to a Dark One, and they know it. But your gifts and abilities make you a threat. You're on their radar now, and they're afraid. When you battle them, when victory or loss hangs in the balance, they show you their true face because fear is their most powerful weapon . . . That's Ben's and my theory anyway."

"It makes sense. If you can distract or intimidate your adversary at the crucial moment in battle, it could buy you that critical second to deliver the death blow," Jed said.

"This is a really big deal, Jed. We see something special in you, but so do Victor and his boss. Like Mike said, you're on his radar. I'm sorry to be the one to have to tell you this, but you're going to have to really watch your six. Victor is going to be coming for you, probably in more ways than one," Ben said.

"Well, then we have another problem," Jed said. "Because Eddy saw it too."

Ben traded glances with Pastor Mike before turning back to Jed. "Are you sure?"

"Oh yeah, he saw the eyes *and* the demon face, and it messed him up. He was in catatonic mode the whole ride back from the op. Someone should probably talk to him . . ." Jed shifted his weight between his feet, unsure. "Do you want me to try?"

"I think that's a solid idea, actually," Pastor Mike said. "You reassure him he's not crazy, and then Ben can have a follow-up chat with him."

"That's a great plan," Ben agreed.

"Are you going to try and recruit him?" he asked.

"Maybe," Ben said.

"We have to pray about it first," Moore said and with a wry smile added, "But it looks like there might be more than meets the eye when it comes to this Green Beret. The Dark Ones are certainly interested in him because one of them took a shot at taking him out today."

"Well," Jed said, "if you do, I'd welcome him into Joshua Bravo. He's a solid operator and I get a good vibe from him."

"We'll pray on that, too," Ben said with a smile. "Why don't you find Eddy and chat with him before the joint debrief. Then bring him to me after, okay?"

"Roger that," Jed said, still a little uncertain as to what he should say to the Green Beret.

"If he's receptive to the outreach, then feel free to share your story. It's our personal experiences that resonate with like-minded warriors. I think you sharing will go a long way with Eddy."

"Okay."

Pastor Mike turned to David. "Will you lead us in prayer?"

David nodded and with a self-assuredness Jed hadn't seen from his friend since high school, the Shepherd's newest TSL led them in prayer . . . and a compelling one at that.

"Amen," Jed mumbled in unison with the others. He looked

up and found David smiling at him, eyes on fire. Perhaps this had been God's plan for David all along. His charisma, penchant for risk, and endless thirst for adventure growing up suddenly seemed ironically suited for the journey they were on. Strangely, Jed wasn't sure how he felt about that.

He nodded and slipped back around to the front of the TOC, searching for Eddy among the operators securing weapons, gear, and body bags.

"All good, bro?" Eli asked, clasping him on the arm.

"Yeah, just looking for Eddy," he said.

"I saw him head to the shower trailers around back," Eli said, jerking a thumb in that direction.

"Thanks, bro," Jed said, fist-bumping his teammate.

He rounded the corner and saw a door slightly ajar on one of the trailers housing showers and toilets, harsh light streaming through the gap in the predawn night. Jed mounted the steps and opened the door. Eddy startled from where he leaned, both hands on the edge of the sink, water dripping from his face. Then he recognized Jed and shot him an awkward smile.

"Hey, Eddy," Jed said, grabbing a handful of paper towels and wetting them to scrub the grime from his face at the adjacent basin.

"It's Edwin, actually," he mumbled, staring at Jed in reverse in the mirror, his warrior's eyes dark and brooding.

"Oh," Jed said.

"The team calls me Eddy because they know I hate it. Team room stuff."

"Right," Jed said, shaking his head and grinning. "Team room stuff. Listen, I'm glad to run into you, Edwin."

"Yeah, well, I'm glad I ran into you, too," the Green Beret said, forcing a grin and an air of confidence onto his face. "I want to apologize for how I acted back there at the X. I think I had some weird ass hallucination or something. I don't know what that was all about, but I promise you I've never . . ."

"Let me stop you right there. I saw it too," Jed said.

Eddy froze. "In that case, I don't want to talk about it," he said stiffly. "And no one can *ever* tell my team . . ."

"Look, Eddy . . . I mean, Edwin . . . it's okay," Jed said. "I'm not telling anyone, but I couldn't leave here having you think you were going crazy. I remember what it did to me the first time I saw a demon . . ."

Edwin jerked upright, practically snapping to attention. "Demon? Is that what that was?"

"Yes," Jed said simply. "Look, man, I know this is bizarre. Believe me when I tell you I know just how you feel. What you saw—it's real. And it's also something that not everyone can see. It's rare and it's special."

"Special?" The Green Beret laughed, a bit hysterically, Jed thought. "In what way is that special?"

Jed took a moment to choose his words, suddenly wishing Pastor Mike—or maybe even David—were with him.

"Are you a spiritual man, Edwin?"

Edwin sighed. "I'm a believer. But honestly, I've drifted from my faith these last few years. All I've seen and done . . . it's become harder and harder to find God in the world we live in, bro."

Jed nodded. "I get it. And I've been there. But I can tell you that God is here, right now. He's with us. And so are the evil forces, because Satan is just as real. There's a war raging all around us—a war that most people can't see. But some of us can. The enemy showed you his face today, Edwin. What happened on the X was no accident."

"Why are you telling me this?" Edwin asked, but his face suggested he might already know.

"I'm telling you this, brother to brother, in the hope that it doesn't take you more than a decade to find your way back to God and the answers you're seeking like it did me."

"So this spooky outfit you're with," Edwin said, nodding as the pieces began to click into place. "They're all dudes who've seen what we've seen?"

"Dudes and ladies," Jed said with a chuckle. "It's not the same for everyone, but let's put it this way: they're all read in on the cosmic goings-on."

"And you guys travel around and hunt these things?"

"In a nutshell, yeah, pretty much."

"Hmm . . . I suppose I could get behind that."

"Tell you what, if you're willing to talk to my boss—Ben Morvant—he might be able to help sort you out. He's way better at all this stuff than me."

Edwin looked at him closely but seemed much more in control now. "Yeah, all right," he said, his voice more defiant than resigned. "I'd like to talk to him."

"Cool," Jed said. "Now, we should probably head over to the conventional debrief. I imagine they're waiting on us."

"Sure," Edwin said and followed him out of the shower trailer and into the nascent pink glow of the rising sun. "Your boss, he's not a SEAL or nothing, I hope?"

"Oh, he's a SEAL all right," Jed said with a wry grin. "I mean, you wouldn't expect God to put Army in charge."

This comment got them both laughing and earned Jed a back-slap from the Delta operator who he hoped, God willing, would soon be part of his Shepherd family.

CHAPTER
TWENTY-THREE

The warm nostalgia of the post-op celebration enveloped Jed like a favorite blanket on a chilly night. He'd been in the back of so many cargo planes, returning home from so many missions, celebrating with so many SEAL Team brothers, that he felt a poignant, almost-disorienting wave of emotion from the good feelings swirling around him.

"I'm just saying that Nisha was totally badass," Carl said with bravado, accepting a bottled beer from Eli. "She was number two in the door, cleared our left flank, and then was through to the second room like a shot, engaging bad guys like a true Raider, or dare I say . . . a frogman."

"Frogwoman!" Bex corrected with a chuckle and clinked her bottle against Nisha's.

"The thing is, *I* wasn't even on your X, so I'm not sure how you can make that comparison," Hyeon said with feigned indignation.

"Maybe not," Johnny said, winking at Carl, "but if the Colonel was here with his kill house leaderboard, sounds like Wonder Woman would have outscored your sorry frogman butt . . . as usual."

"Ouch," Hyeon said, pulling an imaginary dagger from his heart, but the twinkle in his eye said he was loving the banter. "Until now, I didn't realize Army could count."

"We can count to ten on our fingers and read words real good too," Johnny replied and tipped back his own beer as everyone laughed and Bex slapped Hyeon on the shoulder.

Jed smiled. One mission under their belt and already they were talking smack and sharing war stories. And that was a very, very good thing.

They were becoming a team.

"All right, Joshua Bravo, listen up," boomed Ben's voice, and Jed turned from where he sat on a camo poncho spread out on the steel floor of the cargo jet. "I've got an announcement."

Everyone settled down, curiosity and maybe excitement at whatever operational insanity might be on tap for them next.

"As you know," Ben said, hands on hips and Pastor Mike standing beside him, "we pulled you out of training before finishing Jericho Basic. There were nearly two weeks remaining in phase one, a tough two weeks of simulated combat mission sets culminating in a real-world, live-fire exercise."

The team exchanged glances, but Jed noticed Eli looking down with a smile on his face.

"I've consulted with the veterans, and they unanimously agreed that, especially in light of your performance in Tal Afar, this team is ready to leave Jericho Basic behind and become permanent and active members of Joshua Bravo team. Congratulations."

The already-buoyant mood elevated tenfold, as the team whooped and high-fived one another. The normally reserved Nisha fist-bumped with Hyeon, and Bex even gave Johnny a hug.

"Strong work, everyone," Ben said. "Nevertheless, there's still considerable training ahead in the pipeline. Finishing Jericho Basic is akin to graduating BUD/S and advancing to SQT. Each of you is now officially a Shepherd and has earned the right to wear the crook and cross, but there is still much to learn—advanced techniques important to our unique tactical environment that you cannot learn anywhere else."

Jed chuckled at that comment, his mind picturing the Dark One flying through the air at Edwin and fighting like a Tasmanian devil after having its neck sliced open.

Unique tactical environment indeed.

"The point I'm making, people, is that it typically takes eighteen months, depending on the deployment tempo and training cycles, to get you through everything our training pipeline has to offer. But during that time, your team remains deployable for specific missions for which we feel you're best suited."

The gravity of that sank in, and everyone glanced at one another with what Jed was glad to see appeared to be confidence and unity.

"Also, with Jericho Basic behind you, y'all can move out of

the training barracks and the four nuggets can find permanent housing," Ben continued. "My wife, Christy, and I live on base with our kids and we love it. I think you'll find the Trinity Loop housing options convenient and well-appointed. In addition, your rent is heavily subsidized—you won't find anything comparable in town at the price point—and there's a security advantage in living on the complex. I know that none of you nuggets are married with kids yet, but it's still something to consider. If you elect to live out in town, you must be within thirty minutes of the Trinity complex, so Nashville, especially the West End, still works. Your TSL David and his family, because of unique circumstances, have already been living in family housing for two months, so feel free to ask him questions about his experience."

Jed looked over at David with surprise. He had no idea they'd left their house in the West End. But given everything that had happened to Sarah Beth and the bloody attack at that house, it made sense why they'd already moved on base.

"We love living on Trinity Loop," David said when Ben gave him a nod. "Like Ben said, it's the best option in town. And to prove the point, I'll be hosting a Jericho Basic graduation barbecue at our house."

"Oh yeah," Johnny whooped. "That'll be awesome."

"Your definition of awesome is any meal you don't have to cook yourself," Eli joked before turning to David. "We'll be there for sure, David. Count me in for two adults and three kids, and I hope you don't have much that's breakable."

"Beer, brats, and little tots . . . what could possibly go wrong?" David said, grinning large. "Now all I need is a couple of days to figure out how to make Rachel think the party was her idea."

This was met with good-natured laughter, especially from the married guys.

Despite grinning on the outside, on the inside, the prospect of a cookout at David and Rachel's house made Jed's stomach go to knots.

I don't know if I'm ready for this . . .

With that thought, he felt a hand on his shoulder and turned to see Ben smiling at him.

"Nice work, Jed," he said, leading Jed gently away from the group to talk. "You led your crew through Jericho Basic, and on your first mission as a team leader, you performed like a veteran Shepherd. I know God has big plans for you with us."

"Thanks," Jed said, not sure what else to say.

"I had a good talk with Edwin, by the way," his boss said, lowering his voice.

"Does that mean what I hope it means?"

"Time will tell," Ben said, "but I extended him the invitation."

"How did he react to that?"

"He said he needed some time to noodle on it, but he asked for yours and Eli's contact information in case he had questions. I wanted to ask you before I passed your mobile number along to him."

"Absolutely, boss," Jed said. "And you don't have to ask me for that. Consider this blanket permission going forward. I'm all in here."

Ben nodded. "I know, and I appreciate ya."

At first he thought Ben jumped into his head, but then he realized the converse was true. Jed heard Ben's thoughts, clearly, in his own mind.

I finally feel like I'm not alone . . .

The Shepherd commander flashed Jed an insider's smile and excused himself.

Jed watched him go, pondering the candid and stolen insight that had just humanized the man he'd been keeping on a pedestal. The burden of leadership was real . . . and it appeared that Ben Morvant was ready to share some of the load.

CHAPTER TWENTY-FOUR

Woland leaned back with a sigh on the crushed velvet love seat, which, like so much of Italian culture, prioritized style over function. The back was too straight and the pillows too thin. The arched armrests looked inviting but the angles were uncomfortable. He shook his head, kicked his feet up onto the small coffee table that sat too low to set down a drink, and took a long pull on his glass of Hardy L'Ete Lalique cognac grande champagne. The smooth and powerful cognac slipped down his throat like liquid silk, and he decided this was one thing—one of the few things—the French had gotten right.

He liked drinking in decadence in front of his Muslim guest. He liked taunting men like Rashid, who draped themselves in false piety. He liked rubbing salt in people's wounds. He liked when men such as Rashid knew they were being used and chose to be exploited anyway.

He reached for the crystal decanter and added two more fingers to his glass, then set the bottle on the end table instead of the coffee table–turned–ottoman. He turned to the terrorist sitting in the armchair across the table and was about to speak when the encrypted phone beside him on the miserable love seat cushion chimed. He held up a finger to the man. Rashid nodded while his eyes ticked disapprovingly to the cognac. Woland responded by taking a long, obnoxious sip and savoring the smooth heat down his throat before finally raising the phone to his ear.

"Yes."

"I trust you're enjoying your accommodations." Victor's oily tone suggested he'd been rooting around in Woland's head already. No matter. He'd become accustomed to that feeling of being a vessel—or at least a cohabitor—of his own mind and body.

"They're adequate," he said, lifting the twelve-thousand-dollar crystal bottle and watching the light dance in the golden liquid.

I need a nice cigar to go with this.

"You can have all the cigars you want when this is over. How are the preparations coming?"

Woland thought back to the operation he'd conducted, utilizing connections inside Boko Haram to kidnap the rector's brother's family, then replayed the conversation with the distraught African priest in his mind. With Victor now perpetually inside his head, thinking his answer was the most expedient. The conversation was more a formality than anything else.

"Things are in place," he replied, getting bored with the game. "The assets I need are in Rome already. The logistics proved easier than I imagined. Europe, it seems, is a revolving door for trafficking the types of people I need." Woland glanced to his left and gave a nod to his bearded guest.

"Very well. How much more time do you require?" Victor hissed in his ear.

"That's up to His Holiness now, isn't it," Woland replied, draping his voice with sarcasm. "I don't control the sacred schedule."

Victor said nothing, just breathed into the phone.

"How is the precursor work in Iraq going?" Woland asked. "I saw the news of the first attack, but there has been no mention of a second."

"The second attack was interdicted by the Shepherds. An unfortunate development, but the fury and fervor on cable news and social media suggest the first attack has stirred the requisite emotion and outrage in the Muslim community. Calls for retaliation against Christians are building everywhere and gaining momentum in all the right circles."

Woland frowned. "All due respect, Victor, but if the Shepherds took down the Dark Horizon assaulters, how long will it take them to trace it back to the source? Perhaps it is unwise to utilize Dark Horizon in support of my mission? I can augment with another—"

"Who are you to doubt me?" Victor snapped, and Woland felt a peculiar pressure inside his head.

Is that Victor or my other? he wondered, wincing.

"I'm sorry. I would never doubt you," he said, clearing his mind.

"Remember your place, Nicholas," Victor said, and the pressure in Woland's skull began to ebb. "Dark Horizon is but a tool. As are you. Broken tools can either be remade or replaced."

"I understand. I live to serve," he said as he contemplated the metaphor.

I was remade once already. . . . Would he grant me a second chance?

"Our enemies are gaining strength. New champions are rising in the ranks of the Watcher and Shepherds corps. Sarah Beth Yarnell. Jedidiah Johnson. These are names you would do well to familiarize yourself with. The threat is real. It's time to check your unbridled overconfidence and prepare yourself for the challenge ahead. Assuming you survive this operation, I foresee a great opportunity for you."

"What type of opportunity?" Woland asked, suddenly salivating at the prospect of greater power and influence.

"Prove your *capital* first, and then we'll have that discussion."

"I understand," Woland said, feeling his chest tighten with anxiety. Robotically, he reached for and drained his drink.

"In the meantime, keep focus on the Vatican and be thinking about contingencies and how you'll counter interdiction scenarios. Your skill set and knowledge of the Shepherds is why I broke you out of La Santé. You were born for this operation. Do not disappoint us."

He was about to thank Victor, but the line went dead.

Woland set the phone down and fixed his attention on the bearded terrorist.

He apologized in Arabic and said, "Good news, Rashid. Funding is secured and I have approval for the operation to proceed. Soon the halls of the Vatican will run red with the blood of the infidels who slaughter innocent believers in Allah's sacred mosques."

"This is good news," Rashid said, clapping his hands together. "I will prepare my men for what lies ahead. Victory will be granted from above."

Not from above, you fool . . . most certainly not from above.

"Inshallah," Woland said and rose to his feet as Rashid did the same.

Right hand over his heart, the terrorist bowed to him. Woland returned the respect, then escorted the jihadist out. As he shut and locked the door, his mind went back to Victor's words:

"Sarah Beth Yarnell. Jedidiah Johnson. These are names you would do well to familiarize yourself with. The threat is real . . ."

"Interesting," he murmured as he poured the last of the cognac from the decanter into his glass. "Victor, it would seem, is afraid . . ."

CHAPTER
TWENTY-FIVE

Walking a loop around the perimeter of the barracks, Jed listened to the voice mail from Maria Perez for the second time just to be sure. Yes, he was a big, dumb door kicker, but even he understood the subtext in the Nashville police detective's message. Apparently he'd been on her mind since the events rescuing Sarah Beth, and she was interested in reconnecting. Like most women he knew, she wanted *him* to do the asking, but she'd made it obvious for him by taking the first step and initiating contact.

Although he'd never admit it, the prospect of seeing her excited him. Sure, they'd gotten off to a rocky start—their introduction taking place with him handcuffed in an interrogation room at her precinct—but after that, he'd managed to turn it around. And she'd taken a bullet for him . . .

So there's that, he thought with a smile.

He stared at her number but couldn't quite bring himself to dial it. Like every good operator, he didn't do anything without a plan. How should he greet her? Should he call her Detective Perez or be casual and use Maria? Should he ask her if she wanted to grab drinks together, or was meeting for coffee a better option? Did the former imply a date while the latter was just a friendly meetup? What if her *real* reason for wanting to chat was simply to get an update on Sarah Beth and nothing more?

Probably best to start with coffee . . .

"Stop being such a loser and just call the lady back," he murmured and pressed the Call button.

"Hey, Jedidiah," she said, greeting him casually after the third ring.

"Hey, I got your message," he said, surprised she'd greeted him by name—must have saved his number in her contacts. "How are you doing?"

"I'm doing okay. How about you?"

"Good . . . good," he said, feeling a sudden awkwardness through the phone. "You, uh, healing up okay from that night at the Yarnells'?"

"I'm still on medical leave, but yeah, I could go back if they'd let me. You know how it is—abundance of caution and all that. How about you? If I recall, you took quite a beating that night as well."

"Yeah, but it looked worse than it was," he said, realizing that if they talked much longer, they'd burn up all the easy conversation fodder on the phone. It was now or never. "I'm not sure if I told you, but I'm back in Nashville now—probably for a while. If you want, we could meet up for a coffee and compare scars."

She hesitated a beat before answering. "That's great! I'm so glad you're here," she said. "Maybe we could meet for drinks and a bite to eat. There's a cool place on Eleventh Avenue with outdoor tables and a great view of downtown and the Gulch."

"So long as they serve beer, I'm game for that," Jed said, switching ears with his phone. "When did you have in mind?"

"What about tonight?"

"Hmmm, my schedule is pretty packed these days," he said, grinning. "But it looks like you're in luck. I just happen to have a cancellation and can squeeze you in."

"Oh, well, in that case, what a lucky girl I am."

He chuckled. "What do you say . . . seven o'clock?"

"Let's make it eight," she said.

"Eight it is. . . . What's the name of this place by the way?"

"L.A. Jackson," she said. "Do you have transportation, Jed? If not, I can pick you up."

"Actually, I bought a truck . . . so I'm all good to pick you up if you like."

"Oh, that's sweet, but how about we meet there?"

"Roger that. I'll see you at eight, Detective."

"Looking forward to it," she said, and he could hear the smile in her voice.

"Me too."

He ended the call and turned back to the barracks. On his way in, he ran into Bex and Nisha, who were heading out, backpacks slung on their shoulders.

"What are you smiling about?" Nisha said with a playful look on her face.

"I think somebody's got a date tonight," Bex chimed in.

"I'm that transparent, huh?" he said.

"Like a windowpane," Nisha said.

"Well, it's nothing to get too excited about. We're just friends."

"Where are you and your *friend* meeting?" Bex said.

"Some bar called L.A. Jackson. I've never been."

"L.A. Jackson is not a *we're just friends* kinda place. It's more of a *who's who of Nashville* joint. So don't be wearing your cargo pants there."

Jed pulled his chin back. "Seriously? Dang, 'cause my wardrobe options happen to be extremely limited at the moment, living out of the barracks and all."

"Don't worry, Jed. With your build you can wear jeans and a T-shirt and you'll still impress," Nisha said with that coy lip-curl thing she liked to do.

"Well, unless I can borrow a button-down from Eli, jeans and a T-shirt is probably how I'm going to have to roll," he said. "Hey, speaking of closet space, have both of you figured out where you're going to live? I could definitely use recommendations for decent apartments in town."

Nisha and Bex looked at each other; then Nisha turned to him and said, "Actually, Jed, we're going to room together here on the main campus. We've already lined up a two-bedroom apartment in Trinity Tower."

"Seriously? I just figured . . ."

"You figured what? That two hot babes like us would want to live downtown so we can hit the club scene every night?"

He felt his cheeks flush as they were now clearly having a good time at his expense. "That's not exactly where I was going, but I certainly didn't think you'd wanna live on base. Er, not on *base*—you know what I mean."

"Jed, have you actually bothered to look at the housing here? Have you gone to main campus yet at all?"

He shook his head.

"I didn't think so. Before you do anything, you need to check out the housing options here. You're not going to find anything—and I mean anything—in Nashville with this quality, convenience, and perks for the subsidized prices they're offering us. You're looking at, like, double or triple the price in town. And I don't want to speak for Bex, but I for one am tired of living a double life outside the wire and being alone. Maybe it's just a former spook thing, but I'm really looking forward to being part of a community where I don't have to be guarded and careful all the time. It's just so . . ."

"Exhausting?" he said.

Nisha nodded. "Precisely."

"All good points. Maybe sometime during the next couple of days you could give me a tour of your new apartment?"

"Absolutely," Bex said.

"Where are you staying until you find a place?" Nisha asked.

"The barracks." Jed shrugged, the question not having even occurred to him.

Nisha and Bex both laughed.

"You do remember that we graduated from phase one basic two weeks early," Nisha said, laughing.

"I know."

"Everyone's moving out of the barracks, dude," Bex said.

"Yeah, but I've got at least two weeks, right? I mean, the new class isn't starting yet."

"Soooo you're going to live here by yourself?"

"Yep," he said and then added, "Don't worry. I'll have the Colonel to keep me company."

Bex gave the outside of his upper arm a pat. "Good luck with that."

"Have fun tonight, Jed," Nisha said over her shoulder as they walked away. "Can't wait to hear all about it at the barbecue tomorrow night."

"What barbecue?" he called after them.

"Our graduation barbecue at the Yarnells' house. Don't tell me you forgot already?"

"No, of course not. . . . I'll be there," he said, remembering David's announcement on the plane ride back and also remembering his decision to put it out of his mind until he was emotionally prepared to think about seeing Rachel. Apparently his subconscious had done too good of a job compartmentalizing this one.

Old habits . . .

Nisha shook her head but also smiled as she waved goodbye. He watched her go for a moment before turning and heading inside the barracks. The sleeping hall was deserted, proving the girls right. All the beds were made and locker doors hanging open to reveal empty insides. Everyone had moved out . . . except for him.

Looks like I'm alone, again, as usual.

He walked over to his rack and sat down on the mattress. The metal slats underneath groaned in protest under his weight, echoing loudly in the empty hall. He sighed and checked his watch.

1745. He still had nearly two hours to kill before he had to leave to meet Detective Perez. He thought about taking a nap but dismissed it immediately as the end result would inevitably be (a) him sleeping through his alarm and missing the date altogether or (b) the alarm waking him up in the middle of a REM cycle and him being groggy and grumpy for the date.

It's not a date, dude, the SEAL inside corrected.

"Fine, it's not a date," he murmured. "And now I'm talking to myself. Wonderful . . ."

He looked down at his hands—big and scarred and heavily calloused—and thought about how much damage he'd done both to and with them. How many faces he'd bloodied, how many throats he'd slit, how many triggers he'd pulled. Like most operators he knew, Jed didn't keep count.

But God did, right?

Certainly.

But they were all bad guys.

He inhaled deeply through his nose and exhaled through pursed lips.

Yeah, they were all bad guys . . . and one very bad grandma.

He walked over to his locker and, brain on autopilot, changed into his PT clothes. Despite the fact that he'd already worked out today, he badly needed to go for a run, a luxury he'd missed for the couple of years after he'd damaged his hip and before Ben had healed him—God had healed him, he corrected in his head. He headed out, and when he reached the intersection of the Jericho Training complex access road and Trinity Loop Road, he noticed the Colonel coming around from the north. Jed jogged in place along the curb until Jericho caught up.

"Mind if I join you?" he said as he fell into stride beside the salty instructor.

"Don't mind, so long as you don't slow me down," the Colonel replied.

"If I did, would you wait for me?"

"Nope."

"Then I guess we're good either way."

Jericho actually smiled at the comment, but you had to know what to look for and even then, most people wouldn't call it a smile. Clearly there had been a shift, though—similar, perhaps, to the change that occurred in the SEAL community once you graduated BUD/S. You were no longer a candidate with a 70 percent chance of ringing the bell and washing out. You were part of the community. You'd made it and were worthy of respect and the grueling SQT training that remained to earn your Trident and make you a full-fledged SEAL. Maybe, by completing phase one, he was now a part of the Shepherds community to the Colonel.

"Couldn't help but notice that you haven't moved out of the barracks," the Colonel said.

"It's either sleep there or in my truck," Jed said. "'Cause I don't have a place yet."

The Colonel nodded. "I'm gonna go for an early run tomorrow morning before services start, if you want to join me."

"Sure, I'm game."

They ran for a half mile before either of them spoke again.

"You got something on your mind, son?" the Colonel asked without looking at Jed.

"What makes you say that?"

"No offense, but you're pretty transparent . . . spiritually that is."

Jed thought about the comment for a second, not sure what to make of it, before saying, "Yeah, well, I've got a million things on my mind, but don't we all?"

"No, not all of us. I try to limit myself to one worry at a time."

"Is that right?" Jed said, laughing and throwing his breathing out of sync as he felt the Colonel increase the pace a bit.

"It's called living in the present. You should try it sometime, Johnson."

"You think I don't live in the present?"

The Colonel chortled at this. "Heck no, son. The transmission may be in drive, but you've got your eyes glued to the rearview mirror."

"I don't know about that."

"Well, I do. You're always thinking about what you did wrong. About what you'd do different if you could go back in time and do things over again. A leader can't operate that way, Jed."

"With all due respect, I disagree. A good leader is introspective. A good leader is honest with himself, identifies his weaknesses and mistakes, and works hard to improve and not make those same mistakes again."

"That's true, but that's not what we're talking about and you know it," Jericho said between controlled breaths. "Don't you think it's time for you to offload that backpack full of regrets you insist on carrying around with you everywhere you go?"

Jed didn't answer. To do so would mean admitting something he'd never had to articulate before.

My regrets are the only thing that keeps me going.

"What did you say?" Jericho pressed.

"I didn't say anything."

Does he have that gift, too?

"Uh-huh. You familiar with Philippians 3:13, son?"

"No," Jed admitted. "Sorry."

"Don't be," the Colonel said as he increased their pace again. "It says, 'Brothers and sisters, I do not consider myself yet to have taken hold of it. But one thing I do: Forgetting what is behind me and straining toward what is ahead.' Think about it."

"Wise words," Jed agreed, unconvinced.

"From a man with far more to regret than you, Jed."

Jed grinned as the Colonel ran effortlessly beside him, the older man showing superhuman endurance. A moment later he turned to Jed again, a tight smile on his leathered face.

"Jed, to lead in the Shepherds, you need to leave your regrets behind. Clinging to guilt from the past will limit you here. Frankly, it's not a biblical way for any Christian to live, but here in the Shepherds, it's dangerous."

"Dangerous?" Jed asked with surprise. "How so?"

"In 1 Peter 5:8, it says, 'Be alert and of sober mind. Your enemy the devil prowls around like a roaring lion looking for someone to devour.' When you hold on to the guilt and regret that should be buried at the cross with your sins, then you don't walk awake with God. And that makes you vulnerable, my friend. The lions are on the prowl and you must be vigilant. For you, that starts by letting go of your past. Always remember, the vigilant mind is a mind unburdened."

Jed nodded but said nothing, the conversation a little too honest and him a little too winded to want to continue. So they ran in silence for the remainder of the loop. When they got back to the training complex, they walked the access road together for their cooldown, Jed's mind turning furiously over the things this man had shared. They felt right but also nearly impossible.

"What time tomorrow?" Jed asked.

"0600," the Colonel said.

"See you then."

Jericho nodded and they parted company, with Jed heading into the barracks and the Colonel going to his living quarters—which Jed had not seen but understood from Eli was a fully decked-out apartment above the barracks sleeping hall. Once inside, Jed showered, brushed his teeth, and dressed for the evening. Turns out he did have one 5.11 polo-style shirt to wear with his jeans, so at least he didn't have to show up in a T-shirt for the date.

It's not a date, bro, the SEAL in the mirror reminded him as he combed his hair before walking out into the cool night air.

"Right, it's not a date," he said, still content to argue with himself. "It's just two people who fought demons side by side, nearly died in the process, and are now having drinks together. All perfectly normal stuff."

CHAPTER TWENTY-SIX

Jed arrived early but decided to sit in his truck in the parking lot until eight. Instead of obsessing over what he was going to say to Perez—which would have been normal for him—he couldn't stop replaying the conversation he'd had with the Colonel. And that irritated him because it proved the man's point. The Colonel was a man of few words, but the ones he spoke hit "on time, on target" with deadly accuracy. Critiquing his past and thinking about what he'd do over was Jed's modus operandi and somehow he'd become blind to it.

Is regret the only lens through which I know how to view my life? I've got to try to unburden myself. David seems to be moving on . . . why can't I?

Movement outside the driver's window snapped him out of his ruminations. He turned his head to see Detective Perez walking up. He smiled, opened the door, and climbed out to greet her.

"You know this place is not like a Sonic," she said with a playful smile. "They don't bring your drinks to the car. You actually have to go inside."

He chuckled and glanced at his watch. "Well, you know, I wouldn't want you to think I was too eager."

"Too bad I caught you waiting in your truck then," she said, laughing and stepping in for a friendly hug, which he reciprocated.

She was shorter than he remembered and, feeling her torso against his chest, a tad softer than he'd imagined. Of course, he had been hanging out with Bex and Nisha for weeks now, so his perceptions were skewed.

"You sure did heal up nicely," she said, stepping back from the embrace. "In fact, I'd argue you're even slightly more handsome now, after having your face pummeled, than you were before."

"Hey, look at that, you're a detective *and* a comedian," he said, playing it up. Man, did he love it when girls could dish it out with the best of them. "All right, your turn. Lemme see that belly scar. . . . I know you're dying to show it to me."

"Wow, folks, he hasn't even gotten me liquored up yet and already he's trying to get my shirt off," she said as if addressing the crowd in an invisible comedy club.

This comment really got him laughing.

If things keep on like this, it's definitely going to be a fun night, he thought and realized that all the tension and awkwardness he'd been worried about simply weren't there.

"I am a door kicker," he said. "Direct action is what I do."

"Too bad, because we've got to save something for later," she said with a grin and gave his sleeve a tug to get him moving toward the restaurant entrance.

"Would you like a table inside or outside?" the hostess asked as they checked in.

Jed looked at Perez. "Your call."

"I brought a jacket. You're the one in short sleeves. So it's up to you."

"I say outside," he said. "I'm hot-blooded that way."

"Okay," the young woman said with a smile. "Follow me."

The hostess sat them on the rooftop patio at a table for two with a great view of downtown. Despite the cool evening, the outside dining area was mostly full. Jed pulled out Perez's seat and then sat down opposite her. Their server arrived before either of them managed to squeeze a word in.

"I'm Stuart and I'll be your server tonight," a bearded Xennial with a man bun said as he stepped up with menus. "Can I get you a craft cocktail or something to drink?"

"I'll have a No New Friends," Perez said without looking at the menu.

"Not your first time here, I presume?" the waiter said.

She shook her head. "Definitely not."

"Excellent choice, and you, sir?" the waiter said, turning to Jed.

"I'm usually a beer guy, but I guess I'll try what she's having . . . unless it's served with an umbrella and a cherry."

"No, certainly not. It's rye bourbon with aperol, cynar, orgeat, and bitters," Stuart said.

"I have no idea what most of those things are, but okay, I guess I'll give it a try."

"Two No New Friends coming right up," the server said and departed with a cordial nod.

"You really don't get out much, do you?" Perez said with a grin.

"No, not really . . ."

"It's good to see you, Jed," she said, leaning in to rest on her elbows.

"You too, Detective," he replied, maybe a tad too quickly.

"You know you can call me Maria."

"All right, Maria," he said, glad to finally get that over with.

"I was nervous to call you," she said, shifting her gaze away from him and out to the downtown skyline. "Considering everything that happened and all."

"Yeah, but I'm glad you did. It's a strange world we live in," he said, deciding that maybe he'd walk Alice right up to the proverbial bunny hole and see if she took the leap with him.

She looked back at him. "I wasn't sure if my being a little older than you might be a turnoff," she said coyly.

"I didn't really think about it," he said, laughing off the comment. He knew some women were more self-conscious about their age than others, but he found her interesting, attractive, and funny. She might have beaten him to mile marker forty, but what was *not* to like about Maria?

"Good to know," she replied with a nervous laugh.

"Guess I thought we were probably around the same age," he added, hoping to put her at ease.

She smiled. "I know this is probably going to sound weird, but I think maybe you and I were destined to meet."

"What do you mean?"

"Well, I was having coffee with Rachel Yarnell, and your name happened to come up in the conversation. I don't know . . . Just from the things she shared, it seems like you and I have a lot in common."

A flash of heat ran up his neck.

She had coffee with Rachel? When did that happen, and what sort of things did Rachel share?

"You had coffee with Rachel?" he said, barely able to get the words out.

"Yeah, I was concerned about Sarah Beth—well, maybe more curious than concerned. You never know how something like that will hit a kid, but in general they seem pretty resilient. So I followed up with Rachel directly and she suggested we meet up and talk. I'm so glad that Sarah Beth has been able to move on and is in a better place, both emotionally and spiritually. Don't you agree?"

Jed fidgeted in his chair.

Perez smiled, but when Jed didn't say anything, she raised an eyebrow at him. "You've got nothing to say on the matter?"

"Well, I just—" He stopped midsentence as their server returned with their bourbon cocktails.

"Two No New Friends," Stuart said, setting a drink in front of each of them. "Can I get you something from the kitchen?"

Jed looked at Perez, letting her decide on the question of dinner.

"I'll have the hanger steak," she said.

"Excellent choice, and you, sir?"

Jed's stomach growled at the question. "I haven't had a chance to look at the menu, but you guys wouldn't happen to make a decent burger, would you?"

Stuart smiled. "The best in town. Double stack with cheese, onions, tomatoes, pickle, homemade aioli, and french fries."

"I'll take that, but hold the pickle and give me a double order of fries."

Stuart nodded. "I'll get your order in right away,"

Jed turned back to look at Perez, who was already holding up her cocktail glass for a toast.

"To new friendships," she said.

"To new friendships," he echoed and clinked her glass, the irony of her choice of words juxtaposed against the name of their cocktails not lost on him.

He took a sip to consummate the sentiment and was surprised how nice the drink was. "This is really good," he said and took a second sip. "I've never tasted anything quite like it."

"That's kinda the point of tonight," she said.

He met her gaze and suddenly wondered exactly what she thought was going to happen. Yes, he was interested in getting to know her better, but he'd hoped she wasn't looking at this as a prequel to a hookup. One-night stands had never been his thing, and neither was moving a relationship along at warp speed. Now that he was rediscovering his faith, those things were more important to him than ever. She must have picked up on his reticence, because she reached out and patted the back of his hand.

"I'm just messing with you, Jed," she said with a self-deprecating smile.

"Sure, yeah, I know," he said, smiling back. "So . . . you had coffee with Rachel?"

She leaned back in her chair and shifted her angle to uncross and then recross her legs the other direction. "It was good for us to connect. I needed it for my own peace of mind—to hear that Sarah Beth was doing okay—but I also think Rachel needed it too."

"What do you mean?"

"With David's new job and him traveling, and Sarah Beth attending boarding school, I think Rachel is feeling alone. I think it was nice for her to have another woman to talk to and confide in."

Jed resisted the urge to screw up his face at what he was hearing. Everything Perez was saying simply didn't jibe with the Rachel he knew. The Rachel *he* knew was a fiercely private person. She wasn't insecure or needy and hated nothing more than to sit around and gossip. The idea that she'd gush to Perez, a literal stranger, over coffee just didn't compute . . .

Dude, the Rachel you knew was a teenage girl. What do you know about Rachel the woman? Absolutely nothing. You've been out of her life for more than fifteen years, the voice in his head argued back. *You have no idea what she needs or is feeling right now.*

"Did I say something wrong?" Perez asked, leaning forward with a sudden look of concern.

"No," he said, couching his reply. "I'm just surprised to hear you two hit it off so well, having just met and all."

"You shouldn't be. After all, Rachel and I are very much alike. We both grew up tomboys. We're both confident, independent women with a strong faith. And apparently we even have the same taste in men," Perez said through a laugh. "Strike that, sorry. That's the alcohol talking."

Jed glanced at her cocktail glass and saw that she'd completely drained it. When he looked back up at her face, he could see that she was embarrassed. Thankfully, their waiter arrived to interrupt the awkward moment.

"Can I get you another cocktail?" he asked Perez.

"Yes, thank you," she said.

"Sir?" Stuart asked, despite Jed's glass still being two-thirds full.

"I'm good for now, thanks."

"Your food should be out momentarily," the server said and then departed, taking Perez's empty rocks glass with him.

Jed looked at Perez, who'd shifted her gaze out to the city skyline. Looking at her in profile, he had to admit she was striking—high cheekbones, bronze skin, chestnut-colored hair, and full lips—all things he'd somehow not noticed when he'd been dealing with her professionally.

The Colonel's advice suddenly came back to him now. Maybe the salty drill instructor had been right. Maybe Jed was falling into the same old paradigm trap he always did, living in the past and letting his regrets about abandoning Rachel drive his interaction with this woman here and now. Perez—no, *Maria*—was making an effort with him. Sure, maybe she was being a little too aggressive for his taste, but who was he to judge? He'd not had a meaningful romantic relationship since he'd run away from home and joined the Navy. Maybe it was time he opened himself up to a woman. If Rachel trusted Maria, then why shouldn't he? After all, she had literally taken a bullet for him. He knew what kind of person that made her.

"I'm really glad to hear that you and Rachel hit it off," Jed said, trying for a reset. "It's great that you care about Sarah Beth and that you were there for her as a sounding board. Rachel and I used to be close, but that was before I joined the Navy. We didn't really stay in touch over the years."

Maria turned and met his gaze. "Yeah, I pieced together as much."

"Did you really talk about *me*?" he said with a theatrical cringe.

"All good stuff, I promise," she said.

He shook his head. "Great, that's exactly what I need—you having a free pass with Rachel to learn all my secrets from the past."

"Don't worry. Your secrets are safe with me," she said and crossed her heart.

Their food arrived a few minutes later along with Maria's second cocktail. The burger was out-of-this-world delicious, and the exclamation point came when Maria carved him off a quarter of her hanger steak after claiming she was too full to go on. She didn't, however, have any problem polishing off a third cocktail while Jed painstakingly nursed his first, quenching his actual thirst with three glasses of water. He'd never been much of a drinker, and he had zero tolerance for drunk driving. Seeing how tipsy the pretty detective across the table was becoming, he decided he was now responsible for getting her home safely.

"So, Jed," she said, leaning hard on her elbows and looking up at him. "I know you're some sort of task force–type operator from all that happened with the Yarnells and then the attacks here in town. Tell me about this supersecret outfit you work for."

He recoiled a little at the question. Yes, he knew it was the alcohol talking, but still. "Ah, c'mon, Maria, you of all people know I can't talk about that. It would be like me asking you about an active case . . ."

"I know," she said, smiling at him from under drunken eyelids. "But being in law enforcement and living here in Nashville, I've heard so many rumors about Trinity Loop. It would be nice to know what's going on in my own backyard. You know what I'm saying?"

"Sure, I get it, but there's really not that much to tell. We're like Triple Canopy, except we specialize in training and readiness."

"Oh, Jed, we both know that's horse pucky. Training and readiness contractors don't stop terrorist attacks on Catholic churches in downtown Nashville before the FBI and metro PD know about it. I was there, remember? And I was at the Yarnells' house the night those men tried to take Sarah Beth. Jed, please, I need to know what's going on."

He swallowed and fixed her with a hard gaze. "In that case, I'm going to answer your question with a question—what do *you* think is going on?"

"A battle for the soul of mankind," she said, slurring *mankind* as she did.

He slow-nodded. "I think that about sums it up, Maria."

"In that case, I want in," she said, holding his eyes.

"You what?"

"I want in," she said again with conviction, sobering up a little as she spoke the words.

"It doesn't work that way. You have to be recruited."

"Then recruit me."

He blew a snort of air out his nose. "Sorry, recruitment ain't my department."

"Then can you at least throw in a good word for me?"

He thought about it for a moment before answering. "Okay. I think I can do that."

She reached out and squeezed his hand. "Thank you."

"You're welcome."

"I have to go to the bathroom," she said.

"Thanks for sharing . . . or do you want my help with that too?" he said, suppressing a grin.

"Nah, I should be able to handle this one by myself," she said, and they both laughed as she scooted her chair back from the table.

What have I gotten myself into? he thought as he watched her walk away and disappear into the restaurant. *Hopefully something good.*

In her absence, he took the opportunity to close out the check and preempt her fighting him over the bill. And in doing so, he also stymied her from ordering another drink—a drink she probably didn't need.

When she did return, it was with narrowed eyes.

"I just tried to pay the bill on my way back from the ladies' room, and Stuart said you already settled the tab," she said, standing at the tableside with her hands on her hips.

"Guilty as charged," he said and stood up.

Her expression softened. "Thank you, Jed."

"You're welcome," he replied with a little bow of the head. "How about I give you a lift home? I think you've probably had too much to be driving."

"I agree," she said and stuck out her elbow to him.

He took it and escorted her to his truck, where he opened the passenger door for her.

"Truck's got a lift, so watch your footing and use that nerf bar to step in," he said.

She slapped his hand away as he tried to help her. "You think I've never climbed into a pickup truck? What kind of girl do you think I am?" Then, under her breath, she murmured, "I've done all kinds of things in pickup trucks. Stuff you don't even want to know about, Jedidiah Johnson."

Grinning, he shut the door behind her.

Gotta love drunken, brutal honesty . . .

He climbed into the driver's seat, put on his seat belt, and started the engine. "Where to?" he said, glancing over at her.

"Just drive. I'll tell you where as we go," she said. "GPS is for losers."

"Roger that," he said with a chuckle.

Drunk Maria was really beginning to crack him up.

As it turned out, she didn't live far. She directed him turn by turn through downtown, then out to the West End and a luxury apartment tower called Twenty & Grand. He pulled into the circular drive in front of the building.

"You gonna have any trouble getting back to your car tomorrow?" he asked, putting the transmission in park.

She shook her head. "I took an Uber to dinner. My car's in the parking garage."

"Oh, smart," he said.

"You gonna walk me to the door?" she asked.

"Absolutely."

He opened the door, climbed out of his seat, and walked around to open the passenger door for her.

"Thank you," she said as he helped her down. She held his arm as he walked her to the glass doors through which he could see a well-appointed lobby. Apparently Nashville detectives did pretty well financially.

She stopped, turned, and looked up at him expectantly. "Would you like to come up?"

"Maybe next time," he said.

She nodded. "I had fun, Jed."

"Me too."

"Thanks for dinner," she said and tipped on her toes, ostensibly to give him a peck on the cheek, but she still wasn't tall enough. He knew this well from experience, however, and bent at the waist so she could reach.

"You're welcome," he said and turned to leave. When he got halfway to his truck, he stopped and turned back to look at her. "You know, we're having a team barbecue tomorrow night at the Yarnells' house. Do you wanna be my plus one? I'm sure Sarah Beth would love to see you."

A broad smile lit up her face. "Are you sure? I wouldn't want to impose."

He shrugged. "I'm not worried about that. You and Rachel already get along, and you and I . . . obviously get along. Plus, it would give you a chance to meet some of the other folks on the team to, you know, see if there's a possible fit for you."

"Oh, Jed, that's really wonderful of you. Thank you."

"Yeah, don't mention it."

"What time?"

"How about I pick you up here at four thirty. The barbecue starts at five thirty, but we're gonna need to allow time to get you through security."

"Hold on—this is happening on Trinity Loop campus?" she said, her eyes going wide.

"Yeah, why? Is that a problem?" he said.

"No, no, not at all," she said. "It's just I've never been invited on campus and I've always wanted to see it, so this is great. Thank you, Jed."

"Yeah, I'm sure everyone's going to be excited to meet the woman who took a bullet for me."

"That reminds me," she said with a coy smile, looking down at her belly. "Since you're leaving, you're not going to get to see my scar."

"Another time, maybe," he said with a boyish grin back at her.

"Third date it is," she said and winked, and Jed shook his head with a blush, the implication uncomfortable.

She waved goodbye and he watched her disappear into the elevator before climbing into his truck. Before pulling away, he synced his phone to the Silverado's infotainment center and cued up his country music favorites playlist. He was proud of himself for tonight, taking a chance and not letting his regrets screw up another potential relationship before it even got started. Smiling large, he drove away, tapping his thumbs on the steering wheel and singing along with John Rich as he belted out the words to "I Thought You'd Never Ask."

Tonight had been an unexpected blessing.

He couldn't wait to see what tomorrow would bring.

CHAPTER
TWENTY-SEVEN

Jed shifted his truck's transmission into park, took his foot off the brake, and sighed. Nothing, it seemed, was ever easy.

"I'm sorry, Mr. Johnson, but your guest is not on the approved entry list for today," the security guard, Sanderson, said.

"But I submitted pre-authorization paperwork this morning," he said.

"I believe you, but it's Sunday, which means a reduced staff, and so it's likely they weren't able to complete the vetting process. The first time takes the longest because they have to run a background check as well as other kinds of checks."

"What are our options?" Jed said, trying to keep his tone professional.

Sanderson shook his head. "Your best bet is to check back tomorrow, preferably after lunch. By then, there's a good chance her paperwork will be through the system."

"But that doesn't do us any good. The barbecue is tonight."

"I understand that, but these safety protocols are in place for a reason."

"It's okay, Jed," Maria said from the passenger seat. "I can just come back another time."

"No, it's not okay, because coming back another time defeats the purpose." He grabbed his mobile phone from where it was sitting in the center console cup holder and, while staring at Sanderson, called Ben.

The Shepherd commander picked up on the second ring. "Morvant . . ."

"Hey, Ben, it's Jedidiah calling."

"Hey, Jed, how are you?"

"Frustrated," he said, no longer trying to hide his irritation. "I'm at the front gate and trying to get my guest for the barbecue cleared through security, and she's not on the approved visitor list."

"When did you submit the paperwork?"

"This morning."

"Well, that explains it. Sunday is a day of rest, Jed. You know that. The offices are closed; only a skeleton crew is on duty today."

"I know, but I just was hoping we could get her cleared so she could come to the barbecue."

"Who's your guest, Jed?"

"Detective Perez of Nashville PD," Jed said, glancing at Maria with a smile. "You remember her from a few weeks back. She was in charge of—"

"The Yarnell kidnapping," Ben said, cutting Jed off. "Yes, I remember Detective Perez."

Jed picked up something in Ben's voice—an uneasy sentiment he couldn't quite place. When he didn't add anything else, Jed felt compelled to prompt him. "So is there anything you can do to help grease the skids here, boss?"

Silence hung on the line for a long moment before the Shepherd commander said, "Let me make a couple calls and get back to you."

"Thank you, sir," Jed said and the line went dead.

Jed glanced in the rearview mirror to see if a queue was forming while he blockaded the checkpoint with his obstinance. Thankfully, nobody else had pulled up behind him.

"I don't want to cause any trouble. It was a last-minute idea, and it didn't work out. Really, it's fine, Jed. We should just go," Maria said, reaching out to give his forearm a squeeze.

"Let's give Ben a chance to work his magic first. If he still says no, then we'll abort and try again some other time. Okay?"

"Okay."

Jed turned to look at Sanderson, but he'd gone back inside the guard shack while Jed was talking to Maria.

"How's your head?" Jed asked, swiveling back to her.

"My head? Fine . . . ," she said, her tone suggesting she didn't catch his non sequitur. But before he could explain, she made the connection. "Ah, you mean how's my hangover?"

He nodded with a grin.

"I don't get hangovers," she said proudly.

"What? Seriously?"

"Yeah, seriously. I don't get hangovers. Maybe if I polished off a whole bottle of bourbon, I would, but a few stiff drinks like last night . . . I don't feel anything the next day."

He was about to comment when he heard the guard shack door open and Sanderson stepped outside.

"Here's her guest pass," Sanderson said, handing Jed a printed single-day pass in a badge holder on a lanyard. Then the guard passed him Maria's leather bifold with her police ID and badge, which she'd handed over on arrival.

"Thank you," Jed said, accepting both items and passing them to Maria.

"Ma'am, you'll need to wear that lanyard at all times while you're on the property," Sanderson said, looking past Jed.

"Understood," she said and slipped the lanyard over her head. "Thank you, and you have a nice night."

"You as well," Sanderson said as he stepped away from Jed's truck and raised the gate.

Jed nodded at Sanderson, put his transmission in drive, and pulled through the checkpoint and onto campus. Earlier that day, he'd done a test drive to find the Yarnells' house so he'd know where it was. It had taken him by surprise when he'd learned that Rachel and David had moved to campus housing. Not because it didn't make sense—it made perfect sense given the events with Sarah Beth and the attack at their house in Nashville—but because he'd only learned of it on the flight home from Iraq, and then even Maria had mentioned it at dinner. They'd been on the campus for weeks and David hadn't bothered to tell him they'd moved.

"Have you been to Rachel and David's new house?" Maria asked, seemingly reading his thoughts.

He shook his head.

"Can't blame them for moving, after everything that happened and all," she said.

"Yeah . . ."

"Do you know if Sarah Beth is going to be at the barbecue tonight?" she asked as he turned off Trinity Loop Road and onto the spur that led to a little neighborhood of single-family houses.

"I would assume so, but I don't know for sure. I hope so."

"It would be nice if she was. You and the girl certainly have a connection."

He glanced sideways at her. "Why do you say that?"

"I mean, it's obvious, Jed. You saved her life . . . twice."

"Yeah," he said, nodding slowly. "You know, I didn't think to ask you this last night, but what did you ever find out about the men that tried to abduct Sarah Beth the night you got shot?"

"Disappointingly little. None of them had prior criminal records and I couldn't find any professional or social ties between them. It was almost as if somebody grabbed a bunch of random guys out of a bar, gave them guns and cash to abduct a girl, and turned them loose. But I should probably be asking you the same question. You're the one who works for the spooky task force."

"It's above my pay grade. Besides, I'm not the detective here," he said with a frown, wishing her answer had a little more meat on the bones.

Why was it that Nashville PD had been so impotent on Sarah Beth's case? Did Maria know more than she was letting on? Had internal affairs ever investigated Corporal Alexander's appearance at the terrorist attack at the Cathedral of the Incarnation, or had his death that day closed the case, making an investigation moot?

He still had plenty of questions, but he'd been letting them simmer on the back burner. With Jericho Basic and everything else going on, he'd not had a chance to dig into any of them. The fact that the Dark Ones had infiltrated at least one of their own into Nashville PD was disturbing. Were there others? And if so, how many?

"You want to hear something kinda sad?" Maria said, suddenly sounding weary. "Just because you have a badge and the title *detective* in front of your name doesn't mean you're given special treatment. Sure, this badge opens more doors than a private investigator's license, but you'd be surprised how many doors it doesn't. I try to keep my chin up, but truth is, I'm just a little fish in a big pond."

Jed parked along the curb in front of the Yarnells' house as the driveway was already full. He killed the engine and turned to look at Maria. Half her face was bathed in sunlight, the other half dark with shadow.

He felt a sudden pull from her and the desire to kiss her swelled inside him. "Your eyes are . . . beautiful."

She demurred. "They're nothing special—just brown, like five billion other people's eyes."

"That's not true," he said, noting how the sunlight revealed complex bands of honey, copper, and rich cognac on the brightly lit side. "I see so much color . . . so much light."

She abruptly looked away and grabbed the door handle. "Ready to head in?"

"Sure," he said, wondering what he'd said that upset her.

He exited the truck, didn't bother locking the doors, and walked around to meet her on the passenger side. She smiled at him and he smiled back, but she did not reach for his elbow or hand as they headed for the front door. Country music and a happy ruckus could be heard emanating from the back of the house. A waft of charbroiled meat hit Jed's nostrils an instant later and his mouth immediately began to salivate.

"Maybe we should just walk around to the back?" Maria said, stealing his thought. "Sounds like this party has already gotten started."

"Agreed."

"Smells like burgers and brats," she said and with a grin added, "You gonna be all right having burgers two nights in a row?"

"I could eat a burger every night and never get sick of them."

"Why does that not surprise me?"

Rounding the corner of the house, a scene right out of a movie greeted them—the perfect backyard barbecue, with a handful of kids running around in the yard and clusters of smiling men and women, drinks in hand, chatting on a wide patio. In synchronized unison, the assembled adults turned to greet Jed and his plus one. He caught flashes of surprise on most faces, but the looks disappeared almost instantly, replaced by welcoming smiles.

"Hey, Jed," David said, walking up to meet them.

"Hey, David," he said.

"Detective Perez, so nice of you to come," David said, sticking out his hand to greet Maria. "Jed phoned earlier and mentioned you might be coming. Welcome to our *new* home."

"Thank you," she said, shaking his hand. "It's a very nice house you have here."

"Oh, thanks. It's quite an upgrade from what we had before," David said with a chuckle. "Anyway, make yourself at home. Rachel is in the kitchen with Sarah Beth if you want to say hi."

"That would be lovely," Maria said, and then she turned to Jed and smiled up at him.

"She insisted on coming home for this. She didn't want to miss the opportunity to see Uncle Jed," David said happily, without any of the insecurity or jealousy Jed had read from his thoughts on the plane.

"Let's go say hello," Maria said, gesturing with a turn of her head toward the back patio door.

"Sure," Jed said and nodded at David.

On his way across the patio, Jed traded hellos with Eli and Grayson and waved at the trio of his fellow rookies—Hyeon, Bex, and Nisha—who chatted together in a tight group. Jed's gaze lingered on Nisha, who was wearing a vacant smile and staring at Maria instead of him. A tingle chased down his spine as he walked through the open patio door and into the kitchen. Inside, Rachel and Sarah Beth stood together at a food-prep island, placing cut strawberry wedges on top of what he guessed to be a shortcake. The instant Sarah Beth saw him, her face lit up and she ran to him.

"Hey there, partner," he said as she threw herself at him, more like a five-year-old, and wrapped her arms around his midsection.

"It's so good to see you, Uncle Jed," she said. "I missed you."

"Ditto," he said, hugging her back.

Then, as if a bug had just flown into her mouth, Sarah Beth's expression soured when her gaze ticked to Maria, who was standing to his right.

"Hi, Sarah Beth. I'm not sure if you remember me?" Maria said. "My name is Detective Perez."

"I remember you," Sarah Beth said with what Jed recognized as *This is the smile I use with grown-ups I don't like.*

Maria stuck out her hand to Sarah Beth, who looked at it for a long second before finally shaking it.

"Maria, we're so glad you could make it," Rachel said warmly. Unlike her daughter, Rachel seemed relaxed and unperturbed by Maria's arrival. The two women hugged before Rachel finally turned to acknowledge him. "Hi, Jed."

"Hi," he said, then quickly shifted his gaze to the strawberry shortcake and added, "Wow, check out that cake. Looks delicious."

"C'mon, Uncle Jed," Sarah Beth said, grabbing him by the hand and tugging. "I want to show you my new room."

"I don't think so," Rachel said sharply. "We don't have strange men in our bedrooms, Sarah Beth." She shook her head but tried to smile at Jed as she rolled her eyes.

"He's not a strange man—he's Uncle Jed," Sarah Beth protested with a child's innocence.

"Look, Sarah Beth—" Rachel said, now avoiding looking at Jed.

"Your mom's absolutely right," he said to cut off the awkward moment. "Let's go out back and we can catch up, okay?"

"Okay," she grumbled. "I had some things I wanted to show you. Growing up sucks."

"Watch your language, young lady," Rachel scolded but shot Jed a grateful look.

"You have no idea," Jed said with a laugh. He let Sarah Beth lead him to the back door, and as he did, he turned to Maria and gave her a *Whatcha gonna do* shrug.

Outside, Sarah Beth made a beeline for the far corner of the yard where a small, round cement table—more decorative than functional, Jed thought—sat unused with untrimmed grass growing thick at the base. With some difficulty he folded himself onto the uncomfortable round bench across from her, his knees almost to his chest.

"Is everything okay?" he said.

"Yes," she said, but then without warning her eyes rimmed with tears. "Actually, no . . ." She glanced around to see if anyone might notice she was crying, but no one seemed to be paying any attention to them.

"What's going on? Do you want to talk about it?" he asked, but as the words flowed from his lips, something unexpected happened.

In his mind, he reached out to her and images flooded his consciousness like a runaway train practically barreling him over. They were memories . . . not his own. Memories through Sarah Beth's eyes at what he knew was St. George's Academy. And even though he'd never been there before, an uncanny familiarity came *with* the memories—as if somehow her familiarity transferred itself to him.

A group of girls staring, whispering, and laughing at him from a neighboring lunch table.

A woman teacher embarrassing him in front of the class.

Corbin giving him a hug at his locker, while tears streamed down his cheeks . . .

These were Sarah Beth's memories but they felt like his own.

What are you doing, Uncle Jed? she scolded. But her lips weren't moving. *I didn't invite you in . . .*

"I . . . I didn't mean to," he said, recoiling back into himself.

"Don't ever do that again without permission," she chastised, talking aloud to him this time.

"I'm sorry, Sarah Beth. I didn't mean to," he said, feeling terrible about it.

"It's okay." After a moment, the serious look on her face melted away. "I didn't know you could do that."

"I didn't either," he said. "Something weird is going on with me lately."

"You're turning into a Watcher!" she said in a hushed tone, tinged with excitement. "Very few grown-ups can do it."

"Yeah, I don't know about that . . ."

She nodded as if she'd made up her mind on the matter.

"So . . . St. George's hasn't been all unicorns and rainbows for you, huh?" he said, changing the subject back to her.

She looked down at her lap. "I thought they'd all be nice to me, you know, because they're like me. I don't get it, Uncle Jed."

He nodded, his heart breaking at this unexpected turn of events.

"Corbin says it's because they're jealous of me. She said most of the kids there are way behind what I can do. And this one teacher, she really hates me for some reason and always tries to make me look stupid in front of the other kids, but I have no idea why."

"But Corbin is looking out for you?"

"Yeah, if she wasn't there, I don't know what I'd do. Unfortunately, she's been gone for a little while . . ." She gave him a knowing smile, and he felt her rather than heard her add, *And we both know where and why.* "I hate it when she's not around. Not the school, I mean, just . . . I don't know."

Jed smiled at her. The problems she was having seemed to be everyday sort of middle school problems, actually. In his mind, that was probably a good thing.

"And there's nobody else you've made friends with?"

"Not really . . . Well, there is this one boy, Max. He's in my grade and he's pretty cool. I mean, he's not as good at Watcher stuff as me, but he can definitely do things. He doesn't care if I'm better at stuff like some kids—says it's not a competition. We snapchat all the time."

"Hold on—they let you use your phones in class?"

"No, silly, *Watcher snapchat,* like what we just did. That's what we call it at St. George's."

"And all the kids can do it?"

She laughed at this. "Not even close. That's kind of the problem. Most kids there can't do much. That's why they're jealous. Some kids act like they can do more than they can, and other kids who can do a lot hide it. It's weird. Is that what it's like for you with the Shepherds?"

He thought about the question and the real-world parallels for a moment before answering, "You know what? Yeah . . . it kinda is."

She nodded, the answer seeming to please her. "You wanna try again?" she said, perking up.

"Try what again?"

"Watcher snapchatting," she said. "Only this time with my permission."

"Sure, I guess, but like I said, I'm not really sure how I did it. I don't have control over it like you do."

"That's okay. I'll teach you," she said happily, apparently loving their role reversal. "You just sort of reach out and look for—"

"For an invisible thread?" he asked, interrupting her.

"Exactly . . . when you find the invisible thread, you just follow it to the end and you'll run into a bubble kind of thing. That's, like, the boundary," she said. "Last time you went inside, all the way into my private thoughts. This time just kinda stop when you find me. Otherwise it's rude."

"Okay," he said, chuckling at being schooled by a kid. He closed his eyes and, like a blind man in the dark, felt around until he found the invisible thread.

Is that you, Sarah Beth? he asked in his mind.

Yep, it's me, she said.

Am I doing this or are you doing it? he asked, unable to identify the locus of control.

We're both doing it.

Is this what it's like when you and Corbin connect?

Yeah, kinda, she said. *Everybody's mind is different.*

It's weird . . . because I can't see . . . but I can kind of see at the same time, he said.

I know, totally! And it's even weirder when you do it with your eyes open.

He opened his eyes and everything mixed together into a weird dreamlike state. Vertigo washed over him and he quickly shut them again. *I don't like that. Maybe with more practice I'll get used to it.*

Yeah, it definitely takes practice, she said.

They didn't talk for a few seconds; then a question came to him, which she answered before he could even ask it.

Because I don't trust Detective Perez, she said.

Why? She tried to save you that night. She took a bullet for us, remember?

Did she? she came back. *I'm not so sure.*

What? he said, confused, but a voice outside gave him a start and he slurped back into his normal headspace.

"Jed . . . Sarah Beth . . . ," Rachel called from the deck on the back of the house. "Y'all are going to miss dinner if you gab much longer. I know Jed must be hungry because I can hear his stomach growling from over here."

He lifted a hand in acknowledgment and despite the distance could see her smiling.

The awkward moment from earlier when she'd referred to him as a *strange man* was seemingly water under the bridge now. But he got it. Boundaries with kids, especially young women, were paramount.

"Your mom makes a good point, Sarah Beth. Besides, I don't want to miss getting a piece of that strawberry shortcake. It's one of my favorite desserts."

"I know. Mom told me," Sarah Beth said with a smile. "That's why we made it."

He glanced from Sarah Beth to Rachel, but she'd already turned to go back in the house. "Really? That was nice of you."

Sarah Beth shrugged. "You did save my life," she said, popping to her feet.

Jed laughed, contorted himself off the awkward round bench, and followed her to the back patio, where the majority of the gang was congregated. He headed to where David was working the grill while he entertained the crowd with a stage-worthy comedic routine. Seeing David flipping burgers, turning dogs, and cracking jokes struck a discordant chord. Jed was the team leader, but tonight David was apparently the life of the party. In high school David had been the funny one—a helium balloon of charisma to Jed's paperweight of dutiful earnestness—and that old feeling came back to Jed like indigestion after a delicious meal.

Grayson sidled up beside him as he joined the group. "Dude, I didn't realize David was so hilarious. His Jim Gaffigan impersonation is legit."

"Yeah, he's always had a talent for impersonations. You should hear his Eddie Murphy," Jed said, putting on a smile.

"There's the big guy," David called, his gaze locking onto Jed. "Grab a plate, buddy, I've got a couple burgers and brats with your name on them here."

Jed nodded and turned to Grayson. "I am starving. Lemme grab some food and circle back."

"Go, dude, before they're all gone," Grayson said through a laugh.

Nodding to various teammates on the way, Jed headed over to the grill.

"Did you have a good catch-up with Sarah Beth?" David asked as he loaded a doubled-up paper plate with two burger patties and two brats for Jed.

"Yeah, it was good. She told me all about St. George's. She seems happy there. I think you definitely made the right call with enrolling her and moving on base," Jed said, and when David didn't immediately answer, he added, "About earlier . . . if the whole 'Uncle Jed' thing makes you and Rachel uncomfortable . . ."

"I think it's great," David said, meeting his eyes. "I'm glad you're back in our lives."

"Oh . . . yeah, me too," he said, unconvincingly.

"You know, Jed, when Sarah Beth was born, Rachel and I talked about—well, fought about, actually—asking you to be her godparent. Obviously the invitation was never extended, but as far as I'm concerned, the way Sarah Beth has taken to you, it's proof that she needs an 'Uncle Jed' in her life."

Jed could scarcely believe the words coming out of David's mouth. He nodded, unsure what to say as he remembered the shock and angst he'd felt upon getting Sarah Beth's birth announcement all those years ago—a birth announcement he'd received secondhand, when his parents had forwarded theirs to him in Virginia Beach in a resounding statement.

"Rachel's going to take a little while to come around," David said. Then, straight from the dude-friendship handbook, he simply added, "But from my perspective, we're all good, Jed."

Jed nodded and quickly cobbled together a complimentary response. "Sarah Beth's lucky to have parents like you and Rachel. She's got a good head on her shoulders, David. She's full of life and light, and she's going to be an amazing Watcher. You should be very proud."

"We are," David said with a comfortable, knowing smile. Then, turning to look at the condiment table, he added, "The ketchup and chips and the like are over there. And there's a couple of Igloo coolers with drinks. Feel free, obviously, to help yourself to whatever you want."

"Thanks," Jed said and wandered off, wondering why he felt annoyed despite David's genuine and gracious attempt at reconciliation.

Upon reaching the picnic table covered with sides and condiments, he opened a hamburger bun and loaded it up with fixings. Next, he ladled a scoop of yellow potato salad onto his plate, and as he did, his mind shifted back to Colonel Jericho's sage advice:

"To lead in the Shepherds, you need to leave your regrets behind . . ."

Tonight, David had done just that and, in doing so, had proven himself to be more of a leader than Jed. Maybe there was something to Ben pairing them as "cocaptains" of Joshua Bravo after all.

He turned and spied Eli by the drink cooler.

The veteran waved Jed over and, using a Bottle Breacher— a polished .50-caliber shell made into a bottle opener—popped the top off a cold Budweiser longneck. "This Bud's for you," he said with a goofy grin and handed it to Jed.

"Thanks, bro," Jed said, then glancing at the Bottle Breacher, added, "I gotta get me one of them."

Eli slipped the Breacher back into his blue jeans pocket. "Bottlebreacher.com. The company was started by one of your frogman brothers, I believe."

"Cool, I'm definitely checking that out," he said.

"Your date and Ben sure seem to be hitting it off," Eli said with a chuckle, redirecting his gaze to the opposite corner of the deck, where Ben, holding a beer, and Maria, sipping from a glass of white wine, were chatting off by themselves.

"Yeah, I think she's interested in being recruited. After what she's seen, I'm not surprised."

Eli pursed his lips and nodded but didn't say anything.

"What?" Jed said.

"It's nothing . . ."

"Does she rub you the wrong way?"

"Mmm, not really. It's just in my experience, the ones who lobby to be recruited aren't a good fit. I'm sure there are exceptions," Eli said, then, excusing himself, asked, "You seen Grayson around?"

"Yeah, he's over there talking with Carl, I think," Jed said.

"I'll catch ya later, bro."

"Yeah, man."

Jed thought about joining Maria and Ben but instead vectored back to the condiment table to look for tomato slices and mayo, which in his distracted state he'd forgotten. To construct his double burger properly, he had to set his beer and plate down, which he did on an open patch at the edge of the table.

"Man, I should have had you make my burger," Nisha said, walking up beside him. "That looks good."

"You eat hamburgers?" he said, turning to her.

"I'm a Christian, Jed, not Hindu."

"Sorry, of course," he said, shaking his head at his own stupidity. "I'm an idiot."

"It's okay," she said with a chuckle. "You seem a little bit distracted. Is everything okay?"

"Yeah, yeah, everything's great. I'm just starving," he said, disappointed to learn he was so transparent. "Once I get my blood sugar back up, I'll be right as rain."

"Who's your date, by the way?"

"She's not my date," he said and then, digging the hole a little deeper, added, "She's just a friend . . . more of a work colleague, actually."

"Mmm-hmm," Nisha said and did the little spooky lip-curl thing she seemed so fond of. "And what is your 'friend, more of a work colleague's' name?"

"Detective Maria Perez. She worked the Yarnell case for Nashville Metro and was there the night—" He cut himself off. "I probably shouldn't say anything."

Nisha nodded. "Sure, I understand . . . classified and all." She chuckled and shook her head. "Oh, look, here she comes now."

Jed glanced at his plate longingly. He just wanted to eat his stinking burger while it was hot and not have to play these little games, whatever these little games were. Was that too much to ask?

"Hello," Maria said, stepping up beside Jed. In the corner of his eye, he noted how she looked Nisha up and down before adding, "I'm Maria."

"Nisha," the spook turned Shepherd said and shook Maria's outstretched hand.

"Do you work with Jed?" Maria asked.

"I do."

"Oh, that's nice. Jed's not mentioned you."

Nisha smiled. "Well, it's mutual."

Maria parried with a closed-lip smile of her own and shifted her gaze to Jed's cooling burger. "Almost as big as the one you had last night on our date at L.A. Jackson. I wonder which will be better?"

"I'm not picky," he said, hating all the innuendo flying around. "I'm sure I'll like both."

"You're with Nashville PD, I hear?" Nisha said, resetting the conversation.

Jed picked up his burger and took his first bite. His teeth sliced through the bun, lettuce, tomato, and the two charbroiled patties. Heavenly burger grease flooded his mouth along with juice from the tomato, ketchup, and mayo.

"I'm a detective," Maria said. "And what is it that you do?"

"I'm a training instructor. I work mainly with former military personnel who have transitioned to the private sector in contract security, but also with active-duty law enforcement seeking to elevate their tactical and operational skills and proficiency," Nisha said, rattling off the Shepherd party line with practiced efficiency. "Who knows, maybe someday you'll be one of my students."

"I somehow doubt that," Maria said, her frosty tone not lost on Jed.

Mouth full of food, he glanced disapprovingly at her.

"I'm sorry. That came out wrong," Maria said, correcting herself. "What I meant is that my department doesn't have a contract with Trinity, so it would be unlikely that our paths would cross in that capacity."

Nisha nodded and did her lip-curl thing. "Not to worry. I caught your meaning."

Jed was about to attempt to break up their lexical melee when his mobile phone vibrated in his pocket. At the same time, he heard Nisha's mobile vibrate and she glanced down at her own pocket. A quick scan revealed that all the other Shepherds in attendance were being summoned simultaneously. Jed's heart rate picked up and his stomach sank. He knew what this was. He'd lived a short-fuse mobilization a myriad of times with SEAL Team Ten.

With a sigh, he put his burger down and was about to reach for his phone, but Nisha already had hers in her hand. She looked at the screen, then shifted her gaze to Jed, telling him everything he needed to know in a glance.

"It was nice to meet you, Detective," Nisha said, turning back to Maria. "You'll have to excuse me, but it looks like something has come up."

"I understand," the detective said and tapped her own pocket. "Duty calls."

Nisha stepped away as Jed turned his attention to Maria. "I'm so sorry about this. Looks like I'm going to have to run you home."

"It's okay, Jed. I completely understand," she said, but she wasn't looking at him. Instead, her attention was fixed on Morvant, who strode rapidly in their direction.

"I hate to be the party crasher, but it looks like I have to steal Jedidiah," Ben said as he stepped up, still smiling his Sunday-afternoon-barbecue smile.

"I'm her ride tonight," Jed said.

"Not anymore. I've got a car pulling up out front to take Detective Perez home," Ben said, his voice cordial but firm.

It was not a request.

"Understood," Jed said.

"It was good to see you again, Detective," Morvant added, then turned and headed over to caucus with Eli and the other veterans.

"Well, it sounds like I need to be off," Maria said with an uneasy smile. "Will you please give Rachel and David my thanks and say goodbye to Sarah Beth for me?"

"I sure will," he said and started walking her off the patio and around the house.

"You wouldn't happen to know what this is all about, would you?" she asked as they got out of earshot from the rest of the team.

He recoiled inside at the question but tried not to show it. She knew better than to ask such a thing.

Aw, she's probably just curious because she's here and still doesn't know what we really do, he told himself.

"No idea," he said. "But even if I did, I couldn't say."

"Sure, sure. OPSEC, I get it," she said. "I shouldn't have asked."

When he spied a black Tahoe pulling up in front of his pickup truck, he stopped and waved at the driver. The driver, who was looking at them, waved back.

"I have a feeling that's you," he said.

"Yep," she said and leaned in.

He bent so she could give him a peck on the cheek, just like she had last night. But this time she let her lips linger a half second longer and gave him a hug too.

"Be safe," she said when she stepped back from the embrace.

"I will."

Jed watched her jog to the Tahoe. Before she climbed inside, she turned and waved to him. With a tight smile, he raised a hand in goodbye. Then, with lingering warmth from her lips still on his cheek, he turned to rejoin his team and prep for whatever emergency had just spoiled their first party as a team.

As he headed back toward the house, an invisible call made him look up. He spied Sarah Beth, staring down at him from her bedroom window, a strange look on her face.

I think something bad is going to happen, she said in his mind.

That gave him pause. *How do you know?*

I just know.

Do you know what it is? Have you had a vision like you did with the church in Nashville?

No . . .

Okay, well, if you do, reach out to me—you know, Watcher snap-chat—and let me know.

Okay.

He thought about that for a moment and about Rachel's comment earlier.

But if you do, you need to let your parents know. If we're going to stay in touch like this, you need to tell your mom and dad. Your mom knows how it works, he reminded her. *You talk to her this way sometimes, right? But I'm not a fellow student and I'm not your dad, so promise me you'll tell her, Sarah Beth.*

Okay, I promise.

And then she was gone from the window. He felt a heaviness from her he didn't understand, but it seemed important. As he walked back to join his team, he couldn't help but wonder what new dark plot they were up against now.

CHAPTER
TWENTY-EIGHT

Maria Perez paced back and forth on the gray hardwood floors of her apartment in her stocking feet and tried to get control over the myriad of competing emotions she felt. Frustration, anger, confusion, fear, a fair measure of lust, and . . . something else. It was the something else that kept her heart racing and her mind reeling, looking for what she might be missing.

It's that meddlesome little girl. Sarah Beth and her weirdly codependent relationship with Jed is keeping me from succeeding in my mission. I hate that little brat.

She swung a fist at the lamp on the end table beside her modern sofa, instantly grateful when she missed it. Then she sighed and dropped onto the couch, leaning forward and placing her face in her hands. The departure of the Shepherds, especially on such a short fuse, must mean something important—and something Victor would want to know. But what? Could it be related to his operation in Europe? To Woland?

The thought of the bad-boy operator made her flush with excitement, but then a weird sort of regret swept over her as she thought of Jed.

"What is wrong with me?" she asked the empty room, louder than she meant to.

The phone, the special phone she had placed on the coffee table to call Victor and report the movement of the Shepherds, chirped at her, setting her heart racing again and flooding her with a whole new set of emotions, this time fear at the top of the list.

"Hello?"

An uncomfortable pause hung on the line—a tactic Victor used often and seemed to enjoy. Finally, like the encroaching buzz of a swarm of killer bees, he spoke.

"You seem troubled, my dear," he said, and she pictured him popping one of the dates he liked so much into his mouth with those long, bony fingers. "Did you execute poorly?"

"Not at all," she said, keeping her voice steady and her mind as closed as possible. "Things are moving in the direction we want, but the timeline might be slower than anticipated."

"I understand," he said, leaving her to wonder if he knew already or simply wanted to make her squirm.

"I've formed a relationship with Jedidiah Johnson—in fact,

it proved easier than I anticipated." She pictured the reaction of the Indian woman, Nisha, when they'd been introduced on the Yarnells' patio. Maria couldn't read minds, but Nisha's hostile suspicion had been impossible to miss.

"And . . . ," Victor prompted.

"I gained access to Trinity Loop," she said, her voice full of self-congratulation. "Jed invited me to a team barbecue on campus. But the opportunity was cut short when Jed—and his whole team, for that matter—had to leave suddenly."

The pause that followed was agonizing and she finally gave in.

"That's the reason I called you—er, intended to call you before you called me. The Shepherds are mobilizing on short notice. I knew you would want to know and was concerned it might be related to your operation in Europe."

The pause again, but having nothing else to reasonably add, she was forced to endure it.

"You've done well, Maria," he said, and she imagined him staring at his long nails as he spoke. "And yes, this is important information for us to have. Knowing the movements in and out of Trinity Loop is why we so desperately want you inside for us."

She smiled tightly. He seemed genuinely pleased.

"Is there something troubling you?"

"Why?" she asked, not sure what Victor meant.

"I sense there is another obstacle to your mission, but I'm having trouble seeing what it is."

"It's nothing I can't handle," she said, realizing she did have another concern and marveling that he knew before she could even articulate what she'd been thinking about only moments ago. "It's the girl."

"Sarah Beth?" Victor asked.

"Yes," she said. "She was there, at the party. She has a rather unusual bond with Jed and I sense she doesn't like me, but I can handle it."

"Sarah Beth is a growing threat to us," Victor said, and his tone sent a chill down her spine. "It was why I ordered her taken in the first place. We should have killed her instead of trying to turn her. That was a mistake."

"She's been accepted into the Watcher academy."

"Of course she has," he said. "Figure out her homecoming patterns. That's when she'll be vulnerable."

"I will," she said and ran a finger across her lower lip, "and I'll use all the tools at my disposal to put a wedge between her and Jed."

"Yes," he said. "We cannot penetrate the girl's mind. She's being protected and growing stronger by the day."

"Understood," she said and sensed he had more to ask of her.

"I want you to leverage your budding relationship with the new Shepherd to collect intelligence and infiltrate the organization. Prove your worth and worthiness to him . . . Try to get yourself recruited."

"That's my plan. I've dropped hints, and tonight Jed introduced me to his boss, Ben Morvant. That seemed to go well . . ."

"Be very careful around Morvant," Victor hissed. "He has powers like a Watcher and you should lock your mind when you are near him."

"I thought second sight only existed in children," she said, confused.

"There are exceptions to every rule," Victor said with reproach.

"Okay, I'll be careful."

The line went dead.

Discontentment replaced her fear as she silently judged her performance on the call.

Could have gone better . . .

But a little anxiety was nothing a few drinks couldn't cure.

Hopefully she could be back at work soon. Detective work gave her another much needed outlet and kept her mind busy. In the meantime, she would continue to seduce Jed when he returned and work the recruitment angle. Perhaps another coffee with Rachel was in order—not only for this new mission to keep tabs on Sarah Beth, but also to wiggle her way into the web of relationships that seemed to define the organization.

The Shepherds were a tight-knit group.

Like a family . . .

With a heavy sigh, she rose from the sofa.

Family had never been one of her strengths.

PART III

You believe that there is one God. Good! Even

the demons believe that—and shudder.

JAMES 2:19, NIV

And I will execute great vengeance upon them with

furious rebukes; and they shall know that I am the

Lord, when I shall lay my vengeance upon them.

EZEKIEL 25:17, KJV

CHAPTER TWENTY-NINE

Jed jerked awake in his seat.

The turbulence shaking the plane's fuselage was terrifyingly in sync with his nightmare that the plane was on fire and being ripped apart in midflight. He scanned the cabin and, seeing nothing of the sort happening to their plane, collapsed back into his seat with a sigh of relief.

"You all right, big guy?" Johnny said, leaning over from the seat behind Jed. "You've been twitching and making noises like crazy over there. If I didn't know better, I'd have thought you were having a seizure."

"Leave him alone, Johnny," Nisha said from her seat across the aisle. "Count yourself lucky you don't have to battle demons in your sleep."

"I didn't ask for your opinion, Nisha," Johnny snapped.

"That's never stopped me before," she fired back.

Jed was about to say something to break up the tiff, but the pilot's PA announcement that the aircraft was on final approach did the job for him. The tension on the plane was palpable, and Jed understood why. Back-to-back short-fuse ops with limited information had that effect on a team. The intel brief given by Ben and Pastor Mike midflight had been high on stakes but low on details. Watcher intelligence presaged that an attack on the Vatican was imminent, but they had precious little to go on beyond that. Ben hadn't explained why he'd tapped Joshua Bravo to augment their sister unit Joshua Alpha for the op, leaving Jed to wonder if the kill house simulation they'd run in Jericho Basic had something to do with the assignment.

The same kill house simulation I failed miserably . . .

He turned and looked out the porthole window at the Italian countryside as they came in for a landing. As a SEAL, he'd flown through NAS Sigonella dozens of times, but this would be his first time in Rome. The corporate biz jet bobbled a little in the wind just before the wheels chirped, and the fuselage shuddered on touchdown as the pilot engaged the thrust reversers. As the plane finished taxiing, Ben addressed them from the front of the cabin.

"All right, everybody, grab your go bags and let's regroup on the tarmac. I expect our hosts will have transportation ready and waiting. Let's hump the hard cases out of the cargo hold ourselves so we don't have to wait on the ground crew to do it."

"Roger that," Jed said, answering for the group as he got to his feet.

He arched and twisted his back to work the kinks out from the flight, but unlike inside the cavernous C-17 they'd flown on to and from Iraq, he couldn't stand up straight in the fancy Bombardier without hitting his head. After Johnny cleared the aisle, he opened the overhead bin, pulled out his backpack, and moseyed his way to the front of the aircraft. On his way out, he thanked the pilots and then trudged down the airstair to the tarmac.

Just as Ben had said, ground transportation was waiting for them in the form of four Fiat Ducato cargo vans—each labeled Caggiano Construction—and one Alfa Romeo Stelvio SUV.

The passenger door of the sleek Italian SUV opened, and a dude in a suit and sunglasses stepped out. His square-jawed good looks, polished appearance, and confident presence garnered everyone's attention but drew lingering stares from the women in the group.

Ben's face lit up with a brotherly smile and he embraced the Italian with a hug. "Vincenzo, it's been a long time, my friend."

"Too long," the man said with Italian-accented English. "I've missed your light, my brother."

"The feeling is mutual," Ben said and turned to the group. "Let me introduce you to my team. Everybody, this is Vincenzo Rossi. He heads up the Italian office for Shepherds Europe and we are very fortunate to be working with him."

Jed nodded, along with the rest of the team.

"Welcome to Roma," Vincenzo said. "I only wish it was under better circumstances."

"Whatever you need from us," Jed said. "We've got your six."

"Thank you," the Italian Shepherd replied and then gestured to the column of vans idling nearby. "Each van has seating for seven plus cargo, and I can take four more in the Stelvio."

"All right, you heard the man," Jed said, taking charge. "Let's load the hard cases into those vans and saddle up."

The combined sixteen operators from Joshua Alpha and Bravo made quick work of the hard cases, transferring their weapons and gear from the cargo hold in the belly of the Bombardier to the vans. Eli slipped in next to Jed on one of the two bench seats in the lead van and Nisha took the seat on the other side. David, Carl, and Hyeon crammed into the other bench seat, leaving Bex, Grayson, and Johnny to hop in the van behind with the other Shepherds who divided up in the remaining vans. Ben and Pastor Mike were joined by Corbin and her Keeper, Pastor Margaret, in the Alfa Romeo.

The trip took thirty-five minutes, taking them northwest and across the Tiber River to San Gioacchino ai Prati Castello—a church where they would be staging for the op. The church was conveniently located off Piazza deui Quiriti, just over a kilometer from the Vatican.

"This church is dedicated to St. Joachim, the father of Mary," the Italian Shepherd driver told him over his shoulder as the vans braked to a stop on Via Pompeo Magna.

Jed scanned the two-story facade fronted with six Corinthian columns and an impressive exterior frieze above rendered in full color. In addition to the architecture, he noted construction barricades and tape blocking pedestrian traffic. Scaffolding was erected inside the portico and a couple of workmen appeared to be working on the arch.

"Is the church being renovated?" he asked.

"No. This is just an excuse to close the church to the public while we temporarily occupy the premises," their Italian driver explained and tossed a plastic bag stuffed with class 2 neon-orange safety vests into the back. "Each of you put one of these on before you get out."

Jed nodded.

OPSEC was important, and every measure they took to minimize their footprint helped increase their chances of success. The Italians had gone to the trouble of creating a construction narrative to help keep them safe, and he was grateful for the foresight. He handed out the vests to each of his colleagues and everyone complied before opening the slider door and disembarking.

"Unload our gear now or later?" Jed called to Ben, who was standing on the sidewalk with Vincenzo, David, and Mike. Ahead, Corbin smiled at him over her shoulder as her Keeper led her into the church.

"My guys will do it," Vincenzo said. "For now, everyone follow me."

Jed nodded and walked with the group of sixteen operators and support staff through the open iron gate, up a couple of granite steps, and into the church. Inside, they were greeted with sunlight streaming through intricate stained-glass windows, towering marble columns, and a richly painted decorative ceiling. He wasn't an architecture guy, but he appreciated fine craftsmanship and recognized beauty when he saw it.

The Italian Shepherd, Vincenzo, led them through the nave and then to the left out of the main sanctuary, through a doorway and down a flight of steps to a cavernous basement where an impromptu TOC had been set up. In addition to three computer workstations and a cluster of flat-panel televisions mounted to metal poles, their host had staged a sleeping area with rows of folding cots and a dining area with folding chairs and card tables. Two long buffets, positioned end to end, were loaded with provisions, food, and bottled water. A half-dozen operators—Italian Shepherds, Jed presumed—were already present and greeted their American counterparts with cordial nods.

"Welcome to your home for the next twenty-four hours," Vincenzo said once they were all assembled. "I apologize for the spartan accommodations, but this is the best we could do on short notice. Once the threat has been neutralized, I promise to treat you to *real* Italian hospitality. We have access to a country estate that is *magnifico* and you can stay as long as you like."

Ben walked up beside his Italian counterpart and put a hand on the man's shoulder. "No apologies necessary, my friend. My guys are happy sleeping in the dirt and using their go bag as a pillow. Heck, for most of them, this is an upgrade."

The comment earned a round of laughter from the group and set the tone of cooperation and understanding that helped grease the proverbial skids for the joint operation to come. They were guests here, and this was certainly no vacation. Vincenzo nodded thanks to Ben and seemed to relax with that out of the way. Jed noticed that without his trendy sunglasses on, the man's demeanor was totally different—the *GQ* trendsetter vibe replaced by a contemplative tactician with the weight of the world on his shoulders. A dark-haired, attractive Italian woman wearing glasses and a black pantsuit spoke with Vincenzo briefly before taking a seat at one of the computer terminals. As she went to work, imagery populated the television monitors.

"Okay, let's go," Vincenzo said, clapping his hands together and facing the assembled Shepherds. "The situation is not a good one. You're not going to like it. We don't like it. Nobody likes it, okay, but this is how our job is . . ."

Jed felt himself nodding. Short fuse, incomplete tactical picture, nothing deconflicted, and so on . . . that was the operator life. No point in complaining about it or wishing it were different. Vincenzo got it, and so did Jed's team.

"What we know is that the Dark Ones are planning an attack on the Vatican sometime in the next twenty-four hours. We don't know the target. We don't know all the players. We don't know the size of the force we're up against."

"Basically, they don't know jack," Johnny whispered to Carl.

Jed turned and shot the veteran a look, which Johnny returned with a glare of his own. Instead of things getting better with Johnny since graduation from phase one, Jed sensed the tension between them ratcheting up. The dude hadn't been shy about letting everybody know his opinion on Jed, "the nugget," stepping directly into a leadership position in Joshua Bravo. Jed still wasn't entirely clear on how advancement and hierarchy worked in the Shepherds, but it shouldn't matter. The head shed had made him the combat team leader and that was the end of it.

Or it should have been.

He turned his attention back to Vincenzo, who was speaking again.

"It is important for you to understand that our relationship with the Roman Catholic Church is long and complicated. Keep in mind that the Shepherds and the papacy have been interacting for five hundred years. Some popes have embraced our existence and our charter, while others have not. None, however, have overtly supported our mission—at least not in the last few hundred years. We do not have time for a history lesson, but tactically speaking it is critical for you to understand that we have no official standing and limited influence inside the walls of Vatican City. We do not provide security for or counsel to His Holiness. The Swiss Guard is responsible for the pope's personal safety and the security of the Apostolic Palace. Whereas the grounds and institution of Vatican City is secured by the Corpo della Gendarmeria."

The platoon leader of Joshua Alpha, a former Marine MARSOC operator named Scott McGuirt, raised his hand. Jed didn't know Scott personally yet, but the man had a stalwart reputation as both a conscientious operator and a servant leader.

"*Prego,*" Vincenzo said, gesturing to Scott. "Ask your question."

"We appreciate the delicate situation you guys are in with the Vatican, trying to manage your anonymity while also needing to execute the mission. So please, rest assured, we're going to trust you to manage that interface and not stick our nose in where it doesn't belong. That said, I do have concerns about the tactical implications of trying to operate inside Vatican City. I'm worried we're going to end up in a potential blue-on-blue scenario, where our presence puts everyone's lives at risk and also introduces confusion and chaos that the Dark Ones can exploit. The last thing we want is Gendarmerie GIR shooting at us while we're trying to help them," Scott said and then with a chuckle added, "Because I hate to be the bearer of bad news, but none of us speak Italian. I suspect us running around kitted up with assault rifles, jabbering in English on the radio, is going to be hard not to notice."

"*Sì*, my friend, this is the nightmare scenario. Welcome to my world!" Vincenzo said.

When the Italian Shepherd didn't elaborate, Scott tried again, "Again, not trying to get into your business, but what's the mitigation plan? Do you have embeds in the Gendarmerie, Swiss Guard, and papal staff who are going to be running interference? Or is the plan for us to augment GIR using some NOC?"

Vincenzo pressed his lips tight together and didn't say anything for a long moment. "*Sì*, we have a plan for this, which is to use the confusion to our advantage. Maybe you already know, the Carabinieri has its own special forces unit called Gruppo Intervento Speciale or GIS. This is different than the Gendarmerie GIR, but it is a sister unit that is specializing in counterterrorism operations. And it is a sniper unit as well. So in a situation where there is a terrorism event at the Vatican, it would not be unreasonable for GIS to arrive and augment the GIR response."

Scott nodded to Jed, who nodded back. He agreed with the Alpha platoon leader's concerns but saw where the Italian Shepherd was going. "Okay," Jed said, "so what I hear you saying is we're going to fall in under Carabinieri GIS as some multinational joint counterterror task force?"

"Not exactly," Vincenzo said with an uneasy smile. "We're going to *pretend* to be a multinational counterterrorism task force working with GIS. Ben and I have decided to use blended teams, so there will be native Italian speakers on every squad."

"Hold on," Jed said, unable to take it anymore. "Pretend? That sounds really risky. What happens if the real GIS shows up?"

"*Così è la vita*," Vincenzo said with a smile. "Which is why it is important to work fast."

Jed turned to his counterpart. The former Marine's eyes said it all. This was the exact kind of amorphous craziness that the Italians were known for. Just like the insanity that was navigating traffic in Rome, managed chaos seemed to be the de facto Italian solution for problems that were simply too difficult to tackle with rules and a roadmap.

Jed rolled his eyes, and Scott chuckled.

"This is no different than the myriad of situations we've operated under domestically and in the Middle East," Ben said, jumping in. "We're going to use the nature of compartmentalization and the fluidity of joint operations to our advantage. Everyone will assume us to be what we appear, because it is common now—a joint, multinational counterterror task force under GIS. By the time local law enforcement and the media figures out what's going on, we will have exfiltrated."

If you say so, Jed thought to himself and prayed Vincenzo knew what he was doing.

The rest of the brief focused on scenario planning based on traditional intelligence collected over the past twenty-four hours and input from a pair of Italian Watchers—identical twin girls in their late teens. One twin had dreamed about a terrorist attack in St. Peter's Square, while the other had glimpsed the pope bleeding from the side of the head. Vincenzo had decided to give both scenarios equal weight, and so the rest of the day would be dedicated to developing plans to counter two possible attacks simultaneously.

When they broke for lunch, Jed sought out Corbin, who was with Pastor Margaret eating in an office away from the main group of operators. He knocked on the frame of the open door.

"Would it be okay for me to talk with Corbin for a moment?" he asked, his gaze going to Margaret.

"Of course," Margaret said with a genuine smile. She gestured for him to take a seat across from them.

"How are you doing?" he said, sitting in the empty chair.

"I'm good," Corbin said, dabbing at her chin with a napkin and then setting her paper plate on her knees. "I love going on missions, but it drives my dad crazy. He was a Watcher when he was a kid, but I regularly have to remind him of that. Parents— whatcha gonna do?"

Jed chuckled and wondered how many multigenerational families of Watchers were out there. On the one hand, being a Watcher before becoming a Watcher parent would make the job easier. But on the other hand, sometimes not knowing was an easier pill to swallow.

If I had a son, would I want him to be an operator? Jed wondered. *Hard to say . . .*

"Corbin, what's your take on this? You've gotta have a vibe on something," he said, crossing his legs in the comfy chair. "You didn't chime in during the Watcher brief. Did you have nothing to add?"

She smiled at him and he sensed that she liked the fact that he had come to her for her opinion. "You really want to know what I think?"

"Absolutely I do," he said. "You're an equal member of this team and there's nobody I'd rather have in my ear on an op."

She blushed. "Thank you, Jed. That means a lot to me."

"All right, now spill it," he said with a chuckle. "I can see you got something on your mind."

She glanced at Pastor Margaret, who smiled and patted her on the shoulder, and then said, "Those two girls are totally famous Watchers and used to be really good, but . . ."

"But what?"

"They're aging out and they don't want anyone to know," she said with a conspiratorial tone, much like a high schooler might use when spreading gossip about classmates who had kissed.

"Are you sure?"

She nodded. "They're trying so hard to hide it that it's like a beacon. I couldn't help but read their anxiety."

"So what are you saying—that they made this all up?"

"No, never," she said. "It's just that usually when you have a dream or catch a vision from a Dark One, you can follow the thread and, you know, find the guy and follow him, look through his eyes, try to figure out what else he knows. Like what me and Sarah Beth did before the attacks in Nashville. Remember?"

"Of course I remember." Rubbing his chin, he asked, "Okay, so they're aging out. What exactly does that mean?"

"It hasn't happened to me personally yet, but my old Keeper, Father Maclin, said it's like forgetting a safe combination. At your peak, you can access your gifts like second nature, without even having to think about. Later, you find yourself having to think harder to access them. Eventually it's like you forget the combination to the safe completely and can't access anything, even though you can feel the abilities inside your head, if that makes sense. From what I'm reading, these girls are, like, almost done."

"Hmm . . . does Ben know?"

"Yeah, he knows."

"But not Vincenzo?"

She nodded.

"Okay, this is good to know," he said. "Can you augment them or help them remember the combination in some way?"

"I don't know. I never really thought of that." After a beat, her eyes flickered with hope. "Maybe I can follow one of their threads, you know, in case it's still active, but they can't feel it anymore."

"That's a good idea. Why don't you try," he said. "We don't have a lot to go on here."

She took a deep breath and let out a shaky exhale. "Okay."

"You nervous?" he said with a chuckle.

"A little. The twins are kinda like European Watcher rock stars. They're probably going to throw salt on me."

"If that happens, you let me know and I'll have Vincenzo set them straight. Because you're an American Watcher rock star. Never forget that."

"Yeah, you're right," she said with a self-affirming nod. "Thanks, Jed."

"Easy day," he said and got to his feet, his thoughts turning to his own looming confrontation—the one where he hashed things out with Johnny.

But not today, he decided, kicking that particular can down the road. Increasing friction ahead of the impending combat operation would be a terrible idea. The conversation would have to come eventually.

Just not today.

CHAPTER
THIRTY

Sarah Beth sat on the edge of her bed, annoyed and staring at Darilyn's back as her roommate took her good, sweet time getting ready for breakfast. She didn't dislike the girl—not really—but she disliked how Darilyn treated her. She expected more from someone who'd been at St. George's as long as Darilyn, someone who could have—with very little effort—made her initiation period so much easier. Having been inside her roommate's mind more than once undetected, which she supposed said as much about Darilyn's gifts as her own, she knew that it had very little to do with what

Darilyn thought of Sarah Beth and way more to do with what the girl thought of herself. Despite how pretty she was, Darilyn was very insecure. So Sarah Beth had tried to be empathetic and give the girl grace, but there were times when that was harder than others.

She knew that at least some of her foul mood came from lack of sleep. She'd been having nightmares about Victor and Fake Grandma and the compound in the woods where she'd been abducted. Pastor Dee, from whom she was required to get counseling for an hour twice a week—just one more thing for the other kids to wonder and gossip about—told her that the nightmares were a form of PTSD. She wanted to believe her, to believe that Victor was not still getting inside her head somehow despite the techniques she'd learned to block him out, but it still felt so real. It didn't *feel* like nightmares . . . and so much of her new life was driven by feelings, whether of peace or terror.

She watched Darilyn pull a perfect ponytail out of the hairband she'd just put in to start over from scratch. Her willpower finally depleted, Sarah Beth sighed.

Loudly.

"I'm hurrying, Sarah Beth," Darilyn said curtly. "Just chill."

"I'm sorry," Sarah Beth said sweetly. "I'm just tired. Take your time. I'm not even that hungry."

Her stomach growled audibly, refuting the white lie she'd just told, and she felt Darilyn's silent satisfaction at keeping her waiting. Sarah Beth was *starving*. She was always hungry after a Victor nightmare or after using her Watcher gifts. Maybe it took a lot of energy to do those things even though her body was still?

The door swung open and their other roommate, Elizabeth ("do *not* call me Beth") stuck her head in.

"OMG, Dari," the girl said. "You take longer than my mom. Come on, I'm starving."

Sarah Beth smiled at the comment and rose from where she sat on the edge of her bed, smoothing the covers in case their house-mother decided to check on the cleanliness of their rooms. She liked Elizabeth, even though the girl didn't try too hard to get close to her. Sarah Beth got it—Darilyn could get kids to turn against you quickly and already had it out for Sarah Beth. Best to keep your head down and not provoke the queen bee of seventh grade.

She sent a warm thought to Elizabeth, who suddenly smiled a soft smile, then screwed up her face, apparently confused as to where it came from.

"I'll be ready in less than five minutes," Darilyn said with a *What is your problem?* tone. "Relax."

Sarah Beth shrugged to Elizabeth, who checked to be sure Darilyn wasn't looking and then shrugged back.

"I'll be waiting at the end of the hall with Olivia for you guys," Elizabeth said, referring to another classmate—one Sarah Beth liked a lot but hadn't gotten close to yet. Other than when she was with Max, the one boy at St. George's she had a real connection with, she still felt mostly alone. Her mom told her *everyone* felt alone in middle school, and maybe it was true. The other kids' thoughts she peeked at from time to time certainly supported Mom's theory.

With a headshake at Darilyn's antics, Elizabeth headed back into the hall, leaving the door cracked as a reminder to hurry, perhaps, while Sarah Beth stayed behind.

Her mind drifted to Uncle Jed, maybe her favorite person on the whole planet, other than her parents. Jed was the opposite of Victor in pretty much every way imaginable, so she guessed it made sense that her mind automatically redirected to him whenever thoughts of Victor crept in. And it was probably a little bit of hero worship for the man who'd saved her from pure evil. Oddly, in that moment, her thoughts meandered from Jed to Detective Perez, and she felt a sudden unease in the middle of her chest. Instead of ignoring it, she did as Pastor Dee insisted and confronted the feeling. According to Pastor Dee, heart feelings were one of the ways the Holy Spirit spoke to people.

There's something not right about Detective Perez. Something . . . off.

She knew how grateful everyone was to the detective and that she should feel grateful too. The policewoman had, literally, taken a bullet for her. And risked her life to save Mom and Uncle Jed.

Or had she?

Sarah Beth bit the inside of her cheek.

There's one way to find out. Maybe . . .

She closed her eyes, let out a slow breath, said a silent prayer to find the right thread, and . . . there it was. Breathing slowly, hands clutching the sides of her St. George's Academy blue-and-white plaid skirt, she let herself drift along the thread, trying to hurry without rushing—a critical piece of advice Corbin had taught her.

Snooping was dangerous business . . .

When she reached the end, she slipped inside.

Inside Detective Perez.

She mentally blinked and tried to make sense of what she was seeing through the detective's eyes. A white sofa, super clean and modern—the kind Mom would love and Dad would hate. And a pair of legs, crossed at the knee, with the right foot bobbing nervously in the air.

Our foot. No, her foot . . .

Man, this is so weird.

A phone sat on the coffee table beside the foot, but not exactly a cell phone. It seemed bulky and had a bent-over loop of metal at the top—a weird antenna perhaps.

New images then mixed in with the visions from the detective's eyes. Memories, maybe? She saw Uncle Jed, sitting across a table, smiling and laughing. Plates of food on the table in front of her. The city skyline beyond. Other people eating outside in some sort of patio dining room. Then it blurred and she was in another place. Looking at another face, this one very close and looking down at her. The man's face was handsome but intimidating. His intense eyes were dark in color but then flared with a hint of orange around the irises.

Who is this man?

Is he a Dark One?

She felt the detective pull away from her and she slipped outside the bubble of the woman's mind. Then she floated in the darkness along a new and different thread.

No, wait—I need to know more. I need to go back!

But there was no going back because the pull of the new thread was too powerful, like the current in a river impossible to swim against. She gave up trying, deciding the thread ended at something important God wanted her to see somewhere else.

She slipped inside a new mind bubble.

Through different eyes, she watched a livestreaming video on a laptop computer. The video showed an African woman, her clothes torn and bloody, her face bruised, holding a very young boy in her lap. The toddler cried loudly and beside her an older boy—perhaps eight or nine—knelt on the dirt floor beside them, begging his brother to be quiet. A thin, angry-looking African man stared down at the trio, a rifle clutched in his hands, and when the boy said something to him, the man smashed his rifle butt into the boy's face. The boy collapsed in the dirt beside the mom and the younger brother.

A hand with thick, scarred fingers used the computer touch pad to close the video window.

"The pope's calendar has not been updated," the voice said, perhaps into a phone. "And so still they suffer."

"The offer was extended. His Holiness accepted. I promise he will be there. I cannot control how and when they update the public calendar," another voice said in heavily accented English in their ear—definitely over a phone. "Please, you have to believe me. I'm begging you not to harm them. I've done everything you've asked of me."

"He better be there, Rector, or their deaths will be slow and agonizing, and the next time you see them will be in pieces."

She heard sobbing and the call ended.

Their gaze went to a phone sitting on a coffee table—a strange-looking phone not unlike the one Detective Perez had in her apartment. She—no, he, reached for it. His arm was covered in a sleeve of demonic tattoos—no, not demonic, but Satan himself, the skin gray and the eyes glowing scarlet in contrast to the glowing gold scars over the body of the classic devil. The shoulders and arms were studded with horns.

Sarah Beth felt herself gasp.

The man's other arm, also wrapped in a sleeve of tattoos, set a normal-looking cell phone on the table beside the laptop. He pressed the number one on the glowing number pad and she heard the phone dial.

"Yes?" said the voice on the other end of the line, a voice that took Sarah Beth's breath away and filled her with such fear she momentarily thought she had peed herself. She stifled a gasp, certain if she so much as breathed, Victor would find her.

"It's done," came the man's voice. "Tomorrow."

"What about the calendar?" Victor said, his voice a serpent's hiss in their ear. "Are you sure it's happening?"

There was a pause and she sensed more than felt a brief wave of uncertainty, but then it was gone.

"He assures me the pope has accepted the invitation," the man said.

"Good."

"What do you want me to do with the brother's family?"

"Kill them. Kill them all."

She felt tears spill onto her cheeks.

And heard another voice.

"Sarah Beth? Are you okay?"

Darilyn . . .

"Are you alone, Nicholas?" Victor asked, his voice rising with alarm.

"Yes, why?"

Sarah Beth squeezed her real-life eyes shut and concentrated with all her might.

She slipped out of the dark bubble of the man's mind into the murky ether. She thought she smelled incense, but she couldn't be sure if that was real and felt herself being pulled backward at incredible speed like a fishing lure reeled in through the water by the hand of God Himself.

She opened her eyes, and Darilyn was staring at her, fear on her face.

"Dude, are you okay? You want me to get the RA?" her roommate asked.

It was the most genuine concern she'd ever felt from Darilyn, and Sarah Beth struggled to put a smile on her face.

"No, I'm okay," she said and massaged a thumb into her left temple. "I get these terrible migraines sometimes, is all. I think I need to skip breakfast."

"Do you want me to get the nurse?" Darilyn asked, all her pretentious smiling and jealous insecurities evaporating. In that moment, Sarah Beth knew that one day she and Darilyn would be friends.

"No, but thank you so much, Dari," she said, using the popular girl's nickname for the first time. To her delight, Darilyn didn't bristle.

"Are you sure?" the girl asked with true empathy Sarah Beth could almost feel. Perhaps that was Darilyn's gift—she was an empath.

How strange . . .

"It'll go away in, like, thirty or forty minutes if I just lie down and close my eyes," she said and did just that, laying a forearm over her eyes. "Thank you so much, Darilyn. I'll see you guys in first period."

"Okay," Darilyn said, unsure, and for a moment Sarah Beth worried the girl might stay with her. "I'll turn the light out," her roommate said finally, doing so, and then Sarah Beth heard the door close softly.

Instantly she was sitting back up, her head in her hands, eyes closed, sending out a message to the only one who would believe her—other than Corbin, who was away on a mission.

Uncle Jed, it's me—Sarah Beth. I need to talk to you. I need to tell you something really important.

For a moment, she thought she felt Jed start to answer back, but then the connection broke, like someone rejecting an incoming phone call.

"His Holiness . . . ," she murmured. "That has to be the pope, right? Like the one in Rome? If they're going to do something to the pope, I have to tell Jed before it's too late."

She closed her eyes to try again, but thoughts of Detective Perez snuck in. Why? Maybe she was a little jealous of the woman.

That can wait.

She forced her mind back to the thick, tattoo-covered arms of the man with the laptop who'd been talking with Victor. This man was very dangerous, and she had to warn the Shepherds.

Please, Uncle Jed . . .

CHAPTER THIRTY-ONE

Jed popped two Aleve into his mouth and dry swallowed. He'd heard people use the expression "My head feels like it's in a vise," but he'd never actually experienced such a headache.

Until now.

"There's bottled water on the table right over there, Jed," Nisha said, sidling up beside him and nodding at the two buffet-style tables loaded with food and drinks.

"Yeah, I know, but I've been popping pills like this in the field for years, and you know what they say about old habits," he said.

"I do indeed," she said. "Headache?"

"Yeah," he said, massaging his temples. "A bad one."

"Strangely, I've been battling a headache all day myself. We're probably dehydrated, another reason to grab a water."

"Fair enough," he said and called for Eli—who happened to be standing by the Igloo cooler—to toss them a couple of bottles, which he and Nisha both caught midair. "Thanks, bro."

Eli gave him a two-finger salute and went back to chatting with Grayson.

Clutching the cold, wet plastic bottle, he turned back to Nisha. "At least Vincenzo was finally able to get clearance for us to enter Vatican City tomorrow."

"Provisional access," she said, correcting him. "The Gendarmerie want us to station outside the walls until needed."

"Adapt and overcome, I guess . . ." Jed cracked open the cap on his water. Nisha was right; he was dehydrated, he realized as he chugged half of the ice-cold water. He let out a satisfying *aaaah* and then smiled at her.

"What?" she said.

"Nothing, just smiling."

"Oh, okay," she said and opened her own water.

"How are you feeling about all of this?" he asked with a sweeping gesture indicating basically everything.

She took a contemplative sip before answering. "It's funny—if you would have asked me that five years ago, I would have chastised you and told you what I was *thinking*, because Nisha of five years ago hated questions about her *feelings*. But now . . . I'm not so sure."

He found her response both honest and insightful, especially given her background in intelligence. "You're not so sure about thinking versus feeling, or you're not so sure what you're feeling?"

"Yes, to both. What about you—how do *you* feel about all of this?"

"Have you ever heard the expression 'It ain't what you don't know that gets you into trouble. It's what you know for sure that just ain't so'?"

"Mark Twain?" she said, raising an eyebrow.

He nodded. "Well, I'm feeling like in our case it's going to be *both* what we don't know and what we know for sure that gets us in trouble."

This candid statement got her laughing. "Yes, Jed, I think you might be onto something."

Their eyes met and he felt a connection—her invisible thread. Curiosity getting the better of him, he started to follow it . . . before thinking better of the decision and pulling back into himself.

Spiritual gifts. For God's work, not my own curiosity . . .

"What was that?" she said, her eyes narrowing at him.

"What was what?" he said, playing dumb.

"Just a second ago. It felt like . . ." She looked over her right and then her left shoulder as if trying to catch someone sneaking up behind her.

"Like what?"

"I'm not sure. A presence . . . or, like, an undertow."

Jed shrugged his shoulders. There would be a time and place to let Nisha in on his secret, but it wasn't here and now. Still, he thought that when the Watchers snuck into someone's mind, they did so undetected. But Nisha had felt something and he'd not even really made it inside or whatever the Watchers called it. He frowned. Maybe it hadn't been him at all.

"Was it something dark? Something threatening?" he asked.

"No, I don't think so." She shook her head as if releasing the thought and the concern.

He hesitated a heartbeat, thinking he should maybe say something, but then, in the corner of his eye, he saw Corbin walking up to join them, Pastor Margaret right at her side as always.

Another time.

Seeing the teenage Watcher caused a pang of guilt to blossom in his gut for ignoring Sarah Beth all day. He'd felt her reach out a couple of times since he'd arrived at the church, but he'd been too busy to "Watcher snapchat" with her. While he sure didn't have control over any of this, he found the ability to block her came easily. Jed knew she was having a rough go of it integrating socially at St. George's. He deeply cared and wanted to listen, but now was not the time. He knew from his years as a SEAL that an operator had to be focused or mistakes got made, which meant lives could be lost. Once this Vatican threat was neutralized, he would carve out time for Sarah Beth, but for now he needed to be on mission.

The rest of the European Shepherds had arrived midday and they'd collectively spent all afternoon on mission and contingency planning. Little details and insights, from both conventional and Watcher ISR, continued to stream in, but the picture was still muddy. Vincenzo and Ben had each conducted afternoon briefs, and the focus was on preventing a terrorist attack that, as best they could tell, would target St. Peter's Square.

"Hi, guys," Corbin said as she stepped up to join them. Then, shifting her attention to Jed, she asked, "Can we talk?"

"Sure," he said.

"I'll catch you later, Jed," Nisha said, excusing herself. She gave a smile to Corbin and a nod to Margaret, then headed off across the room.

Jed nodded at her and then shifted his attention to Corbin. "What's up?"

"I did what you said—talked to the twins," Corbin said.

"And how did that go?"

"At first, they were total witches to me, but after I showed them some compassion for what they were going through and told them what I could do to help, they agreed to work with me. We've been at it for hours, and I think I got something."

"Don't keep me in suspense, sister—read me in," he said, excited for the news, amazed as always at the maturity and poise of their teenage Watcher.

"It's kind of random, but I *know* it's connected to the Vatican attack. I can feel it," she said and then bit her lip.

"Well, tell me what you got," he said. "In the Teams, we have a policy that anyone shares anything on their minds if they think it might possibly be important. Talk to me."

Corbin seemed to relax. "Well, so the twins were working a thread they discovered that, from what they can tell, is here in Rome. They weren't able to really get much from it—like I said, they're aging out—but they felt really strongly that it was related. So I went on the thread with them."

Jed's mind immediately turned to a memory of Corbin and Sarah Beth, holding hands in the Yarnells' old living room as they snooped around the spiritual ether together, looking for Victor.

Crazy stuff.

"Anyway, it worked. I followed them on the thread, and I was able to get inside the target's headspace. Pretty easily, in fact," she said, though he detected no arrogance or pride.

She opened the sketch pad she seemed always to be holding, and Jed was once again awestruck by the quality of what could only be described as pure art.

"That's St. Peter's Square," he said, looking at the pencil sketch.

"Yeah," she said. "This was about thirty minutes ago. We were walking the square . . ."

"We?" he asked, confused for a moment.

"Yeah, you know . . . me and the target. I think his name is Rashid. His emotions were intense—pride, anticipation, fear. It felt like he was confirming the layout for an attack and he was very excited for 'tomorrow,' which I think means the attack is coming and it felt like in the morning—like late morning or maybe lunchtime? It was hard to tell."

"What do you mean 'felt like'?" Jed asked, fascinated.

"Well, you know, it's not like he's going to clearly think something like 'Tomorrow at ten we will attack from the east' or whatever. He *knows* stuff, so he doesn't think about those details. I got some names, like, 'Mohamad's team will come from this direction' and 'Abbas will come from behind there'—stuff like that. I noted those things on the sketch."

"How sure are you that this happens tomorrow?" he asked.

Corbin seemed to bite the inside of her lip, and he thought she might be unsure until she answered, "More than 90 percent, I guess."

"This is awesome, Corbin. Great work. I'm not sure how Ben or Vincenzo spins it to the Vatican, but this should get us on property."

"There's more," Corbin said and flipped to the next sketch. The detail was insane—a man sitting on a love seat, a drink in his hand, smiling out at them. The face was chiseled and the eyes, despite being drawn in black-and-white, seemed to stare directly through him. He could almost imagine a faint-orange glow around the irises.

"That," Corbin said, looking up from the drawing with narrow eyes, "is Nicholas Woland."

"What?" Jed said, his mouth dropping open. "How can you be sure? Where did you see this?"

"From Rashid's memory. He came back to it again and again and it seemed to excite and frighten him. He knows him under an alias, the one who is sponsoring the attack, but that's Woland for sure."

"How do you know?"

"Because," Corbin said simply, beaming with pride, "every Watcher on the planet was given images of Woland and instructed to do whatever we could to find him. As far as I know, no one has had any luck. Until now."

"This changes everything," he said. "C'mon, we've got to read Ben in on what you've discovered. If Woland is here, this is bigger than a terror attack on St. Peter's Square."

CHAPTER THIRTY-TWO

Woland adjusted his black necktie inside the starched collar of the white Gendarmerie police shirt. He'd not put on a uniform in years. Even while still in the Army, operators in the Unit rarely wore uniforms—or cut their hair and shaved their beards, for that matter. Such things were reserved for funerals and retirements. Just going through the motions this morning dredged up a hurricane of long-forgotten emotions.

Honor, integrity, respect, mission before self . . .

It made him want to vomit.

What a bunch of self-deluding garbage. The rank-and-file troopers in today's armed forces were nothing but cannon fodder, just like they'd been in every armed conflict since the earliest days of the standing army.

Core values. He scoffed at the thought. *Nothing but propaganda to make the weak and stupid feel good about the forfeiture of their mind, body, and soul to whatever head shed they serve.*

There'd been a time he'd been one of those fools. When he joined the Shepherds, he'd believed it would be different. In God's army, he'd thought his talent and ambition would finally be recognized . . . finally be rewarded. But the Shepherds were no different from any other army. From day one, they'd all been jealous of Woland's talents and threatened by his confidence. As soon as that pious impostor Morvant realized that Woland was God's chosen one, he'd politicked to have Woland kicked out of the organization. He'd never forgiven the Shepherd commander for that, and today he was going to make Morvant pay. He was going to make them all pay . . . including this new golden boy, Jedidiah Johnson, he'd been tipped off about.

He smiled at the thought as he tucked his shirttails inside the waistband of his trousers and cinched his belt. Next, he donned the dark-blue tunic-style jacket. Similar to an American dress uniform, this one had epaulettes—hard shoulder boards indicating his fictitious rank of *vice ispettore*, an officer rank equivalent to an O4 in the US military. He'd never worn an officer's uniform before and couldn't say that it pleased him to do so now. He would have preferred to be dressed as a corporal, one of dozens roaming the grounds, so as not to draw attention to himself. But for today's operation to succeed, he needed to be able to command respect, give orders, and knock down any challenges to his authority.

That the operation had been scheduled for morning today was no accident. The Dark Ones did not have many assets embedded in the Vatican Gendarmerie, but the one they had—Lorenzo Cattaneo—was ideally positioned. Cattaneo had risen through the ranks to watch commander, a supervisory position inside the security and operations center. Like all shift work billets, the watch commander rotated every twenty-four hours. Catteneo had come on duty yesterday at noon and would turn over with his replacement at noon today, which meant that the attack and the kidnapping of the pope had to take place in the morning.

It was Catteneo who had been dialoguing with an Italian GIS representative—a man named Vincenzo Rossi—and alerted Woland to increased counterintelligence activity. The GIS inquiry was no coincidence, and Victor's rising alarm was proof that the Shepherds were here in Rome. From this point forward, Woland would operate under the assumption that Vincenzo Rossi was from Shepherds Europe and that GIS was a NOC for the combined North American and European units.

It is exactly what I would do.

He had told Catteneo as much, and the man had promised to restrict Rossi's men to staging outside Vatican walls. That combined with the distraction of a real terror attack on civilians in St. Peter's Square would give him the time required to complete his real mission. Catteneo would also give Woland's own team of Dark Horizon operatives, dressed up as Gendarmerie, access to the Vatican Gardens. From there, they would ambush the Shepherds, when and if they presented themselves. Woland assumed that the

Shepherds had personnel embedded in the Gendarmerie and Swiss Guard, but whoever these assets were, they did not appear to have any influence over Catteneo, because he'd encountered zero resistance thus far.

Round one went to the Dark Ones.

He finished dressing, holstering his service weapon on his left hip in the "cross-draw" style preferred by the Vatican police, and inserted the micro earbud, bone-conduction transceiver deep in his left ear canal. When he performed a radio check with his team, the call was answered promptly and came with a report that his ride was ready and waiting outside. With two fingers, he pulled back the curtain and looked out the window to confirm the van idling on the street below.

An upswelling of anticipation buoyed his step as he headed out the door and down the stairs to the lobby. Everything was proceeding exactly according to plan, just as Victor had foreseen. The tattooed-over Scripture from Luke's Gospel on his forearm itched like it did so often, but he resisted the urge to scratch it. They thought they were so clever.

So special.

So enlightened.

We'll see how enlightened you are when you're stuck outside the walls taking fire from the GIR while our attack and plans for His Holiness unfold.

"In bocca al lupo," he said to himself, smiling as he stepped out of the building into the bright morning sun, the Italian coming to him from some long-lost memory.

Into the wolf's mouth.

CHAPTER
THIRTY-THREE

"Questions?" Jed asked when he'd finished briefing the team.

He scanned the faces of the assembled operators—Americans from Joshua Alpha and Bravo as well as their European counterparts—and the support people behind them. David stood, arms folded on his chest, his face tight with tension, beside Corbin, who shot Jed a thumbs-up, which made him smile. He watched Pastor Mike whisper something to Ben, but the Shepherd commander shook his head to whatever it was.

"Fine, if nobody else has the guts, I'm gonna say it," Johnny said, scanning for an ally among his teammates. "I don't like splitting the teams. We have no idea the size of the force we're facing or how they'll be armed. We only have two dozen of us as it is, and we have to cover all of St. Peter's Square and the surrounding buildings. That's a lot of surface area, people. We're too thin as it is. Now Johnson gets to make the call to split the teams and stage Joshua Bravo away from the action. The Watchers saw an attack in the square. That intel is golden. We have nothing indicating a second attack anywhere else. We should all be in the square."

Jed turned to Ben to see if the Shepherd commander wanted to field the rebuttal, but Ben's eyes fell on him.

Lead.

The single word echoed loud in Jed's mind.

Jed had lobbied hard with Ben for this tactical deviation, and it definitely was a tactical deviation from their original plan. Johnny made valid points, and normally Jed would be inclined to agree with the veteran, but these weren't normal times. Deep in his chest, he felt that the kill house exercise Ben had created placing them in the Vatican Gardens was a spiritual premonition. The quickest infil to the location in the gardens where they'd battled in the simulation was just outside the south wall along Viale Vaticano. Jed felt staging his element there was the right call. That feeling, that spidey sense he'd convinced himself for years was just a warrior's intuition, had saved his life and those of his teammates too many times in the last decade and a half to ignore. Since becoming a Shepherd, he learned that his gut feelings were much more than just *intuition*. Everything he'd seen and experienced since rescuing Sarah Beth had finally allowed him to believe that these feelings were a gift of the Holy Spirit.

He should just say as much, right?

But he didn't.

Instead, he said, "In addition to our teams, Johnny, we also have the Vatican police and Gendarmerie, whom we're coordinating with. That's a sizable force. But more importantly, like I said in the brief, we have strong reason to believe that Nicholas Woland is involved in the planning and execution of this attack. We can't lose sight of the forest for the trees. It is not unreasonable to assume that the St. Peter's Square attack is a distraction and there's another component to Woland's plan. The Dark Ones have a long game, and this is the Vatican, after all."

"So your plan is for Joshua Bravo to sit and wait outside the wall in case something happens while our brothers and sisters are fighting for their lives in St. Peter's Square?"

"From that position, we can breach the wall into Vatican City Gardens but still have rapid access as a QRF to augment the operation in St. Peter's Square if our support is needed. Staging at the selected waypoint gives us the best coverage for both scenarios."

"But by the time we get there, it would be game over," Johnny came back, unable to contain himself.

"With the Dark Ones, things are never straightforward," David said, shooting Johnny a stern look, surprising everyone and Jed most of all. "Like Jed said, if Nicholas Woland is planning this hit, we should expect the unexpected. Jed's plan seems to give us the best flexibility. Spiritually speaking, it resonates with me."

Johnny opened his mouth as if to argue but said nothing.

Jed stared at David, gobsmacked at how resoundingly his TSL had shut Johnny down.

"We're going with Jed's plan. Time to load up," Ben said, the matter settled. "I'll be in the mobile TOC with Vincenzo. Joshua Alpha will be with Team Europe in the square. Joshua Bravo will be, as briefed, to the south of the wall. Move it, people."

The teams split up, low chatter filling the room as they all finished kitting up, checked their weapons, and then headed toward where the four Fiat Ducato cargo vans waited to take them to their respective staging areas. Jed let his hands fly over his own kit, checking extra magazines, his pistol, blow-out kit, lights, and grenades, with a fluidity born of years of combat operations.

A hand on his shoulder jolted his attention left to where Ben was grinning at him. "Good job with the brief."

"Thanks," he said. "I just hope I'm right."

"I have faith in you," the Shepherd commander said simply. "I trust in God and I trust in you."

"That simple, huh?" Jed said with a snort, slipping his Sig Sauer assault rifle over his head by its sling.

"Does it need to be more complicated?" Ben said with a wry smile, before calling David over to lead them in prayer.

They bowed their heads and David put a hand on Jed's right shoulder and the other on Ben's left.

"Father God, we ask that You protect our warriors as they battle darkness and evil in Your name. Guide their steps. Fill them with Your Spirit and direct them in each decision. Fill them with peace and confidence that can only come from knowing who it is we serve. We lift this in Jesus' name—amen."

"Amen," Jed said and felt a calm settle over him. His worries about the tactical decisions he'd made evaporated and he smiled at David.

Maybe there is something to this partnership after all.

"Thanks for having my back in there," Jed said.

"That's what we do. And I'll try my best to have your back out there as well," David said, giving a nod in the direction of Vatican City.

"I know you will," Jed said. "Pass along any guidance you feel compelled to share. I'll be listening."

"You got it, Jed," David said and clapped him on the upper arm.

"Be careful, Jed," Ben said, his voice tinged with something that caused Jed to turn back to look at his boss. "Watch out for blue on blue. If this goes south, there will be a lot of chaos to deconflict with Vatican police and Gendarmerie. And if you engage Nick Woland, don't make the mistake of underestimating him."

"Understood."

"One more thing."

"Yeah, boss."

"Where Woland goes, Victor won't be far behind. Remember what you learned from the kill house. Don't let him get inside your head."

"I won't," Jed said with a nod, but as he turned toward the vans, he felt cold doubt creeping in.

CHAPTER THIRTY-FOUR

Nobody stopped them—Woland plus his seven highly trained killers dressed as Gendarmerie—as they made their way through the Vatican Gardens to the Ethiopian College. It wouldn't be long until bombs rang like devil's bells in St. Peter's Square and chaos reigned inside the walls of the Vatican. Two hours from now, the world would finally understand what he had accepted years ago . . . that God didn't care. He didn't care about the pope and the Roman Catholic Church, or any other Christian church, nor the billions of His followers around the world for that matter. Today's operation would send a message to all that God was nothing but a voyeur. And a perverse one at that, preferring to watch His lambs be slaughtered rather than lift a finger to help them in their time of greatest need.

Either God is callous and cruel, or He's a coward. . . . There's simply no other way to spin it.

Thankfully, Woland had switched sides and was finally playing for the winning team. So long as he did what he was told, the Dark Ones and Satan, their Dark King, always had his back. When divine intervention was called for, chaos was happy to intervene. Just like today. As an operator, Woland both loathed and admired chaos, having been both its victim and beneficiary at various times. Loathed because of its unpredictable nature and admired because of its raw, destructive power. When savaging the enemy, it was tempting to think of chaos as an ally, but to do so was a miscalculation. Like a rabid dog, chaos could, and would, turn on you without warning or provocation. As a Shepherd, he'd always been wary of trying to harness the power of chaos, but now he no longer feared it the way he once had.

Chaos was the devil incarnate, and Woland could see his hand everywhere he looked.

Every member of Woland's team had cleared security and rendezvoused at rally point Inferno next to the Gardener's Lodge on schedule. In a brilliant stroke of coordinated preemptory mayhem, Victor's remote team had created a half-dozen personal crises across Rome impacting key Gendarmerie personnel. A wife in a car accident, a nanny breaking a hip at the market, an apartment fire, a bomb threat called into a primary school . . . these unfortunate and unpredictable events had thinned the on-duty ranks by requiring the impacted officers to be relieved by Dark One confederates over the last several hours. The watch commander, Cattaneo, had responded like an orchestra maestro, rejiggering duty assignments and personnel on the watch bill to fill the holes while at the same time creating even more confusion.

Bureaucratic malevolence!

Woland glanced at the bilingual Italian asset striding on his right—a man everyone called Rocco—who was second in command for the operation and responsible for any radio or face-to-face exchanges where Italian fluency was required. "After we have the pope, I intend to split the team," he said. "You're going to lead the mop-up crew."

Rocco frowned. "To what end?"

"To safeguard our exfil with the pope and kill as many Shepherds as possible. It's unlikely all of them will be eliminated in the square. They have Watchers guiding them, after all."

"That's a suicide mission. Is this order coming from Victor or from you?"

"Does it matter?"

"Of course it matters. You might have tactical authority, but I work for Victor. This is a deviation from the original plan, which was for all surviving assaulters to exfil as a team via the tunnels."

"Don't test me," Woland said, his eyes boring into the other man. "You won't like the outcome."

Rocco must have seen Woland's snarling *other*, because he acceded with a nod.

As they entered the courtyard at the entrance to the Ethiopian College, a carnal energy electrified the former Shepherd—worming up through the soles of his feet, zipping up his legs into his core, where it flowed into every fiber of his being. And with the power came the thirst . . . the thirst to dominate, to destroy, to kill. Restraining the beast within had become more and more difficult with every operation, and the desire to do so was also eroding. Why try to control it? Why not let the beast loose to do as it would?

Because the beast is reckless, his operator self warned. *The beast cares only for sating its own appetite . . .*

He performed a round of four-count tactical breathing to center himself before climbing the stone staircase leading into the college. The Pontifical Swiss Guard—the smallest army in the world—were charged with protecting the Apostolic Palace and serving as the pope's personal protective detail. While many of their duties were ceremonial and they dressed up like clowns and carried swords, they were not to be underestimated. Beneath the pomp and circumstance, they were highly trained soldiers and their complement had evolved with the times. They employed technology, used counterterrorism protocols, and fielded undercover, plainclothes agents who conceal-carried lethal Sig P220s instead of shiny halberds and silly hats. And being Swiss, they took their job quite seriously. Which made what Woland was attempting quite tricky and required some careful misdirection.

For this operation, he had access to two independent comms circuits. The radio on his belt was Gendarmerie standard-issue and gave him the ability to communicate with Watch Commander Cattaneo directly in the security center, but also access to the Swiss Guard and GIR team channels. His *other* circuit—the one requiring the micro transceiver in his ear—used the cellular network and was linked to his Dark Horizon team and jihadi commander in St. Peter's Square. So far, both circuits were working flawlessly.

He pulled the radio from his belt, keyed his mic, and gave the kickoff command. *"Centro, Uno—cominci."*

"Inteso," came Catteneo's clipped acknowledgment.

He switched channels to the Swiss Guard frequency and listened as Cattaneo issued his first alert of the day—first in Italian and then repeated in English—that a possible terrorist threat had been detected and Centro was raising the threat level from green to yellow. Woland's team, posing as Gendarmerie, had been dispatched to the Ethiopian College to augment the Swiss Guard papal protection detail.

Woland took the granite steps leading up to the entry portico two at a time, moving now with urgency. Two Swiss Guards posted to the main entrance, dressed in the brightly colored Renaissance uniform and wearing halberds on their belts, popped to attention. The pair wasn't wearing radios and would be easy to dispatch when the time came. It was the plainclothes agents and Holy See protection detail commander inside who would be the problem.

Woland paused at the threshold, just long enough to inform the door guards of the elevated threat level and instruct them to be vigilant.

"Reposition to the front of the courtyard," Rocco ordered as they passed the men. The two hustled down the steps and jogged to the corners of the inverted U-shaped building.

"As soon as we're inside, lock the doors behind us," Woland barked as he reached for the door. Footsteps on marble echoed in the grandiose lobby, marking the hurried approach of a pair of plainclothes agents jogging up to meet them, both men wearing worried faces.

"We just got the alert," the taller of the two said in German-accented English. "His Holiness is having tea with Rector Senai and the bishops in the dining room on the third floor. I was just going to recommend to Centro that we move His Holiness to the bunker via the tunnels."

Grinning on the inside, Woland gave the man a solemn nod and gestured toward the staircase beyond. "Lead the way," he said in Italian-accented English. "We'll augment your team as you escort His Holiness out."

CHAPTER
THIRTY-FIVE

Sarah Beth knew long before she screamed that this was not a normal nightmare. It felt so real, like she—her corporeal self—was actually *there*. She ducked down behind the corner of the oversize cabinet in the ornate lobby and watched the group of uniformed police officers shuffle inside. Even from this far away, the red glow burning in the eyes of the muscular man at the head of the group was visible. She recognized him immediately as the man from Detective Perez's memories.

Two other men, both wearing suits instead of police uniforms, jogged across the marble floor—worry on their faces—as the uniformed men locked the large doors between the gold columns. She watched as the agents in suits addressed the officers. If she were inside the head of any of them, she would know what they were saying, but she was observing from outside. The two agents seemed to be receiving instructions from the leader, who she now confirmed was definitely a Dark One, as his eyes flickered like flame in the dim light of the lobby.

The two men in suits turned and hurried the group toward an ornate staircase. As the group of men moved through the lobby, she tried to make herself small, surprised as she did that none of the men spotted her. Walking behind the agents in suits, the leader with glowing eyes drew a knife. He grabbed the closer of the agents by the hair from behind and plunged the knife at an upward angle so that the blade went all the way into the man's brain. As the dead agent fell, the leader took a step backward. While the second suited man spun around in confusion, one of the policemen pulled a gun with a long black tube on the end of the barrel and shot him. Instead of a loud crack, she heard only a muffled thud. The second agent's head jerked backward, spraying a horrible mess of blood and other things onto one of the tapestries that hung like oversize oriental rugs on the marble walls of the foyer.

That was when she screamed.

Reflexively, she covered her mouth in terror, but too late to muffle her scream. Her eyes darted around the huge lobby, finding plenty of wooden doors but nowhere to hide. She took a panicked step to run toward the nearest door, knowing they would catch her easily before she got there, but her survival drive was strong.

She felt herself hyperventilating as she ran, but when she reached the door, she glanced over her shoulder and realized no one was chasing her or shooting at her.

She stopped and turned slowly at the sound of the leader's calm voice as he gave instructions in English.

"Hide the bodies," the man said to one of his men.

The leader showed no apparent concern for the screaming girl who had just watched him kill two men in cold blood. She'd seen killing before. She'd seen Uncle Jed kill the bad guys that came for her. But this—somehow this was different. She stood and stared, amazed that no one was trying to grab her.

"Rocco, take their radios and respond to any Swiss Guard queries. They may be on a separate comms channel."

The leader scanned the room, and her chest tightened as his eyes passed right over where she stood, obvious in her pajama pants and the Six Flags T-shirt she'd worn to bed. But he didn't react at all. It was as if . . .

He doesn't see me!

In that moment, she realized she wasn't really there, wherever *there* was. She was in her bed, in the dorm, and for a moment she could feel the warm blanket tucked under her chin and thought she heard a soft snore from Darilyn.

I must be awake. It's not a nightmare; it's a vision. God wants me to see this. But where am I?

Two of the men were dragging the guards through one of the now-open wood-paneled doors across from her while the other three waited. She walked slowly, silently, toward the men, still wanting to stay away from them, but needing information about this location. There were no signs over the doorway behind them, which she could see now led out to a courtyard with brick arches on either side.

She stopped, not wanting to get any closer to the men, especially the large man with the knife. They were dressed in uniforms, but not exactly like American policemen; they wore white shirts, dark pants, and hats. Sarah Beth turned in a slow circle, looking for something, anything with writing on it. If she could figure out where she was, then maybe she could leave.

The two men came back, smoothing their uniforms, and closed the tall wooden door.

"Where is he?" one demanded.

The man in charge seemed irritated. "Were you not listening? The third-floor sitting room, about to have tea."

"Why is the pope having tea in the Ethiopian College, exactly?" another man, who'd been silent until then, asked.

"Because I arranged it," the leader barked. "Now let's go. We need to time this perfectly so that we're in position the moment the attack in the square begins. We'll take him out in the chaos."

They shuffled past her, one of the officers nearly bumping into her, but then she realized that would be impossible, right?

I'm not really here . . .

She tried to follow them up the marble stairs, but a powerful force pulled her back. The acceleration and speed of travel was overwhelming. She gasped as she snapped back into herself, only to find herself sitting up in bed, clutching her blankets to her chest. A chill chased down her spine, and she knew it had nothing to do with the temperature in the room.

The Ethiopian College—that's what the killer had said.

The pope. They were going to kill the pope at some college

somewhere. *That's what "take him out" means, right? And the man with the tattoos, the man I saw through Detective Perez's mind, is a Dark One and he's in charge.*

Sarah Beth grabbed her notebook computer from the desk beside her bed, the room suddenly glowing with blue light as she opened the screen and logged in. She quickly searched *Ethiopian College* and immediately was directed to multiple sites. Sarah Beth clicked on *Images* and gasped again when a picture in the top row caught her eye. She bent over, inspecting closely the ornate lobby of the Papal Ethiopian College, as the picture was labeled, matching the room she had impossibly been in just moments ago.

She closed the screen, and the room went dark. Then, squeezing her eyes shut, she reached out for Jed.

Uncle Jed, it's an emergency. I need you!

CHAPTER
THIRTY-SIX

Jed shifted in the high-backed leather seat of the Ducato crew cab van, grateful they'd taken two vans to the staging area south of the Vatican wall. That meant only four guys in his van, which allowed him to slide the seat back as far as possible without cramping someone in the row behind him. And *that* meant that he was, well, almost comfortable despite being fully kitted up, with a Sig MCX Tread in his lap.

In the front, Eli chatted with the Italian Shepherd who occupied the passenger seat, listening to the man talk about his family, who lived on the Shepherd compound in Berlin. As fascinated as he was by stories of how the man's youngest daughter—now two and a half—knew her colors and shapes before her second birthday, he desperately wanted to know what was going on with the Dark Ones and Nick Woland. He'd tried, twice, to find Corbin out there in the spiritual ether and had eventually succeeded, only to be rebuked with a *"Hey, Jed—I'm pretty busy here. You'll be the first to know if I have something."*

He keyed the mic on the encrypted MBITR radio on the left side of his kit and called Carl, who was providing sniper overwatch atop the service roof of an apartment building beside them.

"Eagle," he queried. "This is Bravo One. Sitrep?"

"One, Eagle," came Carl's soft voice, with the same smooth timbre of every sniper Jed had ever served with. "All quiet. I have good lines to the Governatorato building north of us and west all the way to the Vatican radio station. No threats, just priests milling about so far. I also have a nice line on the north side of the square at six hundred yards, so I'm in range to assist if things go bad. It's packed with tourists, but nothing unusual happening so far."

"Roger, Eagle," he mumbled, wondering if the comment about his line to the north side of the square was meant to be a jab about their position, but he didn't know Carl well enough to tell. The dude seemed, like most snipers, to be quiet and introspective—so it was a coin flip whether the comment was passive-aggressive. Regardless, it was comforting to have the former Marine shooter in position to lend firepower wherever needed.

"At least *someone* from Bravo will be in the fight when this thing goes down," Johnny muttered from beside him.

Jed was about to tear into the Shepherd beside him when Sarah Beth's voice came to him—so loud and clear he was almost surprised to not see her in the seat behind him.

Uncle Jed, it's an emergency. I need you!

I'm sorry, Sarah Beth. We're on mission. I'll call you later, he answered, aware that *call* might be the wrong word. He appreciated the fact that she was struggling to make friends at school, but whatever adolescent melodrama she was dealing with today would have to wait. He was about to push her out of his headspace when her urgent reply chilled him to the bone.

I know you're in Italy at the Vatican. That's what I need to talk to you about, Jed. Please, just listen, before it's too late!

Jed's chest tightened and he looked over at Johnny, who met his stare and frowned.

Jed pulled the handle and yanked the van's slider door open. He stepped out onto the dirt lot in front of the building where actual construction work had been happening before they took over the position using their contractor cover story. He slid the door shut with a hard whomp, cutting off Johnny's protestation of "Where are you going?" in midsentence.

Acutely aware that a kitted-up SEAL would draw attention from cars passing by on Viale Vaticano, he jogged into the empty lobby of the nearby building being renovated. Standing in the partially drywalled foyer, he reconnected with Sarah Beth.

How did you know where I am? he asked, suddenly very concerned about the OPSEC of their operation.

I had a vision inside the Ethiopian College, she said. *There's a Dark One pretending to be a policeman. Bad things are happening.*

The what? Tell me exactly what you saw.

I mean, I could try to explain it . . . or I could just show you.

Really? Even from so far away?

I think so. Close your eyes.

He complied and felt around in the ether for her thread.

I'm right here, she said in his mind, and he found her glowing and magnificent.

Unlike his previous headspace interactions, this one was definitely enhanced—like going from watching a 1980s-era CRT television to a 4K HD flat-screen.

How are you doing this? he asked.

We're doing it, Uncle Jed. Together. It's like the power of trust. The power of two . . .

The experience took him back to the night when Corbin and Sarah Beth were sitting on the sofa in the Yarnells' old West End house, working together to find Victor. He'd only been able to listen to Sarah Beth's expressions of wonderment at the time, but now, experiencing what she had, he finally understood.

It's like a force multiplier, he said.

Exactly. . . . Now c'mon, follow me and don't use my name.

Roger that, he said, remembering the mistake he'd made in the kill house exercise.

No sooner had she spoken than he was whisked away, cruising at warp speed along whatever thread Sarah Beth had found. A heartbeat later, he experienced a rapid metaphysical deceleration, and they were hovering near a dark, human-shaped void in the light.

Where are we? he said.

She shushed him. *Thoughts can be loud or quiet, just like voices.*

Sorry.

I'm trying to find the right thread . . .

Her voice was a soft whisper and he just hovered beside her and waited. The thought of what they were doing suddenly seemed crazy and doubt crept into his head. The moment it did, the ether seemed to tighten around him and he felt a pronounced sweep of nausea.

Stay still, Uncle Jed.

Her voice was scolding—like a parent to a child—and Jed relaxed. He might not fully understand what was happening, but he believed it was from God. And after everything they'd been through together, he certainly believed in Sarah Beth's spiritual gifts.

There's another thread that intersects with the one I'm looking for in the Ethiopian College. Let's try it instead . . .

Suddenly they slipped through a bubble into someone's mind and Jed was looking through the person's eyes. He saw dark hands resting in a man's lap atop the folds of a black priest's cassock, fingers knit together tightly. Then everything went dark as the man squeezed his eyes shut.

"Is everything okay, Rector Senai? You seem anxious," a kindly voice asked.

The eyes opened and as the lids came up, Jed immediately recognized the face of the pope sitting opposite him, a soft smile of concern on his aged face.

"I apologize, Your Holiness," the rector said. Jed realized that the rector was not speaking in English, and yet he somehow *knew* what was being said. "I am just tired. My work has been all-consuming these last few days. I am delighted at the honor of having tea with you."

"I am eager to hear all about your work here at the college," the pope said, "but first, let us relax and enjoy our tea."

Jed felt a malign intent from inside the rector.

He's hiding something, he told Sarah Beth.

I know. I feel it too, she said. *I'm going to try to talk to him in his mind . . .*

No, don't, he said, but it was too late.

What are you hiding, Rector?

Jed realized it was Sarah Beth asking the question, but her voice was disguised and somehow not her own. This little trick was definitely something he'd have to ask her about later.

No man should have to make such a choice—between his God and his family, the rector said.

What choice? she asked, and when the rector didn't answer, she spoke directly to Jed. *I think men with guns kidnapped his family. Or maybe his brother's family. I saw a terrible video . . .*

Many men have been asked to make such choices, Rector, another voice said, one that Jed vaguely recognized. *Know that you are not alone. Have faith in the Lord and He will light a path for you.*

Ben? Is that you? Jed said, immediately regretting the mistake. A wave of dread washed over him and he felt an omnipresent malice.

I see you, an oily, familiar voice echoed everywhere around them.

Jed felt his chest tighten again and his heart pounding at the sound of Victor's voice.

We have to go, Sarah Beth said, grabbing him. *He's here.*

Jed felt her fear—or Rector Senai's, he could not tell—as she plunged them backward out of the rector's mind with such velocity and intention that when Jed slammed back into his own body, he almost tipped over backward. He blinked twice and found himself back in the construction site.

Sarah Beth? Are you still there?

Yes, she answered, and her voice sounded small and far away.

That was Victor, wasn't it?

Yes. Ever since you rescued me from the compound in the woods, I feel like he's been hunting me. He comes to me in my dreams.

Jed clenched his jaw. The same had been true for him. He knew better than to imagine it had been simple nightmares, and that meant Sarah Beth had been bearing the burden of Victor's visits alone. They were living eerily parallel lives, it seemed, in more than one way. Both starting over in new organizations, both looking for acceptance and validation from their peers, and both fending off Victor's unwelcome incursions into their minds at night.

Sarah Beth's not a kid anymore, he realized, picturing her young face. *Maybe on the outside, but on the inside she's a warrior.*

Who is Rector Senai? he asked.

I looked him up online. Rector Feiven Senai is in charge of the Pontifical Ethiopian College, she said, collecting herself. *Which, as far as I can tell, is like a graduate school for Ethiopian priests.*

Okay, well, what does all of this have to do with an attack on the Vatican?

Uncle Jed, the Ethiopian College isn't in Ethiopia. It's in Vatican City. The rector is having tea right now with the pope and I saw something else—bad men. They killed two people already. It was horrible. I think they're inside the Ethiopian College right now. I think they want to kill the pope.

Jed closed his eyes tightly, his mind reeling. His instincts had been right—there was more to the attack than just the terrorists attacking the square. He needed to mobilize his team right now.

Sarah Beth, you did great. Listen to me. Go right now to Pastor Dee and tell her everything.

Do I have to, Uncle Jed? What if she doesn't believe me?

Go now, Sarah Beth, he ordered. *It's super important. Stay with her until you hear from me—do you understand?*

Yes, Uncle Jed. Please be careful. And try not to hurt the rector.

And she was gone.

Jed sprinted back to the van, keying his mic as he ran.

"Joshua Variable, this is Bravo One," he said, reaching the van and jerking the door open. "Everybody—weapons check and get ready to go. We're moving now."

"What's going on?" Johnny asked.

Jed held up a hand as Ben came back in his headset.

"One, Joshua Variable—I heard. You have the green light."

"The secondary target is the pope," Jed announced into his mic, switching his radio now to VOX and informing everyone of this new development on the open channel. "He's in the Ethiopian College as we speak, having tea with a Rector Senai. It's happening now. I need data on the location of the Ethiopian College ASAP."

His teammates poured out of the vans and fell in on him.

"Bravo One, Joshua Variable—you'll recognize the Ethiopian College from the simulation. It's the building you never it made it into. When you're over the wall, I'll guide you in."

"Roger that, Variable. Bravo is moving now," Jed said, gesturing a hand over his head, telling his team to be ready to move.

"I missed it, Bravo One," came Corbin's tight voice on the radio. "I'm sorry."

"Don't be. I had some help. I'll tell you about it later. Joshua Bravo is over the wall in two minutes."

"What's the play, boss?" Eli asked as they ran.

"Grappling and ascenders over the wall," Jed answered, pointing. "Variable leads us through the gardens to the X. Variable, we need deconfliction with GIR and Vatican police. We don't want to get shot going over the wall and crossing the gardens."

"On it, Bravo One," Ben said.

They dashed across the Viale Vaticano as a group, seven Shepherds from Joshua Bravo and their Italian-speaking teammate on loan from Shepherds Europe.

"Bravo is clear to the wall," Carl said in his ear. "I got your six on the breach," the sniper assured him.

"Copy, Eagle. Get ready, Bravo," Jed said and bowed his head while Hyeon passed out ascenders and harnesses.

Father God, guide us. Don't let us be too late. Make our aim true. And please, please keep Sarah Beth safe.

CHAPTER
THIRTY-SEVEN

A stone-faced Woland, leading four operators moving in a chevron pattern, strode down the hall toward the two Swiss Guards who were standing watch outside the college's dining room. Neither of them had their weapons drawn and ready . . . a mistake they would pay for with their lives momentarily.

"Where are Andreas and Peter?" the closer of the guards asked, scanning past Woland's men with a dubious look on his face. "They should be with you."

"They're not coming," Woland said, pulling a pistol with a suppressor from the small of his back.

He squeezed the trigger at the same time as a suppressed round fired by Rocco whisked past his left ear. Both bullets hit their marks, dropping the two Swiss Guards where they stood while they belatedly reached for their holsters. The three other Dark Horizon operators moved into breaching positions outside the closed dining room door.

"Kill everyone but the pope and Rector Senai," Woland said robotically and gave the go signal.

The largest of his men splintered the decorative wooden door with a single, well-placed kick, and the three shooters plus Rocco went in with guns blazing. Woland waited until the shooting had stopped and then entered the room with a pleasant smile stretched across his face as he surveyed the carnage. The room looked like the set of a slasher movie, with blood spatter everywhere, including all over the pope's white pontifical garb and left cheek. Nine corpses, in delightful variations of limp repose, littered the room. Most were collapsed in their chairs at the table, but two plainclothes agents and one of his Dark Horizon shooters were sprawled in growing pools of crimson on the floor.

Woland pursed his lips and locked eyes with the pope. To his surprise and disappointment, instead of quaking with fear, His Holiness glared back with composure and judgment.

"Such pointless violence," the pope said in accented English. "You need not have murdered them. I would have come with you had you only asked."

Woland gave a wordless snort in reply and shifted his gaze to Rector Senai, who was quaking in his chair. "You did well, Rector," he said. "The Dark Ones will welcome you with open arms."

The pope turned to Senai, a surprised and woeful expression on his face.

"I'm so sorry, Your Holiness," Senai said, eyes rimming with tears. "I had no choice."

"We always have a choice, but I forgive you, my son, nonetheless," the pope said and crossed the air in front of the Ethiopian.

"What about my brother's family?" Senai said, his voice cracking as he looked from the pope back to Woland. "Did you release them?"

Woland shrugged. "Sorry," he said with a dark grin as he leveled his pistol at the man's forehead. "No conscience-easing consolation prizes today, Rector."

Woland pulled the trigger.

Upon this final execution, the pope closed his eyes, bowed his head, and began to pray.

"Get him up," Woland barked and then traced a circle in the air with his index finger. "Time to move."

The satellite phone in his pocket vibrated. Frowning, he retrieved it knowing it could not possibly be good news.

"Yes?"

"I take it you have the package?"

"Yes, we are about to move now. All is going according to plan."

"The Shepherds are there," Victor hissed in his ear, but his voice held excitement rather than concern. "They are coming now."

"How do you know?"

"They were inside the head of the man you just killed. I can't tell you who the Watcher was—someone quite resilient as I couldn't penetrate the mind. The other one was the new Shepherd, Jedidiah Johnson."

"I'm ready for them," Woland said with a smirk. "I anticipated this."

"Do not, under any circumstance, engage the Shepherd prodigy. Focus on your exfil, and leave Johnson to me," Victor said and the line went dead.

I wonder what that's all about.

Rocco and another operator quickly fell in behind the pope and hoisted him to his feet by grabbing under his armpits. Unlike his portly predecessor, this pope was lean, bordering on gaunt. Despite his years, he was a handsome man with penetrating blue eyes and sage features.

"Unhand me," he said, swatting away their gloved hands. "I can walk."

"We don't have time for that," Woland said and directed two operators to pick up the holy man in a litter-style carry. "Oh, and, guys, not a mark on him. My instructions were very clear—we are to deliver the prize unmolested."

Rocco and the five remaining operators returned stoic nods. They understood the price of disobedience and had no intention of drawing Victor's ire, even if it meant forfeiting the once-in-a-lifetime opportunity to leave a scar on the world's most famous living man of God.

"The Shepherds are here," Woland said to Rocco. "They're either en route from the square or they might be in the gardens already. Regardless, take these five and intercept them. Your uniforms will work to your advantage in the chaos."

"So this is the 'mop-up crew' mission you referred to?"

"Yes," Woland said. "Kill the men that hunt us and then meet me in the tunnels."

Rocco scowled at him but said nothing before turning to lead the remaining operators down the hall.

As the hit squad left, he was surprised how much he regretted that he could not be the one to kill the new Shepherd himself. And what if Morvant was here, personally? What a waste to miss the opportunity to confront his old nemesis. He turned to the pope, slung like dirty laundry between the two contractors. On this cue, he felt the beast inside tug at him, urging him to violent action.

No, he told his other. *Patience. We're playing the long game now.*

No matter the price, he would do whatever it took to stand beside Victor as equals when the prince of darkness established the ultimate kingdom.

"Your plan will fail," the pope said, meeting his gaze.

Woland laughed at the hollow threat, started a timer on his watch, and made the call to the jihadist commander to commence the attack in St. Peter's Square. Then, intoxicated by the adrenaline and power, he did the "Ali shuffle," quick shifting his feet, and executed a combination of shadowboxer punches at the air less than an inch from the pope's face. This party was just getting started . . . and he couldn't wait to get his groove on.

CHAPTER
THIRTY-EIGHT

Jed craned his head back and looked up the thirty-nine-foot stone wall surrounding Vatican City.

"Thanks a lot, Pope Leo," he murmured, remembering the name of the pontiff who'd ordered the fortification built over eleven hundred years ago. A lot had changed in counterterrorism operations over the past millennium, but scaling a forty-foot wall was still as much a pain in the butt now as it was then. Well, perhaps not just as painful . . .

"Joshua Variable, Bravo One—sitrep on getting clearance to breach the garden between the Marconi Radio Tower and Shell Fountain?" Jed said into his boom mic as he prepped his ascender.

"The Gendarmerie watch commander is not responding to our queries," Ben came back from the TOC in the church basement where he was coordinating operations with Vincenzo, Corbin, David, and the other support personnel. "Still working the problem."

Jed gritted his teeth. He didn't have time for this. They needed to go and go now.

Screw it, he decided. *We're going.*

Jed turned to Eli and gave the order. "Hooks."

The veteran shepherd nodded and picked up a specialty launcher the size of a SAM unit that, instead of firing a missile, used compressed air to launch a tethered grappling hook.

"Please work," Eli said and squeezed the trigger.

The launcher made a whump sound and fired the weighted grappling hook projectile toward the top of the wall. A hundred feet of Kevlar-woven, cut-resistant Novabraid cord trailed behind it as it sailed over the top of the wall and disappeared.

"Hooah!" Grayson shouted and immediately began working the rope while Eli loaded another hook projectile from a coiled, ready pile of line on the ground.

A second whump echoed as another line sailed over the wall. Grayson continued taking in slack until he felt the hook catch. He pulled it tight, then checked the hold with his body weight. "Set."

Hyeon worked the second line in parallel, while Eli fired a third grappling hook up and over.

"Prep ascenders," Jed ordered, referring to the toaster-size power-assist climbing devices designed for vertical infils like this.

A series of explosions to the east shook the ground and set off car alarms all over Rome. A bolus of adrenaline flooded Jed's bloodstream as the call came in from the Joshua Alpha team leader. St. Peter's Square was under attack, just as Corbin had predicted.

"Variable, Bravo One—we're going over the wall," Jed called in. "Tell GIR not to shoot us."

"Copy, Bravo, but be advised we still do *not* have comms with GIR. Proceed with caution," Ben said.

"Eagle, Bravo One," Jed said, radioing Carl, the team sniper in his roost across the street. "You're our eyes. Provide covering fire if GIR tries to engage. Warning shots only."

"Eagle, copy," Carl came back.

Jed turned to the first flight of breachers and chopped a hand toward the top of the wall. "Go."

Johnny, Grayson, and Nisha—whose ascenders were already clipped to the three lines—took off running up the wall aided by the gravity-defying tech. Jed jogged to the line dangling below Nisha and fed the Novabraid rope into his ascender's serpentine drive mechanism. Next, he clipped the safety traveler to the line below the ascender and squeezed the trigger. The power pulley mechanism grabbed, took up tension, and jerked him forward. Given his linebacker-size body, he waited until Nisha cleared the top before starting his ascent. The hooks and lines were rated for five hundred pounds but that was assuming optimal tine engagement. If the hook broke loose, Nisha falling from that height could kill her.

The instant she was up and over, Jed squeezed the trigger on his ascender and the battery-powered drive mechanism pulled him into the air. Leaning back, he managed to keep his body nearly perpendicular to the stone face as he "ran" up the wall. Feeling very much like a superhero, Jed glanced left at their Italian Shepherd augment, checking the man's progress, and then right at Bex, who was ascending beside him. *This job is so cool,* he thought randomly as he caught her grinning. Eli and Hyeon, the last men on the ground, covered their six from below as they made the four-story ascent. Up top, Johnny, Grayson, and Nisha scanned their respective sectors for threats from kneeling firing stances. As soon as Jed reached the top, he unclipped his ascender and quickly checked the hook to make sure he'd not dislodged the tines.

"Topside secure," Johnny reported.

He acknowledged the report and waved Eli and Hyeon up. With Bex at his side, Jed sighted over the wall, scanning the streets of Rome below to cover their final two operators on ascent.

"Bravo, Watcher One," Corbin said, her voice a tight cord. "You've got incoming."

"Where?" he asked as a suppressed round whizzed by over his head.

"From the northwest. They're taking covered positions around the Vatican radio tower and behind Leonine wall—that stone wall connected to St. John's Tower," she said.

The timing couldn't be worse as Eli and Hyeon were still ten feet from the top. Cursing under his breath, Jed held his position, leaving himself vulnerable to being shot in the back rather than putting his ascending brothers in that danger.

"I got 'em," Johnny said, gesturing to their ten o'clock. "Uniformed Gendarmerie."

A lump formed in Jed's throat. This was exactly the scenario he'd dreaded—a blue-on-blue, friendly fire deconfliction nightmare.

"Bravo," Jed said, addressing the entire team, "Try to keep

them pinned down with covering fire, but do not engage. I repeat, this is a zero-casualty engagement."

"One, Eagle—I got your backs," Carl came back and a heartbeat later Jed heard him going to work with his sniper rifle.

"Variable, One—we need you to get on the horn with the Gendarmerie watch commander and tell the guys shooting at us near Marconi Radio Tower to stand down," Jed radioed in just as Eli and Hyeon reached the top of the wall. He extended a helping hand to Eli and pulled him up and over at the top where transition was the most difficult.

"Copy. Is it GIR engaging you or regular police?" Ben asked.

"Regular police force," Johnny said, answering for Jed. "These guys are not kitted up and are engaging us with pistols."

"We can't stay here, One," Grayson hollered as he hit the ground to Jed's left. "We're in no-man's-land."

The veteran was right—they were sitting ducks on this slab of wide-open nothing beside the wall.

"Last man over," Hyeon shouted, dropping into a low crouch beside Jed, Johnny, and Bex.

"Bravo, reposition east to cover," Jed shouted over the gunfire and chopped a hand toward Shell Fountain, which was surrounded by trees and heavy shrubbery.

"Covering fire," Carl said, and the cadence of rounds from his sniper rifle picked up.

Their seven-operator team plus their Italian augment sprinted along the wall and then doglegged right. As they did, however, the firing angles changed—allowing the Vatican police to better engage them from their covered positions, where they didn't have to risk exposing themselves to Carl's sniper fire. In a normal engagement,

Jed would have split his team and sent a squad around to the north, flanking the shooters and putting his adversary in a cross fire kill box between two elements and his sniper. But in this case, he didn't have the luxury of shooting back.

Hyeon grunted beside him as they scrambled down a berm toward a crescent-shaped cluster of trees and dense shrubs. Jed's mind filled with both marvel and dread at the familiar scene, nearly identical to the virtual reality scenario in the kill house.

No coincidences . . .

Then they were packed together in the scant cover of the grove of trees in the garden.

"You hit?" Jed asked Hyeon as bullets zipped by overhead.

"Took a round in the back, but it hit my vest," Hyeon said. "I think I'm good."

Jed settled into a kneeling firing stance beside a tree trunk and brought his rifle up in a scan to mark the positions of the Vatican police shooters. As he tried to work the problem and figure out what to do, his head suddenly got swimmy. Along with the vertigo, a wave of nausea roiled his insides. His guts felt like someone was putting them into a twist, like the way one wrings out a wet towel.

He groaned and buckled at the waist.

There you are, an oily voice oozed in his mind.

Victor?

Who else? the Dark One said through a laugh. *Did you think God was going to help you? He certainly doesn't care about the pope, so why would He bother with a sinner and coward like you?*

"Jed, dude, are you okay?" somebody asked him.

He blinked hard and shook his head.

You're weak. You don't have the stomach to be a Shepherd and your incompetence is going to kill them all.

It was happening all over again, playing out almost identically to the scenario he'd botched so badly during Jericho Basic. Just like before, he was leading his team through the Vatican Gardens, pinned down by local security forces, with a spiritual assault on his psyche . . . only this time he was in a different grove of trees, with more teammates to worry about, and the person rooting around in his head wasn't Ben Morvant pretending to be Victor, but the actual Victor.

You're weak. You're powerless. You're a fool . . . and God has abandoned you.

He felt his rifle slip out of his grip and hang limp from the sling on his chest.

Get out of my head! he screamed in his mind, palms pressed to his temples.

His mind reflexively reached to Corbin for help, but he shut it down immediately, severing the thread to her. He'd made that mistake the last time and wouldn't jeopardize his Watcher again. He had to face Victor alone.

A series of explosions shook the ground and Jed assumed they'd just been hand-grenaded by the Gendarmerie. He was certain that when he opened his eyes, he'd be surrounded by body parts and the dead eyes of his teammates.

"Variable, Alpha One—we're engaged with multiple terrorists in the square!" the Joshua Alpha team leader reported on the shared comms channel.

That's right, Jedidiah. They're all going to die and there's nothing you can do about it, Victor taunted.

"Alpha, Watcher One—you've got a suicide bomber at your two o'clock, thirty yards from your pos," Corbin reported.

Despite the agony, this made Jed smile. His Watcher was distracted now, engaged in another fight, following different threads. He felt a hand on his shoulder.

"Jed . . . Jed, are you okay?" a woman's voice asked . . . Nisha, he thought.

"I can't . . . ," he groaned, the sound of his own voice very far away.

"Jed, we're going to die if we don't do something," she said. "We need to deconflict this right now."

Take the easy road and save yourself. No one has to know. It will be our little secret. You're already a murderer; what's a few more innocent souls?

"Victor is in my head," Jed said through gritted teeth. "I'm all alone and I don't know how much longer I can hold on . . ."

"You're not alone," a different voice said in his earpiece—a soothing, familiar voice, a voice filled with confidence and certainty. "I know I let you down that day in the basement . . . I froze. I was a coward and let you and Rachel battle that demon alone. I'll never forgive myself for that, but I'm here now."

"David?" Jed croaked as he felt himself losing control, his mind being sucked down a black vortex of defeat.

Give in to me and I'll take away the pain, Jedidiah. Stop fighting and accept who you really are, Victor said, pressing into him.

"I don't have your gifts, Jed," David continued, "or your training or your tactical experience. And I can't help you fend off Victor like Corbin or Sarah Beth, but I want you to know I believe in you. You've always been the strongest of us. You were always our protector. Now is not the time for uncertainty. Now is not the time for doubt. Reach for the Spirit, Jedidiah, and the Spirit will give you light."

Jed grabbed onto David's words, like a life preserver in a raging sea, but Victor responded immediately, boring into him. Jed felt his body contracting, his guts twisting, and Victor screaming in his mind. So much noise, so much chaos, so much pressure to surrender . . .

"What do I do?" Jed called out, clutching his head.

"Just reach," David said, his voice a pillar of certitude.

To survive Victor's assault, he needed to be closed and hard and small—like a turtle pulled into its shell. What David was asking was the opposite of what every fiber in his being was screaming for him to do. And yet in his heart he knew David was right. Victor wanted him closed and small and alone. The paradox was a trap and David understood this.

With great effort, Jed unclenched his right fist . . .

And then his left.

He inhaled deeply and—shedding his fear—opened himself. He opened his mind, his heart, and his soul. Not to Victor, but to the Holy Spirit.

God, help me. Please.

And the light found him. He felt it. He reached for it. He let it in. And when he did, a calm certainty flowed into and through him. His twisted, contracted muscles unbound themselves, and the deafening chaos in his head went quiet and still.

Jed turned to the dark, evil thing orbiting his mind. *I don't answer to you, Victor. Get out.*

The darkness snarled at him just as the light bleached it out of existence . . .

"Jed? Jed, can you hear me?" Nisha said, her hand on the back of his neck.

Like waking from a nightmare, his proprioception grudgingly returned. He opened his eyes and found himself kneeling, hunched forward, looking down, his assault rifle lying on the pine needle carpet in front of him. He inhaled deeply and grabbed his rifle from where it hung on his chest.

"I can hear you now," he said, turning to lock eyes with her.

"Are you okay?" she asked, crouching as low as possible beside him.

He nodded and everything clicked into place. Deep inside, he already understood what was happening all around him, but uncertainty had turned it into a probability game paralyzing him from taking action. The Gendarmerie watch commander, Cattaneo, was compromised, which explained why he wasn't answering their calls and why they had been one step behind from the beginning. Everything the guy had done since Vincenzo had made initial contact had worked to confuse and undermine the Shepherds' efforts. But by opening himself, Jed had purged the paralyzing doubt and indecision that had crippled him in the kill house and was crippling him once again in the garden today.

Enough!

He was certain the men in Gendarmerie uniforms assaulting them were Dark One confederates working for Woland, but before shooting his way out of this mess, he needed confirmation.

"What are you doing?" Nisha said with incredulity as he popped to his feet.

"Going to get confirmation," he said with a wry grin. "Cover me."

"What? Jed, have you lost your mind?"

"Nope, be back in a second," he said and took off north on a flanking maneuver.

To his surprise, Nisha fell in beside him and matched his advance stride for stride. Instead of chastising her for recklessly accompanying him on his reckless maneuver, he read her in.

"We're going to look one of these shooters in the eyes," he said. "It's the only way to be sure."

"If they glow, you know," she said tightly.

"Exactly," he said and then called Eli. "Two, One—turn up the heat and see if you can motivate these jerks to seek new cover."

"Copy that," Eli came back.

A moment later, assault rifle fire from the crescent stand of trees picked up dramatically, and Jed's plan worked. Multiple Gendarmerie shooters scattered from their hides like roaches fleeing a flashlight beam. One of the men abandoned an outcropping of bushes and headed directly toward them. Jed locked eyes with the man and saw the other man's irises flicker the color of flame.

Nisha's rifle burped beside him, her 7.62mm round dropping the Dark soldier with a head shot a split second before Jed's finger moved off his trigger guard.

"You snooze, you lose," she said with a satisfied certainty.

He grinned sideways at her as he made the call: "Bravo team, you are weapons free. The guys trying to murder us are confirmed Delta-Oscar tangos. Shoot to kill."

"Bravo," Eli answered, a tacit acknowledgment for the group.

An immediate shift in firing patterns served as tactical confirmation. Now on the offensive, Joshua Bravo quickly turned the tide, taking out the last three enemy shooters in short order. As soon as the last enemy tango was down, Jed redirected Bravo to the Ethiopian College building. As they sprinted through the gardens, the battle for control of St. Peter's Square raged on. The conflict was so intense, with such heated comms, that Jed migrated Bravo to a secondary frequency. He needed a clear channel for breaching the college, because it was entirely possible they were walking into a trap.

Not liking the tactical geometry of the front entrance—a three-sided courtyard with zero cover where they'd be fish in a barrel if Woland had snipers—Jed opted to breach the building in the back. To his surprise, they breached without meeting any resistance. After entry, he split his team into two elements to systematically search the college for Woland and the pope. Inside, they found neither. What they did find, however, were plenty of dead bodies as well as a handful of survivors sheltering in place. When they finally discovered the third-story dining room, Jed's heart sank.

Scanning the carnage, he called it in: "Variable, Bravo One—Rector Senai is dead and so is everyone else who was having tea with the pope. The pope is missing, presumed kidnapped by Woland's team. Please advise?"

"Pursue and recover," Ben came back, the instruction both simple and direct.

"Roger that," Jed said and then under his breath murmured, "Easier said than done."

"Well, ain't this just wonderful," Johnny proclaimed, throwing his hands up in the air. "While Jed had us farting around in the bushes, Woland got away with the pope. Vatican City is only a hundred and nine acres. I'm sure we'll find him lickety-split."

"Shut up, Johnny," Nisha snapped. "Complaining doesn't help anybody."

Jed turned to their Italian compatriot—a Shepherd called Franco. "Franco, I need your help. If the Dark Ones wanted to get the pope out alive without being seen, what's the fastest and stealthiest way to do it?"

Franco rubbed his chin for a moment, then said, "There is an underground railroad tunnel; we crossed directly over it on our way here from Shell Fountain. It is not used anymore, but it is possible to exit that way."

Jed nodded and closed his eyes.

"What are you doing?" Franco asked.

"Checking," Jed said as he reached out with his mind, searching for the invisible thread leading to Nick Woland. It was a long shot, but if he concentrated enough and was lucky . . .

Got you, he thought, surprised to find Woland's tether a few moments later.

As it turned out, all he had to do was tune to the thread vibrating with the most rage. He took a deep breath and accelerated himself along the thread like Sarah Beth had taught him until he found the former Shepherd. He hovered around the dark void, questioning the sanity of what he was about to do.

Just do it, the SEAL inside barked.

Jed plunged himself headfirst into Woland's mind.

"It's not the railroad tunnel," he said, talking aloud but with his eyes closed. "There are no tracks that I see. It's some other kind of tunnel. Looks more like a catacomb."

"They're in the Templar tunnels," Franco said, "a network of tunnels built a thousand years ago under the Vatican and added to over the centuries. It is a better, more secret way to exit Vatican City. The train comes out in only one place, but the Templar tunnels have multiple exits and many places to hide. Tell me exactly what you see, Jedidiah."

Looking through Woland's eyes, Jed waited and watched for something identifiable.

"I see a split in the tunnel. There's an ornamental chair against the wall at the junction. The chair is old and made of gilded wood with a gold seal of some sort at the top of the seat back. Does that mean anything to you, Franco?"

"I know this place," the Italian said, tense excitement in his voice.

Jed retreated back into himself with a jolt. His eyelids popped open and he was looking at Franco. "Can you lead us there?"

"I've only been in the tunnels once, but I will try. The closest access point is under the Palace of the Governatorate, not too far from here," Franco said. "It is probably how they entered."

"All right," Jed said, bringing his rifle up. "Let's go get the pope back and put an end to Nicholas Woland once and for all."

CHAPTER
THIRTY-NINE

Some secrets are easier kept than others, Woland thought as he led his exfil team and the pope through the tunnels. The whole world knew about the ancient necropolis discovered under St. Peter's Basilica in the 1940s, rumored to hold the remains of the famed disciple himself. And there was also the secret tunnel in the Vatican Palace leading to the Passetto di Borgo—a 2,600-foot-long elevated escape passage built between the Vatican east wall and Castel Sant'Angelo. But the true architectural wonder—a subterranean catacomb and tunnel system snaking everywhere beneath Vatican City—remained a closely guarded secret.

One of God's little miracles . . .

With an emphasis on "little" because those are the only kind God can manage.

"I need to rest," the pope said, taking a seat on an ornamental chair positioned against the stone wall at the crux of the Y-shaped junction ahead.

Woland glowered at the man. Once they'd made it below-ground, he'd let his guys on litter duty set the pontiff down so he could walk under his own holy power. Weighing the tactical priorities, Woland decided he needed the two extra rifles at the ready more than he needed the extra speed. That calculus still held, so long as they didn't stop.

But the pope didn't know that.

"Carry him," Woland barked to his men while taking the opportunity to check the hand-sketched map he was using to navigate.

"No, that won't be necessary. I need but a moment to catch my breath," the pope said, waving them off.

"That moment is over," Woland said, validating that they were supposed to go right at this particular junction.

The pope nodded but kept his backside planted firmly on the chair.

Anger flared inside Woland at the man's tacit stonewalling. The pope wasn't sweating, nor was he out of breath. The old gee-zer's level of fitness was definitely better than he pretended, which meant this little rest break was a sneaky attempt to slow their progress so that the Shepherds could catch up. He'd lost comms with Rocco almost immediately after entering this labyrinth, which was not unexpected. Without repeaters, even the best comms gear in the world was no match for five meters of granite and earth overhead. And yet despite having received no report on the matter, Woland knew Rocco's team was dead.

He also knew that the new Shepherd called Jedidiah Johnson was leading the team in pursuit. Victor had explicitly warned him not to engage the Shepherd—a practice that was entirely out of character for Satan's right-hand man.

If you could call Victor a man . . .

As much as Woland hated to admit it, the order had gotten under his skin. Not because he was afraid of Johnson—he wasn't afraid of any man, including Morvant—but because he could not help but worry that Victor's warning might have been born of prophecy. Had Victor foreseen Woland's death? Victor had referred to Johnson as a Shepherd prodigy. Was the former SEAL that good? Was the only engagement Woland could win against Johnson the one not fought?

To hell with fate, he thought.

"Get up," Woland growled and grabbed the pope forcefully by the upper arm, jerking the man to his feet. "Break time's over."

The pope flashed him an unflappable, apologetic smile and then started walking down the wrong tunnel.

Woland stopped him and shoved him toward the right-hand branch. "We're going *this* way."

"My apologies," the man of God said as he dawdled off. "I don't know my way around these tunnels."

Sure you don't, Woland thought, bringing his rifle up and pointing it at the pontiff's back. He imagined squeezing the trigger and ending this charade right here and now. Things would be so much easier if he did, but a stab of heat in his chest stayed his finger—his master reminding him of the price of disobedience. Victor had grand plans for the pope, plans that would horrify the world and usher in a new era of chaos, hate, and religious warfare. The New Crusades versus the global jihad—2.4 billion Christians trying to kill 1.9 billion Muslims and vice versa.

Oh, the glorious chaos . . .

Grudgingly, Woland lowered his weapon to bring up the rear of the caravan as they headed north under the Vatican museums. There would be plenty of time for unbridled killing . . . and when that day came, he, Nicholas Woland, would finally be able to show the world what he was capable of.

They'd traveled thirty meters or so down the tunnel when the echo of pounding footsteps ahead froze Woland in his tracks. He immediately took a knee, held up a closed fist, and sighted over his pistol down the dimly lit corridor. The tactician in him imagined two possible scenarios unfolding. Scenario one, the Shepherds had deduced their exit plan and sent a second team, which meant he would be boxed in by two converging assault teams. If that was the case, it was game over. Scenario two, this was his exfil team falling in on his position, in which case he was about to have four more shooters to augment his force.

"Hold your fire," he said over his shoulder to the two fighters flanking the pope.

The footsteps ahead went quiet.

The converging assault force had stopped just outside of visual range, weapons undoubtedly up and ready. Both parties were in a tenuous and dangerous standoff until identities could be confirmed. Instead of calling out a code word challenge-response to validate friend from foe, Dark Ones had a simpler and foolproof method. Woland summoned the beast inside, stoking a fire of rage and hate until he felt that old familiar burn behind his eyes and a pulsing red halo appeared around the periphery of his vision.

A pair of glowing amber eyes flashed back at him in reply.

"Let's move," Woland said, popping to his feet and chopping a hand forward.

The augment team didn't wait for him in place, running instead toward his position and meeting him in the middle.

"What's going on?" Woland asked, addressing the leader of the exfil unit, a juggernaut of a man called Lucius. "You were supposed to wait for us at the exit."

"The exit is blown," Lucius said. "The Carabinieri have arrived. I think they're securing the perimeter."

"You think, or you know?" Woland snapped.

"I counted three patrol vehicles and sirens are wailing all over Rome."

The beast inside Woland burned with anger and he felt the compulsion to be reckless and go out guns blazing, but he quelled the impulse and forced himself to think strategically. He pulled out the map and traced the path of an alternate tunnel he could use as a backup exit. Originally he'd deemed it riskier, as it emptied into the wine cellar of an operating hotel and required a trek through the lobby to get to a vehicle, but that might work to his advantage now.

A plan began to formulate in his head.

"Okay, here's what we're going to do," he said, addressing the group. "Lucius, you and the pope come with me. We're going back to the other tunnel and try to make the alternate exit. The rest of you find fortified positions here and then make plenty of noise to draw the Shepherds into an ambush in this tunnel. After you dispatch them, double-time it to the other tunnel and follow us out. If that exit is viable, we'll know by then."

Lucius nodded, the corner of his mouth curling up almost imperceptibly as he well understood the subtext. Only a select handful of them were making it out of this labyrinth alive, and for that to happen required martyrs.

Woland grabbed the pope just above the elbow and pulled the man of God after him in a stumbling run as he and Lucius back-tracked. Time was not on his side now, and their only hope was to reach the fork and disappear down the other tunnel before the Shepherd team arrived at the junction and cut them off.

CHAPTER FORTY

Jed snapped his NVGs into place as he stepped through the ancient-looking iron door and descended the worn stone steps into the darkness below. Immediately the world came to life in shades of green and gray—Eli clearing left as they descended and Jed reflexively clearing right. At the bottom of the stairs they paused, each clearing behind them in their respective corners, then taking a knee as Grayson and Bex surged forward, clearing ahead and center. Then he was up again, moving in a diamond formation down the ancient corridor.

They moved swiftly, scanning sectors and recesses without needing to speak, their movement fluid, in concert, and understood. A part of his mind, the part not occupied with the work at hand as a single segment of an eight-piece hunting and killing machine, marveled at the craftsmanship of the tunnel they moved swiftly along. The stacked stone walls were perfectly cut, the seams uniform and even and spreading into the arches spaced between the rounded stone ceiling every fifteen feet or so, smoothly and perfectly. Had the stone tunnel beneath the Vatican been built in the modern era, the workmanship would be laudable. That it had been created a thousand years ago was nothing short of miraculous.

"Bravo One, Variable—comms check," Ben's voice said in Jed's ears, the signal broken, causing short, annoying breaks in the transmission.

"Variable, copy you broken. Without repeaters, looks like we're going to lose comms," Jed whispered into the boom mic by his mouth as he moved. With the amount of stone and mortar overhead, he wasn't surprised.

How do you read Watcher One, Bravo One? came Corbin's crystal clear voice in his mind, putting his mind at ease.

Perfect, Watcher. Nice to have you in my head.

He felt her smile.

They came to a junction and cleared the intersecting branches reflexively, like the well-oiled assault team they had become. Dim light filled the tunnels now, from what he deduced were motion-activated battery-powered lights affixed to the stone walls at regular intervals. Jed flipped his NVGs up onto his helmet and took a knee on the left side of the dividing wall until Grayson called, "Clear" in his headset, then rose.

We have to move faster.

Jed chopped a hand forward and then took the lead, accelerating down the tunnel. Evenly spaced amber-colored emergency lights turned on sequentially, illuminating the way as they passed into each lantern's detection cone. After fifty meters, he abruptly halted them and took a knee.

"You see something?" Eli whispered, kneeling beside him.

"Yeah, the lights are still on ahead," Jed whispered back. "They must be motion activated and on a timer that automatically shuts off after some preset duration."

"Which means Woland's been here and we're catching up."

"Yeah, but we've got a problem," Jed said, scanning the Y-shaped intersection ahead where the tunnels split into left and right branches thirty degrees offset. At the junction, he recognized the antique chair with the gold seal, the exact chair he'd seen through Woland's eyes when he'd briefly penetrated the former Shepherd's mind.

"Which is?" Eli said.

"Both branches are lit . . ."

"Dude, good catch," Eli said, then blew air through pursed lips beside him. "So . . . you think Woland split his team to confuse us?"

Jed shrugged. "Maybe, or maybe he sent a runner down one so he'd force us to pick."

"We could split our team?" Eli said. "I can take four right and you take four left."

"I don't know," Jed said, chewing the inside of his cheek. "I'd rather stay together and pick correctly than hedge."

"I hear ya, but the clock's ticking."

"Let me check with Watcher One," Jed said and tried to reach out to Corbin for guidance, but she didn't respond.

Strange . . .

"I can't reach her," he said, glancing at Eli.

"Variable, Bravo Two—do you copy?" Eli said, trying to reach Ben on the radio, and when they got no answer, he added, "No comms."

Jed nodded. "Looks like we're on our own."

"What's your gut tell you?"

Jed was about to answer when a cry for help followed by angry voices echoed from the right-hand tunnel. He glanced at Eli and with a grin said, "My gut says go right."

"Mine too," the veteran said, popping up into a combat crouch.

Jed chopped a hand toward forward-right and the team advanced as one.

Upon reaching the junction, he turned to Nisha. "Cover here and watch our six," Jed said, thinking it prudent to leave a ready shooter in position just in case Woland had any tricks up his sleeve.

"Check," she said and took a knee against the tunnel wall facing back into the nexus created by the intersection of the three passages.

Thighs burning, Jed hugged the left wall as he advanced, quick shuffling in a combat crouch. On the far side of the right wall, Eli matched him in mirror image. Fifteen meters into the tunnel, rifle fire erupted in a deafening roar amplified and reverberated by the stone walls. Muzzle flashes dotted the dimly lit passage ahead and the tracers crisscrossed the tunnel as enemy fire tore down the passage.

"Heavy contact," Grayson called from behind him, though of course everyone on Joshua Bravo knew that by now.

The tunnel geometry, combined with the complete lack of hides or covered firing positions, made this firefight an absolute nightmare. It was like being trapped in a firing range—naked targets at the end of a lane.

"Return fire!" Johnny shouted, unloading in earnest with his MCX.

Jed understood the compulsion, as the only defense they had was a good offense. The only problem with that plan was the pope, who was down there somewhere.

"Back, back, back!" Jed shouted, backpedaling. "And hold your fire. We can't risk hitting the pope."

"Are you crazy!" Johnny shouted, dropping prone on the ground. "You're going to get us killed."

Dread washed over Jed.

"Aim high," Grayson barked. "We need suppressing fire, but One is right: we can't hit the pope."

"Jed, we're all going to die if you don't get confirmation," Eli shouted as tracers zipped past them. "We have no comms with Variable. It's up to you and Watcher One. Use your gifts—it's now or never."

Jed dropped prone beside Eli and, despite the maelstrom around him, closed his eyes and reached out to Corbin. *Watcher One, we need you!*

The pope's not with these men, Corbin said.

Are you sure?

Pretty sure, she said. *Ben thinks Woland took the pope in the other tunnel. This force is a decoy to ambush you. I tried to reach you, but something or someone has been blocking me. Ben and I had to work together to find you.*

"Weapons free!" Jed shouted, hearing all he needed to hear. "Return fire."

The Shepherds returned fire with a synchronized and deafening volley that put the distant attackers on their heels.

Is Ben with you now? Jed asked Corbin, glancing back over his shoulder at where Nisha was still holding at her post.

No, he left the TOC.

Where did he go?

He wouldn't tell me. He said there was something that only he could do.

"He's going after Woland," Jed muttered and then turned to Eli. "Take control of Bravo and take these guys out."

"Where are you going?" Eli asked, but his face seemed content and trusting.

"I'm taking Nisha and we're going to search the other tunnel. Watcher One thinks Woland has the pope and is trying to sneak out. These guys are the hit squad he left behind to kill us."

Before Eli could object, Jed popped up and sprinted back to where Nisha was dutifully covering their six.

"C'mon," he said, waving her to fall in on him. "You're coming with me."

CHAPTER FORTY-ONE

Woland's headspace was a war zone—where a desperate and dirty battle between duty and self-preservation raged. As an elite operator, the mantra of *mission before self* had been pounded into his psyche. Both the Army and the Shepherds had brainwashed him into believing that sacrificing his life in service of his tasking—no matter how asinine that tasking might be—was the highest and most noble calling an operator could hope for. That was, of course, both stupid and absurd. Since joining the Dark Ones, he'd flipped that mantra on its head and lived by the converse: *self before mission.*

But now, trapped in the underbelly of the Holy City, surrounded by enemies with little hope of either mission success or survival, he wondered which dictum his masters expected of him. Which outcome would please Victor most? Which outcome would better serve the Dark Prince's long-term machinations? Was delivering the pope alive or Woland's survival to fight another day better for the cause? Surely they didn't expect him to die in vain. There were martyrs and there were *martyrs*, and he had aspirations to be neither. Everything he'd accomplished with this operation, whether he delivered the pope alive or executed him in the name of Allah in the tunnels, would achieve the desired goal. The fear, anger, hatred, and racism that would erupt from the kidnapping and murder of the pope would feed the cycle of religious violence for decades—and ruin the faith of millions. Regardless of the specifics, the outcome would be the greatest triumph for the Dark Ones in a millennium.

I certainly don't need to die to be a hero.

Behind him the sound of gunfire erupted in the tunnels, confirming his fear that the Shepherd squad led by Jedidiah Johnson had survived the ambush by Rocco and his team of spiritual mercenaries. Escaping the second ambush he'd laid for them, however, would be much more difficult. And yet what if Johnson did? His mind went back to Victor's warning. Paranoid thoughts that his own death might have been foreseen by the devil himself flooded Woland's brain. Then, an emotion he'd not felt in years crashed over him like a breaker in the surf . . . panic.

He needed to get out of here at all costs.

The beast inside him stirred and he felt it clawing to the surface and vying for control. It wanted to hunt, to fight, to kill. His gaze ticked to the pope, whose mouth Lucius had covered with a piece of silver duct tape.

He stopped walking, standing fully erect, his head turned upward.

Something was wrong. He had a sudden and overwhelming sense of being watched. He squinted into the darkness ahead of him, scanning for threats with the eyes of the beast.

"What's wrong?" Lucius whispered.

He held up a hand, silencing the brute.

He wasn't being watched from the outside. He was being watched from the inside!

It's Morvant. . . . It has to be him.

He closed his eyes tightly, affording Morvant no visual cues as the Shepherd tried to steal his eyes.

Gunfire behind them was raging now.

Harnessing the power of the beast inside him, he forced Morvant out with a violent shove and locked down his mind like a vault. When the presence pulled away, he opened his eyes and met the burly operator's amber gaze.

"What did you see?" Lucius said, his voice a throaty growl.

"I am being hunted," Woland said. "Stay here. I need to check the exit."

"No way. I'm not letting you abandon me down here."

"If the exit is compromised, if the Shepherd commander is waiting for us with a squad of shooters, then this is all for nothing."

Woland scanned the right and left tunnel walls. Ten meters down on the right, he spied an alcove flanked by rusted wrought iron stanchions still in place after almost five hundred years.

"Wait for me in there," he commanded. "If I don't return in fifteen minutes, kill the pope and save yourself."

Lucius smirked, seeming to like this idea. "It will be done."

Woland nodded to his fellow demon soldier and jogged down the corridor, smashing the motion-activated lights and throwing the tunnel into total darkness as he went. Despite what he'd said, he had no intention of coming back. He glanced over his shoulder at the mammoth of a man waiting dutifully in the tunnel, his glowing red eyes tracking Woland in the darkness.

He smiled.

If you want me, Morvant . . . you'll have to go through that monster first.

CHAPTER FORTY-TWO

Jed stopped running and took a knee, his right shoulder pressed into the tunnel wall as he scanned over his rifle.

His head was noisy—way too noisy for battle—and he needed to center himself. As a SEAL this sort of thing had rarely happened to him, but as a Shepherd it felt like he carried all his interpersonal baggage into the fight with him. All the people in his life whom he'd forged or renewed bonds with over the past short months— Sarah Beth, Corbin, Ben, David, Rachel, Eli, Nisha, Maria—he could feel their invisible threads tugging. As a natural loner, this was a new experience for him. Being part of a SEAL Team platoon was one thing, but this—this was so *intimate*.

He blinked hard and performed a round of four-count tactical breathing to center himself and cloister the noise.

Inhale, hold, exhale, hold . . .

Nisha took a knee beside him, and he felt her hand on his shoulder.

"Everything okay?" she whispered.

"Yep, just centering myself for what's ahead," he said and turned to look at her.

She shifted her gaze from his face down the tunnel. "The lights are out down there. They either timed out or it's a trap."

"If they timed out, by logic these lights here at the front of the branch should have gone out first," he said.

"Agreed. We need to stay frosty."

"You want the left or right wall?"

"Right wall," she said and flipped her NVGs down over her eyes. "Let's go save the pope."

He nodded, dropped his own NVGs into place, and chopped a hand forward. A heartbeat later, they were both up and moving in mirror-image combat crouches down the tunnel, scanning over their rifles. As they advanced and left the battery-powered lanterns behind, the ambient light dropped to zero in the subterranean corridor. In the default mode, NVGs worked by amplifying low-level light and required a minimum lumen threshold to function. He was losing resolution fast and his visual field was washing out with grainy green-gray static.

He was reaching up to switch to infrared mode when he saw a flash of fiery eyes across the corridor. He heard a guttural roar, followed by Nisha's scream and then what sounded like a hundred-pound bag of cement hitting the ground. Jed brought his rifle up and scanned where he'd last seen the glowing eyes, but before he found a target to shoot, he was hit by what felt like a Ford

F-150. He flew backward through the air, but instead of hitting the ground, he slammed into the tunnel wall. His back hit first, followed by his head, which whiplashed into the stone. His Kevlar helmet saved his melon from cracking in two, but a flurry of white stars swirled in his vision.

Duck! Corbin shouted in Jed's mind.

He did and the brute's fist crashed into the stone wall above him. Capitalizing on the moment, he drove up with his legs and rammed his left shoulder into the dark warrior's chest. He executed a football tackle, bringing the full mass of his heavy frame on top of the other man as they crashed onto the stone floor. The contract killer grunted on impact and Jed heard something crunch underneath him. The landing knocked Jed's NVGs askew, but he didn't have time to mess with them. He scrambled into the mount position and started pummeling the snarling thing below him with closed-fist blows. In the pitch-darkness, the only thing he could see was a pair of glowing red eyes, so that's where he aimed.

He landed strike after strike with brutal and punishing force, the TPR knuckle guards in his Mechanix tactical gloves allowing him to punch without restraint. The glowing eyes began to dim and in that instant, Jed tasted certain victory. Then the eyes pulsed with raging fire, and he felt his body suddenly become weightless as the beast beneath him flung him across the tunnel like a rag doll. He slammed, back first, into the wall on the opposite side of the tunnel so hard this time that it knocked the breath out of him. As he slid down the stacked granite blocks gasping for air, he lowered his NVGs and switched to infrared mode.

In grainy green-gray monochrome, he watched his opponent get to his feet. The warrior was no ordinary man; he was a juggernaut—taller, thicker, and heavier than Jed himself. He'd assumed he'd been fighting Nicholas Woland this whole time, but now he realized that was not the case. This adversary he did not recognize. The demon soldier spat a bloody glob onto the floor, wiped his mouth with the back of his hand, and laughed with unhinged malice. Jed reached for his rifle, which hung limp by the sling, but the man closed the gap between them before Jed could bring the muzzle all the way up. The dark warrior caught the rifle by the forestock and wrenched it free, breaking the sling's swivel hardware, and flung it down the corridor. A booted foot careened straight at Jed's face, but he dodged left and crabbed on hands and knees to get some fighting separation. He wasn't fast enough, however, and the man's next kick connected with Jed's midsection. He grunted, taking the blow, while his mind subconsciously computed his next move based on years of close-quarter combat training. The next kick came with furious speed, but Jed swiveled and it glanced off his hip, giving him the precious seconds he needed to pop to his feet and square off against the dark soldier.

Jed surveyed his enemy, looking for any vulnerability he could exploit. Where he was decked out in full battle rattle—with helmet, pistol, bowie knife, kit with plate carrier, and tactical gloves—his opponent was dressed in the service uniform of a Vatican police officer. On paper, the Dark One didn't stand a chance.

On paper . . . I should have already won.

"I'm going to rip you apart, Shepherd, piece by piece," the demon soldier growled, his eyes burning red embers in the dark tunnel.

"Bring it on," Jed fired back as he shifted into a close-quarter combat stance.

And then it began . . .

The beast of a man came at him fast, furious, and with a ferocity that took Jed by surprise. He didn't have time to pull his pistol before the dark warrior was all over him. The battle happened at reflex speed—driven not by premeditated thought but by training, muscle memory, and combat experience.

Block, elbow, knee, block, punch . . .

After the first few seconds, Jed was on his heels, backpedaling. Ducking and weaving was impossible; the man was a cyclone of fists and feet, elbows and knees—a combination of an obvious operator pedigree strengthened by the demon inside. It was all Jed could do to keep his forearms up to protect his face and neck. The blows came with the speed and sharp intensity of semiautomatic rifle fire. Stabs of pain blossomed in his forearms, ribs, thighs, and shins as he took a pounding from top to bottom. Between deflections, he tried to exploit the gaps and slip in strikes of his own, but hitting the man was like trying to punch the wind.

As Jed tired, the dark warrior's strikes began to find their marks. He felt his right eyebrow split open and warm blood snake down beside the corner of his eye. Pain blossomed in his lower abdomen as a gut punch landed below his kit. Jed's guts burned with the blow and dread flooded his consciousness. He was outmatched and losing . . .

Focus, the SEAL barked in his head. *Synchronize and slow it down . . .*

Like many operators, Jed believed in something called the *cadence of combat* and that the key to special operations was synchronizing the cadence of the mind with the cadence of war. In doing so, chaos finds structure . . . tumult becomes tempo. In the Teams, some guys liked to say, "Slow is smooth and smooth is fast." In Jed's experience, this seemingly paradoxical advice was about synchronization—a mantra about finding the rhythm of combat. The goal was to match the mind's processing rate to the velocity of battle. When the synchronization happened, the paradox took hold—time appeared to slow down. Movements felt smooth. Temporal clarity, the ability to perceive cause and effect, and the power to anticipate outcomes were reestablished when the operator synchronized the cadence of combat.

Find the frequency . . .

He forced his gaze up.

A fist clutching a long stiletto blade streaked toward his face.

He ducked his head and the dark warrior's fist slammed into the crown of his helmet. The sound of a bone breaking echoed in the tunnel, followed by the clatter of the knife hitting the cement floor, and the man grunted. Jed felt a shift and finally slipped into the cadence of combat. Like a sine wave, he could now perceive the crests and troughs of battle.

Trough—he drove an open palm strike up into the man's nose.

Crest—he blocked an incoming right hook.

Trough—he snapped a front kick to the midsection, driving the dark warrior back.

Crest—the behemoth of a man drove a kick at Jed's front knee, but Jed sidestepped clear.

After the miss, the dark fighter disengaged and looked Jed up and down. His eyes flashed with flame and he laughed.

"I know you," the mercenary said, but Jed knew immediately it was the demon inside that spoke, the voice suddenly transformed with a supernatural timbre as a demonic double visage appeared on his face.

Jed's eyes went wide with recognition and gooseflesh stood up on his neck. "And I know you," he said, his voice a baritone growl. The demon snarling at him had the same face as the fiend he'd battled in Kenny Bailey's basement all those years ago. Was it possible? Was this really the same demon inside this foe as the one that had tried to rape Rachel? Or was this just a mind game played on him by the devil?

Did it matter?

"Ready for another go at it?" the Dark One said.

In reply, Jed's right hand found the hilt of his SOG bowie on his kit and he unsheathed the blade.

"That's the spirit," the demon said with a malevolent grin and charged.

Like before, his adversary closed the gap with blinding speed. Jed was ready, but it really didn't matter. Like his previous battles with Dark Ones, the possessed had superhuman strength, power, and endurance. As the fighter crashed into him, Jed drove his blade deep into the possessed man's abdomen.

Which changed nothing.

The Dark One tackled him and drove him backward to the ground. In a reversal of fortune, the beast leapt into a straddling position on top of him. The blows rained down savagely and with preternatural speed. It was all Jed could do to shield his face with his left arm, while he twisted the hilt of his bowie knife with his right. He whipped the blade around inside his assailant's guts before violently pulling it out.

The man, or perhaps the demon inside, howled and a foul-smelling crimson stream gushed from the gaping wound, spilling all over Jed's torso.

Jed took a shot to the mouth, splitting his bottom lip open, but he maintained his wits and stabbed again. The blade found its mark, going again into the man's abdomen, this time just below the rib cage. Jaw clenched, Jed drove the blade up to puncture the diaphragm and shred lung tissue. The demon-faced warrior bellowed again but this time grabbed the knife hilt over Jed's hand and yanked it out. With a sharp twist, he wrenched the blade from Jed's grip and tossed it down the corridor.

"Die, Shepherd," he screamed and clutched Jed about the neck with both hands, thumbs pressing so hard Jed thought his trachea would implode.

Jed hammered at the powerful, thick forearms, trying to break the other's grip, but it was as futile as punching an iron beam. The darkness of the tunnel began to close in all around him as the blood flow to his brain dwindled. He frantically searched all his invisible threads, broadcasting cries for help.

Your gun, Uncle Jed, Sarah Beth said, her voice bright white. *You still have your gun.*

And as he felt himself slipping into a dark, deep abyss, he dragged his right hand along his side until his fingers found the grip of his Sig Sauer P229. He pulled the weapon from his drop holster and, with the last vestige of muscle memory, angled it up and squeezed the trigger again and again and again . . .

The pressure on his neck eased.

As blood flow renewed, Jed's wits and vision returned. The demon warrior on top of him rematerialized, its body convulsing with each strike of the hammer. The Sig in his right roared and kicked as his trigger finger indexed on automatic pilot, emptying the entire magazine. When the final round kicked off and Jed felt the slide lock open, he bucked his hips and threw the man off of him. Rolling clear, he scrambled to his feet to face the bloody heap of possessed flesh on the floor.

Like a nightmare he couldn't wake up from, Jed watched in horror as the possessed warrior rose impossibly back to his feet.

"No," Jed murmured, shaking his head. "Not possible."

The dark warrior looked like something out of a zombie movie—damaged beyond repair, oozing black blood, flesh ripped from bone, and yet still somehow ambulatory. Jed steeled himself, exhaled, and brought his fists up for another round. The dark warrior took a step toward him, and then something happened Jed did not expect. The man, skin as pale as a corpse now, stumbled to a knee. The demonic double visage shrieked with rage and frustration, then detached from the man it possessed. It swooped in a loop around Jed before smashing into the ground, leaving a fiery stain behind.

Like a puppet whose strings had just been cut, the killer collapsed to the ground with a shocked look on his face. He met Jed's stare momentarily, but then his gaze went vacant as he died in a puddle of blood.

Jed scanned the tunnel for Nisha and found her lying splayed and motionless on the floor by the right-hand tunnel wall. He rushed to her side and checked her neck for a pulse. He sighed with relief upon finding a strong heartbeat but didn't dare move her for fear the dark warrior had broken her neck.

"Nisha?" he said, snapping his fingers in front of her face and then caressing her cheek.

He saw her eyeballs twitch beneath her closed lids momentarily as she came to. She opened her eyes but couldn't focus on him.

"Jed? Is that you?"

"Yes, it's me," he said. "I'm here."

"I can't see," she said, trepidation in her voice.

"I know . . . that's because it's pitch-black in here," he said, grinning in the dark.

"So I'm not blind?" she asked, bending at the waist to sit up and groaning for her trouble.

"No, and thankfully, not paralyzed either," he said.

"It threw me against the wall like I was a toddler," she said. "How long have I been out?"

"A couple minutes," he said, "but don't worry. I fought him off by myself while you took your nap."

She tried to laugh at this but winced and clutched her chest instead.

Jed suddenly felt a presence behind him and whirled, ready to engage a new attacker only to find the pope, duct tape over his mouth and hands out in front, feeling blindly in the darkness.

"Just stay there, Your Holiness," Jed said. "We're the good guys and I'm coming to you."

He pulled a couple of chemlights from his kit, flipped up his NVGs, then cracked and dropped the glow sticks on the ground to provide some much-needed illumination. Next, he gently removed the duct tape from the pontiff's mouth.

"Are you hurt?" he asked, looking the pope up and down for bloodstains.

"No," the pope said, sadness ringing in his voice like a tower bell. "But many other innocents are, I fear."

Jed nodded, the words prompting him to action.

Reaching out with his mind, he searched for Ben. When he

couldn't find the Shepherd commander's thread, he looked for Corbin instead.

I have the pope, he said. *He's secure. But Woland is missing. We need to find him.*

I know, Corbin said in his head, her mind voice full of tension and frustration. *We're all looking for him.*

And Ben? Have you heard from him?

He hasn't checked in, she said. *I can't reach him . . . and that's not for lack of trying.*

Jed balled his fists in frustration. *I can't let Ben face Woland alone.*

You don't have a choice, Jed. Your orders are to shelter in place with the pope and wait for backup. That comes from Pastor Mike directly.

Copy, Jed grumbled, really hoping that the "grumble" part translated over Watcher snapchat.

"Jed, are you . . . you know?" Nisha said, placing a hand on his shoulder.

"Yeah, checking in with Watcher One right now," he said, tapping his temple.

"What are our orders?"

"Secure the pope and wait here for the rest of Joshua Bravo to join us, which, from the sounds of the boots I hear coming, should be any second."

Just to be safe, he found his rifle, raised it, and peered down the tunnel into the darkness in the direction of the incoming footfalls.

"Bravo One, Bravo Two—enemy neutralized, east tunnel secure," Eli called.

Jed exhaled with relief and lowered his rifle. "Enemy neutralized here, too. The Holy Package is secure," he called back and heard Nisha stifle a laugh beside him at the latter part of the report.

Probably never going to hear the end of that one . . .

"You're safe now, Your Holiness," Jed said, turning to the pope and forcing a grin onto his bloody face. "It's over."

The pope crossed himself and nodded to Jed and then to Nisha. "God is with us. Thank you both for your courage and your light in these dark, dark times."

CHAPTER FORTY-THREE

Woland had no supernatural gifts—and certainly no "gifts of the Spirit," having abandoned the Holy Spirit and the rest of the Trinity years ago—but he didn't need them to know that whatever had gone on back in the tunnel had gone badly. He could only hope that, before dying at the hands of the infernal Ben Morvant, Lucius had at least dispatched the pope. If so, his mission was still a success, and surely Victor would see it as such. They knew getting the pope out alive would be a long shot, but the terror attack in St. Peter's Square, the short-term kidnapping of the pope with the execution of his security team as well as several bishops and Rector Senai, and the murder of His Holiness in the tunnels beneath the Vatican—these were immense accomplishments for a single day. He imagined Victor would be very pleased indeed.

He pressed his ear to the ancient, corroded iron door and listened. Hearing nothing, he grabbed an old-fashioned brass key that hung from a peg by the door. After inserting it into the clunky antique lock, he rotated it a quarter turn clockwise. He felt the lock mechanism disengage, then grabbed the handle and tugged—the heavy door swinging slowly open on massive, rusty hinges. He slipped inside an antechamber, which he presumed led to the wine cellar beneath the boutique hotel. After closing the tunnel door behind him, he noted that the lock was keyed for operation only on the inside. He wondered if the next door was configured similarly for security purposes and he would become trapped in this little stone holding cell—a prison between two worlds—until Victor saw fit to get him out. Flashbulb memories of his cell in La Santé filled his consciousness and a wave of claustrophobia washed over him.

No, I will never be caged again. I'll go back and face the Shepherds in the tunnels if it comes to that.

He steeled himself and walked across the antechamber to the modern door and studied the lock and handle configuration. To his surprise, this door had a dead bolt lock with a thumb-turn tumbler on his side, which meant it was likely keyed on the other.

A victorious grin curled his lips as he put his ear to the slab and listened.

Hearing nothing, he disengaged the bolt, turned the doorknob, and opened the slab. His senses on high alert, he slipped out into a dimly lit wine cellar.

"Hello, Nick," an old, familiar voice said, stopping Woland's breath in his chest.

Not . . . possible. Not even the anointed Ben Morvant could be in two places at the same time.

His body, honed as a weapon over decades, tensed and prepared for battle as he assessed the situation. Morvant stood alone under an arched stone doorway, across the rectangular-shaped cellar stacked with shelf after shelf of wine bottles and at least a dozen cask barrels. He held an assault rifle at the ready across his chest but not yet raised.

The beast inside stirred with anticipation and Woland smiled.

By not killing him immediately, Morvant had made his first mistake.

Woland resisted the urge to reach for the pistol in his waistband—he was quick, but not that quick. To turn the tables, he would need to prey upon and exploit Morvant's greatest weakness—the same weakness that made all Christians such easy marks: compassion. Always turning the other cheek, always ready to forgive, no matter how egregious the offense . . . yes, this was the key to victory. He would exploit Morvant's godly impulses and then take the greatest pleasure of his life in ending the mighty Shepherd who stood so relaxed and overconfident before him.

"I'd hoped we would meet, Ben," Woland said and let his shoulders sag, signaling defeat, though his arms remained tense—coiled snakes, ready to strike. He made sure to slip subtle conflict into his voice. "I . . . I guess I had, at first, hoped to be able to confront you. But now . . ." He sighed, looking down at his feet and feeling hope and satisfaction that Morvant had still not raised the rifle. "I've made terrible mistakes, Ben. There is a darkness in me, something not of God, that I would give anything to purge. I just . . . I just don't know if it's too late for God's grace—for God's mercy. I feel nothing but judgment now. Judgment from God, but also . . ." He worked harder than ever to put grief and regret onto his face. "From you. For everything I've done. For losing my way. Can you help me? Can you guide me back to the light?"

"My job is not to deal death and judgment, Nick," Morvant said, his voice soft, even gentle.

I have him.

Inside, the beast growled with hunger at what would come next.

Morvant took a step toward him.

Is he so naive that he would actually embrace me?

"Judgment is only for God," Morvant continued.

Woland nodded penitently and opened his arms wide to his former mentor.

But instead of coming to him, Morvant stopped still ten paces away. The Shepherd commander brought his rifle up swiftly, the flash of red from the target designator sweeping across Woland's eyes as the beam found his forehead. With cool certitude, Ben pressed his cheek into the stock of his rifle as he leaned forward into a shooter's stance.

"But as His servant, I'm obligated to arrange the meeting."

Woland's heart skipped a beat.

No, I won't go down without a fight.

He harnessed his hatred. He would savage the Shepherd, rip the flesh from the man's bones, and when he was done, dance on his corpse. The fight was not over; this was only the beginning. He'd not failed Victor nor the Dark Prince. To the contrary, he'd struck a fatal blow to the sanctity of the Roman Catholic Church and forever cast doubt on the impenetrability of the Vatican. And now, by harnessing the power of the demon within, he would topple the leader of the Shepherds as well.

He growled and tried to muster the beast, but the surge of inhuman power did not come. The burn behind his eyes that he expected, that he craved, that he *needed,* did not happen. Instead, a crippling and overwhelming explosion of nausea roiled his insides as his other abandoned him, vacating his chest with searing pain and leaving a dark, frigid void behind.

"What's happening?" he murmured, his mind and body both in shock. "I have served loyally. Why, in my moment of greatest need, do you abandon me?"

His gaze found Morvant's eyes and epiphany struck Woland like a thunderbolt. The beast had never served him; his body had been nothing but a vessel. The power, the preternatural strength, the sense of invincibility—all a deception.

What he had always mistaken as weakness in Ben now radiated as strength.

Hollow, desperate, and depleted, the former Shepherd did the only thing he could and reached for his gun.

As his fingers found the pistol grip, the muzzle of Morvant's rifle flashed bright white, and the universe exploded with light and color as the bullet tore through his skull.

CHAPTER FORTY-FOUR

Jed probed his still-swollen lip with his tongue as he stared out the porthole window at the top of the bright-white cloud deck below. His body felt pretty beat up, but no worse than after his last battle with the Dark Ones at the Yarnells' old house. He'd been better prepared this time, both tactically and spiritually, and it had made a difference.

And he'd had allies . . .

How Sarah Beth had found him in the fray, he had no idea, other than the tether between him and the girl who called him uncle. Fighting the possessed was a terrifying proposition, but he'd had multiple engagements now and he'd managed to survive all of them.

Faith, firepower, and friends . . . you needed all three in excess to come out on top when battling the Dark Ones.

All things considered, despite their fits and starts, the operation in Rome had been a success. They'd saved the pope and prevented the attack from becoming a bloodbath. While he'd been battling the demon-possessed man in the tunnels, Joshua Alpha platoon, the team from Shepherds Europe, and Gendarmerie GIR had worked together to put down the terrorist attack in St. Peter's Square. Innocent lives had been lost and one Shepherd killed, but the civilian casualties totaled in the dozens rather than the thousands. Rector Senai and several bishops had been murdered by Woland, but the pope had been saved and the plot of his kidnapping kept secret. And somehow, using prescience that must surely have come from God, Ben had been in the right place, at the right time, to confront Woland. Ben had shared little about the battle that must have ensued, saying only that the former Shepherd was no longer a concern. Unlike Jed, he seemed unscathed, so his battle must have gone better. Perhaps his powers were just so much more under control.

He let a finger drag across the stitches on his pummeled face where his skin had split above his eye, weirdly relishing the burning pain it brought. They had another victory, and that was all that mattered. Just hours ago, they'd learned that a fire team from the Tier One SEALs had rescued the Senai family, held hostage in Ethiopia, and that all would recover physically, though the psychological trauma sustained was another matter. Most important of all, the pope had responded in the aftermath with both empathy and leadership—calling for peace, disarming rising rhetoric, and quelling any and all calls for retribution. The Dark Ones' plan to topple dominoes with a Vatican attack that would kick off an all-encompassing global war between Christians and Muslims had been averted . . . for now.

Whatcha doing?

Sarah Beth, is that you? Jed said.

Duh, who else?

He shrugged and smiled. *Good point. How you doing, kid?*

Good. I have a math test I should be studying for, but I wanted to check on you.

Well, I appreciate that . . . and if you must know, I look like somebody used my face for a punching bag.

What else is new, she fired back, and he could practically feel her laughing at him.

Ha-ha, laugh it up, pip-squeak. A comfortable pause lingered between them before he said, *Thanks, by the way.*

For what?

For being there for me when I needed you. If not for you . . . I'd be dead right now.

All I did was tell you to use your gun, duh.

He chuckled. *Yeah, in that moment when the demon was choking the life out of me, you were the light in my darkness.*

That's what we do—I watch your back, and you watch mine, she said before adding, *But, Uncle Jed . . .*

Yeah?

Please don't tell my mom.

Don't tell your mom what?

You know . . . that I'm doing Watcher stuff without permission.

And that we're snapchatting all the time. Pastor Dee and the head-master want me to focus on school and making friends at St. George's and stuff.

Jed chose his words—or his thoughts, he supposed—carefully.

Sarah Beth, first I need you to know that neither of us can keep secrets from your parents. Me because it's wrong, and they're my friends and my teammates now.

The word *friends* came to him naturally. He wanted it to be true—prayed soon it really would be.

But, Uncle Jed, they don't understand. You're the only one who understands.

That is simply not true, Sarah Beth, which brings me to number two: They love you unconditionally and support everything you're doing as a Watcher. And if Pastor Dee believes you need time to focus on school and your training, then she knows best.

Well, that's dumb, because you just said if it wasn't for me, you'd be dead.

I know, but this isn't a game. The Dark Ones are very powerful, and Victor has already gone after you twice. Maybe it's best if you focus on school and develop your skills until you're Corbin's age and officially move into the Watcher rotation.

I'm already better than most of them.

There's more to being a Watcher than raw talent.

Is that a backhanded way of saying you think I'm immature?

You're twelve going on thirteen, not twelve going on seventeen. It's okay to grow up one year at a time.

Jed decided in that moment he needed to speak with Ben, and then maybe even Pastor Dee, about Sarah Beth. Twice now, only Sarah Beth's "disobedient" involvement had allowed crucial missions to succeed. That had to mean something, right? What was going on with Sarah Beth was both spiritually powerful and strategically significant. Wasn't it Ben who liked to preach that God gives gifts to prepare His people for the tasks in store for them? And if that was true, God was calling Sarah Beth to something important already. Nonetheless, this was a decision for Ben and Pastor Dee.

She didn't answer and for a moment he thought she'd severed their chat.

Okay? he prompted.

Okay, she finally said.

Okay what?

Okay, I won't snapchat you anymore.

Now hold on, that's not what I meant, he said. *I said I agreed with Pastor Dee and your headmaster that you should be focusing on school, not doing Watcher stuff without permission. That doesn't include cutting off contact with me. I spoke with your dad and he's fine with it, and you said you would clear it with your mom, so when you've done that, let's stay in touch.*

Do you really mean that?

Yes, 110 percent I do.

I'll tell Mom about my dreams and how I seem to be tuned into the moments when you and your team are in danger. I owe her that, and maybe she'll even have some ideas about it.

I agree, he said, proud of his adopted niece.

Oh, shoot, I'm gonna be late for class. Bye, Uncle Jed . . .

Jed chuckled. Thank God for youthful naiveté and that she still had some growing up left to do. *Later, kid.*

In the seats behind him, he could hear Eli and Grayson arguing about pickles. This time they were really going at it and were soliciting allies to their respective sides about whether pickles were a gift from heaven or a culinary plague on this Earth. Jed shook his head and couldn't help but laugh at the wonderful absurdity of it all. He'd loved being a SEAL, but being a Shepherd was all that and more. Jericho Basic and the missions they'd executed had opened his mind and his heart to putting his fate and his trust in spiritual elements he couldn't touch, see, or explain.

The very definition of faith, he supposed.

He'd let go of his control, let go of his doubt, and opened himself to the wisdom and guidance of others and their gifts and insights. Trusting was hard for him—being vulnerable, even harder—but he'd done both, and in the doing, he'd found strength. Only God knew where his journey as a Shepherd would take him next, but he was ready for that next step.

A wave of drowsiness suddenly washed over him.

Smiling, Jed leaned back against the headrest and closed his eyes. Content with the certainty that the world would survive for the next few hours without him, he surrendered to sleep and let himself drift off for a hard-earned, well-deserved nap.

EPILOGUE

TWENTY & GRAND APARTMENTS

2000 GRAND AVENUE, WEST END

NASHVILLE, TENNESSEE

2105 HOURS LOCAL

Maria paced along the floor-to-ceiling window in the living room of her apartment. Holding a glass of red wine in one hand— her fourth—while she tapped a nervous cadence in sync with her pulse against her hip with the other.

She should have heard something by now.

From someone. Right?

It had been a long time since her handler, a man now serving in the US House of Representatives from the great state of Tennessee, had contacted her. At some point his guidance and instruction just stopped.

Lately, she heard only from Victor himself.

Whether that had represented a promotion or simply meant Victor wanted direct control over her, she didn't know.

And . . . could never ask.

Victor communicated what he wanted when he wanted. He didn't "keep her in the loop" if there even was such a thing. Her professional existence was the literal definition of "need to know," and right now she clearly didn't.

Tired of pacing, she set down her glass and collapsed onto her designer sofa, pulling her legs up under her. She leaned her head back and made a loud *"arrrrrr"* sound, staring at the ceiling. What was it she hoped to hear, anyway? That her warning to Victor had ensured the success of the mission? That because of her, they'd been ready for the Shepherds and rebuffed their intervention? If that were true, it also meant Jedidiah Johnson was likely dead.

And that we won. Both of which are good things, right?

But the thought of Jed dying didn't feel good.

Not at all.

She shook her head, then took a long pull on her wine.

What was wrong with her? She'd chosen her side. There was no going back. There was no defection from Victor. Despite what they taught you in Sunday school, there wasn't enough grace in the universe to turn a blind eye to the role she'd played in the ever-raging battle between God and Satan. Hope was propaganda—a delusion.

Hope always, always ended in pain.

So why was she so upset?

The phone rang, startling her and causing her to slosh wine onto her hand, which she tried to slurp up with her lips before it could drip onto her white leather sofa. She hurried to the breakfast bar, set down her glass, and grabbed a napkin to blot up the rest as she sprinted to her office.

"Hello?" she said, her voice a tight string as she connected the call.

"Who did you expect?"

"You," she answered, squeezing her eyes shut.

Of course, you. Who else would call on this phone?

"No one," he hissed in her ear, again pirating thoughts from her mind. "But perhaps not who you hoped."

"All went well?" she asked, refusing to play his games tonight.

"No," Victor said, and she felt the weight of his rage even through the phone. More than rage. The kind of hatred that had caused wars, had caused genocides, had left the world's people ravaged, bloody, and hopeless for millennia. "I am afraid not. The Shepherds have grown in power, and I fear that you may be our best next hope to stop them from meddling in our affairs. The world is meant to be our dominion, and for us to enjoy the fruits of our labors, we need them destroyed."

"I'm working on it, I assure you."

"I know you are," Victor said, letting the words float around her a moment. "Your lust for the gifted Shepherd will serve us well, if used properly. But you must maintain control. You cannot let yourself be seduced by the light. Only you are in position to infiltrate their ranks. With you on the inside, we will finally have the means to breach their citadel and burn it to the ground."

"I understand," she said, forcing away any thoughts of Jedidiah that might betray her inner struggle to Victor.

"Do you really?" he said, his voice dripping with superiority and judgment. "Because I'm starting to wonder if you might have forgotten your place."

"I serve only you," she said, her stomach suddenly an acid bath.

"In that case, I have another mission for you, one that must be completed in tandem. If forced to prioritize, this mission takes precedence."

"What is that?" she asked, confused. What on earth could possibly take precedence over toppling the Shepherds?

"The key to infiltrating Trinity is Jedidiah Johnson. But it appears that he has found himself a guardian angel."

"Morvant?" she asked, still confused.

Victor hissed a serpent's laugh. "No, Sarah Beth Yarnell. We grossly underestimated her power. We should have never tried to take her. Her faith is young, pure, and unshakable. Despite all she has suffered, her light shines bright. She is bound tightly to Jedidiah and must be eliminated before he can be exploited."

Maria nodded. Victor might well be right. There was *something* about that girl.

I've felt her probing, looking into and through me, perhaps.

"What do you want me to do?" she asked.

"Kill her," Victor said, "and make it look like an accident."

The line went dead.

She set the phone on her desk and a cold chill chased down her spine.

Kill her . . .

Despite her sour stomach, she shuffled to the kitchen and topped off her glass of wine. Her head swimmy, she walked back to the wall of windows to stare at the Nashville city lights and drown herself in alcohol until the schizophrenic chorus of voices in her head went quiet.

KEEP AN EYE OUT

FOR THE NEXT THRILLING READ IN THE SHEPHERDS SERIES BY

ANDREWS & WILSON

AVAILABLE IN STORES AND ONLINE FALL 2022

JOIN THE CONVERSATION AT

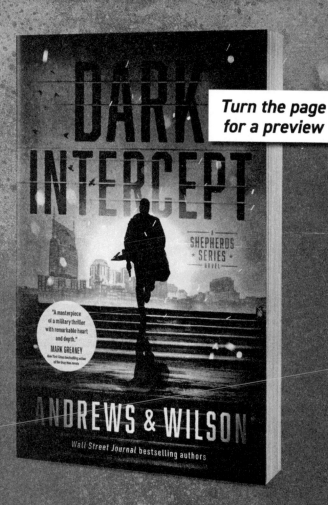

CHAPTER TWO

Navy SEAL Senior Chief Jedidiah Johnson loosened the tie on his dress blue uniform and slid onto a barstool. He raised a hand to the girl behind the bar.

"Hey, Jed," she said and pulled a Corona from the cooler. She slid it to him across the counter. He caught it and then licked some spilled suds off the back of his hand. "Big day, right?" the girl said with a wink and a smile—the same pretty smile that earned her thousands in tips and hundreds of unsolicited phone numbers scribbled on cocktail napkins from the legion of Navy SEALs who called this bar their home away from home.

"Yeah," Jed said. "Big day." He took a long pull on his beer and looked around the bar. In minutes, the joint would be swelling with his teammates—*former* teammates, actually. He would have to get used to the word *former*: former teammate, former Navy SEAL, former senior chief. He sighed and smiled at the bartender. "Whaddaya say we get out of here? Run away to the Caribbean and drink Coronas on a real beach."

"Nuh-uh. No way, Jed," she laughed. "You're not getting out of this one. I promised the boys I'd lock the doors if I had to."

A resigned smile curled his lips and he shook his head. For a Navy SEAL, retirement was as difficult as it was inevitable. Being a SEAL was like being a professional athlete, and the human body, as amazing as it was, could only take so much abuse. At thirty-five, he would still be considered a young man in most professions. But in special warfare, seventeen years of hard service and a shattered hip had left him a bit long in the tooth. After taking a 7.26mm round to the left hip, the docs had said he'd walk with a cane for the rest of his life, but he'd proven them wrong and rehabilitated himself back into fighting form. And yet, it was important to be honest with himself. Could he still do his job? Yes. Could his brothers without chronic pain, scar tissue, and flaring arthritis in their hips do the job better? As much as it stung, the answer was also yes. Retiring with grace was not the same as being retired. Passing the torch was not the same as quitting. These were the things he'd told himself, and they were true . . .

But why didn't it feel that way?

"What's up, Senior?" A voice interrupted his rumination, and the slap on his back sloshed beer onto the back of his hand. He looked up into the smiling face of a teammate ten years his junior—a lifetime in the SEALs. "Is this a party or a wake?"

"He's right, Jed," a familiar voice beside him boomed, and Jed felt himself reflexively straighten up at the sound of the Group Two Commander, Captain Mike Jared. He had served with the senior officer on and off his entire career. Jared was one of the SEALs Jed respected most, and he was confident the man would make admiral and one day command all of WARCOM. "You okay, Senior Chief? Not having second thoughts, are you?"

"No, sir," Jed said with a forced grin. "I'm good."

"Well," the officer said, "if you change your mind, let me know. I've got enough rank to make your retirement package disappear." Captain Jared smoothed his dress blues as he took the barstool beside his former platoon leader. Like the rest of the SEALs funneling into the room, Jared would be more comfortable in BDUs or blue jeans. In the Teams, the dress uniforms were little more than dust collectors in between funerals and retirements—more of the former than the latter since 9/11.

"I'm sure you could, sir," Jed said. "Like we made that bus disappear in Qatar that one time."

"Easy now," Jared said but laughed at the memory. "We agreed never to speak of that, shipmate."

Jed nodded and took a pull from his Corona. He loved his brothers more than anything in the world. Maybe he was making a mistake. What kind of life could he ever have apart from these men? Then a parade of faces marched past his mind's eye—the brothers lost and the lives he had taken. The same faces that harassed him in his dreams every night.

Jed sighed. *No, it's time.*

"What are you gonna do, Jed?" the younger SEAL asked.

"Still working on that," Jed said and looked away, not sure what else to say.

"My offer stands, Jed," Captain Jared said. "I have a lot of friends at the Agency and others working in contracting jobs. One quick call and I can have you in a six-figure job doing what you do best."

"I appreciate that, sir," he said, feeling uncomfortable now. "I may take you up on it, but I need to look around a little first. My whole life has been Navy. . . . I just need to see what else is out there."

Jared nodded. "Completely understandable. Look around and see what your options are. Just know I'm a phone call away if you need me."

Jed's phone vibrated and then rang in his pocket, giving him a perfectly timed out. He retrieved the phone and checked the caller ID but didn't recognize the number. Nonetheless, he'd take a call from the devil himself to get out of questions about what he planned to do with his life now that he was a *former* Navy SEAL.

"Excuse me a moment, sir," Jed said to Captain Jared and slid off his stool. He walked quickly to the door and stepped outside before pressing the green button on the screen.

"Hello?"

The relative quiet of the outside was shattered by the roar of an F/A-18 fighter jet screaming in from the ocean and then breaking in a ninety-degree turn directly over him before heading toward the runway at Naval Air Station Oceana a few miles away. When the vibration stopped and the ringing in his ears eased, he tried again.

"Say again," he began. "I couldn't hear you."

"I'm sorry. Maybe I have the wrong number?" The voice on the line sounded tight and strained. The owner was clearly under stress—maybe even duress—and Jed looked again at the screen, hoping the seemingly random string of numbers would become enlightening.

He put the phone back to his ear. "Who's calling?"

"Is this Jed?" the voice asked, and Jed suddenly felt something familiar about the voice, but he couldn't place it.

"This is Senior Chief Jedidiah Johnson," he said coolly. "Now who is this?"

"It's David," the trembling voice replied. He thought the man on the other end of the line might even be crying.

"David who?" he demanded.

"David Yarnell," the voice answered, and Jed felt the blood drain from his face. "I'm sorry to call, Jed. I know it's been a long time, but I need your help. I desperately, desperately need your help."

Anger, indignation, and a wave of other conflicting emotions swirled in his mind and made his guts ache.

"How did you get this number?" he asked and instantly realized what a ridiculous and inappropriate question it was. As far as he knew, his childhood best friend still lived in Murfreesboro and David's parents still lived three doors down from the house where Jed had grown up. Even if David had moved, he could still just call Jed's parents to get Jed's mobile number. It had been a long source of strain on Jed's relationship with his parents that they'd stayed in close contact with David all these years, despite his own bitter estrangement from his childhood friend.

"Please, Jed." David's voice choked. "You have to help me. They took her."

Jed felt his chest tighten as if he had just taken a blow to the ribs. "Took who—Rachel? Is Rachel okay?" he blurted.

"No, not Rachel," David said. "Sarah Beth—our little girl. They took my little girl. Please, Jed, you have to help us get her back."

Jed loosened his tie even further and started down the block, walking away from Hot Tuna, toward the corner where he could cross over to the beach side of the road.

"Take a deep breath, David," he said. "Start from the beginning and tell me exactly what happened."

He heard only uncontrolled sobbing from the other end of the line.

"David, listen to me. I can't help you if you don't talk to me."

His *former* best friend coughed and cleared his throat. "Okay . . . I'm okay . . ." David breathed, gaining his composure. "I didn't know who else to turn to. The police are looking for her, but so far they've got nothing. I know you're a Navy SEAL, and I . . . I just thought that if anybody could find my baby girl, it would be you."

Jed swallowed hard, but the lump in his throat persisted. None of the memories swirling in his head were pleasant. Old wounds reopened and the once-extinguished anger at the betrayal he'd suffered rekindled. And then there was the other memory—the one he'd been running from his entire adult life—that usurped all others and filled his mind with dread. He squeezed his eyes shut. How could he possibly go back to Nashville and face all the unresolved matters that awaited him there? And besides, he was a Navy SEAL, not a miracle worker, and he was certainly no investigator. What did he know about finding missing kids? Give him a target package and a location, and he and his team of SEALs could unleash the wrath of God, but what David was asking for was no counterterrorism operation.

"Are you there?" David said.

Jed let out a long, quivering sigh. He felt nothing but animosity toward the man on the phone, a man he'd vowed to never forgive. But this wasn't about David, was it? A little girl was missing. *Rachel's* little girl. And try as he might, he'd never been able to stoke a fire of anger toward Rachel. The connection they'd shared had been powerful and special. He'd never experienced anything like it with any other woman in the years since.

"Jed, please. She's only twelve years old. You have to help us."

The sound of a father weeping for his missing daughter eroded his defenses. No matter what had happened between them, no matter how painful unpacking the past might be, how could he walk away from the man he'd once loved as a brother?

"Okay," Jed said at last. "Tell me exactly what happened, and you have my word I will do whatever I can to help."

GLOSSARY

18 Delta—special operations medic

AR—augmented reality

BUD/S—basic underwater demolition/SEAL training

CAG—Combat Applications Group (First Special Forces Operational Detachment-Delta—aka Delta Force, the Unit), the Army's elite special operations force under operational control of the Joint Special Operations Command

Carabinieri—the national gendarmerie of Italy or national police

CASEVAC—casualty evacuation

CIA—Central Intelligence Agency

CL or CTL—combat lead / combat team leader

CO—commanding officer

CONUS—continental United States

CSO—chief staff officer

DNI—director of National Intelligence

DoD—Department of Defense

exfil—exfiltrate

FOB—forward operating base

Gendarmerie or Gendarmerie Corps—the police and security force
of Vatican City and the Holy See

GIR—Gruppo Intervento Rapido, the rapid response and
counterterrorism special unit of the Gendarmerie

GIS—Gcoruppo di Intervento Speciale, a special forces unit of the
Carabinieri

HUMINT—human intelligence

HVT—high-value target

IC—intelligence community

indoc—indoctrination

infil—infiltrate

IR—infrared

ISR—intelligence, surveillance, and reconnaissance

JSOC—Joint Special Operations Command

JSOTF—Joint Special Operations task force

KIA—killed in action

MARSOC—Marine Corps Special Operations Command

MBITR—multiband inter-/intra-team radio

NOC—nonofficial cover

NSA—National Security Agency

NSW—Naval Special Warfare

NVGs—night-vision goggles

OGA—other government agency; frequently refers to the CIA or
other clandestine organizations

OPORD—operations order

OPSEC—operational security

QRF—quick reaction force

PT—physical training

ROE—rules of engagement

RPG—rocket-propelled grenade

SAPI—small-arms protective insert

SCIF—sensitive compartmented information facility

SEALs—sea, air, and land teams; Naval Special Warfare

SecDef—secretary of defense

SF—special forces; refers specifically to the Army Special Operations
   Green Berets

SIGINT—signals intelligence

sitrep—situation report

SOAR—special operations aviation regiment

SOCOM—special operations command

SOF—special operations forces

SOPMOD—special operations modification

SQT—SEAL qualification training

SWCC—special warfare combatant-craft crewmen; boat teams
   supporting SEAL operations

TAD—temporary additional duty

Trinity Global—the official cover entity for the Shepherds
   organization

Trinity Loop—the headquarters facility for Trinity and operational
   command of Shepherds North America

TRP—thermoplastic rubber

TS/SCI—top secret / sensitive compartmented information; the
   highest-level security clearance

TSL—tactical spiritual leader

TOC—tactical operations center

UCAV—unmanned combat aerial vehicle

UAV—unmanned aerial vehicle

USN—United States Navy

ACKNOWLEDGMENTS

We again want to acknowledge our families; our amazing agent, Gina; the incredible team at Tyndale House; and our ministry partners who lent us counsel. But more than anyone, we want to acknowledge you, the reader, for joining us on this journey. We have been overwhelmed by the feedback, support, and prayers for this series of books, and we are grateful that you are with us for this adventure!

ABOUT THE AUTHORS

Andrews & Wilson is the bestselling writing team of Brian Andrews and Jeffrey Wilson—the authors behind the Shepherds series, the Tier One and Sons of Valor series, and *Rogue Asset*, the ninth book in the W.E.B. Griffin Presidential Agent series. They write action-adventure and covert operations novels honoring the heroic men and women who serve in the military and intelligence communities.

Brian is a former submarine officer, entrepreneur, and Park Leadership Fellow with degrees from Vanderbilt and Cornell. Jeff worked as an actor, firefighter, paramedic, jet pilot, and diving instructor, as well as a vascular and trauma surgeon. During his fourteen years of service, Jeff made multiple deployments as a combat surgeon with an East Coast–based SEAL Team. Jeff now leads a men's military ministry for a large church in Tampa.

To learn more about their books, sign up for their newsletter online at andrews-wilson.com and follow them on Twitter: @BAndrewsJWilson.

BOOKS BY BRIAN ANDREWS AND JEFFREY WILSON

THE SHEPHERDS SERIES

Dark Intercept

Dark Angel

SONS OF VALOR SERIES

Sons of Valor

TIER ONE SERIES

Tier One

War Shadows

Crusader One

American Operator

Red Specter

Collateral

Scars: John Dempsey (a Tier One Origins novella)

W.E.B. GRIFFIN PRESIDENTIAL AGENT SERIES

Rogue Asset

THE NICK FOLEY SERIES (AS ALEX RYAN)

Beijing Red

Hong Kong Black

PARTNER PAGES

Andrews & Wilson actively promotes and partners with veteran-owned small businesses that demonstrate a mission of giving. The organizations featured here donate and support the health and well-being of US service members as well as their families. We encourage you to learn about and support our partners and spread the word about the important and uplifting work that they do.

BONEFROG COFFEE/CELLARS

A veteran-owned and -operated premium, small-batch coffee roastery and vineyard located in the Pacific Northwest.

After serving twenty-five years in the Navy, former SEAL Tim Cruickshank created Bonefrog Coffee and Cellars as a tribute to the "brotherhood" of US Navy SEALs, the Naval Special Warfare community, and to all Americans who bravely served, or who are currently serving, in the United States Armed Forces. Each label they create tells a story to remind us of battles fought and great American heroes who answered the call, and proceeds from every sale support those who served in the Naval Special Warfare community and their families.

bonefrog-coffee.com

bonefrogcellars.com

ALL SECURE FOUNDATION

Founded by Army veteran and retired Delta Force Tier One operator Tom Satterly and award-winning filmmaker Jen Satterly, the All Secure Foundation provides resources, education, post-traumatic stress injury resiliency training for active-duty units, warrior couples workshop retreats, and family counseling for special operations warriors and their warrior families. They believe that every family member deserves tools to heal from war trauma and that no one is left behind on the battlefield or the home front.

allsecurefoundation.org

COMBAT FLAGS

Founded by US Army veteran Dan Berei, Combat Flags began as an idea to connect veterans and give back in a meaningful way. Combat Flags is dedicated to helping stop soldier suicide (stopsoldiersuicide.org) and Dan's personal mission is to leave the world a better place than he found it.

In addition to the store, Dan interviews veterans and talks leadership, life lessons, and service on the Combat Flags podcast.

combatflags.com

STAY UP-TO-DATE ON NEWS FROM ANDREWS & WILSON AT

andrews-wilson.com

TYNDALE HOUSE PUBLISHERS IS CRAZY4FICTION!

Fiction that entertains and inspires

Get to know us! Become a member of the Crazy4Fiction community. Whether you read our blog, like us on Facebook, follow us on Twitter, or receive our e-newsletter, you're sure to get the latest news on the best in Christian fiction. You might even win something along the way!

JOIN IN THE FUN TODAY.

 crazy4fiction.com

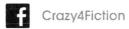 Crazy4Fiction

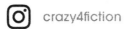 crazy4fiction

 @Crazy4Fiction